# THE REFLECTION

To Susan,

It has been such a
pleasure getting to know you.
You're really quite wonderful.

Joe Bright

# THE REFLECTION

*A Novel by Joe Bright*

Writer's Showcase

San Jose  New York  Lincoln  Shanghai

# The Reflection

Writer's Showcase
an imprint of iUniverse, Inc.

For information address:
iUniverse, Inc.
5220 S. 16th St., Suite 200
Lincoln, NE 68512
www.iuniverse.com

ISBN: 0-595-24949-3

Printed in the United States of America

Dedicated to the memory of Adrian Bright, my beloved brother and friend

## House of the Unholy

The screaming skulls of North Yorkshire
Have alas consumed the final squire
Have bled him out, have purged his veins
Then dragged him down to hell in chains
What's left, we ask, inside these walls?
What ghouls and phantoms fill these halls?

When night comes down upon the moors
Who creeps among the corridors?
Death, it moves, I smell its sin
Drawing nearer once again
The beast breathes still in the abyss
What name is next upon the list?

—Bernard Phelps
Resident poet, Lurkdale, England

# PROLOGUE

*F*rom outside the study, he could see down the corridor and into the kitchen. With the exception of the grandfather clock ticking behind him, the only sound he could hear was his own breathing. His face was beading with sweat, yet his hands were cold. He looked over his shoulder again, into the living room. He knew the American still had to be in there, but he'd already looked three times and had found nothing.

There was a splotch of blood on Earl's white shirt. He hadn't gotten the worst of it, though. Inside the study, face down on the floor, lay Thomas Windfield. The man had blood all along his arm and a lot more pooled up around his midsection, where the knife had gone in. He was dead, and Earl knew it, but that didn't stop him from checking. He put two fingers against the man's neck and found no pulse.

It was the first dead body he'd seen outside of a coffin.

He returned to the living room for the fourth time, still thinking he'd find the American. But he wasn't there. Just a bunch of furniture and that long mirror that filled the room's inner wall. Staring in at his reflection, he wiped at the bloodstain on his shirt. All it did was smear. How did he get that on him anyway? He couldn't remember. Everything had happened so fast. And now what was he supposed to do? What was he to tell the others? Not the truth, that was certain.

Regardless of how unbelievable it seemed, he knew what he'd seen, and there wasn't a soul alive who would believe him.

He went to the kitchen and stood at the windows that overlooked the backyard garden with its pathways lined with statues, hedges and flowers. It was beautiful out. Thomas's wife and two children were out there with the stable boy, Berney Phelps. They were happy in their ignorance, not knowing what had taken place inside the home.

Earl rubbed a hand across both cheeks, brushing the tears away. He wasn't a man who cried much, but watching Mrs. Windfield made him feel sick inside.

He stepped outside and pulled the door shut behind him. Heather, the daughter, was the only one who looked back toward him. He watched her stand up and touch her mother on the back of the arm, both of them now looking at him come toward them, concerned by his crying.

He wasn't sure how he was going to tell them, but the words just came out. "He's dead." The words caught in his throat. "The American killed Thomas."

# CHAPTER 1

*D*an Adams was a fat man with little hair and little patience for people who wasted his time. Most of his clients were losers. He tolerated them strictly because he made his living off them. He was in his office staring at the clock on the wall while he chewed at the end of his ballpoint pen. He'd sent his secretary home an hour and a half ago. He'd be home himself if his appointment had shown up on time. Instead he had to sit around staring at the walls, wondering if the man was going to show at all. Worse yet, he didn't even like the man.

Adams was once a handsome man, or so his "late" wife used to say, back when he had all of his hair and weighed a hundred pounds less. He liked to refer to her as his "late" wife so everyone would assume she'd died, rather than suspect the truth, which was that she'd gotten tired of watching his body grow fat and his hair grow thin. Worse than that were the seven years he'd spent trying to get his law practice rolling while they lived on her teaching salary, which barely paid the bills.

After she left, he became a successful lawyer just to spite her.

Setting his pen on the desk, he opened a drawer and rummaged around until he found a stick of gum, which he unwrapped and stuffed in his mouth. It was a stick of gum that had gotten him in this whole situation in the first place. He'd been up in the White Mountains of New Hampshire, viewing the site of a logging accident that had put one of his clients, a man named Mark Fenley, in a wheelchair for life. Adams was questioning some of the loggers, hoping to find someone who would give him a straight answer about what they'd seen. What he found was that none of the men cared much for Mr. Fenley and that no one was willing to say anything that would aid his lawsuit. One of the loggers, a young blond man with hair down over his ears, was chewing a stick of gum as Adams asked his questions and jotted down everyone's names and phone numbers in his small notebook.

It looked to Adams as though the blond had something to say but didn't want to say it in front of his buddies. So he handed the guy a business card and told him to call if he thought of anything he felt was relevant. The man pulled the gum from his mouth, stuck it to the business card, wadded it up and tossed it on the ground. That won a few smiles from his coworkers, but Adams didn't much care for it. In his notebook, he put a checkmark by the man's name so he'd remember it for future reference, in case he was ever in a position to do the man some harm. Adams liked to make lists of enemies. His grandest dream was having one of them need his help one day, just so he could turn him down.

He wasn't going to be turning anyone down this evening, but at least he was going to get the opportunity to teach the man some respect. When the door to his office opened, Adams stared at his watch to emphasize the lateness of the hour and said, "Funny, I could have sworn we set this appointment for five o'clock."

It'd been two months since the incident with the business card, but Adams recognized the man on sight. He was cleaner this time, but still had the long hair and that smug look on his face. By the looks of him, he'd just showered and put on a fresh change of clothes.

"You *are* Bren Stevens, I presume," said Adams, standing up behind the desk.

The man nodded as he closed the door and came into the office.

"We've met before, haven't we?" Adams referred to this as his deflation technique. Never let the enemies know that you remember them. It was his way of letting the air out of their egos, get them thinking that they hadn't made much of an impression.

"Yeah, I met you up in the mountains. You were asking about Mark Fenley's accident." Bren Stevens sat on a wooden chair in front of the desk as he watched the fat man, waiting for him to recall the incident. "You gave me one of your business cards," he prompted, but Adams just furrowed his brow and nodded, looking like he was trying to remember but couldn't. It took all the fun out of it. Everyone up on the mountain had talked about it for days afterward, and here the fat lawyer couldn't even remember it. What a disappointment.

"I understand Mark Fenley is asking for five million."

"We're still negotiating the price." Adam retook his seat and gathered some papers that he had spread across the desk. "Personally, I think five million isn't enough."

"Of course you don't."

"And what do you think? You think five million dollars is worth your ability to walk?"

"No, but that's not really the point here."

"No?" Adams feigned an expression of confusion. "We've got a young man with a crushed spine who's sitting at home right now in a wheelchair, and that's where he's going to be spending most of his life. What other point is there?"

"What you seem to be forgetting," said Bren, "is that Fenley brought this upon himself. Everybody knew that tree was coming down, including Fenley. He's one of those guys who think none of the rules apply to him. This time it got him hurt. Now he wants somebody else to pay for it."

Adams bobbed his head and rubbed his chin, looking like he was giving Bren's advice some thought. "Do they have that phrase carved on a tree up there on the mountain somewhere? 'Cause all your friends gave me that exact speech, almost verbatim."

Bren liked Adams less now than he did when he first met him two months ago. His fancy suit and piggish face made him look a bit like a caricature of Winston Churchill. The man had money; there was no question about that. Just a glance around at the wooden furniture in his office revealed a lot about his bank account. But all that money didn't make him any less deplorable.

"I didn't have to come here, you know?" said Bren.

"Is that right?" Adams had a look that he'd practiced, one he used whenever he wanted someone to feel like they'd just said something stupid. He could see it working its magic now, making Bren turn red in the face.

"I can see we're done here." Bren got to his feet. "It's been a real pleasure, but I've got someplace else I have to be." He started for the door and felt the heat rising in his cheeks.

"You mean you didn't get all dolled up just to come talk to me?" That won the lawyer a nasty glance and a frown, which gave him a warm, fuzzy feeling inside. Getting under people's skin was what he liked best about his job. He let the blond get all the way to the door before adding, "Why do you think I asked you here, Bren?"

"I really don't know, because there's nothing I can tell you that you haven't already heard a dozen times from my coworkers."

"You're right about that." The lawyer was on his feet now, moving around to the side of his desk. "And I sure didn't ask you down here just to waste my time and see how much of a smartass you can be."

"No?" Bren feigned surprised. "That's too bad, 'cause that's the only reason I came."

It came out sounding like sarcasm, but Adams figured there was more truth in it than Bren wanted to admit. "Why don't you take a seat and let me tell you why you're here?"

"I'm in a hurry."

"Your birthday party can wait." Adams watched Bren take his hand from the doorknob and look back with mild surprise. "I'm a lawyer. I get paid to know things. Now have a seat."

"You like telling people what to do, don't you?"

"Yes, I do. That's why I became a lawyer. Now have a seat. Please. You're going to want to hear what I have to say."

"I can only stay a minute."

"If I don't have your attention within a minute, feel free to get up and walk out." Adams waited for Bren to retake a seat in front of the desk before sitting down himself. He put on a pair of wire-framed glasses and removed a white envelope from his center drawer. "Right now you don't like me much, but when I'm finished with you, you're going to be loving this fat man." His puffy lips contorted into a little smile, but got nothing but a stone expression from the blond man. "This meeting has nothing to do with Fenley. I suppose I should have had my secretary tell you that on the phone when she scheduled this appointment, but after you used my business card as your personal garbage disposal I felt no obligation to do you any favors."

"Then you do remember me?"

"Of course I remember you. I'm not a stupid man." He sat back in his chair and took off his glasses before continuing. "Your being here has nothing to do with Mark Fenley. That's strictly a coincidence." He gave Bren a long stare. "As a lawyer, sometimes it's fortunate to be blessed with the last name Adams, strictly so I can be listed first in the phone directory. A lawyer in England contacted me a few weeks ago, needing someone here in New Hampshire to get a hold of you. I offered my services, despite your bad manners up on the mountain." He paused for an apology but didn't get one. "I'm afraid, Bren, that I've been elected the bearer of bad news. Good *and* bad actually."

He could see that he had Bren's full attention.

"I've received word from England that Thomas Windfield has died." He paused again, this time for impact, not sure now if Bren was aware of the death. "I've been asked to take care of things on this end. If it's okay with you, I'll be acting as your lawyer in this matter." He still wasn't getting much more than a blank stare from the blond man seated across the desk from him, so he clarified himself by adding, "I'm asking if you'd like me to represent you."

"I caught that part." Bren nodded and leaned forward on his chair. "But in what? I mean, who's this Thomas Windfield guy, and what does he have to do with me?"

Dan Adams felt the color go out of his face. This was a man who made his living by always having the right words to say, but he couldn't think of anything brilliant at the moment. Instead, he sat back in his chair, took his gum out of his mouth and dropped it in a trashcan that stood next to the desk.

"You don't know Thomas Windfield?"

"Should I?"

"I would think so." Adams watched Bren give him a shrug. "You ever been to England?"

"No."

"You have British ancestry?"

"Perhaps. Somewhere along the line. Why?"

Adams was slowly shaking his head, uncertain about what to make of what he was hearing. "Well, perhaps you didn't know Thomas Windfield, but he certainly knew you." He slid the envelope in front of Bren and watched him pick it up and turn it over in his hands. "It's a little gift from Thomas Windfield—to you."

"You already opened it," said Bren.

"It came that way," Adams lied. The British lawyer had sent everything in a cardboard box. There were two envelopes inside, one addressed to Dan Adams, the other to Bren Stevens. Adams had read his personal letter but wasn't satisfied with that. In the back office he had a coffee pot, which he'd used to steam open the second envelope. He'd known what he'd find inside but wanted to see it first hand.

Now, staring across the desk, he watched Bren withdraw the sheet of paper, unfold it and scan the paragraphs, with a glazed looked of confusion.

"Consider it a birthday present," said Adams. "I received it nearly two weeks ago from the lawyer in England, who requested that it not be given to you until your twenty-fifth birthday. Today."

"This is a will," said Bren.

"I'm aware of that. I've read it. It's a fairly large estate: a house, a good deal of property, and one million pounds, all of which he's giving to you." Adams raised his eyebrows. "Quite a healthy sum from someone you don't know, wouldn't you say?"

"Are you sure you've got the right person here?" Bren looked again at the will. The paper bore his name, address and the day's date: June 11, 1994. "Why me?"

"I thought you'd know that," said Adams. "Lenard Berke, the English lawyer, called about a month ago wanting to know if I'd be willing to do a little research for him. I was prepared to tell him no, until he mentioned your name. He had your address, wanted to know if I'd go over to your place and find out if you actually existed. I told him that wouldn't be necessary, that I already knew you existed." Adams grinned. "I still remembered you from the mountain. So he asked if I'd pass the will along to you. I told him I would." He pointed to the paper in Bren's hand. "That's not a complete will you have there. It's only one page out of several. It's not even dated."

"Where's the rest?"

"In England, I suppose. I tried to call Lenard Berke back after I read the will, see what more I could find out, but he wasn't in. I left a message for him to call me. I'm still waiting. I can give you Berke's address and phone number if you'd like."

"I would."

On the desk sat a small green filing box filled with names and addresses. Adams removed a card from it and started copying the English lawyer's information down on a post-it note.

"You get the house and some of the money now. But as you'll read in, I believe it's paragraph three, the majority of the money can't be withdrawn for another year."

Bren scanned down to the third paragraph, which read: *While living in the house for the first year, the beneficiary is entitled to withdraw ten thousand pounds a month for living expenses and to facilitate in any needed restorations to the home. After the beneficiary has abided in the home for one full year, the remaining balance of the account will then be made available in full.*

"So what do you think of the fat man now?" asked Adams as he handed Bren the note containing the information for Lenard Berke.

"You're getting better by the minute," said Bren. "But don't go telling any of my friends I said that."

"Don't worry, I won't let it out that you were in here acting like a human being." Adams winked, then bent over, lifted a briefcase from the floor and placed it on the desk. "This is also yours." He pushed the worn case over to Bren. Its once black leather had now faded to a dusty gray. Cracks split the leather, and two tarnished locks held the lid tightly into place. "There wasn't a key," explained Adams. "And I have no idea what's inside."

He'd spent half an hour one day looking the thing over, wondering how he could get those locks open so he could take a peek inside. In truth, getting them open wasn't the real problem; it was getting them closed again without leaving traces that they'd been forced open that presented the real challenge. So it remained closed.

Adams pulled open the center drawer of the desk and pulled out a screwdriver that he'd put there a few hours earlier, just for this occasion. He handed it across the desk and was disappointed when Bren didn't reach for it.

"I think I'll do this at home, if you don't mind."

Adams looked like a man who had just swallowed a mouthful of sour milk. He nodded, thinking it'd be best not to let on how disappointed he was. Then he thought better of it and said, "You're not honestly going to cheat me out of this moment, are you?"

Bren picked up the case and rattled it. It was lighter than he'd expected. Looking across the desk at the fat man, he could see that the lawyer was serious about wanting to see inside the case, but rather than respond Bren stood and put his hand out.

"You know why I took this assignment?" asked Adams, sitting back in his chair, away from Bren's outstretched hand. "It surely wasn't for the money. The English lawyer offered me a few hundred dollars to see that the will and briefcase got to you. It's hardly worth my time. But I was curious. Now I find out you don't even know this dead man. Well, that makes me more curious. Some Englishman you don't even know put you in his will and sent you a briefcase. I'd like to know what's inside."

"I'm late for my own birthday party." Bren tucked the briefcase up under his arm and reached out to take a business card from a small tray that Adams had on his desk. But before he could snatch one up, the fat lawyer pulled the tray away.

"Your business card is lying in the dirt up there in the mountains and has a wad of gum stuck to it. You want it, go up and get it."

"What if I need to get in touch with you?"

"I'm in the phone book." The fat man offered a half-smile. It wasn't much, just a simple business card, but it was nice being able to say no to the blond man after all. For forty-two, Dan Adams had the spiteful heart of a nine-year-old, and he knew it. Not that this knowledge ever prompted him to change. The fact was he enjoyed getting the best of the argument. It was one of those simple pleasures of life that he never grew tired of—like putting too much hot fudge on his ice cream or watching the defendant leave the courtroom in tears after the jury returned a verdict of guilty. Satisfaction was satisfaction no matter where it came from.

# CHAPTER 2

$\mathcal{H}$e sat in his car, staring through the windshield up at the sky. There was something eerie about the moon, the red tint and the way the line of clouds was drifting past. And it was so large, like it was closer to the Earth than normal. The look of that moon summed up his whole mood, surreal and dubious. His head kept telling him that he should be elated about what had just transpired at the lawyer's office, but at the moment, all he felt was confused—like he'd opened someone else's Christmas present and now knew he had to give it back, but had no idea who to give it to. His name and address on the front of the envelope didn't offer much comfort in the matter.

Next to him on the front seat sat the briefcase, still unopened. He'd already looked in the glove compartment for something he could use to pry open the latches, but all he'd found were a few maps and some receipts for maintenance he'd had done to the engine.

The envelope containing the will was sitting on the dashboard. He'd given it a lot of thought on the drive over from Dan Adams's office. The most logical explanation was that they'd gotten him confused with some other Bren Stevens. Not that the name was all that common. Though he doubted it was entirely unique either. Bren had come from a long line of hard-working, yet unsuccessful men—"Losers," his mother always said—and it seemed unlikely that he'd be the one to break that losing streak.

His grandfather had settled a farm in lower New Hampshire. He worked long hours, putting seed into the ground, irrigating and harvesting. In return for his hard labor, the government was kind enough to step in and take his farm away. So he and his family moved to Littleton, where he took a job as a mechanic. He raised three boys, who would all grow up and disappoint their mother: the first by being stupid enough to get himself killed in Vietnam, the second by spending time in the state penitentiary for (accidentally?) shooting one of his friends while deer hunting, and the third by not having sense enough to move out of Littleton. The third was Bren's father, Ruben Stevens: the lumberjack, the drinker, the smoker, the TV watcher. "The worst of the litter," Ruben's mother used to say. "If he's going to make a wreck of his life, at least he could have enough respect to do it somewhere where I don't have to look at it."

Ruben's mother was dead now, and that was fine with him. One less critic nagging at him, telling him to get off his duff and do something with his life. His wife had that job now and was very good at it. She'd tell him about all the potential he had and how he was wasting it because he was too damn lazy to go out and make something of himself. Instead he stuck around their small town, setting a bad example for Bren, his only child, who was most likely going to grow up and be just like him.

Bren didn't like listening to his mother nag any more than his father did, which was why he spent as little time as possible around his parents' home. His father was just as critical. Sitting in front of the television with the volume up loud (a bottle of beer in one hand and a cigarette in the other), he'd tell Bren about how great the economy was now, about how kids nowadays were out starting their own businesses. It was different when he was younger, he maintained. Otherwise he'd have done something more with his life, but Bren had no excuse. He was born in an age of opportunity, yet he was wasting his time up in the mountains cutting down trees and making somebody else rich.

He was only twenty-five and already the people who loved him most were telling him he was a failure. The problem was he believed it. Leaving Littleton was his greatest ambition. He'd gotten himself into a rut, and as far as he could tell, there was no getting out of it. He talked a lot about saving up his money and going to college, but after paying his rent and other bills, there never seemed to be much left to put in the bank. He'd always been a smart child. He read a lot and caught on to things faster than his friends, which was why his mother was so disappointed in seeing him follow in his father's footsteps.

He got out and shut the door of his Ford Mustang, a piece of junk that his uncle, the ex-con, had sold to him, telling him that all it really needed was a new paint job and it'd be just like new. He'd failed to mention all the problems with the engine.

Across the street was a house owned by a friend of his. It was a small place with wood siding and a few mangy bushes out front. The music was up loud, and judging by the number of silhouettes he could see passing the windows, the house was full.

A neighbor's dog started barking at him through a chain-link fence, so he moved off to the side of the house, away from the streetlight, in case someone should happen to glance out the window. He passed through a gate and into the backyard, which was dark except for two rectangles of light coming from the kitchen windows. Inside, a woman was putting cookies on a plate. It was Julia Eastman, a girl he'd dated off and on back in high school and who now dated his best friend, Paul Danes. She still harbored some bad feelings toward Bren, but she mostly kept it to herself.

He tapped at the window and held his finger to his lips when Julia looked up at him. She smiled as she came around the counter and unlocked the door.

"What are you doing at the back door?" She was a short girl with dark eyes and thick eyebrows.

"I need to talk to Paul."

She looked behind her at the kitchen door. It was open, revealing the short hallway that led to the living room. "Everybody's in there waiting for you."

"I know," he said. "Don't tell anyone else I'm here, okay? Only Paul."

He remained in the backyard and watched through the window as she crossed through the kitchen and exited down the short hall. It was a warm night, even with the breeze. A mosquito was buzzing in his ear and he could hear the chatter of people inside the house. It sounded like they were having a good time, probably drinking beer and retelling the same stories that they told whenever the group got together, reminiscing about high school, baseball or summer camp. It was always the same, yet no one ever seemed to mind. To Bren it was just another facet of the rut, a feature he never complained about but always found unbearable.

It only took a moment before Paul was coming through the kitchen, shaking his head at him, wearing that mildly amused expression that was so typical of Paul. "You're an hour and a half late," he said as he stepped out the back door. He was a thin man with dark hair and a thin mustache that he'd been trying to grow for the past six months.

"I had my appointment with the fat man today," said Bren.

"How'd that go?"

"Not so bad."

Paul looked through the kitchen window at Julia, who had come back to fetch the plate of cookies. "They're threatening to eat the cake without you," he said.

Bren didn't look as though he cared. He said, "I've got something you're gonna wanna see. You got a screwdriver?"

"My house is filled with guests, Bren."

"I know that."

Paul nodded and went back inside the house. He knew Bren well enough to know how to read him, and judging by his tone of voice and the look in his eyes, he had something up his sleeve. They'd been friends since they were children and trusted each other more than they did their own flesh and blood, which wasn't saying much, considering their families. The two of them had come from bad stock, that's the way they saw it, and that gave them a tight bond.

Bren stood at the edge of the house, looking again at the moon and trying to think if he'd ever heard the name Thomas Windfield before. As far as he could recall, he hadn't. Windfield could have been a distant relative, but something inside him told him that wasn't the case.

Hearing the back door close behind him, he turned and found Paul coming toward him in the dark, with a screwdriver in hand.

"This better be good," he said.

The neighbor's dog barked again as they crossed through the street, to the Mustang. Bren slid in behind the steering wheel, leaned over to unlocked the passenger door, then pulled the briefcase toward him so Paul would have a place to sit. As always, the first things Paul did were roll down the window and scoot the seat all the way back to make room for his long legs. He was taller than Bren, and thinner, and he never hid the fact that he didn't like confined spaces. Not claustrophobic per se, but close to it.

"Where we going?"

"Right here." Bren turned on the dome light before taking the envelope off the dashboard and handing it to Paul. "I don't want everyone else to know about this. Not yet anyway, not until I have time to figure out what to make of it. The fat man gave it to me."

"I thought he wanted to talk to you about Mark Fenley."

"So did I."

Opening the envelope, Paul removed the paper, unfolded it and tilted it toward the light so he could see the fine print. It only took the reading of the first paragraph for him to realize what he had in his hands. He raised his eyes a moment, as though he had a question to ask, but he said nothing, just put his eyes back on the page and read down to the bottom. His first thought was to dismiss it, but Bren wasn't the type for pranks. In fact, if anything, Bren was often too serious. Fabricating a will didn't seem his style.

"Is this for real?"

"According to Dan Adams it is." Bren took the will back and stuffed it into the envelope. "Apparently a lawyer in England sent it to Adams a few weeks ago and asked him not to give it to me until today. He also sent this." He patted the briefcase.

"What's inside?"

"That's what the screwdriver's for."

The sound of crickets swept in through the open window as Bren put the briefcase on his lap and proceeded to pry open the latches with the screwdriver. They were tarnished, even appeared to have a trace of rust on them. The man had sent a will worth several million pounds, but couldn't afford a decent briefcase. That was one of the details that Bren didn't trust. Yet at the same time, it was the very thing that made him think there just might some merit in all of this. The kind of man who would give his house and money to a stranger was most likely eccentric enough to send everything else along in a tattered briefcase.

It didn't take much effort to get the latches open. Just a few twists of the screwdriver and they popped right up. The interior of the case had the smell of musty leather, yet appeared in better condition than the exterior. The contents consisted of a set of keys, a metal object, several black and white photographs, and a letter, handwritten in black ink and signed, "Thomas James Windfield." It read:

☙

Dear Bren, my trusted friend:

I can only suspect that my death has come as a surprise to you—as I'm sure it did to me. However, I do not doubt that my death isn't what is troubling you most at this moment, but it is my life that does the troubling. Who am I and why have I bequeathed my possessions to you, a stranger? These are undoubtedly the two foremost questions on your mind. Am I right? I do not doubt your answer to be yes.

I would like to explain everything to you, but this is impossible, since doing so may interfere with my request. What request?—you ask. Well, the one I am about to petition you for: avenge my death.

I would like to say that my eternal peace depends upon it, but, not being dead at the time I write this letter, I do not know whether or not such a statement would be true. But surely, you, as my friend, will rest more peacefully if this request is carried out. So good luck and have a pleasant journey to England.

Your friend eternally,

Thomas James Windfield.

"My god." Paul was sitting sideways on the seat, his face half lost in shadows, his mildly amused expression gone. He was quicker to buy into the absurdity than Bren, yet he could think of no words to express his feelings, other than to repeat "My god" a few more time. The will had aroused his curiosity, but the letter had struck a nerve. Paul was one of those men who believed that the divine intervention spoken of in the Bible was what people nowadays called luck or chance. Whatever was happening was fate—a little out of the ordinary yes, but it was most definitely fate.

Bren wasn't apt to believe that God was up there pulling the strings and bringing this all into play, but he did believe that it was significant—and that alone was enough to make the hairs on the back of his neck stand on end. It was one of the rare moments in life when he could actually see the cogs clicking into place and know that his world was ready to take a radical turn. Like most people, he generally never knew an event was significant until long after it'd passed and he was able to look back on it with the prospective of how it'd changed the course of his life. This time was different, which excited him nearly as much as it frightened him.

He set the letter aside and took the metal object from the briefcase. It was a scrap of silver, about the size of a ballpoint pen, with metal teeth protruding all around it. It didn't look like anything he recognized.

Next, he grabbed the stack of eight by ten, black and white photographs. Nine in total. The first photo was of a three-story gray granite mansion, with a turret on one side and a stretch of ivy climbing the other. It was a beautiful home, surrounded by trees and plenty of grass. It shamed the nicest houses that Littleton had to offer. It was one of those solid European structures, built over a century ago, one that looked as though it could withstand war and weather, and perhaps had done so.

"You think that's the house?" asked Paul.

"I hope." Bren's eyes brightened for a moment, until he turned to the second photo, which sent a chill running the length of his spine. It showed a group—five men, two ladies—standing within the door of a white gazebo. What drew his attention was a young man in his mid-twenties, positioned at the right of the group. He had blond hair and light eyes.

"My god." It was Paul talking again, this time in a whisper, as he took the photo and held it closer to the light to get a better look. It was a face he knew too well, and seeing it in that photograph, surrounded by strangers, made his jaw fall slack. "If it weren't for the hairstyle—" he trailed off and looked at Bren. "You think that's Thomas Windfield?"

"That'd be my guess."

"My god." Paul was shaking his head. "The man could be your twin."

Bren's sentiments exactly. It was almost like looking in a mirror. The chances of Thomas Windfield being a relative seemed indisputable now. He flipped the picture over. On the back, someone had handwritten the date August 16, 1964. In a little over two months the picture would be exactly thirty years old.

The third photograph showed his twin, the man he assumed to be the young Thomas Windfield, sitting on a stone bench next to a brunet. They were in a garden with lots of flowers and hedges in the background. The girl was lovely, perhaps twenty years old, with long hair and dark eyes.

Several of the pictures were of a middle-aged man, who'd also been present in the gazebo photo. He had a distinguished face and graying hair. There was a shot of him standing in an elegant room next to a long mirror, another with him behind a desk, and a third showing him standing in a large library. None of the photographs had anything written on the back. In fact, other than the gazebo photo, only one other picture had been dated, and it bore the exact same date, August 16, 1964. It showed a view of the back of the house. Framed within a second-floor window stood the young Thomas Windfield, staring down at the camera. He looked horror stricken, like he'd just seen someone jump to his death. This was the photograph that Bren found the most disturbing. Something about that expression on his twin's face, the genuine angst in the eyes, made the muscles in Bren's chest tighten and brought a shiver across his scalp. It was an odd sensation, somewhat akin to déjà vu.

He looked out through the windshield again, up at the large moon, and suddenly wondered if Paul's view of fate didn't hold some merit after all. The strangest feeling washed over him. It was as though his life were out of his hands, that he was being pulled by some invisible force that had its own aspiration about where his life should lead. He couldn't say how he knew it, but he was certain his life would never be the same. It was the best feeling he'd felt in years.

# CHAPTER 3

✿

$\mathcal{I}$t was late afternoon when the bus rolled into Lurkdale in North Yorkshire and left Bren standing on the curb near the one-room bus station. On the flight over, he'd restudied the photographs and the letter. He didn't know much more now than he'd known the day he sat down with Dan Adams in his office, but he knew enough to convince him to come to England and have a look at the house for himself. He'd left the keys to his car and to his apartment with Paul, telling him that if things went well that he could have what he wanted and sell the rest.

So far he liked what he saw.

On the bus from London to Lurkdale, he passed many quaint villages, medieval castles, and thatched-roof cottages lined with flower gardens. Lurkdale itself appeared as though it'd come straight out of a storybook, with its gray limestone buildings lining narrow cobblestone streets and the steeple of a large gothic church towering over the rooftops. The village was lovely, and nothing in its appearance could have warned him of the sinister worm eating away at its core.

Lurkdale, a once lead-mining community, lay upon the rolling hills in northern England, with a river that cut between the hills and drew a curved line right through the center of the village. Three stone bridges connected the two sides, and cobbled streets branched up the hillsides away from the bridges. At the edge of town, a ruined mill sat at the river's bank.

He crossed through a side street and found himself on Moorland Avenue, the main street of the village. It was a canyon-like street that twisted past tight-fitting seventeenth-century shops. Nearly every building bordering the avenue stood slightly askew, tilting off in one direction or another. Their leaning shadows fell across the street beneath the falling sun. Several people strolled along the thin side-walks, looking at Bren carrying a large suitcase in each hand and a new briefcase under one arm.

Within the shadows of the sidewalk, a lady stood in the doorway of a shop where mannequins wearing red bonnets and blue dresses stood poised behind the windows. The lady's back was to Bren, but he could see her fiddling with a collection of keys, sorting to find the proper one to lock up for the evening. Across the street, in front of a butcher shop stood a young boy of no more than ten. He was hold-ing a broom twice his size and pushing the dust from the sidewalk into the gutter while a man with bushy eyebrows and little hair stared from the window between dangling sausages and a cut of pork.

"Lost, are you?" said a voice, and Bren flinched at the plump gen-tleman who stood with a loaf of bread cuddled under his arm, obscured within the doorway of a bakery.

"It's that obvious, is it?" Bren set his bags on the walkway. "I'm looking for Windfield Manor."

The man, with the fat of his face all contorted, looked Bren over suspiciously, focusing on the suitcases for a moment. "And what would a lad like yourself want with a foul house such as that?"

"Foul?"

"Like no other."

"I own it."

"Right. And I own Buckingham Palace." The man laughed as the smell of pastries drifted from the open door behind him.

"Is it near here?"

"Going to stick to that story, are ya? Do as you like. That'll be the street you want." He pointed with his nose, over to a narrow lane that veered down the hill.

"You know where I can get a taxi?"

"Not in Lurkdale, laddie." The man grinned. "But if ever a stranger could lend a word to another, I'd say the tavern is better lodging." The man winked and strolled away, whistling.

"Good enough," the bushy-browed man called from the butcher shop doorway across the street, and added, "'Bout time Mum had tea on." The boy wiped his face on his sleeve and took his broom inside.

Bren descended the hill, down through the residential area of the village. The fading sun sat just above the red rooftops, where lines of smoke twisted up into the sky. The air was cool and smelled as though it'd rained not long before, though the street and sidewalks were dry. The cottages were quaint and close together, with manicured hedges and flower gardens. Not many people were out, just a few children playing in the street and a couple of elderly women seated in rocking chairs on the porch of a small home. They said nothing as Bren passed, just nodded, and eyed him coldly when his back was to them. It wasn't often they got strangers in this part of town, especially one carrying luggage. Even the boys in the street, who had been kicking a soccer ball along the cobblestones, had to pause and give him a look, watching the stranger set his suitcases on the sidewalk, which was little more than a strip of cement pressed up flush against most of the houses.

"Would you boys happen to know where Windfield Manor is?"

One of the boys stopped the ball under his foot and pointed down the road. "You're going right, mister. Just a few kilometers out of town."

"Out of town?" Bren stared off toward the edge of the village, where trees speckled the darkening hillside. "How far's a kilometer?"

That won him a laugh, but no explanation.

The day after his birthday, after reading the will and viewing the contents of the briefcase, he'd called England, trying to get in touch with Lenard Berke, the lawyer who had sent everything to New Hampshire. Berke was out, but his secretary was able to answer the most vital questions, stating that the will was legitimate and so was the house. That was enough to convince him to come to England and check it out for himself. As for the briefcase, the secretary could only say that she'd never seen it open.

At the bottom of the hill, the road connected with one of the three bridges that spanned the river. From there, it twisted to the right and led out of town, up into the green hills and trees. That's where he got his first glimpse of the house, far off in the distance, its roof rising above the trees. Beyond it, above the chimneys rising up from the roof, there was a hint of red in the sky. It wouldn't be long and that too would vanish, leaving him with nothing but the moon. He didn't like the thought of arriving at the house at night, but there was nothing that could be done about it.

The road from the village to the house was paved and deserted. Along the way, he passed a few farms, which were set back away from the road, with rock walls sectioning off the property lines. Two miles out, a small lane branched off toward the mansion through a thicket of trees. He passed under the branches and came out at the front of the house, which faced the village. It was large, just as the photographs had portrayed it. Yet it wasn't the same. A ten-foot high wooden fence surrounded the home, and the third-story loft glared over the wall, with the moon rising above it. There was a stench wafting toward him, from inside the fence. It was rancid, like dead animals.

He was standing on the old parking area, which was inlaid with reddish bricks that now had long grass growing up between them. It didn't look as though anyone had been here in years. From where he stood, he couldn't see much of the house, just the fence, all cracked and splintered. The white paint had turned gray and was curling away from the wood. And from what he could see, there didn't appear to be a gate in it, at least not along the front section.

He had no idea who Thomas Windfield was, but he'd developed a love/hate relationship with him already. More hate than love at the moment.

Between two of the wooden planks, Bren found a small notch that he could see through. It was dark and the notch didn't provide much of a view, but it was enough to know that things were much worse than he'd imagined. He kicked at one of the boards several times until it snapped, the sound echoing, sending birds fluttering from the trees.

He pulled the broken plank from its frame and stared in at the house. It was a sorrowful sight. Only fragments of glass remained in the window frames. The lawn lay heavy in growth and weeds, and trash was strewn throughout the yard, mainly along the front end of the lawn, where teenaged villagers had thrown their garbage on dark nights as they stood outside the fence telling ghost stories. The living trees needed pruning, and in the center of the front yard, a large oak had completely withered, its bare branches all gnarled and hauntingly appropriate. The ivy on the north wall of the mansion was now only a mass of shriveled twine, dangling across the side of the granite wall.

"Thank you very much, Thomas, whoever you are," Bren said as the growing wind sucked the shredded curtains out through the broken glass then blew them back in again. "My own little plot in hell." He could feel the jetlag overtaking him and he hoped things would look brighter in the morning after a good night's rest, because they sure looked bleak right now.

A twig snapped outside the fence and drew his attention. He gazed down the wooden slats to the trees. There in the darkness stood the figure of a person.

"Hello," he called.

No answer.

"Who's there?" He kept his voice steady, trying to sound calm.

The figure pulled a cloak snug over its head, stepped back among the trees and disappeared.

# CHAPTER 4

With the early morning sun rising behind them, Eric and Lug ambled into the Lurkdale Tavern, which doubled as a hotel and diner. Lug, who had earned his nickname by his inexplicable ability to swallow everything in sight and never get full, pulled a single cigarette from his shirt pocket and plopped it in his mouth. He didn't light it, just let it hang over his bottom lip as he'd seen James Dean doing in a poster that he used to have when he was a kid.

From the tavern's lobby, the two men stepped inside the dining hall, whose front windows overlooked Moorland Avenue. Eric Starkey cupped a hand over his eyes to ward off the sun that was slanting through the glass and glaring across the red and white checkerboard floor. He'd had too much to drink the night before and his hangover was still in full bloom. His eyes were puffy and as red as his hair.

It was still early, and so far the only people in the room were Fanny (the waitress) and the gaunt-faced Mr. Dowry, who was taking a break from his morning milk run. Most of the village was still in bed, which was precisely where these two men would have been if the judge hadn't sentenced them to community service, which in their case consisted of city clean-up duty. Two hours a day, from 6:30 A.M. to 8:30 A.M.

"You look like death." The waitress pointed them to a table in the sun. They opted for a table against the far wall instead. Eric wanted to stay as much in the dark as possible. He cursed himself for leaving his sunglasses at home, and even more, he cursed the mayor, who had accused them of the crime that brought about their punishment.

"Get that stupid thing out of your mouth." The waitress plucked the cigarette from Lug's lips and crumbled it in her fingers. "Makes you look utterly daft."

"He is daft," said Eric.

"Bah," replied Lug and grumbled at his Auntie Fanny for destroying his last cigarette. This was his mother's sister, but that still didn't give her the right to demolish his personal property. Yet he said nothing, other than to place his order of spaghetti on toast while his companion chose his standard eggs, crumpet and black coffee.

The two men did indeed look like death. Neither of them had gotten more than five hours of sleep a night all week, yet only Lug's aunt thought they looked any worse than they did on a normal day. Down both legs of their blue jeans were parallel slashes that they'd intentionally put there themselves. Eric wore a purple T-shirt that clashed with his hair, and Lug wore a crucifix earring in his left lobe. He wasn't a religious man, but most people found his display of Jesus hanging from the cross sacrilegious. Nothing could have pleased him more.

A week earlier, the two twenty-two-year-olds had driven Eric's rusty pickup east to Scarborough, where they purchased three cans of black paint. They'd gone to Scarborough because they knew that tracking down the buyer of paint purchased in Lurkdale would be much too easy. At two in the morning, the two young men parked down the street from a lovely home that had a silver Oldsmobile parked in the drive. With a can of paint in one hand and a brush in the other, the two proceeded to cover each window with thick black paint. It took just over an hour, and the job was far from professional. When they were finished, the house looked like a picture from a children's coloring book. Behind the house, in a metal box attached to the back porch, they found the main circuit breaker.

They flipped it off for a few seconds, long enough to screw up any electric alarm clocks, then turned it back on. Before going home to bed, they drove out of town to Windfield Manor and chucked the paint cans and brushes over the high fence that surrounded the house.

When Mayor Tuttle hadn't shown up for work, his secretary called to see if he was all right. He snatched up the phone beside his bed and grunted out a hello. "Ten o'clock?" he muttered, squinting over at his nightstand, where his electric alarm clock was blinking on and off at him in the blackness of the room. "Are you out of your mind? It's still dark outside." Five minutes later when he was standing outside in his bathrobe inspecting his house, the first words out of his mouth were: "Eric and Lug." His flabby checks smoldered red. There was a longstanding relationship of hate between him and the two young punks. In his mind, this enmity alone was enough to convict them. What furthered his conviction was the fact that two days before the painting incident he'd been in the department store ordering a new alarm clock that had a battery backup in case of a power outage. Just after the clerk had notified him that it would take a week to get it in, the mayor turned and found Eric Starkey standing behind him, grinning slyly beneath his mop of curly red hair.

Lug checked his watch. 5:45 A.M. By 6:30 they were to be at the town hall to meet with the city crew that they'd be spending the day with.

When their food arrived, Eric downed three more aspirin with his coffee and leaned back and waited for his head to explode. He prayed that it would, just to put him out of his misery and get him out of demoralizing himself by walking around the city picking up other people's rubbish. He knew his friends would never let him live it down. They'd only served three days and already the gang at the local pub was referring to them as the *Clean Team* and *Generation Clean-X*. It could only get worse from there.

A few more people trickled in and ordered breakfast. About 6:10 a haggard-looking man wandered in, dressed in a wrinkled shirt. His blond hair was mussed and he hadn't shaved. Lug slurped in a mouthful of spaghetti as he watched his Auntie Fanny point the stranger to a table next to him. A tourist, thought Lug. Lost and frustrated. Either headed to Scarborough or Leeds. Got in late and just woke up and realized he was in Hades. Lug knew just how the man felt. He felt that same way every day.

"Morning, gov." Lug was happy to see that morning had taken its toll on someone besides himself. "Looks like you've had a rough night."

The man said nothing. He merely nodded and gazed out the window at Moorland Avenue until Auntie Fanny came over dressed in her waitress apron, checkered red and white to match the floor. Staring down at the stranger, she grabbed a notepad from the pocket of her apron and pulled a pencil from behind her ear, not saying a word as she waited for his order. For a moment, the man regarded the table, which was supplied with salt and pepper shakers, a napkin dispenser and a set of silverware—but no menu.

"Bacon and eggs—toast—a glass of orange juice?" It was more a question than a statement.

As his aunt returned to the kitchen without writing down the order, Lug stared across the table at Eric, then looked at the stranger. They both looked as though they were suffering from the same malady.

"Where you from, mate?" asked Lug.

"America. New Hampshire." Bren Stevens had taken the counsel of the bread-carrier and had spent the night in the Lurkdale Tavern. He hadn't slept well and he couldn't blame it all on the hard bed. No matter how hard he tried, he couldn't keep his mind from coughing up images of the house and the dark figure lurking near the trees.

"We've got a bleedin' Yank right here in our presence," Lug related to Eric, who merely grunted his tone of disinterest. Lug waved a dismissing hand at him and turned his attention back to Bren. "Lost, eh?"

"Why do you say that?"

"That's what everybody says. You ask any foreigner why they're here and they all give the same answer—they're lost. Otherwise, nobody stops in Lurkdale, mate."

"Is that right?" Bren glanced out the window into the street, where he could see an elderly gentleman setting out his wares by the sidewalk as he prepared to open up shop for the day. "Looks like a nice enough town to me."

"Nice," said Lug satirically. "You'll get right tired of *nice* real soon, believe me. We've got only one pub. And unless you're an alcoholic like me mate here, that ain't even a whole lot of fun."

"I'm no bleeding alcoholic, you sod." Eric's eyes were half closed. "I'm a social drinker. I just happen to be very social is all."

"You're right. I am lost." Bren rubbed the sleep from his eyes. "You two heard of a man named Thomas Windfield?"

Lug dropped his fork onto his plate. Even Eric came to attention with this question. This was a topic not approached by the average passerby. Just the sound of an outsider mentioning the name made the men uneasy. They gave each other a disconcerting look, picked up their plates, glasses and silverware and moved over to Bren's table. Have they heard of Thomas Windfield? Ludicrous! They'd heard it all. And they'd seen enough to make their skin crawl. For most people in Lurkdale, the Thomas Windfield story was pure legend and fascination. But for Lug and Eric it was more than mere hearsay—it was life. They'd seen things that to this day still made the hair on the back of their necks stand on end.

"What's this about Thomas Windfield." Eric was leaning across the table, staring the stranger in the face.

"He's the reason I'm here."

"I thought you said you were lost."

"I am. Figuratively speaking." Bren paused as the waitress came and shoved a plate of runny eggs and toast in front of him and plopped down a glass of orange juice. There was no bacon as he'd ordered. Instead there was a large mushroom about half the size of his fist. Bren thanked her and she grunted in response as she walked away.

"She's a talker, isn't she?" said Bren.

"That's me Auntie Fanny." Lug checked his watch. 6:20. They had ten minutes to get to the town hall. But he couldn't leave now. Not when the conversation had just gotten interesting. "How long are you staying in town?"

Bren shrugged. "Yesterday I'd have said I was moving here. But now I don't know."

Eric laughed. It hurt his head, but he laughed. It was more of a snort actually. Lurkdale wasn't the kind of place that attracted foreigners. Sure it had a superficial charm to it. But once you broke beneath the quaint surface, all you were left with was the writhing heart, and Thomas Windfield was what gave it life.

Eric pushed his plate aside and extended his hand across the table. "I'm Eric. This disgusting creature beside me here is Lug."

"Don't be calling me names in front of strangers."

"What? You think he won't figure it out on his own? You've got the foulest mouth in Lurkdale, mate. You think he's not going to notice?"

"Ain't nothin' foul 'bout me mouth," said Lug. "Don't listen to me mate here. He spent too much time in the sun yesterday. He's got this pale-moon skin that fears the sun, and the heat always distorts his thinking."

Eric feigned a smile, his hair dangling across his face. "What's all this business about Thomas Windfield?"

"I take it you're aware that he died." Bren paused for a reaction and watched them regard him as though his comment were totally absurd. "Anyway, he left me a few things in his will."

"Such as?" asked Eric.

"His house. His money."

"Rubbish." Lug was playing with his fork, tapping it against the side of his plate. "How old are you?"

"Twenty-five."

Hearing this made Lug feel better. It confirmed the fact that the American was lying, which he'd hoped he was. The last thing he wanted was any more complications to this already complicated issue. Setting his fork down, he sat back in his chair and put his hands on his round stomach.

"You know how long Thomas Windfield's been dead?" he asked and watched Bren shake his head. "I didn't think so." Lug checked his watch again. They were now ten minutes late for clean-up duty. "Should've done yer homework 'fore you come claiming some thirty-year-old corpse mentioned you in his will."

Bren cocked his head as if he'd misheard him. "Come again."

"That's right, matey. Thirty years. Nice try though." Eric looked much more awake than he had when he first entered the diner. "If you own Windfield Manor, why you sleeping in town?"

"I arrived late."

"Ah." Lug nodded and looked at Eric. "He arrived late. Course you'll be staying there tonight."

Bren said nothing.

"Course he'll be staying there, Lug. He owns the place, doesn't he? Can't expect the owner of Windfield Manor to go spending his nights in town when he can be out there living it up in such a fine home."

"Yes indeed." Lug wiped a napkin over his lips as he stood. He tapped his plump finger on his watch, indicating to Eric the need to run. But before leaving, he leaned his weight on the table and looked Bren in the face. "Tell me this, mate." He lowered his voice to a whisper. "Why would you want to pretend you own that defiled house of horror? Got a soft spot for the wicked, have you? It's a beastly place, that. A maggot-infested carcass of a purified pig." He cringed at his own words. "Got a worm in its core, and it's just begging some fool to take a bite. If I was you, I wouldn't be so eager to be that fool."

# CHAPTER 5

"Thirty years," Bren repeated as he stood at the fence and gaped in at Windfield Manor, which favored a harrowing version of a country inn, with its many chimneys rising up from the roof. Rain clouds gathered overhead. He pulled another board from the fence, stepped through and set his suitcases down on the garbage-covered walkway that led to the front door.

The stench from the night before lay visible in the light: a rotted fish, a half-eaten slice of pizza, a diaper speckled in ketchup, and a slew of nameless, indistinguishable items, all shriveled and bug-crawling.

He jangled the house keys from his pocket and climbed the three steps to the front door, which was already unlocked. Home, sweet home. He pushed the large oak door open and breathed in the musty air. Glancing up at the sky, he hurried back down the walkway and grabbed his suitcases and brought them up the steps and set them inside the door so that the oncoming rain wouldn't drench them. Inside the entryway a carved mahogany staircase coiled to an upper floor, and a web-covered chandelier hung from the high ceiling at the center of the stairs. In front of him, a corridor burrowed through the center of the house, with an offshoot trailing off to the south wing library and conservatory.

He tried the light switch at the foot of the stairs near the front door, but nothing. Leaving the door open, he walked down the corridor, where he looked in at the living room, and then crossed over into the study, where empty bookshelves lined the walls. A dark patch stained the carpet in front of an oak desk. It looked as though it could be old blood or perhaps some sort of syrup. Behind the desk, a small window looked out through the dead ivy and onto the side lawn. He'd just started toward the window when a thunderclap shook the house.

He wasn't the sort of person who scared easily. It was just thunder after all, and that alone was nothing to worry about; however, there'd been something else, something upstairs. He could hear several doors banging open, and—

He strained to hear.

It was more than the wind. Footsteps perhaps. He exited the study, where the storm had darkened the corridor. A gust of wind blew up from the kitchen at the back of the house and slammed the front door. In front of him, a large arched doorway led into the living room. To his right, the mahogany staircase twisted up to the second floor, where something moved. He crossed the living room, to the fireplace, where he retrieved an iron poker and brought it back with him to the entryway. The house fell silent for just a moment. He stared at the top of the stairs, at the balustrade, then pulled the door open again and propped it with his two suitcases. Outside, the rain was coming down hard and the scent of rain blew in with the breeze as the sky rumbled.

He rounded the stairs all the way to the top. A hallway cut about a quarter of the way through the house, with doors on either side, then twisted into a labyrinth of corridors, nooks and chambers. He came down the hall with his iron poker held above his shoulder. The first door stood open and was ceaselessly banging back and forth against the wall and a white tennis shoe that was keeping it from closing. The next two doors were doing the same, one held open by a box of clothes, the other by a can of varnish. He pushed the next door open. Nothing but a mirror, a bed and an overturned dresser.

Ahead of him, a door squeaked open and something thudded upon the floor inside the room, followed by what sounded like the shrill of a bird. Then nothing. The hallway was thick with shadows. At Bren's back, beyond the balustrade and the spidery chandelier, a shattered circular window looked out over the front lawn. The dim light that shone through did little more than add a gloomy ambience to the hallway. He moved forward and paused in front of the door where the sound had come from. It was quiet now.

Listening, he tightened his grip on the metal poker before kicking the door wide open and charging in.

The first thing that staggered him was the sight. The smell didn't register until a moment later. At the far end of the room, six yellow cats tore at the remains of a freshly killed bird. A crow, Bren surmised, judging by the size as well as by the black feathers scattered about. And by the stench and the shear amount of remnants of claws, beaks and feathers, he figured this wasn't the first bird they'd slaughtered inside this room. When he first charged in, four of the cats immediately scrambled out. The other two scampered then came back to the bloody carcass and fought over which one would have the honor of carting it off. They hissed and swiped paws at each other until Bren screamed and chased them from the room.

The window was totally in tact, unlike those along the front of the house. He opened it to vent the stink, put his head outside and took a few deep breaths. The rain was still drizzling down. Below him lay a garden filled with statues, fountains and pathways. Every inch of it was overrun by weeds and vines. It actually had a charm to it, nature ravaging the creations of man. From the second floor, he could see out beyond the fence that encircled the yard. Directly behind the house, past the fence, stood a hill roughly twice the height of the house. To his right lay a field of heather. It was beautiful—even in the drizzle and beneath the dark sky—all wet and purple.

The sight made him forget the house for a while, and made him remember that he should be enjoying himself, if for no other reason than the fact that he was in a foreign country far from home. Far from his father, who had told him he was wasting his time and money coming to England. He'd told Bren that he'd give him a week before he came crawling back home to New Hampshire. Two weeks tops. The only thing the old man liked more than making predictions was rubbing it in everyone's face whenever he was right.

Mr. Stevens was one of those men who loved to come home after work, sit on the sofa and have his wife bring him everything. She'd be chatting on the phone or knitting an afghan when he would tell her to get into the kitchen and get him a beer. She'd always argue, tell him she wasn't his slave. Then she'd get up and get it for him. He loved to bark, but he wasn't a violent man. He'd never struck his wife and had only beaten Bren once in his entire life, the day he caught Bren deflowering Julia Eastman in his upstairs bedroom, and there weren't many who faulted the old man for that.

The day Bren showed him the will, Mr. Stevens had been sitting in front of the TV with a cigarette in his mouth. He took one look at the photographs and the letter and declared them all fake. "What kind of man plays who-done-it games with his will?" he asked. "And what the hell would you want to live over there in England for anyhow? You got everything you want right here in Littleton." He was always saying things like that, one week telling Bren to get out of Littleton and make something of himself, the next week asking why in heaven's name anyone would want to leave this nice little community. He was the only one who failed to see the contradiction.

Bren left the window open and stepped back into the hallway, where a gust of wind came through the window behind the chandelier and sent a whirl of dust and paper spinning down the hall. The banging of the doors ceased for a moment, and in the silence he could hear a flutter of wings. Ahead of him, where the hall angled off to the right and disappeared into another section of the house, a crow settled down on the wooden floor and strutted a few steps. There was unquestionably something alien about this house. Something he'd never felt in his twenty-five years. Not frightening exactly. Just foreign. As he moved forward, the bird entered an open bathroom doorway at the end of the hall, then came back out, flapped its wings again and disappeared the same way it'd come.

Following the direction of the crow, Bren rounded several corners and discovered another set of stairs that went up to the third-floor loft. At first, he could hear no more than a single pair of wings beating the air; however, as he climbed, the whole room above him seemed to stir. He could hardly believe his eyes as he hit the top of the stairwell. He thought six cats were bad, but try sixty crows—all fluttering and perturbed that someone had invaded the nest. The sound of the wings unnerved him. There was an energy in that room that Bren could only describe as malicious. Yet he had no idea how malicious it could be until the first bird swooped at his face.

He couldn't believe it, a damn bird. He'd had a dog attack him once, got its teeth into the back of his leg, but this was nothing but a stupid bird, yet it had his heart pumping.

He swung the poker and caught the crow in mid-flight. It hit the soiled carpet with a dull thud. More birds took to the air. He was backing down the stairs now. They came at him in droves. Not as an organized mass, but as a swarm of insects intent against the same enemy. Hitchcock's *The Birds* kept going through his mind. He would have never believed that he could be so afraid of a bird, or that they could be so malicious. The way they were coming at him—and the noise. He swung again and again, missing more than he hit. All it would take was one wrong step, one fall, and they'd be all over him like buzzards, tearing at his flesh.

He stumbled backwards down the steps, tripping over himself and halfway falling. They were everywhere, coming at him from all sides. One was in his hair, clawing at his ear. He slapped it away with his open hand. Another one fluttered into the stairwell, swooping at his face. He jabbed the poker into its chest and left it flopping on the stairs as he turned and bolted back toward the front of the house while half a dozen crows pursued him down the hall. Rushing into one of the open bedrooms, he slammed the door shut behind him. It was unbelievable. He had blood running from his ear and arm, and there was a claw mark along the side of his neck.

He hadn't even had time to catch his breath when he caught sight of a man from the corner of his eye, standing near the wall. His reflexes were good. He swung the poker in a swift fluid motion, putting his full weight into it. A split second before he landed a solid hit he realized that he'd made a big mistake. But it was too late. The poker struck the mirror right at the point where it reflected his own face. The glass fractured and a large section fell from the wall down to the carpet.

Seven years bad luck, just what he needed.

The small fire in the living room fireplace provided the only light in the dark house. The wind was up outside. It blew through the broken windows and swayed the curtains at his back. He was in a wooden rocking chair near the window, writing in his diary. At the end of the room, beside the fireplace, stood a grandfather clock that no longer worked. Next to him sat a rain-stained sofa. Across the room, a large mirror filled the inside wall and reflected the sway of the curtains and the flicker of firelight.

Even though he was alone at night in the house, he didn't feel as frightened as he thought he would. His search of the house had turned up nothing more than the crows nesting in the third-floor loft. Even the sounds of the house creaking and of the curtains flapping didn't bother him much as he held his diary on his lap and scribbled out his thoughts. He wrote about the large mirrors that hung in nearly every room of the house. He wrote about the furniture he'd found scattered throughout the various rooms and questioned why it'd been left behind. He wrote about the cats, the crows and how he'd spent the rest of the day.

After departing from the room where he'd holed himself up to escape the birds, he scouted out the downstairs dining room, kitchen, conservatory and library. He found a straw broom in a kitchen closet and spent the day sweeping down cobwebs and cleaning one of the upstairs rooms so he could stay the night. He picked a room that contained a large bed and an unbroken window. Since it didn't have a dresser, he dragged one down the hall from another room. He didn't plan on unpacking his suitcases quite yet, but he needed something heavy to prop in front of the bedroom door at night since he'd discovered that the room had no lock, and neither did any of the other bedrooms.

He raised his eyes from the diary and glanced across the room to the mirror. Behind him, the wind flung the curtains aside, then back down, but in that brief glimpse, he was certain he'd seen someone standing outside the window. Setting his diary on the sofa, he went to the window and parted the curtain slightly. Someone was indeed standing in the tall grass inside the fence, the head cloaked in a black cloth, the arms folded inside a coat, the dark eyes gazing upon the front door. The same person he'd seen in the woods that first night.

The black figure moved forward a few steps, stopped and tilted its head toward Bren, who clutched at the curtain and hid his face within the darkness of the room. Even with the fire flickering behind him, he didn't feel that he could be seen. Yet, the way the person turned and stepped toward him, he felt that beneath that black cloth were two eyes focused right at him. It lurched forward, came upon his doorstep and knocked. Bren peered out the curtains. His first night at his new home and already the neighbors were calling. How thoughtful. Who could it be? Cousin It? The Wicked Witch of the North? Jack the Ripper? Surely somebody who would feel welcome among this list of freaks.

Another knock and Bren went to the entryway and stood at the door, which he'd actually locked, despite the fact that if someone wanted in they could easily come through one of the many broken windows. A moment later there was another knock, accompanied by the words: "I know you're there." It was the voice of a woman, yet by no means alluring or lovely. Rather it had a harsh grating quality to it.

He turned the lock and pulled the door open slightly, just enough so he could see out. He stopped it short with his foot. A dark eye stared at him through the crack. The face of an old woman peered out from beneath the black cloak, with rotted teeth nullifying her grin.

"Could I come in?" Her breath reeked, and her voice was as cold and scratchy as the wind at her back.

"What do you need?" Bren closed the gap in the door slightly.

"Just a word. Only a word, that's all." The hag leaned her head toward the crack. "It's pertaining to you and the house." Assuming herself in, she put a hand on the door and pushed her way toward the opening, but Bren held firm, allowing nothing but the wind to hiss through.

"It's a bad night for visiting," he said.

"An even worse one for being left at the doorstep." The woman's grin disappeared behind her cracked lips.

"Perhaps you could come back in the morning."

"Perhaps morning will be too late."

"I'm sorry." Bren pushed the door closed. Her words intrigued and worried him, but the thought of allowing that woman in the door worried him more.

"Leave it be, young man," the hag's voice shrilled outside the door. "Leave it be."

Bren turned the lock and listened for departing footsteps, yet he heard nothing but the howl of the wind. To the left of the door was a small circular window. From it he could see the walkway leading down toward the fence and the hole he'd created in it.

The old woman, however, was nowhere in sight.

He couldn't help but wonder what a person like that would want with him. What she could possibly know. And most important, where she'd gone. The kitchen door was also locked, but she didn't know that. And the windows! All those broken windows! He hurried back to the living room, where he could get a better view of the front yard, and hopefully, a better view of the crone. He pulled the curtain slightly to one side, and there, with her wrinkled face pressed inside the window frame and her wild eyes looking level with Bren's, stood the hag. He scrambled away from the window in horror. The curtain fell closed, but a hand reached through the broken glass and pulled it aside again.

Leaning her face inside, she glared in at the man still cowering toward the mirror on the inner wall. "Stay where you belong. Some lines are best not crossed." The old woman turned away, and the curtains once again fluttered with the wind.

Bren Stevens followed the road back toward Lurkdale, with his hands weighed down by suitcases. The diary entry about the hag would have to wait until he settled back into the Lurkdale Tavern. Stupid biddy. He'd been scared off by someone's shriveled grandmother. He knew it was all in his head, but after the old woman had stepped back through the hole in the fence, the house seemed more alive than ever. Every noise creaking through the hallways sounded like approaching footsteps. When he climbed the stairs to retrieve his two suitcases and briefcase, he could feel eyes watching him from every doorway. He had that same alien feeling that he'd felt when he'd first seen the crow. Only this time it was coupled with terror. All the way back down the stairs, out the front door and across the yard, he watched his back, overwhelmed with the feeling that some presence was breathing down his neck. The feeling never left him until he reached the outskirts of Lurkdale.

With the wind rippling through his clothes, Bren moseyed along the cobblestones of Pepperfield Lane, past a pub that brimmed with laughter and loud music. The sound of other people calmed his nerves, and the sight of a small crowd gathered outside the pub made him feel safe. That is until he saw who they were.

"Oy, mate," a voice shouted and Bren recognized two of the men as the same two he'd met that morning in the diner. Lug was unmistakable with his robust stomach, and though it was too dark to see, he knew that the taller man to Lug's left had red hair.

"Decided to stay in town, did ya?" asked Eric.

"What's wrong? Windfield Manor not good enough for ya?" Lug added and the two of them laughed mockingly as Bren walked on, his shoulders hunched under the weight of the suitcases. "He's the bloke we were telling you about," the voices continue behind him.

He'd started fights over much less and even felt anger swelling inside him, but wasn't in the mood to fight tonight. Instead, he strolled on up to Moorland Avenue, where he clattered through the tavern door and set his bags in front of the counter. A chubby lady came out from the back room and gave Bren a half-friendly smile. She felt a tinge of déjà vu. When she'd checked him in the night before, he'd looked tired and despondent. He looked exactly the same now.

"Back for another night, are you?" The lady pulled a key from the beehive boxes on the wall. "The same room be all right?"

"Sure, that's fine."

"Actually you could have any room you like. Lurkdale's not highly rated by tourists."

"Same one's fine." He took the key and carried his bags upstairs.

# CHAPTER 6

The sign outside "The First Bank of Lurkdale" had remained unchanged for a quarter of a century. The fancy letters were carved deep into the slate of wood, and the once royal purple paint had chipped away, leaving only the raw wood, now darkened and rotted by years of English rain, then dried and cracked by the sun. But no one cared much about the esthetics of a sign. It was a bank, with brick walls, bars in the windows and an iron safe in the back. Anyone in Lurkdale with a shilling to save kept it here, tucked inside the redbrick walls. Even the richest man to ever walk the streets of this quaint English village, Thomas James Windfield, secured his fortunes inside the safe of "The First Bank of Lurkdale," (which, incidentally, was the only bank of Lurkdale). And still, thirty years after his death, many pounds lay inside the vault, waiting for their new owner to come claim them.

Bren shut the door behind him. The bank floor creaked beneath his tennis shoes. A wooden counter stretched from one wall to the other, and portholes for five tellers opened along the face of the counter. However, only the center porthole was ever open for business. The other four remained more for decoration since the bank never saw enough patrons at one time to warrant their opening.

A thin man stood at the counter, dusting, while a plump man with bifocals sat at a desk punching keys on a calculator. Other than that, the bank was empty. Only silence kept the men company, a silence only broken by an occasional brush of the feather duster and the sporadic tapping of calculator keys.

"May I help you?" The teller grinned and set his duster aside. He had sunken cheeks and black poodle hair.

The man at the desk glanced up to see who had come in. The fat on his cheeks gathered into little cottage-cheese mounds as he squinted through his bifocals past the ball of his pug nose.

"Sure." Bren pulled out the will and laid it on the counter. "I believe I have some money in your bank."

The teller looked the will over, and then eyed Bren curiously. Taking the will, he walked over to the man sitting at the desk and mumbled something to him. The tapping of the calculator keys suddenly fell silent, and both men stared over at Bren. The man at the desk adjusted his bifocals, with his eyes magnified behind the lenses. He whispered and the thin man whispered back. Bren could only make out a word or two. The man at the desk studied the will carefully before standing and approaching the stranger, with the teller at his side.

"Bren Stevens?" As the bank's president and owner, Henry Hays took pride in his work. He'd started working for the bank thirty-seven years before, under the direction of his father, and took over after his father's death. Henry was a gentle man, with a wife and three children. He was generally accompanied by a sincere smile, which had abandoned him at this moment.

"Yeah." Bren smiled at the bank owner and received nothing but a cold stare in return.

"Have any ID?" Henry glared intensely, thinking—or more accurately, *praying*—that this was a bad joke, as he watched Bren fumble through his wallet, remove his driver's license and hand it across the counter. Henry squinted at the identification. "What's your relationship with Thomas Windfield?"

"I'm still trying to figure that one out myself," Bren said.

"I beg your pardon?" The bank owner wasn't amused.

"I have no relationship with Mr. Windfield. At least none that I know of. But the will's legitimate, if that's what you're wondering."

"Who was Windfield's lawyer?"

"I have his name and number here somewhere." Bren searched through his wallet and pulled out the post-it note that Dan Adams had used to write down Lenard Berke's information. He handed it to Henry, who went to his desk and called. He didn't look well. He had the look of a man fighting off a bout of the plague.

"Mr. Berke," Henry said into the phone. "Henry Hays here. From the bank. Oh I'm fine, and you?" He stared over to the counter at Bren, and his voice suddenly sounded strained. "Did you by chance handle Thomas Windfield's will after he died? Uh-huh, uh-huh. Yes, he's here. Is that right?" He removed his glasses and rubbed his eyes. "Well I for one don't find it very amusing. This whole thing is absurd. He's no more than a child." His face changed from light brown to sunset red. "Of course we have his money." His tone wasn't convincing. "Yes, I'll see to it that he gets everything specified in the will." Henry placed the receiver back in its cradle and bit nervously at his finger.

"Is there a problem?" Bren called from the counter.

Henry looked up at him. "No problem." His brow folded and he closed his eyes. "None at all."

Henry slumped in his chair as the teller watched innocently. For thirty years, no one had come to claim the contents Thomas Windfield had left in the vault under the name Bren Stevens. For the first seven years after taking over the bank, Henry merely thought about the money and questioned the morality of claiming it as his own. For the next ten years, he praised the antics of the eccentric Mr. Windfield and lived comfortably off the unclaimed treasure. He bought Christmas presents for the children, remodeled the kitchen to his wife's liking, and pampered himself in every restaurant from York to London.

Henry had turned the name Bren Stevens over in his mind for the past thirty years. He liked the name, for it seemed to belong to no one. It was just a name scribbled on the bankbooks, assigned to an account opened by Thomas Windfield not long before his death. But suddenly Henry disliked the name Bren Stevens. And furthermore, he disliked Bren Stevens—the person—the cruel man who now stood at the counter, thoughtlessly demanding his money.

Henry had cheerfully spent thousands of pounds over the past ten years. But what took only ten years to spend would take a lifetime to repay. And now his only option was to borrow money from his own bank to make good on the amount specified in Bren Stevens's account. He expelled a sigh and slouched in his chair with his eyes on the will, reading the idiocy. One million pounds, he thought. But—a glimmer of hope.

"You realize you can only withdraw ten-thousand pounds a month for the first year, don't you?" Henry looked over the edge of the paper to the stranger at the counter.

"Yeah."

"And how much you want today?"

"I suppose five-hundred ought to do," Bren said, then added, "So how much have I accrued in interest over the past thirty years?"

Henry moaned. He would calculate that out later and have a good cry.

Bren left the bank feeling much better about his trip to England and about the absurdity of the will. Nothing like discovering you're a millionaire to brighten your day. He crossed through the street while Henry Hays stared spitefully from the bank window. Henry had never considered himself a violent man, but for the first time in his life he actually found himself contemplating murder. The American had no connections here. He wouldn't be missed. By the time the folks back home realized something was wrong and came over to do some snooping, he could have the body well disposed of. Part of him said he could never go through with it. The other part wasn't so sure.

The realization that Thomas Windfield had actually left him a million pounds made him more intrigued than ever about this whole bizarre situation. Who was this man who had died thirty years ago, leaving his home and a considerable amount of money to someone who hadn't even been born yet? Bren was only twenty-five, for crying out loud! The very thought of it made him crazy. He returned to the tavern and looked again at the photographs and reread the letter. *Avenge my death.* How ridiculous! In spite of the money, he felt no obligation to seek revenge for this stranger, even if this stranger did look exactly like him. What he did feel, however, was complete and utter curiosity. He had to know about this man and about the circumstances surrounding his death.

He took the black and white photograph of the six people standing inside the gazebo doorway and laid it on the dresser. One of the men in the picture was Thomas; he was quite sure of that. He was also quite sure he knew which one he was. Everyone else, however, needed to be identified. With any luck, one or all of them were still alive and living in Lurkdale. Taking a pocketknife from one of his suitcases and opening the blade, he made a cut along one side, so that the picture of his twin (the young Thomas, he assumed) was removed. He planned to question townspeople about the photograph and he didn't want them thinking he was asking about a picture of himself.

Outside, he headed up the street where Tudor-style buildings rose high on both sides, with signs dangling across the sidewalks. There were about a dozen people on the street. He passed all of them. Too young, which made them unlikely prospects for identifying people in a thirty-year-old photograph. What he wanted was someone over fifty. Stopping at an antique shop, he stared through the window at a man standing at the counter polishing a bronze statue. The gray storekeeper looked as much a part of the wares as the antiquities displayed for sale. Perfect. Well over fifty.

A cowbell stationed above the door jingled when he entered.

"Morning," said the old man. "Help you find something?"

"Actually I have a question about a photograph that was given to me. I was wondering if you knew any of these people." He handed the photograph to the man. "It's thirty years old."

The man set his statue on a table and studied the photograph with interest. "Where'd you get this?"

"It's a long and unbelievable story."

"I deal in old photographs, and you've got a gem here. The Windfields were once a prominent fixture in this community. This is them here." He pointed to a couple in their mid-to late-forties and a pretty girl beside them.

"This is Thomas Windfield?" Bren put his finger on the picture of the man with graying hair.

"That's right."

"You're sure?"

"Absolutely."

Bren wasn't sure what to make of that. If the graying gentleman at the center of the photograph was his benefactor, that would make his twin—someone else. Who exactly he didn't know.

"Recognize anyone else?"

"He's put on some weight since this photo." The man brought the picture closer to his face as he narrowed his eye. "But that there's Mayor Tuttle. He was a close friend of the family."

"And where could I find Mayor Tuttle?"

He climbed the steps of the town hall, where large columns held up the arched entranceway and lion statues guarded the double wooden doors. Inside a long hallway, he located the door marked "Mayor" and entered. He found a lady sitting at a desk, typing frantically. She was homely, middle-aged and wore a red dress that gripped her unattractively at the chest and waist. To her left was another door, which Bren assumed led into the mayor's personal office.

"I'm looking for Mayor Tuttle," he said and watched the woman look up from her typing.

"Have you an appointment?"

"No."

"Would you care to make one?"

"He's not available now?"

"He's a busy man." She opened an appointment book that was sitting beside her keyboard and turned a few pages, looking for an opening. "What's the nature of your visit?"

"It's pertaining to Thomas Windfield."

She glanced up at him and closed the appointment book. Getting up from her desk, she knocked on the mayor's door but didn't wait for a response. She pushed the door open and poked her head inside, where the mayor, a stout fifty-six-year-old with a bulldog face, sat at his desk talking on the phone. His shoulders were wide and his body thick and husky. He glared up at the secretary.

"Sir, there's a young man to see you."

"About what?" The mayor cupped his hand over the end of the receiver.

"It has to do with Thomas Windfield."

The mayor squinted curiously and asked her to show him in. Mayor Tuttle stood, turned his broad back to the door and continued his conversation into the phone as Bren walked into the room and closed the door behind him. The room was small and cluttered. A picture of the Queen hung behind the desk. A gray suit coat straddled the back of the desk chair, and the matching trousers gripped firmly at the mayor's bulging waist.

"I'll phone you later," Tuttle said into the receiver with his back turned toward Bren to muffle the sound of the conversation. "You know me, always got somebody wanting my time. I'll be thinking about you. Cheers." He smiled as he turned and hung up the phone. Then his face twitched and he retreated a step as he glared at the man standing before him. "You!" The mayor swallowed hard and held onto the back of his chair. He rubbed his chin in thought and regained his poise. "You—wanted to see me?"

"Hope I'm not interrupting anything too important. I'm Bren Stevens." He walked to the edge of the desk and extended his hand. The mayor slowly did likewise. "I was wondering if I could ask you a couple of questions?"

Tuttle twisted his wedding ring. "I suppose you could always ask." He sat down and invited Bren to do the same. "What's this about Thomas Windfield?"

"Well, I was hoping you could tell me a little about him."

"This is the urgent matter you needed to talk with me about?"

"I never said it was urgent," said Bren and could see that Tuttle didn't care to be corrected. "I have a photograph of the Windfields." He retrieved the gazebo photo, which he'd folded and stuffed into the back pocket of his blue jeans. Unfolding it and smoothing out the creases, he showed it across the desk to Tuttle. "Is that you?" he asked, pointing to one of the young men.

Tuttle snatched the photograph and studied it. He recalled the day this picture had been taken, and he recalled who had been standing to his left, the man who had now been cut out of the picture. "Where'd you get this?"

"It's an odd story. That is you in the picture though, right?"

"That's me. Why?"

"I was hoping you could tell me a little about Thomas Windfield."

Tuttle glared across the desk. The resemblance was unnerving. "What's any of this got to do with you?"

"Thomas Windfield, for some unknown reason, willed me his estate."

The cleft in Tuttle's chin deepened as he gritted his teeth and narrowed his eyes. "Thomas willed his estate to you?" His tone revealed his disbelief. "How old are you?"

"Twenty-five. And I already know, he died five years before I was born."

Tuttle's lip snarled. Wherever this was going, he didn't like it, not one bit. He tossed the photograph back at Bren and said, "So you're suggesting that Mr. Windfield willed his estate to an unborn child?"

"I suppose so," Bren said with some reservation, seeing the mayor's agitation. He folded the photo and stuffed it in the pocket of his shirt.

Tuttle stared at him for a moment, the lines in his face growing harder. "I'm not sure what you're up to, young man. But rest assured you're not dealing with fools here." The mayor stood behind his desk and leaned down toward Bren, fully intending to intimidate, and succeeding magnificently. It pleased him to see the young man cower back in his chair, this man with a face from the past and the audacity to create such an obvious lie. "Thomas Windfield was a personal friend of mine, and I'll not have you making a mockery of his good name by spreading this ridiculous story."

"I have the will." Bren reached in the back pocket of his jeans and pulled out the paper, which Tuttle grabbed and examined.

"He also wrote me this letter." Bren had brought all of them with him from the tavern in case he found someone who could fill him in on their significance.

Tuttle snatched the letter as well and sat softly back down. His lips moved as his eyes followed along the sentences, but he spoke no words—not until he read: "Avenge my death," which he merely whispered, then grinned hideously. "This is preposterous. You wrote this."

"No."

"You think I'm an idiot?" Tuttle theatrically held his hands out to his sides as he posed the question. "How could he possibly know his death would need avenging? And how could he address this letter to you, a nonexistent person?" He studied the stranger seated before him. He thought he could guess what the man was up to, but how? Someone else was behind this, pulling the strings. Someone he'd met long ago. But that face! Even a son couldn't look that much like the father, could he? "What's the real reason you came to see me?"

"I just wanted to find out more about Thomas Windfield is all."

"I'm not one to be toyed with, young man. If you have something to say, say it. Otherwise, get out of my office!" Tuttle threw the will and letter on his desk. He was looking for a sign in the man's face, but the man was giving nothing away. He merely took the will and letter and headed to the door.

"What else did Thomas give you?" the mayor called after him.

"He left me some money," Bren said, turning back toward the mayor.

"How much?"

"Why?"

"Let me ask the questions." The mayor walked around his desk. His bulldog body moved with self-assurance, a man who was used to getting his way.

"He left me enough," Bren said as he turned away from the mayor and reached for the doorknob.

"How dare you walk away when I'm talking to you?" Tuttle grabbed Bren's arm and he flinched from his grip.

"You're the one who told me to get out."

"But now I'm talking to you," said the mayor. "Did he give you a key? A metal contraption about so-big?" He measured with his hands, the same size as the unusual piece of silver sent to Bren in the briefcase.

"Yeah." Bren nodded, puzzled by the term *key* and the mayor's awareness of it. "What of it?"

"Bring it to me. Then maybe I'll believe this business about the will." Tuttle took a step closer. He had a thin grin on his lips, daring this young man to contest his authority.

Bren felt his hand tremble, both from nervousness and anger. He didn't think it would be wise to make enemies in a town he was considering moving to, especially with someone in authority. Yet he couldn't control his tongue. He said, "What do I care what you believe?" Then pulled the door open and stepped out.

The mayor's grin disappeared. His breathing grew shallow and his face contorted into a sour expression. "If you know what's good for you, you'll tuck your tail between your legs and head back where you came from." Tuttle's angry face glared out from his open office door, waiting for Bren to spout off with another wise remark, but he said nothing, never even turned around.

The secretary perked up in surprise and watched Bren exit into the hall. She wisely avoided eye contact with the mayor, who silently closed himself back in his office, returned to his desk and bit at his bottom lip. He pulled a cigar from his desk drawer, lit it, and leaned his elbows onto his desk. With a plume of smoke rising from his lips, he whispered softly to himself, "Thomas Windfield, you mysterious fool. Now what have you done?"

# CHAPTER 7

*B*ren made up his mind to sell the house. Clean up the outside and get rid of it. Let the new owner worry about the interior. For three days, he tore incessantly at the fence with a crowbar and hammer that he'd purchased at the local hardware store. He didn't go inside. Not after his visit from the crone. He spent his days laboring in the warm sun or drizzle. At night, he would take leisurely strolls through Lurkdale before retiring to the safety of the tavern rather than stay within his own home.

By the third day, he'd removed the entire front of the fence and part of one side. The weed-infested landscape lay naked before the world. By next week he planned to make a considerable withdrawal on his account and rent a large truck so he could haul out the thirty years of debris. The dead tree that stood in the front yard also needed to come down.

The ivy that clung to the side wall had withered long ago. It stretched all the way from the ground up to the third-story loft, where a crow was perched on a windowsill, cawing down at Bren. Several more birds fluttered out from the high window and lit softly along a ledge. Their feathers ruffled in the wind as they tilted their faces downward. They looked like the stone gargoyles he'd seen on the church in Lurkdale.

Behind the house, he entered the garden. The house was built in an L-shape, with the south wing, which contained the library and conservatory, making up the shorter end. The garden encompassed the entire L and went all the way back to the hill that rose up high behind the house. Statues and archways, reminiscent of a once-beautiful flower garden, now lay infested with weeds and drooped with dead ivy. Thistles grew around the edges of a fountain that held a statue of a girl holding a dove.

Following the flagstone pathway that ran through the garden, he found the gazebo. The same one he'd seen in the photograph, now half buried in ivy. It was situated near the back of the property, where the pathway disappeared beneath the fence. He hooked his crowbar under one of the planks and pulled it loose so that he could see where the path led. Through the opening, he could see that the walkway passed among a group of trees and continued on down a short flight of steps that led to a field of heather. There, at the foot of a slope, stood the charred remains of a building covered in vegetation.

He'd just started to loosen another board when he heard the sound of engines coming down the lane at the front of the mansion. He figured Lurkdale wasn't the kind of place that would send out a welcoming committee, and when he rounded the house, he found that he was right. A welcoming committee it was not. Three cars and a truck were parked on the brick area in front of the mansion and five men were high-stepping their way through the garbage on the front lawn. Expressions alone told Bren this wasn't a social visit.

A large man with closely cropped blond hair led the way. He looked as though he were leading a military squadron into battle. Bren feared he was doing just that. Bren was six feet tall, and working as a lumberjack had honed his body. In spite of that, the man with the cropped blond hair stood a solid four inches taller than him and outweighed him by a good fifty pounds.

"What the bloody hell do you think you're doing?" The man stopped in front of Bren and slapped the back of his hand against his cheek. Not hard, just enough to taunt him.

"Tearing down the fence." Bren realized that he was stating the obvious and that he would come off sounding sarcastic, but what other answer could he possibly give?

"Who gave you permission?" asked a shorter, yet stocky fellow, with a face filled with stubble and pockmarks.

"I did. I now own this place."

The shorter man hissed between his teeth in a way that communicated his disbelief. The five men regarded each other momentarily. Behind them, on the parking area, the doors of the rusty truck squeaked open and two more men emerged. Eric and Lug. Even from the distance of twenty yards, Bren could see how much they were enjoying the show. They got out casually, walked to the back of the truck, lowered the tailgate and took a seat. Lug appeared to have brought a bag of goodies to indulge himself while he watched the drama.

"You know how long it took this town to build that fence?" asked the blond man.

"Well, you forgot to put a gate in it," said Bren.

"No use building a fence if you're going to put a bleedin' gate in it, now is there?" Toby, the shorter one, kicked defiantly at the trash on the ground but kept his eyes on Bren. He'd come hoping for a fight. He knew that Sean Goodgraves could tear this Yankee boy apart if it came to it. He prayed it would come to it. It'd been a good five months since he watched Sean pound anyone. And that had only been a scruff at the local pub. Who knew what he could do if he really had just cause? And Toby knew that to Sean, tearing down *this* fence was just cause. Sean had more than a casual interest in it. He'd only been a lad of fourteen when the inhabitants of Lurkdale united to erect the fence. But he had a stake in it. For twenty years the fence had stood, only trespassed by Lurkdale youth too foolish to know what awaited them inside.

"I have a mind to rip you apart, mate." Sean pushed his hand against Bren's chest. "And there's not a soul around who'd condemn me for the gesture. You bloody Americans are all the same. Think you can come over here and do anything you bleedin' well please. Well you're in Lurkdale now. And we don't take kindly to strangers coming in and changing things. You understand me?"

Bren said nothing, just let the resentment swell within his throat.

"If there's any trouble, it'll be on your head." Sean tensed his jaw, and the chest muscles flexed inside his light blue T-shirt. Bren saw Sean's fist tighten. If it came to it, Bren would give him a good fight. He was certain of that. He'd fought people larger than himself before and had always faired well. Fighting five men at the same time, how- ever, was a different story. He figured he'd get in a few solid blows to the blond man's lips and nose before his four friends jumped in and sent him to the hospital.

"What are you afraid of?" asked Bren.

"Are you calling me a coward?" asked Sean.

"Not exactly. I was just thinking that if you were afraid of some- thing, what would it be? After all, you're a big man. If there's some- thing about the house that frightens you, perhaps it would be wise of me to be frightened, too. That's all."

"Go back to America. That's all you need to know." He'd expected more resistance and had come prepared to deal with that. He didn't quite know how to handle this passiveness. He looked over Bren's shoulder at the house, the only thing on Earth that frightened him. He could feel its presence. Glancing up at a window on the second floor, he felt a shiver spread across his back. He could still see the body plunging to its death. He could still feel the horror. And here, standing before him, this stupid man dared bring down the fence. He wanted to hit him, not out of anger really, just to wake him up, bring him to his senses. He raised his hand, flexed his jaw, but merely slapped at Bren's cheek again. "Consider this a warning." He turned back toward his car.

Bren's heart was pounding. But the fear had come from more than just the thought of being pulverized by Dudley Dooright and his entourage; it had come from the look in Sean's eyes, the sheer terror that had come over him when he looked at the house. There was something about this place that made grown men shudder. Whatever it was, it was contagious, and Bren could feel it working its way into his stomach.

The redheaded man and his chubby mate waited for the cars to drive off under the trees before hopping off the tailgate and wandering through the garbage. They couldn't recall ever seeing the house so naked before. Although they'd both been there twenty years ago when their parents helped build the fence, having only been two at the time, they had no recollection of it. But they had other memories.

"Been inside yet?" Eric looked past Bren at the house.

"Yeah. Went in the same day I talked to you two in the diner."

"But we notice you didn't spend the night. One thing this town doesn't need, mate, is another coward. Lug here's already got that position filled."

"Bah." Lug sneered. "At least I have the courage to admit I'm a coward. Unlike someone else I know who abandons his friends at the first sign of danger."

"I never abandoned you," said Eric.

"Oh, indeed you did."

"Did not."

"Did so."

"What is it about this place anyway?" asked Bren. "It's just a house."

"Thomas Windfield was murdered in that house," said Eric.

Bren nodded and thought of the stain in the study, on the carpet in front of the desk. He'd suspected it was blood. "And?" he said, prompting the men for more information. "Surely this has to do with a lot more than murder."

The two men didn't appear to have any more to say. They felt vulnerable standing so close to the house with no fence to keep the horror in. They knew what they knew and that was enough for them. Eric slapped Lug on the shoulder and motioned to the truck.

"That's it? A man was killed in the house?" Bren said, following them through the garbage, back toward Eric's truck. "People are killed all the time, but you don't go building a fence around their house and piling garbage in the yard." He stopped and let them keep walking. "You boys sounded pretty tough the other day at the diner and then in front of the bar, but look at you now. A couple of real hotshots."

"Yeah, that's right." Lug stopped and looked back. His cigarette was hanging over his bottom lip. "I'm a coward and I'm bleeding proud of it. Cowards live longer, I always say, and I plan on living to a ripe crusty age."

"Tell me about the house." Bren came toward them.

"No."

"Do you know anything about some old hag that's been hanging around here?"

"Gretchen Wicks was here?"

"Some old crone paid me a visit, yeah. She was a hideous looking thing. You know her?"

"Ah, we know her all right." Lug cringed. "We know her like a leech that has stuck to the bone. She lives in that rickety shack back in the woods up the road. If she's hanging round, it can't be good, can't be good at all. She may have worms in the brain, but she seems to know things—mysterious things. Everyone knows she's a loon, but when she starts talking, people frantically shut up their ears, 'fraid of what she has to say. If she's hanging round, you can bet there's trouble brewing."

Gretchen had made a life out of haunting Lurkdale. With the accuracy of a prophetess, she spouted her words of doom. Cloaked in black, she would amble into town, preach her warnings, and then amble back out again. And she never bore a happy message, only messages of death and sickness and lost fortunes.

"She's a witch, I think," Eric said. "Could be that I'm wrong, but I'd put money on her riding a broom late at night and turning people into toads."

"She smelled something awful." Bren could still picture her face staring in through the broken window. Her rotten teeth and chapped lips.

"She's a scabby old thing, she is." Lug could taste his words. "She's the village defecation. Her breath oozes like vapors coughing up from an open sewer." He spit the taste from his mouth and was disappointed to see his cigarette fall in with the rest of the garbage.

"So what'd she say?" asked Eric.

"Nothing really. At least nothing that made any sense. Just told me to stay where I belong. Whatever that means."

"I'd say that means 'stay out of the house,'" said Lug.

"That was my guess, too. That's why I didn't end up spending the night."

"Wise decision," said Eric. "Now do something even wiser: leave this place. Let the crows have it." He looked to a window in the third-floor loft where three crows sat looking out at them.

"What happened in this house?"

"He's still in there." Lug looked at the dark windows. "Hiding in there somewhere."

"Who?"

Eric shook his head at his chubby friend, warning him not to say any more.

"Who?" Bren repeated.

"Windfield's killer." Lug cocked his head toward Eric, as if apologizing for saying too much.

Bren looked behind him at the house. It didn't exactly look innocent, but from what he'd seen inside, it didn't look lived in either. "There's no one in that house," he argued.

"It's true, mate." Eric was uncomfortable with his own conviction. "As much as I hate to admit it, this ain't just some fairy-tale ghost story. We seen him with our own eyes." He looked at the house and shivered. "Everyone said the place was haunted, but we didn't believe it. So we went inside. We used to go in there a lot—to have a smoke, you know? We thought it was the safest place. Where our mums wouldn't find us. But this one time when we were in there, we were sitting in the living room, smoking, laughing, telling each other what a brave lot we were 'cause we were the only ones that dared go in a haunted house. And out of nowhere comes the Windfield killer."

"Out of the wall. That's where he came from, right out of the bleedin' wall." Lug was looking at the front door of the house, as if expecting the killer to come walking out. "He was a big man, bigger than Sean Goodgraves, and twice as ugly. His hair was wild and he grinned at us and said if he caught us smoking again he'd chew our eyes out. I haven't lit a cigarette since. He even knew our names."

Bren was grinning, not sure what to make of the story. "If you were only twelve," he said, "how would you know what the killer looked like?"

Eric said, "After we told me father what happened, he took us to the library and we looked at the picture in the newspaper. And it was him all right. I swear it. And he hadn't aged a day. And we're not the only ones who saw him. Thomas's daughter was here, a long time back. She saw him. And some of her mates chased him into a water closet. He locked the door, and by the time they broke through, he'd disappeared. Yet that was the only way into the room. We read that in the newspaper, too."

# CHAPTER 8

"He's tearing down the fence!" Sean leaned over Mayor Tuttle's desk, with a group of seven men clamoring behind him, all scowls and bent brows.

"He's got no right being in that house!" another voice exclaimed.

The mayor sat back in his office chair, tapping his foot on the carpeting as he rubbed a finger in the cleft of his chin. Under any other circumstance, he'd have had the whole lot tossed out. Only he had the right to throw tantrums in this office. But this was no ordinary circumstance, and seeing the eight men so riled actually calmed his nerves. Perhaps something could be done about this situation after all.

"Truth is," said Tuttle, his eyes glinting beneath the office lighting, "I don't like him in there any better than you do. But he has a will—signed by Thomas Windfield."

"It's a forgery," said Henry Hays. "He just wants the money Thomas left in the bank."

Tuttle's eyes darkened. "He said something about some money. Why haven't I ever heard mention of this before?"

"Well—" The cottage-cheese mounds on Henry's cheeks gathered and his eyes magnified behind his bifocals. "It's a banking matter. The money's been sitting there for thirty years, untouched."

"Whose name is the account in?" asked Tuttle.

"Bren Stevens."

"This is ludicrous!" Toby hit his fist against the office door, eliciting a frown from Tuttle.

"How large is the account?" Tuttle continued.

"Large," said Henry Hays. "A million pounds."

"Oh, great scott!" Toby threw his arms in the air in frustration. "Let's shoot the bugger and put him out of our misery. I'm sure even the Queen would approve." He gestured to the royal portrait hanging behind Tuttle.

Henry winced in shame. A million was bad enough. If he had it his way, he'd keep what he had to say a secret, but the truth was bound to come out sooner or later anyway. With a hand over his mouth, he added shyly, "Plus thirty years interest."

The mayor, who had been staring at his desk, raised his eyes slowly at the banker. His nerves were beginning to flare again. "Which comes to—?"

"Over three million pounds more," said Henry.

"Just in interest?" shouted Toby. "This has gone too far. Sic your bloodhounds on him, Sean. Send the bugger to his grave."

"It has to be a hoax," Henry said. "He's just a lad. I'm telling you, check the will; it's a forgery. I'm certain of it."

"It's no forgery," said Tuttle. "I spoke with Lenard Berke yesterday. It was he who sent the will on to the American lawyer. I checked the whole thing out. No holes." He'd called every lawyer in town, all three of them. He was as anxious as anyone else to get to the bottom of this. To his dismay, the will was legitimate. Thomas Windfield and his lawyer, a gentleman by the name of Glenn Ward, had sat down and drawn up the will thirty years ago. Before his death, Ward had handed the whole case over to Lenard Berke, who himself had found it ludicrous. After all, his instructions were to seek out an American lawyer and inform him to save the will until Bren Stevens's twenty-fifth birthday. It didn't take a mathematician to see that things didn't add up.

"I, for one, am not going to stand by and watch as some bleeding Yankee frees that beast from the house." The veins in Sean's neck were tense and blue. "He ain't from here. He don't know what evil he's letting out."

The mayor stood and pointed an angry finger across his desk at Sean. "If you decide to take the law into your own hands—" he scolded, then paused with thought and added in a whisper, "don't let me know about it."

# CHAPTER 9

$\mathcal{B}$ ren found a quiet corner of the library and set the newspaper on a table. The pages, worn by time and use, bore the smudged-candy fingerprints of a careless reader. Probably Lug. The black ink had changed to gray, and the white paper had yellowed. The date August 17, 1964 had summoned many viewers to survey this particular issue of the Lurkdale Gazette. A picture of Thomas Windfield was on the cover of the paper, accompanied by the headline: THOMAS WINDFIELD STABBED TO DEATH.

The paper outlined the details of the murder, which took place on August 16, the same date on the photographs that had been sent to Bren in the briefcase. The paper told how Mr. Windfield was brutally stabbed to death by a guest in his own home. How Earl Tuttle, a close friend of the family, had pursued the killer but lost him within the maze of halls. How the police had sealed off the area and searched every corner of the estate. But the killer had vanished somewhere within the home. The article called the killer by name: Stephen Bradson. At the time of the writing, Bradson was still at large, but they suspected it wouldn't take long to track him down. If he'd managed to get out of the house, which apparently he had, the police were sure to apprehend him at one of the many roadblocks they'd established, or at a bus station or airport, all of which were being closely monitored. The article noted that Bradson was an American and that the police suspected he would try to flee back home.

Bren turned the page for the continuation of the story. To this point, he'd found the account interesting at most, but nothing could have prepared him for the photograph on the following page. He let out a throaty gasp and rubbed his mouth. Under the photograph was the name "Stephen Bradson," and the words below that read: *Windfield's Killer.* Here was the man who had stabbed Thomas Windfield in the study. Bren could hardly contain himself. The man, the cold-blooded killer, was none other than the man he'd first mistaken as Thomas Windfield. His own look-alike.

*Stephen Bradson,* thought Bren Stevens. Even the name bore resemblance. He shuddered at the thought, and then shuddered again when a voice whispered at his back.

"I warned you, didn't I?" said the raspy voice. "I told you to leave it alone."

Bren turned to the wrinkled face of the old woman standing behind him, her head wrapped in a black cloth. Gretchen Wicks. Looking as beautiful as an unveiled mummy.

"That night you left me standing in the cold, I warned you. But would you listen? No! And now your curiosity is aroused." The woman seated herself in a chair beside Bren and leaned her face close to his. "An uncalmed mind can be a treacherous thing. It can lead you to hell like an unbridled whore, and keep you smiling each step of the way."

"What do you know about this?" Bren pushed the paper in front of Wicks.

She leaned away and smiled nervously. Her teeth were spoiled, her breath hideous, and her lips were scabbed and cracked. "You don't know, do you?" This point took her by surprise. She had a gift, as her mother used to say, (a curse, everyone else said) that allowed her glimpses into other people's heads and told her things to come. But she hadn't quite grasped the essence of Bren Stevens. She'd suspected that he had more of a hand in the murk that she could sense stirring in his future, but she now felt otherwise. "It's nothing to do with you." Gretchen leaned her head closer. "The house has a world all its own. You should've never come."

"What do you know about the house?" Bren casually cupped a hand over his nose to distill the stench that emerged every time the woman spoke.

"Enough to know you don't belong." She steadied her gaze on Bren's eyes, trying to get a sense of the man. How could his appearance be chance? Even without her gift, she would have sensed that something was amiss. She'd seen his face before, as had others. Even then, thirty years ago, his presence had felt out of place.

"That night," said Bren, not even taking notice of the several faces staring up through the library aisles, watching the stranger converse with the woman known as Lurkdale's witch, "the night you came to the house, you said you had something that would interest me about the house. What was it?"

"The curse." Wicks turned her face toward an aisle and watched two teenaged girls turn briskly away. The hag frowned and returned her attention to Bren. "Something in that house isn't right. I've felt it all me life. Of all the places in the world, only one causes me heart to slow and me soul to shiver, and you call that place home."

Bren snickered. The words seemed overly melodramatic to him.

"Laugh now." She held up a frail finger. "Laugh all you can, for someday that house will steal your laughter. It will build your dreams, your passions; then it will warp your soul and twist you into taking out its vengeance for it. Leave now, lad. Leave before your hands are filled with another man's blood."

"What do you mean by that?" Bren slid his chair a few inches across the floor, away from Gretchen. The chair's legs squeaked across the wooden surface, and the pitch sounded hollow in the quiet of the library.

"If you stay, blood will stain your soul, stain it so crimson that not even years will wash free the guilt. So pack your bags and leave. Leave while you still have free will. Otherwise, passion will swell in your veins and Murderer will be your name. Fate is an already written book. The only way to escape the next twist is not to turn the page. So be off with you before time proves an enemy too fierce to hold back."

Gretchen tucked her head inside her cloak and slunk away. Bren watched as she left, but she never looked back. Her dark eyes were busily darting through the library aisles, searching for more gloom. Faces saw her coming and quickly hid themselves in books so that the soothsaying hag couldn't look into their eyes and see their futures. They knew this woman too well, and nobody wanted to hear the kinds of futures she had to tell.

Bren closed the newspaper and returned to the circulation counter. Handing the paper back to the librarian—a thin, balding man with a pleasant demeanor—he asked if he could recommend any other papers that followed up on the Windfield story. The librarian recommended three, the same three that everyone else requested when researching the Windfield mystery. He brought them up from a room in the basement where important documents and past issues of the Lurkdale Gazette were stored. Returning to the corner of the library, Bren laid the newspapers on the table and opened the first one—this one dated August 12, 1974. On the cover was a photograph of Heather Windfield, Thomas's daughter. She was the burnet pictured in the gazebo photo and in the photo taken in the garden, the girl who'd been seated beside Bren's twin. He found her captivating. In the newspaper before him, her face was still beautiful but more cynical now, her eyes harder, her smile not nearly so bright. WINDFIELD'S KILLER STILL IN HOUSE, the headline read, and on an inside page, the same photo of Bradson stared back at him.

The article gave an account of how Heather Windfield Chandler had returned from Scarborough to retrieve some of her belongings.

She'd recently married and was in the process of moving into a new home in Scarborough. Windfield Manor had been locked up for ten years, ever since the death of Heather's father, Thomas. The family had moved away shortly after the murder, leaving many of their possessions stored in the house. The search for Stephen Bradson had long been forgotten. Authorities speculated that he'd managed to flee the country and was living somewhere in the States in obscurity, probably under a different name. Yet Heather had disproved this theory.

While in the house gathering her things, she made a horrifying discovery—Stephen Bradson had never left. Three men helping Heather move her things out of the house chased Bradson into an upstairs washroom where he mysteriously vanished. The search resumed for two weeks, but no trace of him was ever found. A thorough inspection did indicate that at some point within the last ten years someone had broken into the house through the back door and that the perpetrator had rummaged through the boxes, cupboards and closets. However, it turned up no evidence that anyone had been living in the house. The kitchen contained no food; the beds hadn't been made nor slept in; none of the nine fireplaces had been used; and the house had no electricity. But despite the lack of evidence, her story was taken seriously and a fence was erected around the property.

He opened the next paper and read how periodic searches of the house had been conducted by the police, but they'd never found a thing. The short article also told of two children who claimed to have seen the Windfield killer. No pictures were included of the boys, who had only managed to convince a handful of younger children of the truthfulness of their story. It didn't call them by name, rather it referred to them as the ginger-haired boy and the stout boy. Bren smiled. It had to be Eric and Lug, and the story had to have been concocted. Or so he thought until he looked at the date printed at the top of the page—August 12, 1984, nearly twenty years after the murder and exactly ten years after the first sighting. He doubted that their young minds would have given enough forethought to plot such an elaborate detail.

In the final paper, he read of the brutal murder of a visiting Londoner who had climbed the fence surrounding Windfield Manor and had gone inside the house while cousins and friends watched from over the fence. To their horror, they witnessed the young man fall to his death from a second-story window after being stabbed in the throat with a knife. The onlookers ran for help, but when they returned with the police, the killer had vanished. The newspaper's date: September 20, 1987—which coincided with nothing.

Two days after Bren's visit to the library, Lurkdale's elders and elderly gathered in that same building. They waited until after closing time for a secret meeting on the fate of the young American who had stripped away the fence and left the town vulnerable. They mumbled among themselves, spoke of how evil had come to Lurkdale thirty years ago and how evil had never left. The old copy of the Lurkdale Gazette was summoned from the archives. The page was displayed. The high ceiling echoed back the oohs and ahs as the old folks gazed at the photo. To them, this was a photograph of evil, of a phantom who never aged, and they were certain that Stephen Bradson and Bren Stevens were one and the same. In the thirty years since Thomas Windfield's demise, Lurkdale had become a Mecca of insanity, and Lurkdalians were careful not to let this insanity show when strangers were about. They would smile brightly at tourists and talk about the weather, never mentioning the house. It was an unwritten law that no one would ever reveal Lurkdale's secret horror that pervaded many private conversations. Few people ever broke this law.

"It's actually him," said an old man, looking at the killer's photograph in the paper.

Some of the more feeble conspirators sat on the cushioned chairs, while the more spirited merely leaned on tables.

"What shall we do?"

"Burn him."

"Can a devil burn?" contested a thin man with a cane. "Brought up from hell with all that ash and cinder, you really think a devil can burn?"

"He's mocking us, he is," Henry Hays spoke up, thinking more about the money that this devil was claiming than about the killing he was doing. He adjusted his bifocals as the attention of the group turned to him. "Walking around all innocent and smiling like we wouldn't notice, or if we did notice, like we wouldn't dare confront him."

"*Do* we dare confront him?" asked the man with the cane.

"We can't just leave him there. Let him run amuck though our town with us pretending we don't know." The banker slammed his fist on a table, and his bifocals almost rattled off his face. This gathering had been his idea and he was counting on a bit more spunk from his fellow townsfolk. If this apathy continued, he was going to have to pay four million pounds to a man who resembled Thomas Windfield's killer.

"What if it's not him?"

"Don't be a fool!" Hays ridiculed. "Look at the picture! It's him. No doubt of it. Same evil face. Same evil eyes. Not even a day older. A stake through the heart ought to work." There was hope in Henry Hays's eyes. A hope that someone would latch on to his suggestion and enthusiastically carry it out.

"Good heavens, Henry, the man's no vampire."

Henry frowned.

"So where does this leave us?" Lurkdale's physician sat on the edge of one of the wooden tables and tried to sum up the course. "We've got a known killer living among us. The man's been hiding in that house for thirty years and now he's out again, planning to do heaven knows what. I don't like it; you don't like it. What do we do?"

"Nothing," a voice came from the front of the library.

Matthew Golding, the chief constable, came ambling up the library's widest aisle, where several beams stretched from the floor to the high ceiling. He'd moved to Lurkdale six years earlier and had never bought into to all the superstitions of haunted houses and non-aging devils. He was off-duty and dressed in street attire, but everyone knew not to question his word. He wasn't an overly nice-looking man with his twisted mouth and smashed nose, and this added to everyone's fearful respect of him.

"I'll tell you what you're going to do." Constable Golding weaved through the group and sat on a table. He put one foot on a chair and sat back, looking as comfortable and confident as a teacher instructing his school children on proper conduct. "You're going to put that paper away, walk out of here like good citizens, and forget all about this whole thing. You understand?"

Several moans droned among the crowd.

"Was that a yes?" asked Golding. "You do realize that murder is against the law, don't you? As is conspiring to commit murder." He looked directly at Jonathan Powell, who was ninety-seven and had a tendency to forget his own name from time to time. He figured if anyone needed to be reminded that murder was illegal, Jonathan would be the one. Though he doubted the old man had the strength to kill an earthworm.

Everyone murmured in agreement and nodded, obeying every order except the last. They couldn't forget. They couldn't pretend that they didn't know what they in fact knew. They shuffled home through the streets, cooked dinners on their stoves, and sat before their television sets, but their minds kept turning. And those with a proper view stared from their windows, out to the edge of town where evil lived. And when evil came to town, they kept an alert eye and watched his movements, his ventures, trying to outguess this man of hell and see what no good he was up to, see what evil he had in store for them.

# CHAPTER 10

The animosity toward him built gradually over the course of a week. At first it was no more than disapproving looks or a snide remark made in a shop or along the street. Then at mealtime, in the tavern's dining hall where he ate most of his meals, people began leaving whenever he'd come in. On one occasion, a gentleman not so accidentally spilled his coffee all down Bren's back on his way out of the diner. There was no apology, no look of remorse, just a mild applause from the rest of the diners. That took place at lunch, and no one expected him back, but there he was that same evening, back for dinner.

He was stubborn like his father, and spiteful. He'd once seen his father buy a brand new barbeque grill, just because his wife had told him not to. He brought it home, set it up in the backyard and made her fix dinner on it. He then stuck it in the garage, where it sat ever since. The man behaved like a child sometimes. Bren maintained that he was nothing like his father. His rebellion wasn't childish and obstinate. It was strictly a matter of principle; that was the only reason he came back to the diner that evening, and every day after, for about two weeks, until they made him leave. This happened on a Thursday morning. Even as he came into the diner, he knew something was up. The hostess was polite as she escorted him to a table, and worse yet, nobody got up to leave. Everyone was watching him like he was some sort of entertainer and they were waiting for the performance. They watched him order his breakfast, then whispered about him beneath the din of forks and knives clinking against dishes. He couldn't hear their words, but he could see the eagerness in their eyes.

A lanky man with a mustache rose from a table and crossed the room. Bren watched him, anticipating another dose of coffee down his back. Instead, the man pulled out a chair at Bren's table and took a seat. His face was long, with sunken cheeks and dark, deep-set eyes. His hair was jet black and wavy.

"Good morning." The man placed his elbows on the table and offered an insincere grin. "I was wondering if you needed help checking out this morning?"

Bren couldn't say where this comment was leading, but he was sure it wasn't as polite as the man's tone had indicated. "I'm not checking out," he said.

"Actually, you are." The man smiled, exposing a set of coffee-stained teeth. "Your room has already been booked for this evening—by someone else."

"Who are you?"

The man twisted the black hairs of his mustache. "I own this tavern," he said and watched the anger go out of Bren's eyes. Now all he saw was worry, which he found quite delightful. The Lurkdale Tavern was the only rentable lodging in town, and everyone knew it.

"Just give me another room then."

"*All* the rooms are filled." The man's smile became sincere.

Bren knew the man was lying. Each floor of the three-story building had one bathroom that was shared by everyone staying on that floor. In the entire time that he'd stayed in the hotel, only two nights had he ever had to share the facilities with anyone. And the overweight lady who worked at the front counter had told him that the third floor hadn't been used in over two years.

"Hope this doesn't cause you any inconvenience." The man stared across the table, fully aware that Bren knew he was lying. This knowledge did nothing but intensify his smile. "Don't know why you'd want to stay here anyway when you've got a lovely place of your own." The tavern owner stood and started away, then stopped, turned back to the table and added, "Oh, yes, and I'd also appreciate it if you wouldn't eat here at the tavern anymore. Your presence has been having an adverse effect on business." He walked back to his table and took a seat across from a stout man who had his back to Bren. The table companion turned in his seat with a sly grin. Mayor Earl Tuttle, looking exceptionally pleased with himself. Sunlight streamed through the front windows and fell across the mayor's table and round body. With a wink, he smirked and raised a glass in toast to Bren's bad fortune. He then mouthed the words "bye, bye," and turned back toward his food.

He entered the Bank of Lurkdale, agitated. With the animosity rising against him in Lurkdale, he felt it would be best if he extracted the rest of his ten thousand pounds and lived anonymously in some other city. He could always return to Lurkdale once a month and collect his allowance.

The young bank teller, who was busy helping another gentleman, glanced up at Bren and smiled uncomfortably, then looked around for Mr. Hays, who was nowhere to be seen. Hays had been jovial all day. He'd come to the bank early and had brought some pastries and coffee, which he shared with his assistant.

When the gentleman had finished his transaction, the teller watched Bren approach the porthole. He was dressed in a thick green shirt and had a scowl on his face.

He said, "I need to make a withdrawal."

The thin teller muttered and rubbed the side of his nose, then turned without a word and walked to the back of the bank, where he entered an office. When he returned, Hays was with him. Bren couldn't quite place it at first, but Henry Hays looked different some-how. Younger, perhaps, or more benevolent. His old smile had returned and he actually appeared happy to see Bren standing at the counter.

"Something I can do for you?" Henry asked with a smile.

"I want to withdraw the rest of my money for the month." He was tapping his fingers on the counter. He didn't see Henry's bright atti-tude as a good sign.

"Still staying at the tavern, are you?" Henry's eyes were lit up behind his bifocals.

"No, I'm checking out. Got better things to do."

"Moving into the house?" Henry was genuinely interested.

"I still have nine-thousand-five-hundred pounds left for the month. I'll take all of it."

"Well, now, I don't believe I can let you do that." Henry pinched at the skin on his chin. "After all, you're not living in the house, now are you?"

"So."

"So, I'm just following the law." Henry shrugged as if it pained him to have to enforce this rule. "Apparently I have no choice but to heed the wishes of Thomas Windfield. After all, it was he who put this money in the account in the first place. And apparently he doesn't want me giving it to you unless you're living in the house."

"Is that right?" Bren leaned into the porthole and raised his eye-brows skeptically. "And I suppose Thomas told you this himself."

"He said so in his will."

"No he didn't." Bren had read the will a dozen times and he could think of no line stating that he had to live in the house.

"I'm afraid he did," said Henry Hays. "You have a copy of the will on you?"

"It's back at the tavern."

"No problem. I just so happen to have a copy of it here." Henry casually wandered back to his desk, pulled open a drawer and retrieved a paper. He'd gotten his copy of the will from Mayor Tuttle, who had gotten his from Lenard Berke, the lawyer who had sent the will and briefcase to America. Tuttle, Hays and a lawyer named John Fowler had sat down the evening before, set on picking the will apart, looking for a loophole. It took Fowler precisely five minutes to find what they were looking for, and he was prepared to try the issue in court if Bren Stevens dared to protest it. He knew he could convince a judge to see it his way. Personally, Tuttle and Hays wanted a broader loophole, but they settled for what they had.

Henry laid the will out on the counter in front of Bren. "Let's see. Where was that clause?" He adjusted his glasses and ran his finger down the page. "Oh, yes, here it is. 'While living in the house for the first year.' You see that? Apparently Thomas wanted you living *in* the house. *In*! Not around, not near, but *in*." He raised his shoulders apologetically. "And you have to live there a full year before you can receive the rest of the money."

"That could be interpreted a lot of different ways," Bren contested.

"Can it now?" Henry's voice suddenly became sharp. "Does 'in' mean something else in America? 'Cause me and the lawyers here could only come up with one interpretation: that is, your body inside the house, living there. Until that happens, you're not collecting another shilling from this bank. In fact, I think you should return the five hundred pounds I already gave you."

Bren gritted his teeth. "We'll see about that." He pointed a finger at the banker, turned and stormed out of the bank. This had turned out to be a very bad day indeed. He had no place to stay, and he doubted that he even had enough money to purchase a plane ticket back to the States.

Down the street from the bank, he found a red, wooden phone booth on the corner. Stepping inside he pulled out his wallet and found the post-it-note with Lenard Berke's phone number on it. He dropped some coins in the slot, dialed, and was happy to hear Berke's voice on the other end.

"Mr. Berke. Bren Steven's here. I'm not sure if you know who I am—"

"Of course I know who you are." Berke was seated in his office, staring down at some mortgage papers he had spread out on his desk. He was a tall man with habitually messy hair and reputation for being late for everything, especially bill payments. He'd consistently missed making his mortgage payment on time for the past year, and had been threatened with foreclosure four times. "How's Lurkdale treating you?"

"Not so good, which is why I'm calling. It seems the bank doesn't want to give me the money promised to me in the will."

"Yes, I'm aware of the situation," said Berke. "Henry Hays from the bank called me about it yesterday to get my opinion on the matter. I'd love to help you out, but I'm afraid the law favors the bank on this one."

"You're kidding me."

"Afraid not." Berke didn't like lying, even to people he didn't know, but the bank held the lien on his mortgage and he needed the grace Henry Hays had promised him if he went along with him on this. "Perhaps you should consult another lawyer," he advised. "Perhaps your friend from the States."

"Yeah, perhaps I will." Bren hung up and bit down on his bottom lip. Calling Adams seemed useless, but he dug in his wallet and found a scrap of paper that he'd written Dan Adams's phone number on, since Adams had refused to give him another business card. He dropped some money in the slot and got hold of an international operator who connected him to the lawyer's office back in New Hampshire. He feared that with his string of bad luck Adams wouldn't be in, but he was.

"Bren Stevens calling," he said when he had the lawyer on the line. He and Adams hadn't parted on the best of terms, and he wasn't sure how helpful the lawyer would be. "You wouldn't happen to have a copy of Thomas Windfield's will, would you?"

"Is there a problem?" Adams was sitting at his desk.

"These people. You wouldn't believe the runaround they're giving me. They're refusing to give me my money unless I live inside the house."

Adams sat back in his chair and grinned at the phone. Finally someone on his list of enemies was calling him for help. "Is there a problem with you living inside the house?" he asked as he pulled open a file drawer and searched for his copy of the will.

"Yes, frankly, there is. Old man Windfield bestowed upon me my own little piece of hell. I can't live in that house."

"Own little piece of hell, huh?" Adams liked the sound of that. He located the will and laid it on his desk. "So what am I looking for here?"

"The part about me receiving ten thousand a month while living in the house. The bank here doesn't seem to think they need to give me any money since I don't live in the house."

Adams found the passage and read it through a few times. "Sounds like a technicality."

"So is there something I can do?"

Adams hadn't felt this happy in years. The phrasing of the will was a minor detail, something that could probably be beaten if taken before a judge, at least in the States. He couldn't say for sure how things worked in England. He exhaled a long breath into the receiver and said, "Probably not. It doesn't appear as though Mr. Windfield intended your staying in the house to be a condition; it's more the wording. However, the wording appears to fall more in their favor than in yours."

"What do you suggest I do?"

"The house can't be that bad, can it? I mean, we are talking about a lot of money here. How bad can it be?"

Famous last words, Bren thought as he set the receiver back in its cradle. He didn't like Dan Adam, but he had to admit that the fat man was probably right: one year in that house was a small price to pay for that much money. But by damn, he wasn't going to be spending his nights in the dark.

It was nearly four o'clock when he entered the stone building opposite the town hall. The office in charge of maintaining the city's gas and electricity. He caught several sets of eyes watching him come through the door and immediately knew that he was in trouble. It was the kind of looks you'd expect from a group of school kids who knew the schoolyard bully was waiting for you around the corner. The bully in this case was a short man standing on the other side of the counter. With merely a simple glance he confirmed what Bren had suspected all along: the whole town was conspiring against him. Getting tossed out of the Lurkdale Tavern and being told that he couldn't withdraw any of his money was just the tip of the iceberg.

The short man with the bushy eyebrows and thick lips bobbed his head a few times as Bren explained his situation, but it was clear that he was merely waiting his turn to speak, so he could give the speech that he'd rehearsed. He opened a scheduling book and hardly even glanced at it before saying that it'd take two months before they could get an electrician up to the house to switch on the electricity. "We're very busy here," he said.

Bren looked to the back of the room, where several electricians were gathered around a table, playing a game of cards.

"Are those the busy people you're talking about?"

The short man didn't turn around, just gave a slow nod and said, "They're on break."

"How hard can it be to flip a switch and turn on my electricity?"

"It's not that simple. That house hasn't had electricity in thirty years. We got to have men go through it and inspect the wiring, make sure it's not faulty. Wouldn't want to burn down your house, now would we? That takes time, and we've got a two-month waiting list in front of you."

"I can't wait two months. I'm moving in today. What am I supposed to do?"

"Buy a flashlight." There was a trace of a smile at the corners of the man's mouth.

The muscles in Bren's neck tightened. He wanted to reach across the counter and smack the man on his fat mouth. The only thing that stopped him was the thought of getting tossed in jail. Not that jail would be any worse than the house, but it wouldn't bring him any closer to serving out his year sentence. So instead, he walked out, slamming the door behind him and heard a bout of laughter from inside as he left.

Dark clouds hung in the sky and it was already beginning to sprinkle.

Before returning to the tavern for his suitcases, which he'd packed and had the clerk hold at the front desk for him, Bren shopped the stores of Moorland Avenue, where he purchased a flashlight, bedding, and an ax. The ax was as much for protection as it was for ridding the yard of the large dead oak. The sight of him heading down the road with a suitcase in each hand and sporting a backpack with the red metal of the ax protruding from it didn't exactly foster anyone's trust in him—which was fine with him. Everyone in Lurkdale could rot in hell for all he cared.

When he'd gone in to get his bags from the tavern, Mayor Tuttle had been sitting in the diner with Henry Hays. They were both eager to see what the American would do. They had their money on him hightailing it back to America, since they'd seen to it that he was ousted from the tavern and that his electricity wouldn't be switched on. Who in his right mind would stay in that house in the dark? Plus, it was now the beginning of July and they'd made it clear that he couldn't withdraw another shilling until the first of August.

Both men gritted their teeth when they saw the ax. It could only mean that he was planning to rough it out. But they weren't overly worried. They knew he wouldn't last the month.

Two days later, a crowd had gathered on Oswald Road, which led out of town past the mansion. They watched as bird-desecrated items flew from the top windows of the house. Carpeting, chairs, cushions, and pool cues all heaped on the lawn outside Windfield Manor. Bren had purchased two bug bombs, which he activated and lobbed up into the third-floor loft to clear away the crows. They worked like a charm. He'd also purchased a large roll of plastic to cover the windows to keep out the birds.

There were seven cars parked along Oswald Road now, with nine men standing beside them. Next to Henry Hays stood Mayor Tuttle, chewing on a cigar. His eyes were fixated on the house.

"I really didn't think he'd stay."

"I bet he doesn't last another night," said Toby, the stubble on his face growing longer. "If Windfield's killer doesn't kill him, someone else will." He looked down the road where two more cars were pulling off to the side. "I just bet someone else will," he repeated, staring at his blond-haired mate. "Wouldn't you agree, Sean?"

Sean didn't utter a word. He just gritted his teeth and watched the cascade of debris fall from the window.

# CHAPTER 11

*L*ug was lying on his stomach in the tall grass and staring at Wind-field Manor, with its broken windows now covered with thick plastic. His armpits were stained with sweat and his hair was matted to his neck. His stomach grumbled. It'd been at least an hour and a half since he'd eaten anything and he needed nourishment. Lug was *oral retentive*, his mother always said. He always needed something to pacify him. If not food, it was an unlit cigarette, a toothpick, or a blade of grass, which he was now chewing on. The three men were resting beneath a tree, in the shade, taking a break from clearing away the rubbish from the yard. So far they'd made seven trips to the local landfill. After hearing that Mayor Tuttle wanted Bren out of the house, Eric and Lug decided to do whatever it took to help him stay. It was the least they could do after spending three weeks cleaning Lurkdale's streets at the mayor's orders.

Eric had his back up against the trunk of the tree. His head was back and he was staring up at a broken window on the third floor. It was now covered in plastic, keeping the crows out. "You ever take a look in the library?" he asked. "At those newspapers we mentioned?"

Bren was sitting cross-legged, pulling at the tall grass. He'd been living in the house for two weeks now. He'd chased the cats out the front door and had seen two mice in the kitchen. What he hadn't seen was any sign of Stephen Bradson.

"I read them," he said. "It's quite the story."

"But you don't believe it."

"I'm not saying that. The truth is, I don't really know what to think of it yet. I can tell you this much, though, whoever you saw in the house that day is gone now."

"You willing to bet your life on that?" asked Eric.

Bren offered an ambiguous nod and stared past Eric's truck, which was parked on the lawn and had a bed full of rubbish. Beyond it, the house loomed high above them, looking mistreated, yet innocent. "What worries me isn't the house; it's Lug's girlfriend. I don't like her popping up all the time."

Lug raised his head with interest. "Who're you talking about?"

"Gretchen Wicks. I heard the two of you are a pretty hot item."

"Gretchen ain't woman enough for this much man." Lug sat up and patted himself on the stomach. "She is a pretty thing, though, isn't she? Her baked lips, oozing breath you can almost taste, ripe and eagerly waiting for some handsome American like yourself to lock onto them in a passionate kiss." He sighed and put a hand to his heart.

"You're a sick man, Lug." Bren stood and dusted the seat of his jeans. "She paid me a visit that day I went to the library, you know? I was looking at the photo of the killer when she came up behind me and started spouting off about how the house was gonna twist my mind and make me kill someone. The woman's got some serious mental problems."

Lug didn't like the sound of that. One thing he knew was that Gretchen Wicks's prophecies had a habit of coming true. He despised the woman, but he never doubted her words.

"How long's it been since you two looked at the newspapers?"

"Six, seven years, something like that."

"It's been a while then." Bren grabbed his gloves, which were sitting next to the tree. "So if you passed this Stephen Bradson fellow on the street, you think you'd recognize him?"

"I'll never forget that face," said Lug. "It was like looking into the eyes of evil."

"That bad, huh?" Bren was staring at the front door. "Why don't you come in the house a moment? There's something I've got to show you."

"Not on your life," said Lug. "You tell us you're destined to kill someone, and now you expect us to follow you in the house? How foolish you think we are?"

"You think I'm gonna kill someone?"

"If Gretchen says it's so, then it's so."

"How about you, Eric?"

Eric said nothing, just looked at the house and stayed where he was seated.

"You don't want him in there with you," Lug said. "The first sign of trouble he'll be right out the door while you lie there in a pool of your own blood."

"I never abandoned you that day in the house, and you know it. So just shut up about it, okay?" He stared at Lug long enough to make him uncomfortable, until he was certain his chubby friend knew he wasn't joking. "I'm just tired of hearing about how I up and left you, when we both know it ain't so. It was a bad day that day, but it was a long time ago. It's time to let it go." Eric pushed the hair out of his eyes. "Perhaps it's time for a lot of things," he added, looking at the house. "Perhaps it's time for us to go inside again and face our fears."

"You go face whatever you want, but me, I'm staying right here," Lug said bitterly.

"There's nothing to worry about in that house," said Bren. "I've been living there for two weeks. There's nobody in there."

"You weren't there, Bren. You don't know. You didn't see what we saw. I'm not going back in that house, not ever. And Eric, you should know better. But knowing you, you just want the fat boy to come along, so that if the beast comes chasing, all you have to do is outrun me. And while I'm lying there getting me eyes hacked out, you can be running safely back home for tea. I appreciate the offer, ole chap, but no thanks."

That brought Eric to his feet. He looked like he was going to come over and beat the fat man, but instead he headed toward the house.

"Go right ahead!" Lug called after him. "But if you come out dead, I ain't coming in after you!" He propped himself against the trunk of the tree, in the shade, and watched Bren stand there a moment, looking at him, then turn and follow Eric across the yard. Lug had known Eric his entire life and he knew he wouldn't go through with it. The redhead was all talk; he always had been. He'd get across the lawn, stand at the front door and chicken out, just like he did with everything else in life. Lug watched him climb the three steps to the front door and look back at him. He looked paler than usual. But the idiot went in, and Bren went right behind him.

It'd been ten years since he'd been inside, but Eric remembered it well. He remembered the entryway and the twisting stairs that ended at the balustrade above him. He remembered the long corridor leading into the kitchen. Mostly, he remembered the living room. The sofa was still there, as were the rocking chair and grandfather clock. Very little had changed.

"This is where we saw him," he said. "We were sitting right on this sofa when he suddenly came walking out of the wall over there." He pointed to the far end of the room, where the mirror ended and the fireplace stood. He lifted a cushion from the sofa and could hardly believe it. After ten years, his pack of cigarettes was still there. "Right where we left 'em." He picked up the pack, with its corners gnawed up by mice.

The living room only had one door, which was now at their backs. When Eric and Lug had seen Stephen Bradson, the sofa had been pulled away from the wall and was facing the doorway, giving them a view of the only way into the room. Yet somehow the man had appeared behind them. He could still picture the look on Lug's twelve-year-old face. Just thinking about it sent a shiver up his spine. Even now, as he watched Bren opening the curtains to let some light into the room, Eric could feel a presence in the house. They'd left the front door open and he could feel the breeze on the back of his neck. It was gentle, like someone breathing close behind him.

He turned toward the door and felt the blood drain out of face. Staring him right in the eyes was Lug's fat face, still gnawing on a blade of grass. Both men let out a short scream, Eric from being taken by surprise, and Lug because Eric's scream had frightened him.

"I thought you were going to wait outside." Eric slapped Lug on the arm.

"That's what you want, isn't it? Leave me out there all alone. What kind of friend are you?"

"Bloody hell," said Eric and slapped Lug's arm again.

Bren went upstairs to the master bedroom, where he kept all of his personal belongings. He had unpacked his clothes, hung some in the closet and put the rest in the dresser. The bed was unmade. He didn't sleep well at night, despite the new sheets and blankets that he'd bought in town. He lay awake most nights, thinking about Tuttle and Hays and how they'd taken it upon themselves to interpret Thomas Windfield's will, and how they had appointed themselves the trustees. But mostly he thought about Gretchen Wicks. The old woman was out of her mind—probably senile—but she'd gotten under his skin with her crazy prophecies about his being destined to kill someone. Sure, he had a temper sometimes, but a lot of people did. That didn't make him capable of taking a human life.

Near the window that overlooked the front yard was a small table that he'd brought in a few days ago. It had one drawer in it, which was where he kept the briefcase. He took it down to the living room where Eric and Lug were looking at the grandfather clock and fireplace as if they expected to find a hidden door or some sign of what had occurred there ten years before. It felt nice having other people in the house. In the two weeks since he'd moved in, he hadn't felt much fear, only solitude. Hearing somebody else's voice in the room made it feel more like a home.

"I'd offer you something to drink," he said, "but all I have is bottled water, and even that's warm."

"About time we got home for tea anyway." Lug looked at his wrist as if he had a watch, which he didn't.

"I'll keep it brief," said Bren. "Why don't you have a seat?" He pulled the wooden rocking chair over in front of the sofa and sat facing the two men. They both looked nervous, especially Lug, who was looking at the briefcase as if he was expecting Bren to pull a gun from it and shoot him. "Some presents from the late Thomas Windfield," he said as he set the case on his lap and flipped open the latches. "I don't know what to tell you about any of this stuff I have here, so I guess I'll just show it to you and let you decide for yourself what to think." He removed the letter from the case and handed it to Eric. "Thomas Windfield wrote this to me before he died. Perhaps you can read it out loud if you don't mind."

"Yeah, sure." Eric took the letter, not looking entirely sold on the idea, and held it up in front of him. "Dear Bren, my trusted friend," he read. "I can only suspect that my death has come as a surprise to you—as I'm sure it did to me." He glanced up from the letter and pushed the red hair from his eyes. "You can't honestly expect anyone to believe this."

"Sure I can." Bren was rocking in the chair. "Just like you expect me to believe all those stories you tell me about this house."

"That's different?"

"How's it different?"

"You weren't even born at the time he died."

Bren nodded. "Maybe Thomas didn't write that letter, but somebody did, and they signed Thomas's name to it. And whoever that somebody was also stuck me in Thomas's will, giving me this house and a hell of a lot of money."

Eric hissed out a mouthful of air and put his eyes back on the letter. He read down to the bottom, not liking the rest of it any better than he did the beginning. He'd grown up in Lurkdale and was used to things not making any sense, especially those things pertaining to Thomas Windfield. Yet that didn't make this any easier to swallow.

"Avenge his death?" said Lug. "How're you supposed to do that?"

"It gets worse." Bren took the letter, placed it back inside the case and pulled out the black and white photos. He passed them one at a time to Eric, beginning with the picture of the white gazebo, which he'd taped back together so that his look-alike was reunited with the five other people standing in the doorway.

Eric looked at the photo, then looked at Bren, not sure what he was supposed to say or think.

"Recognize anyone there?"

"Only you."

"That's not me." Bren was sitting forward in the rocking chair. "The picture's thirty years old. That's Thomas Windfield himself standing there in the center with his wife." He leaned forward and put his finger on the man with the graying hair. "And this here's his daughter, Heather."

"Nice," said Lug.

"She's fifty years old by now," Bren said. "You might as well stick with Gretchen."

"Is this your father?" Eric pointed at Bren's look-alike.

"No." He'd considered this possibility himself, but had ruled it out, since he and his father didn't look all that much alike. "That there is Stephen Bradson—the man you saw here in the living room that day." He watched Lug's eyes widen. "How was it you described him? Big and ugly with wild hair? Isn't that what you said?"

Lug gave him a hard look, trying to remember that day ten years ago when he'd glanced over his shoulder and had seen the man standing behind him. The man had seemed bigger, more menacing. He'd have to look at the newspaper in the library again to be sure.

"I don't like this any better than you do." Bren could see that Lug was looking stressed. "I'm sure there are people in town who have already seen the resemblance. And those who haven't, I'm sure it won't be long before Tuttle points it out to them."

"You think Tuttle knows?" said Eric.

"I'm certain of it. That's him right there in the photograph." He put his finger on the young Earl Tuttle. "There are a lot of people around here who don't like me. I don't know if it's because of my unfortunate resemblance or because I tore down the fence and moved in here, but I've got a feeling it's only gonna get worse."

Eric was looking at the picture and shaking his head. He thought he knew all the bad there was to know about the Windfield story, but here he was holding a photograph of the killer and sitting in a room with a man who looked just like him. He didn't like the way that made him feel, like he had worms moving through the pit of his stomach.

"Who'd ever think you'd see Tuttle and old man Phelps together?" he said.

"Who's Phelps?" Bren watched Eric point to the unknown man from the photo. "You know him?"

"I think so. Looks like Bernard Phelps. He owns the used-book store in town."

# CHAPTER 12

*B*ernard Phelps was a frail man with a thin face and thin hair, but a fat heart. He polished the weathered cover of a novel with his sleeve and tucked it tightly on a shelf between similarly worn books. The store was quaint and snug, just a narrow room on Brimlock Street, with a jewelry store on one side and an ice cream parlor on the other. He was wiping the dust from his shirtsleeve when the door swung open and the sound of children laughing swept in from the street. Mr. Phelps looked up and smiled, infatuated with the contagious laughter.

A blurred figure of a man stepped through the door, and Phelps squinted. "Help you find something?" Phelps pulled a pair of glasses from his shirt pocket, put them on, and couldn't believe his eyes. "Oh my God!" Phelps stumbled backwards. He clamped his fingers to a shelf to brace himself and sent a few books tumbling to the floor with a bang.

"It's not what you think." Bren approached, and the old man shied back in fear, retreating behind the counter. "I'm not who you think I am. I just wanted to ask you a few questions."

Bernard Phelps grabbed a crucifix from under the counter and held it up. The old man's face stiffened with determination and the faith of Moses. Had Bren come up from hell, he would have had no choice but obey this God-fearing man and crawl back into his fiery pit. But instead, Bren merely grinned at the absurdity.

"I know I look like Stephen Bradson, but I'm not him. My name's Bren Stevens." He said his own name with chagrin. The fact that it sounded so similar to the killer's made him certain that others would see it as a poor attempt to hide the truth, a pseudonym thought up by a moron. He extended his hand, and Phelps touched it quickly with the crucifix to see if it would burn. But there was no smoke, no sizzle, so the old man lowered his crucifix and went into a back room, returning shortly with a damp cloth, which he patted across his face.

"I've seen that face of yours in nightmares for the past thirty years." He regarded Bren prudently. "I never thought I'd see it walking through my door."

"I'd have left it home but it's the only face I have." Bren smiled, and the old shopkeeper smiled back weakly.

"Don't tell me you're the fellow living in the mansion that everyone's talking about?" Phelps put the cloth on the back of his neck.

"Afraid so."

"Oh, if only Thomas knew the irony of his own pen."

"If he didn't, it's the *only* thing he didn't know." Bren pushed a stack of books aside and leaned on the counter.

Phelps nodded. "That and the fact that he'd invited a killer into his home. I was there that day, you know? The day he died. Me and the whole Windfield family. We were in the backyard garden. Terrible shame."

"What's your relationship with the Windfields?"

"I used to tend to their horses."

The door opened and Bren turned to see a large man with a drooping mustache come in. Mr. Phelps nodded at him and smiled, leaving the man to browse through the aisles.

"How'd he get away?" Bren continued in a quieter voice. "If everyone was there at the house like you say, how could he've left without anyone seeing him?"

"Because he didn't leave." Phelps shot a painful stare at Bren. "They watched that house for three months after the murder and no one ever saw him leave."

"And they searched the house?" said Bren.

"Of course they searched the house. *I* searched the house. Everyone in this whole bleedin' town searched that house. But it was as though he just vanished." Phelps walked around the counter and sat on the edge of a small table that was holding a lamp. "About ten years after the murder, Heather Windfield, the daughter, came back to the house to gather up some of the things, and she and several others claimed they saw the killer and chased him through the house. And several years ago, two boys claimed they saw him again in the house. Course I'm not so sure how reliable those two are, but I'm apt to believe Heather. Then a few years back another boy was killed in there."

"So I've been told."

Bren paused as the customer stepped between him and Bernard Phelps and asked for a book. He nodded at Bren and apologized for interrupting. Had the circumstance been different, Bren would have thought nothing of it when the man mentioned that he was looking for a book entitled *Yankee Go Home*. However, given the animosity building toward him in Lurkdale, Bren couldn't help but consider this a subtle invitation to pack up and get out.

"Sorry, don't believe we have that one in stock," said Mr. Phelps, and the man nodded warmly at the two men and shuffled out of the shop.

Bren stared at Bernard Phelps to see if he would acknowledge what had just happened, to see if he should take offense, but if Phelps thought this was a threat of any kind, his face gave nothing away.

"Would you happen to know how I could get in touch with Heather Windfield? Or I guess it's Chandler now," Bren said, recalling the newspaper article. "She still in Scarborough?"

"Last I heard." The old man rubbed a hand over his thin hair. "Sent me an invitation to the wedding, she did, but—haven't heard from her since. I think she keeps in touch with Tuttle, though. Perhaps you should pay him a visit."

"I already have, thank you. And I'd prefer to have nothing more to do with that man."

Phelps smiled. "My sentiments exactly." He rose and returned to the other side of the counter. "I'm sure you could find her in the directory." Setting a phone book on the counter, he thumbed the pages and came to rest on the name Chandler, Heather. "Husband's name isn't given," he commented.

"Scarborough far from here?"

"About an hour drive." Bernard Phelps turned the phone directory toward Bren and handed him a piece of paper so he could copy down the information.

When Bren left the bookstore, he went from Brimlock Street up through Moorland Avenue. He'd been along this street many times and was becoming familiar with the shops and sights. It seemed different today, however, and it took him a moment to realize what it was. It was midday, yet the street was nearly deserted. There were two women looking out a window at him, and one small boy came running up from a side street, gave him a glance and went inside a store. Even the traffic was moderate.

A knot of fear tightened in his stomach.

The first man he saw was the man with the drooping mustache, who'd been looking for *Yankee Go Home*. He came out of a clothing store and stood in the doorway, looking around as though he hadn't even noticed Bren coming up the walkway. A moment later a second man emerged from a door directly across the street.

Bren stepped off the curb and passed between two parked cars.

There were three men behind him now, two on his side of the street and one on the other. They appeared to be in no hurry and were paying no attention to him.

Slipping his hand into his pocket, he removed his keys and arranged them so they were poking out between his fingers, ready to take someone's eyes out if it came to that. He crossed through the street, keeping watch on the men coming along the sidewalk. He wasn't sure if he should run or not. Perhaps none of these men were actually following him. Perhaps it was just paranoia getting the best of him. He stopped in the center of the street and stood there a moment, waiting to see what the men would do. Down the street about a block and a half in front of him, another five men came out of a building and started toward him.

He remained in the street and headed south, putting all but three of the men at his back. He felt like he was in a movie, a bizarre western set in England with the showdown taking place on this narrow, cobbled road. Only he hadn't read the script and had no idea what the next line was.

A car came from behind him and he stepped aside to let it pass. One of the men coming toward him walked into the street and stood next to a parked car. He had on dress slacks and a tan shirt, not exactly the gang type. Bren watched him remove a set of keys from his pocket, open the driver's door and get in. And that was that. He was officially losing his mind. Half the people in this town were crazy and now he understood why: it was contagious. He'd been here for nearly a month and he'd already had his first psychotic episode. What the hell was he thinking?

He stepped back onto the sidewalk and put his keys away. By the look of the sky it was going to be a glorious day, something he hadn't seen much of in Lurkdale. He turned around, back toward Grover Street—which he generally took down the hill and over the river on his way home—and ran right into to the man with the drooping mustache.

"You should watch where you're walking." The man patted Bren on the chest, a little too hard to be a friendly gesture.

"Sorry." Bren started around the guy, but he stepped in front of him again, not letting him pass.

"There you go, almost ran into me again. You might want to get yourself a pair of glasses."

Over the guy's shoulder, Bren could see one man crossing through the street toward him and three more coming up the sidewalk. He took another step to the side and got the same treatment as before. Apparently his psychotic episode wasn't over yet. Behind him, two more men were closing in. Maybe nobody else was in on this, but he wasn't taking his chances.

"It looks like Mayor Tuttle has something to say to you." Bren stared past the gentleman, as if looking at the mayor. He waited for the man to glance over his shoulder before sucker punching him in the stomach and running past him.

There was a side street between him and the three men up ahead. He took it and headed toward the river. There was some shouting behind him, sounded like they were calling in the troupes. He was flying, not even slowing down at the corners. He glanced back a few time and saw that his paranoia wasn't entirely unfounded. There were possibly seven men back there. Working as a lumberjack had kept him in good physical condition, but he didn't know the streets as well as they did. Lurkdale was one of those old cities that had grown gradually over time, and the roads were more of an after-thought, a way of getting from one house to another. No rhyme or reason to any of them. Once, while coming into town, he'd decided to take what looked to be a shortcut and it had added fifteen minutes onto his journey.

He cut over to Grover Street, since that was the only road through this section of town that he was familiar with. Some of the men were still behind him, others were branching off down a side street—intending to cut him off, he figured. There were only three bridges over the river. Grover Street led to one; the other two were too far to consider. He hoped that if he ran fast enough, he'd hit the bridge before any of those who had taken the shortcut.

He came down Grover Street in a dead sprint. Six blocks to the bridge! He couldn't afford to have even one person beat him there. Even the briefest brawl would slow him down enough for the others to catch up. As he approached each crossroad, he anticipated someone bolting out and tackling him from the side. But this wasn't to be. Instead, two men came out ahead of him just in front of the bridge. They were both thin and long-legged. In their late teens by the looks of them. But they were enough to get him to change his direction. He made a right at the next corner and crisscrossed through two alleys before turning down a winding path that led to the water. He had no plan. When he hit the ledge that dropped off into the river, the best he could hope for was that the two lads would have been drawn away from the bridge, leaving it free for him to double back and cross over. As he came out on the narrow street that bordered the river, he spotted Sean Goodgraves standing one block down from him, frantically rotating his head back and forth like a dog on the hunt.

He smiled when he saw Bren. It was like looking at a prize deer, standing in the clearing, out of breath and out of hope. He could see the sweat on his face. There was a stone ledge that bordered the river on both sides, and a road ran alongside it most of the way, only twisting back a few times, around several houses and the old mill. All three bridges were at Sean's back, and that was the beauty of the situation. A few voices shouted behind him, and he looked back and saw Toby and Denny jogging toward him.

Now Bren was running again, headed toward the old mill. Sean started after him. He was a large man, and athletic, but running had never been his strong suit. That didn't worry him much, though, not even with Bren pulling away. The man had nowhere to go. Sooner or later, he'd tire himself out. But Sean respected his effort. Most men would have lain down and taken their beating, but this man was a fighter. Sean wouldn't have guessed that upon his first meeting up at the Windfield place. He'd expected a quick lashing and then off to the pub for drinks, but this little row was turning out to be quite sporting indeed, like a good foxhunt, which was Sean's sport of choice. He'd always said that a clever fox was much more fun than the dimwitted, which gave up too easily. *This is why men don't hunt cows,* Sean was fond of saying whenever he came across an unworthy opponent. The clever ones prolonged the chase, made the hunter work for his spoils, but sooner or later, they all found themselves in a corner—as would this quarry.

What Sean liked even better was an opponent that surprised him, which was what Bren did when he did a belly flop into the river and swam sluggishly to the other side.

Sean's dive was more graceful, though his swimming was just as sluggish.

Bren pulled himself onto the embankment on the opposite side of the river and drew in several long breaths before he could run again. Sean wasn't far behind him, and three other men were stroking through the water right on his heels. The majority of the mob, however, had turned back for the bridge, so they could cross over on dry land.

He took off down a pathway that cut between two homes and came out in an alley. The place was a maze of streets, alleyways and paths. He wove through the next few blocks, trying to make it hard for them to trail him, but it was useless. Everywhere he went, he left a line of water that dripped from his soaked clothes. Unless it started to pour soon, he didn't stand a chance. But by the look of the sky, that wasn't going to happen. Turning onto a lane called Beekman's Court, he balled the tail of his shirt in his hands and wrung out a stream of water. He could hear the voices closing in behind him.

Beekman's Court was a narrow lane with a slight curve in it, enough to conceal the fact that it led to a dead end. When Bren rounded the curve and caught sight of the back wall, he felt a new sense of panic rush through him. Tall brick walls surrounded him on three sides, caging him in. There were several doors on each side and square windows lining the second story. He was willing to walk right through someone's house if he needed to, but every door he tried was locked.

He started back toward the front of the lane and saw his friend with the droopy mustache coming toward him. The man grinned and hollered out for reinforcements. It was only a matter of seconds before a couple of his buddies were behind him. Then several more stepped in behind them. A thin boy remained at the mouth of the lane, shouting out directions for those lagging behind. There were a lot more of them than Bren had suspected.

"Not so smart after all, are ya?" stated a fat man, panting from the chase. His shirt was untucked and unbuttoned down the front to allow the air to cool the steamy sweat from his chest. His hairy stomach pushed forth over the ridge of his trousers.

"I warned ya, didn't I?" came a voice from the back of the mob. At first, Bren could see nothing more than a crew-cut blond head moving through the crowd. Then Sean stepped forward to the front of the group. His red T-shirt was dripping wet, which caused it to cling to the curves of his muscular chest and arms. "I told you to leave that house alone, but still here you are. Did you think I was joking?"

Bren remained silent. He could think of no words that would save him from the anger standing before him.

"What do I need to do to show you that I'm serious?"

"I say we run his head into the wall!" Toby yelled, and a few voices shouted in agreement.

"I'm not sure that's necessary." A man with a gray beard pushed his way to the front of the crowd and continued civilly, "The whole town helped build the fence, you know? That's why no one's too pleased with you right now."

"Yes, I'm aware of that." Bren shoved his wet hair back out of his eyes and took a few steps toward the men. He kept his eyes on the gray-bearded man, since he seemed the most civil of the bunch. "But it is *my* house, you realize."

"Nobody cares about that. You should know by now what people around here think of that house." He gave Bren a long stare. "If you know what's best for you, you'll head back up to the house and put the fence back the way you found it. Will ya do that?"

Bren could see the earnestness in the bearded man's face. Plainly, there was only one right answer to this question, but it was an answer he couldn't give. He said, "I'm afraid I can't," and saw the gray-bearded man shake his head, his way of saying that he'd done all he could, that he'd given Bren a way out and it wasn't his fault that he'd failed to take it.

Sean smiled. He stepped forward and raised a hand to keep everyone else back. He had a fighter on his hands and he didn't want to see the moment wasted on a mob scene. Like hunting a rabbit with a machine gun. Kind of takes all the sport out of it.

"Why do you care that I'm in the house?" Bren took a few steps back toward the wall and watched Sean strip off his T-shirt, ball it up and toss it to Toby. "You've been running away from this for thirty years. I say we put an end to it. If the killer *is* in the house, then let me find him. Let me flush him out."

"A lot of people would say the killer has already been flushed out, and that he's standing here before us," said Toby.

"But, of course, you know better than that, don't you?" said Bren.

"Stop your gabbing." Sean settled into his boxing stance and batted his thumb against the side of his nose.

"Of course we know better, don't we, gentlemen?" a voice spoke calmly from the back of the crowd.

Eyes turned to Constable Golding, dressed in full uniform. In one hand he held a billy club, which he smacked gently into the palm of the other hand. The crowd relaxed their fists. Sean, however, didn't retreat. He kept his stance and nodded at Bren to step up to the challenge.

"There'll be no fight today, boys." Golding strolled up between Sean and Bren. "If this man chooses to live in his own house, he has every right to do so." Golding turned his gaze at Sean and stared him down. He liked Sean Goodgraves. He'd joined him occasionally on foxhunts and had spent a week with him camping in the highlands of Scotland. But Sean had a streak in him that even Golding didn't trust. "It's over, Sean." Golding stuffed his billy club into a loop on his belt.

Sean stood his ground for another minute. It wasn't over; it was far from over. It may have to wait till another day, but he and the blond-haired American were definitely going to have their day in the arena. He grabbed his T-shirt from Toby and shot a stare past Golding to Bren, who was visibly shaken by the whole ordeal.

"You take care of yourself there, Yankee boy." Sean pulled his shirt on. "Be careful in that big house of yours. It's been known to be very unkind to its residents."

"It's his life." Golding was eager to put an end to the threats.

"Or death," Sean added before trailing his friends out of the lane.

Bren leaned against the back wall at the end of the lane and took a deep breath. His hands shook as he rubbed them through his damp hair.

"How you feeling?" asked the officer.

"Okay." The sun sat midway in the sky at Golding's back, and Bren had to squint to look at the man's face.

"I'm not saying you're wrong for being here or claiming what's rightfully yours, but you'd be better off leaving this whole thing behind you. No amount of money is worth your life."

Bren nodded, but didn't look convinced. "Thanks for your help."

"Ah." Golding brushed the compliment away with his hand. "It's my job. Yet job or no job, I can't always be there. Someday they'll catch you alone, take you out where nobody can hear your screams and—" He stopped there, knowing that Bren's imagination would fill in the rest of the details.

Bren nodded his understanding, but knew he couldn't follow the officer's advice, and Golding realized this.

"You want me to see you back to your house?"

"No, I'll be all right."

Golding nodded despondently. "You be careful. These people are friends of mine, and I'd hate to have to lock them up just because you went and did something stupid like let them kill you."

# CHAPTER 13

*H*e took a bus to Scarborough, a costal city with the ruins of a castle setting on the headlands that stood as a wall between the North and South Bay. A lively fishing harbor nestled below the castle, and streets stretched inland, up the hillside. He didn't know how Heather Windfield Chandler would accept his visit, but he suspected she wouldn't be overly fond of someone who looked identical to the man who had killed her father. With any luck, though, she wouldn't be as unreasonable as many of the folks in Lurkdale.

From a lady in the bus terminal, he got directions to the street where the Chandlers resided. It was up the hill, near an old church. They lived in a two-story, brick house with three gables peeking out from a pointed red roof. Not so grand as Windfield Manor, but nice. He pushed the doorbell and waited. He was prepared for anything; that is, anything except the lovely twenty-two-year-old who opened the door. Bren looked again at the address to make sure he had the right home. He did.

"Could I help you?"

"I'm looking for a Heather Chandler."

"That's my mother." The woman hesitated a moment as if contemplating whether or not she should invite this stranger into her home. She then opened the door wider and stepped to the side. "Won't you come in?"

Bren followed her into the living room, which was decorated in blues and greens. The sun bleeding through the drawn curtains cast orange tones across the furniture. Bren had been calm during the bus ride from Lurkdale and while walking to the Chandler home from the station. Now, however, he was starting to feel jittery. Making a fool of himself in front of Heather Windfield Chandler didn't appeal to him, but he could deal with it. Yet he wasn't sure he could deal with making a fool of himself in front of Heather's daughter. She was an extremely beautiful woman and he thought it would be nice to leave her with a good impression. That wasn't going to happen if her mother reacted toward him the way the folks in Lurkdale had.

"Could I tell her who's come calling?"

"Bren Stevens."

"Bren," the woman said with a slight smile, as though she liked the name. "Why don't you have a seat for a moment? I'll go get her." She motioned to the sofa.

"Before you go—" He bit as his bottom lip, realizing how stupid this was going to come out sounding. "Chances are, your mother isn't gonna take an instant liking to me. I've got this strange effect on people, and I'm pretty sure she'll disapprove of me—hate me actually. But my name's Bren Stevens, regardless of what she says. I just wanted to make that clear."

"Okay." Her voice was filled with misgiving, and Bren had no doubt that he'd indeed come across sounding like an idiot. "Though I think you can relax. My mother rarely hates anyone."

"Trust me. She'll hate me."

As she exited down a hallway, Bren crossed the room to a portrait hanging on the wall above a baby grand piano. It was a portrait of the Chandler family: a loving husband and wife and a lovely, brown-eyed infant. Heather was smiling in the picture. She looked happy, a twenty-eight-year-old mother with her tearful past long behind her.

She was a lovely woman, Bren had to admit—strong features, and refined.

"Bren Stevens?" said a voice behind him.

He turned and found Heather Chandler dressed in a purple blouse, looking like she was preparing to go out, perhaps to a friend's or shopping. She was older now, forty-nine, yet still lovely. Her brown hair was cut fashionably short and curled. The light in her eyes suddenly dimmed, replaced momentarily by shock, and then by fear.

"What are you doing here?" Her words came out in a strained whisper and she appeared to be short of breath. A hand groped unconsciously and grasped her daughter by the arm, bracing herself. Bren could see that this wasn't going to turn out well even before she began shouting. He knew it by the way the fear in her eyes was slowly turning to anger.

"How dare you come to my home?" The beauty he'd seen in her face was now gone. "Where's your shame? I want you out of here now." She pointed to the door and her hand was trembling.

Bren nodded his told-you-so at the daughter, who had put a reassuring hand on her mother's back.

"My name's Bren Stevens, and—"

"I've heard enough of your lies," said Heather. "Now get out of my house!"

"My name's Bren Stevens," he reiterated. "Your father willed me your house in Lurkdale."

This caught the daughter's attention, but she said nothing, merely held tighter to her mother, seeing that she was on the verge of tears, perhaps headed for that nervous breakdown she was always talking about.

"I think it'd be better if you left, Bren," the daughter said.

"Just let me explain."

"Please." She urged him toward the door. "You should go."

Bren nodded, looking at Heather again and seeing the barrier between them. There would be no talking to this woman, no rationale that would make her see how absurd her accusations were. He followed the daughter to the door, allowing her to escort him out. He wanted more than anything to explain himself to her, tell her that he was just as confused by all of this as her mother was, but he knew this wasn't the time, and was quite certain that there would never be a time.

"My name's Bren Stevens," he said once again before the door closed in his face.

This had gone badly. Much worse than he had anticipated. He stood a moment, looking at the closed door, before wandering slowly down the walk. Glancing back, he found the young woman gazing at him from a window. Her brown eyes were lovely and filled with curiosity, and she smiled a faint, confused smile. As he looked at that lovely face, Bren felt incredibly sad, knowing that in a single instance, he'd both met and alienated the most beautiful girl he'd ever seen.

That night as Bren lay in his barricaded room with the covers snug over his shoulders, he was still awake, staring at the ceiling, when he heard the noise. He'd been thinking about the girl he'd met in Scarborough—he hadn't even asked for her name—as the clatter rose up from downstairs. He knew what had fallen: the pots and pans that he'd pulled from the kitchen cupboards and had laid on the counters. He'd started working on the kitchen three days ago and still hadn't managed to get it in order.

Reaching under his pillow, he retrieved his ax and stepped out of bed onto the cold floor. The cookery hadn't fallen on its own; he knew this. With the plastic tacked up over the windows, no cats or crows could have gotten into the house; therefore, he could only conclude that someone had broken in, or else Stephen Bradson had just stepped out of the wall and was scrounging the kitchen for something to eat. He stood near the blocked door and listened. Another pan crashed to the ground. Moonlight twinkled through the window and stretched Bren's shadow across the wall as he moved the bed and dresser aside and opened the door a crack so that he could see out. The hallway was dark and shadowy but empty. In the quiet, he could hear the stairs creak. Someone was definitely in the house—and coming to pay him a visit.

Quickly, he shut the door again and shoved the dresser and bed back in front of it. He moved back near the window, his fingers turning white around the handle of the ax as he gazed toward the dark lawn, contemplating making the long drop to the weedy ground. The intruder was moving slowly down the hallway. Bren could hear the muffled footsteps and the careful opening of doors along the way. He prayed it wouldn't come to it, but if he had to, he'd prove Gretchen Wicks right.

The doorknob of his room twisted slowly. The door inched open and hit against the dresser. There was a short pause. Then the door pushed in again, this time forcibly. The dresser and bed squeaked forward across the floor a few inches. Bren backed up against the far wall with the ax held up over his head, prepared to slice away at whatever came through that door.

The door closed. Bren could hear the wheezing of his own breath in the quiet of the house. For nearly five minutes he stood there in his underwear with the moonlight shining at his back and his ax perched on his shoulder. He hadn't heard the footsteps retreat down the hall or descend the stairs, but he assumed they had. This was something he couldn't be sure of, but he had no intention of looking out into the hall to find out.

Instead, he pushed the bed and dresser snugly up against the door again and lay down on the bed with the ax resting across his chest. Staring at the shadowy ceiling, he waited impatiently for sleep to come. It never did. He flinched at every gust of wind and at each moth tapping at his bedroom window as he waited for the sun to peer over the horizon. That night, darkness overstayed its welcome. When the first rays of the morning sun finally swept across the moors, he pulled on his clothes, moved his barricade and crept out of his bedroom to investigate. This was a big house with plenty of places to hide, but he knew if he didn't check each room thoroughly, he would continue agonizing and wouldn't be able to relax. Holding his ax on his shoulder, he surveyed the second story and third-floor loft. The place was a graveyard.

In the south wing, Bren pushed open the door that led into the library. He came out on a balcony that wrapped the entire second floor of the large room, which was empty except for the wheeled ladders and several dozen books that graced the shelves that had been built to hold hundreds. He came down the winding staircase, exited into the corridor and checked out the conservatory before making his way to the kitchen, where all the noise had come from. The counter had been swept clean. Intentionally, he figured. Pots, pans, strainers, silverware and numerous other items were strewn across the blue tiled floor. But far worse than this was the message he found scrawled on the back wall above the stove.

"Leave My House," it read. It'd been written in what Bren first thought to be blood, but upon closer inspection discovered to be only lipstick.

He scanned the kitchen, barely lit by the morning light. As he came around the counter, his foot kicked something. It clanked forward and sent a surge of adrenalin to Bren's heart. Jumping back and without a moment's hesitation or thought, he swung the ax at the noise and buried the blade deep into the bottom of a saucepan.

He smiled with relief, but he felt far from amused. Someone had been in his house, had scattered the cookery across the floor and had climbed the stairs to his bedroom door. There was nothing amusing about that, and the lipstick scrawls on the kitchen wall frightened him more than he was willing to admit.

He checked every door and found them all securely locked. No one had forced his way through a door, nor had he torn the plastic back away from the broken windows and come in that way. Whoever had stood at his bedroom door last night had easy access into and out of the house, and that's what frightened him most.

# CHAPTER 14

Wearing a violet shirt and a pair of white pants, Natasha Chandler entered the Lurkdale library. The thin middle-aged librarian sat behind the counter with his eyes closed and an open magazine resting on his lap.

"Well, Mr. McCafry," said Natasha, looking over the wooden counter at him. "If I didn't know better I'd think you were asleep back there."

He sat up straight and attempted to look awake as he gazed up at the counter. It took a few minutes for his eyes to focus. Then he grinned warmly. "Why Miss. Chandler, how many years has it been since we've had the honor?" He stood, came to the counter and put his hand on hers. "And you've grown into such a lovely lady, too. If I were a year or two younger, I know who I'd be calling on. My, my, they didn't make girls that pretty when I was a bachelor."

"You'd better not let your wife hear you say that."

He patted her hand. "So what brings you back here? The usual?"

"I'm afraid I'm still as predictable as ever."

"Old habits die hard, I suppose." He turned toward the back room, then stopped and looked back. "You're here checking on the stranger, aren't you? I guess everyone with any connection to this has heard that he's come out of hiding and is trying to pass himself off as someone else. The beast. You'd think he would've at least grown a beard or changed the color of his hair. Something. But he looks just the same." He went to the back room and came back with a newspaper bearing the portrait of Natasha's grandfather, Thomas Windfield, released the day after his death, August 17, 1964.

"How's your mother?"

"She's fine," said Natasha. "She still has her days; you know Mum, never happy unless she's unhappy."

"Tell her to come visit sometime. We miss her lovely face round here."

"I'll do that, Mr. McCafry." She took her paper to a back table. Nearly four years had passed since she last examined the articles, and after Bren's visit, she wanted to reacquaint herself with the photograph of the killer. She opened to the picture before falling gently into her chair. This was indeed the man who had visited her home, the man claiming to have received the mansion from her grandfather. Sitting back in her chair, she scratched at her brow, getting her first real glimpse into her mother's obsession. Ever since Natasha was a child, she could remember her mother telling stories of what had taken place at Windfield Manor back in '64 and how she'd seen the killer once again ten years later when she returned to gather some of the furniture. Natasha had believed it when she was a child, then had grown to believe that her mother wasn't completely sane. Now she wasn't sure what to think.

She drove her yellow Mini out of town to the manor and found Bren pacing back and forth in the tall grass with a lawn mower. A few weeks ago, he'd discovered the mower in the shed around back, but he hadn't been able to get it to run until today, after spending all morning tearing it apart and reassembling it.

A stretch of cut grass lay in front of the house, making the front entrance look nearly dignified with the exception of the dead tree that stood at the center of the lawn. At the base of the old tree sat the ax, put there just in case Bren's nightly visitor returned, as he had three nights in a row. The last two nights, the visitor merely knocked over items and stomped up the stairs and down the halls, then rapped gently at the bedroom door. He didn't try to enter the room as he had the first night, but his antics were no less frightening. As a result, Bren had had very little sleep.

When the car parked in front of the mansion, he looked up from the choking mower, shut down the engine and dusted the grass from his pant legs. The sun was glaring on the windshield, preventing him from seeing much more than a figure sitting behind the wheel.

Natasha opened the glove box and retrieved a steak knife that she put in her purse before stepping out of the car smiling, with her white purse slung over her shoulder.

"Looking good." She crossed the lawn with the sun accenting the blond streaks in her brown hair. "You've really done wonders for the place."

"It's better anyway. Still needs a lot of work, though." Bren looked back at the sun falling across the plastic in the windows and the lifeless ivy clinging to the side wall. "I'm happy to see that the little episode at your home didn't scare you away, Miss Chandler."

"Natasha," she said.

"I'm Bren."

"I remember. You kept repeating it as my mother shooed you out the door, as I recall."

"I told you your mother would hate me."

"That you did. You do make an alarming first impression."

"It's that good ole American charm of mine." Bren was brushing the grass from his hair. "All woman have that same reaction to me."

"Somehow I don't believe that."

"So what can I do for you, Natasha?"

"Just thought perhaps we could talk. That is, if I can pull you away from all this fun."

Bren kicked the old red lawn mower, now covered with grass and dust. "I guess I can make time. There's a gazebo behind the house." He motioned through the uncut grass toward the backyard.

"I was hoping we could go inside, if that's okay."

"You sure?" he said. "Generally I have to bribe people to go inside."

"I should've resisted. Could've walked away with a few pounds."

He grabbed the ax from beside the dead tree before leading the way up the front steps. For three days straight after his nightly visitations, he'd made a thorough inspection of the house. He couldn't understand it; the place was locked up tight, yet someone was waltzing around freely. The second morning he'd found another message, this time scrawled on the living room mirror. This one read: *The Clock Is Ticking. Time Is Running Short*, and it had an arrow pointing to the broken grandfather clock, whose hands had been turned so that it read 11:00. The next morning the message on the mirror simply said, *Tick Tock*. The time on the clock had been changed to 11:30 and there was a dead mouse hanging from the big hand.

Natasha was watching the ax swing at Bren's side as she casually undid the flap of her purse. "I'm surprised to see you living here. I've heard nasty rumors about the place."

"Me, too." Bren opened the door and stepped inside. "But you know how rumors are; they tend to be exaggerated over the years."

"I suppose. But you'd never convince my mother of that."

"Yeah, so I gather." He closed the door behind them and the entryway fell into shadows. "I'd like to apologize for the other day. I really thought after she got over the initial shock of this frightening face of mine, we'd be able to just sit down and talk."

"Oh it's not your fault." She looked up the twisting mahogany stairs where the light flowing through the circular window fell across the balustrade. "In fact I wanted to apologize for my mother. She's generally quite sane. No, that's not true, but she's generally not quite so buoyantly insane. At least not around strangers."

"When you look like me, you actually get used to that kind of reaction from people around here." He led her into the living room where the curtains were open, allowing plenty of light to flow across the worn carpet and sofa. "Have a seat."

"I was hoping for a tour. Or do you need to bribe people for that, too?"

"No, not for the tour. For that, they usually bribe me."

"Is that right?" She was looking at his reflection in the long mirror. "And what kind of bribes do you take, Bren?"

"Oh, a dinner, a movie, but no horror movies. I get enough of that at home."

She smiled. "So why'd my grandfather give you this house?"

"I was hoping you could tell me that."

"Surely you have some idea."

"None whatsoever. If I did, I wouldn't have gone to Scarborough to see your mother. This whole thing's had me baffled right from the start." They crossed the corridor to the study. "First I receive this house from someone I don't know; then I find out I look like the benefactor's killer. It's been a very confusing month."

"So this is the room." Natasha walked over to the dark stain in front of the desk. "I'd heard the bloodstain was still here. How very typical of my family and this town just to leave it here."

"I take it your grandmother and mother moved out pretty quickly after your grandfather's death."

"They never spent another night here." She sat back on the edge of the desk and stared over at Bren, who was standing in the doorway. "They stayed in town for a few weeks while the police searched for this Stephen Bradson fellow. When he never showed up, they purchased a home in Scarborough. They just ran away, the whole superstitious lot of them." She walked behind the desk to the small window, parted the curtains and stared out into the side yard. "This is my first time inside, you know? I drove over from Scarborough a few times with friends to look at the place, but I got sucked right into the myth like everyone else, and I didn't dare come in. And here you are living here."

"Not by choice, I assure you. I'd much rather be spending my nights in town, just like that superstitious family of yours. This town's belief is contagious, and they take it very seriously."

He gave her a tour of the dining room and kitchen and told her all about Mayor Tuttle and Henry Hays and how they'd taken it upon themselves to interpret the will and assure that Bren followed it to the letter. *The King Tuttle Version,* Natasha had remarked and Bren found the title amusingly appropriate. As they left the study and passed down the corridor to the south wing, Bren relayed the Beekman's Court incident and how the police officer had saved him from an almost certain demise.

"Lurkdale can be very cruel," Natasha agreed as they entered the conservatory, a rounded room set in the turret at the end of the house. It was entirely barren except for several torn pages of sheet music scattered across the wooden floor and a fireplace on the inside wall. "I do hope you realize that not all of England is this eccentric. Just Lurkdale and its descendants. And you've got to realize that you scare the wits out of these people."

"I thought scared people were supposed to run away."

"This is their home," she said. "Attacking intruders is the nature of the beast."

"And what about you, Natasha? Aren't you afraid of me? I mean, after all, I could be the same man who killed your grandfather."

"Don't be ridiculous. You're much too young." She refastened the flap of her purse.

"Yes, well, some think my youth proves my guilt." He was looking out the curved window that overlooked the garden and gazebo. "You've seen the newspaper, I suppose. If I didn't know better, *I'd* think I was your grandfather's killer."

"I was just in the library this morning looking at the paper as a matter of fact," she said nonchalantly, joining Bren at the window. He looked at her, surprised at the candor, but she just looked out toward the gazebo and said, "You have a very lovely garden there, Bren."

"Why, thank you. Many hours of neglect went into developing that sought-after overrun look you see before you."

She turned to him and studied his face. She liked the look of him. Her mother had often mentioned how handsome he was, or at least the man who looked like him. The photographs in the paper didn't do him justice. That, and the fact that she'd always known it to be the face of the man who had killed her grandfather, had always caused her to dislike that face. Yet, looking at it now, she felt much fonder of it.

"You do scare me, Bren. When I was young, I believed in all this demon dogma. I think people will believe anything that's fed to them enough. I went to university and cured myself of ignorance, yet now here I am, completely confused again."

"I'm only twenty-five-years-old. You can trust me on that. And I didn't kill your grandfather."

"I believe you, Bren. Sheer logic forces me to believe you. But I can understand why some people don't, my mother included."

When they entered the library, Natasha walked to the center of the room and looked around her in awe. "This place is incredible. No wonder Mother never got over it." She gazed up at the high ceiling and the balcony that wrapped around all four walls. She imagined it in its heyday: polished floor, shelves lined with books, cushioned chairs where you could sit and read for hours. Just the way her mother had described it.

"Your grandfather asked me to avenge his death, you know?"

Natasha laughed, still staring up at the ceiling as she spoke. "My grandfather, the enigma." Her voice sounded hollow in the lofty room. "That's what my mother always calls him: the enigma. I've always suspected that insanity runs in the family. That's why I studied psychology at university."

"You think your grandfather was insane?"

"Don't you?"

"No. I think he was psychic."

"That, too." Natasha pushed one of the wheeled ladders along the tracks to see if it would still move. It squealed terribly. "So what do you plan to do, Bren Stevens? Are you going to avenge my grandfather's death?"

"No. I'm gonna do my best to make peace with Lurkdale and collect my four million pounds."

"Wise man. The less you get involved in all this hogwash, the better off you'll be."

# CHAPTER 15

Natasha Chandler tiptoed through the front door of her Scarborough home. On an end table next to the sofa, a lamp that her mother had left on dimly lit the living room. She shut the door and clicked the lock into place before crossing over to the piano and setting her purse on the bench.

"Where've you been?"

She turned to find her mother standing in the doorway that led into the hall. She was wearing a pink robe over her nightgown.

"Out," she answered casually and headed past her mother toward her bedroom, as if her answer would suffice. She could predict where this conversation was leading and she didn't want to go there.

"Obviously," her mother remarked. "Where?"

"Why?" Natasha's voice remained calm, indicating that she had nothing to hide or to tell, a ploy that her mother was well acquainted with.

"You went to visit him, didn't you? After everything I said, you still went." There was a sadness in Mrs. Chandler's voice. She'd seen the way her daughter perked up when Bren had related the news about being willed the house. She knew her daughter and she knew she wouldn't be able to leave it alone. So with love, and with the wisdom of one who had been down that same road, she warned her daughter to stay away. Yet she knew. She had failed as a mother; she realized this, for she'd raised a daughter who showed no consideration for her elders, and even less consideration for her own mother. "You went, didn't you?" she restated.

"And if I did?"

"You've got no respect." Mrs. Chandler sat down rigidly in the loveseat. "You know how I feel about that place, yet every time I turn my back, you're back there again. That house has ruined my life. Must it also ruin yours?"

"I'm old enough to decide what's best for me."

"Obviously you're not," Mrs. Chandler scolded. "You run off to school for a couple of years and suddenly you're an expert on the world. Well I'll have you know, little lady, that you've still got a lot to learn about life—things that your great university can't teach you. You have no idea what you're tampering with."

"You're wrong about him, Mother."

"Am I?" she said harshly. "You're so set on proving me wrong that you've run right to the killer's arms. If you love me at all, you'll never go back there again." Tears were in Mrs. Chandler's eyes. She wept out of fear and anger, angry at her daughter's naivety. "You have no idea how dangerous this man is. He'll kiss you one minute and kill you the next. Is that what you want? You want me to lose the last person on earth that means anything to me?"

Natasha leaned on the frame of the doorway and folded her arms. She was calm. "I went to the house, Mother, and there is no demon. There's a young man, handsome and frightened, and he's just as confused by this whole thing as you and I are. Yes, he does look like the man who murdered Grandfather, just like you said, but you and I both know that they're not the same person."

"Don't pull your Miss. Freud on me, Natasha. I find it very demeaning. You are not my therapist, you're my daughter. And I find it intolerable to have my daughter, who doesn't even have a degree, treat me like I'm one of her patients."

"Must I have a degree to know something? No I'm not certified, but I do know paranoia when I see it."

"You're a very cruel person, Natasha. I regret I ever asked you to come back home."

"No you don't, Mother. Without me, you'd have no one to feel sorry for you."

"I bet they never taught you to talk that way to your patients in those psychology courses of yours."

"You're not my patient, remember?"

"If you ever become a psychologist, I'm sure you'll show more respect for your patients than you do for your own mother."

"People are always cruelest to those they love most. Didn't you know that? And I do love you most."

Mrs. Chandler rose to her feet, and Natasha could see that her hands were shaking. The woman needed some Valium, and if Natasha had had her psychiatric license, she would have prescribed it herself. Instead, she watched her mother frown past her and shut herself in her bedroom, where she'd probably stay up all night listening to the wind knock against her window while she waited for Stephen Bradson to force his way into her home.

Natasha went to the kitchen and warmed herself a crumpet, which she buttered and ate while sitting at the table and staring blankly at the refrigerator. She'd been raised on the gospel of Windfield Manor, and like all good children, she didn't question the things taught to her by authority. She knew the demon existed in that house just as assuredly as most children know God exists, and her evidence of the fact was just as strong—her mother had told her so.

# CHAPTER 16

When Natasha showed up at the house the next day, Bren was in a flowerbed to the right of the front door, elbow deep in weeds. His bare arms bore signs of warring thistles, which apparently gave a good fight before allowing Bren to pluck them from the brown earth. His shirt was off and his muscular back was baked brown.

"So how does a poor American boy like you clean up after a strenuous day?" asked Natasha.

Bren stood, his chest equally tanned and his body strong and filthy. "I just stand outside for a while," he said. "I know if I wait long enough this darn English weather is gonna pour buckets of water down on me and lick me clean."

"That it will. But what if we don't have time for the weather?" She glanced at the sky where only a few clouds dotted the sea of blue.

"Are we going somewhere?"

"Yes. I'm a girl of honor, and I plan on settling up for yesterday's tour. That is, if I can get you to make yourself presentable. Even Lurkdale has its standards. There's a little restaurant at the end of Pepperfield Lane, not great, but acceptable. I thought a poor helpless bachelor like yourself could use a little pity."

"Ah, so this is a charity date, huh?" He climbed out of the flowerbed and brushed the dirt from the knees of his blue jeans. "Generally

I consider myself above charity, but being the fine gentleman that I am and not wanting to be rude, I accept."

"I'm ecstatic," she said without a grain of enthusiasm. "But unless you do something about your appearance, I'm not taking you anywhere. A girl has a certain image she needs to maintain. I wouldn't want people to think I'm dating a simpleton."

Bren peeled off his leather gloves and tossed them at the front step. "If it's your reputation you're concerned about, missy, I'm afraid you're keeping the wrong company. Because regardless of my cleanliness, Lurkdale thinks I'm the foulest beast to ever grace its streets."

"Lurkdale's always been infamous for its deplorable taste."

Leaving Natasha to wait in her car, Bren retrieved a towel and a fresh change of clothes from the house before hiking up into the trees where a small brook flowed out of the hills. His finding the brook hadn't come by chance. He'd gone looking for a place where he could wash away his filth, since it didn't appear that the mansion was going to have running water anytime soon. Because of the sharp coldness of the water, he kept his bathing at a minimum, only coming to the brook when his own stench got too much for him to bear.

He draped his clean clothes over the branch of a tree, stripped off his blue jeans and stared at the water. In the beginning, he'd sit on the bank and dip his feet in until they adjusted to the temperature before slowly immersing the rest of his body. This had proved to be nothing but slow torture, so he'd changed tactics and went for the full plunge right up front, as he did this time. The cold stole his breath for several minutes. His body stiffened and his skin grew tight. He moved quickly, rubbing his hands over his body to scrub off the dirt. He grabbed a bottle of liquid soap, which he'd set near the edge of the water, and poured some into his hand. It probably wasn't good for the water, but oh well; the brook flowed down into Lurkdale, and Bren couldn't care less if anybody there got a dose of contaminated water.

He rubbed some soap over his face, then immersed his head and came up gasping. He pushed back his hair and wiped the water from his face.

"A true man of the wild." Natasha came walking out from a grove of trees, gaping at Bren's naked chest rising up from the stream. Bren quickly shrank down so that only his head was exposed. "He gallantly lives in a home where murderers are known to rest. He eats food out of cans that he stores in his bedroom, and now I find that the man bathes in the coldest waters in England. I just love the rugged type."

"I thought you were gonna wait in the car." Bren's bobbing head was shivering.

"There's a naked man in the woods, flaunting himself, and you expect me to wait in the car?" She walked over to the brook and looked down on him. "My whole life, my mother taught me how to live the role of a lady, and frankly, being a lady isn't much fun."

Bren smiled shyly. He'd fantasized about meeting such a bold girl, but now that one stood before him, he found himself uncomfortably speechless.

"Aren't you going to invite me in?" she asked.

"Please, be my guest."

She slipped off her shoe and stuck her toe in the icy water. "On second thought, being a lady does have its endearing qualities." She put her foot back in her shoe and looked Bren over pleasurablely, then added, "I'll wait for you in the car."

The restaurant, The Pepperfield Inn, was an old Tudor-style building with black framing striping through the white exterior. The large windows of the dining hall overlooked the ruined mill resting beside the river at the edge of Lurkdale, the spot where Bren had swum across to escape the mob. The host, a tall, thin man dressed in a white shirt and black dress pants, smiled brightly at the sight of Natasha, and then quickly turned his nose up when he saw her company. He escorted them to a table as far away from the windows as possible, a table that was obscured from the rest of the room by a thick brown beam. When the waiter came, he politely asked for Natasha's order, and then coldly jotted down Bren's request, acting as if Bren had inconvenienced him by patronizing the restaurant.

"You ever get the feeling people are staring at you?" Natasha whispered after the waiter had left.

Bren glanced around, and every single face was turned at him. The faces were stern and accusing, twisted like hungry rats eyeing a slab of molding cheese, not sure if they should devour it or leave it alone.

"Personally, I think you're paranoid, Natasha. Lurkdale has the sweetest people I've ever met. I've always felt just like kin ever since I moved here."

"Yeah, you're the demented cousin everyone avoids."

"True," said Bren. "But it's heart-warming just knowing I'm part of the family."

When the food arrived, Natasha's chicken salad could have fed three sumo wrestlers, while Bren's steak could have barely satisfied an Ethiopian with an immensely shrunken stomach. But Bren smiled pleasantly, happy to be sharing a meal with such a lovely companion.

"So what does your mother think of you spending time with me?" Bren slivered off a piece of steak to pace his portioning to that of Natasha's.

"She hates it. My mother has never approved of the men I've dated, but now she's absolutely hysterical. But you've got to realize that my mother isn't exactly emotionally stable. She's always been a bit paranoid, but you've got her out and out delirious."

"How about your father?"

"He's a major part of my mother's insanity." She nibbled at her salad. "My mother's paranoia isn't exactly unfounded. She saw her own father bleed to death when she was nineteen. Ten years later she was apparently visited by the killer. As ridiculous as that sounds, there are others who substantiate her story. What you don't know is that several weeks after she saw Stephen Bradson in Windfield Manor, my father was stabbed to death in the study in our first home in Scarborough."

There was a silence as Bren looked across the table at Natasha, a girl who was only two years old when her father met the same fate as her grandfather.

"After my father's death, my mother was inconsolable. The police claim that the similarities between the two murders were strictly coincidental. My mother doesn't share their view. Every time we go anywhere, I always catch her looking around like some mad stalker is hiding around every corner. She completely alienated me as a child. All my friends used to look at her like she was a mental patient who had escaped from the psychiatric ward. The worst part of it is that I found myself picking up her idiosyncrasies. I'd be with my friends, and without thinking I'd be checking closets and looking under the bed, expecting to find the bogeyman. I went through a long period of hating my mother. Now I only pity her."

"So you went into psychology to cure your mother."

"No, to cure myself. As I'm sure you've heard, psychologists are notorious for being more messed up than their patients. Though not completely true, in my case it's painfully accurate. I've always felt that I was raised a member of a cult, and for the past four years I've been trying to deprogram myself from their indoctrination, which is really hard when your own mother is the cult leader."

The waiter came over and refilled Natasha's glass of water and didn't even acknowledge Bren's existence before walking off, leaving his glass empty.

"You just going to take that?" Natasha sipped her water.

"What do you want me to do, beat him up?"

"Yeah, I want you to pulverize him. He's a skinny little twerp, and he's making a complete fool of you."

Bren looked out across the restaurant where the thin waiter had paused to fill the glass of a portly fellow with long sideburns. "I'm sure the judge would be very sympathetic when they haul me off to court," said Bren. "'So, Mr. Stevens,' the judge would say. 'Why did you break this man's nose and fracture his skull?' 'He wouldn't fill my water glass,' I'd explain. 'And I was very thirsty.' 'In that case, Mr. Stevens, you're free to go.'"

"Do you find yourself entertaining?" she asked.

"I find myself down right hilarious. Are you implying that you don't?"

"Very good." She grinned. "A friend of mine at Leeds University used to ask me that question all the time and I never had a good answer."

"A friend, huh? Was this friend by chance male?"

"Are you jealous?"

"Of course. I was hoping you hadn't even looked at a man until I came along."

She blushed at the compliment. "His name was Harold Doveman. I met him when I was a freshman, but we never started dating until I was a sophomore. It took me nearly a year and a half to realize what a total loser he was."

"I'm beginning to like this man better all the time."

She smiled. "So what about you, Bren? You're a handsome man. Surely there's some broken-hearted girl back in America awaiting your return."

"Nope. See the way these people are staring at me?" He motioned with his eyes to the occasional stranger still brandishing hateful gazes at him. "That's the way most girls look at me."

"I can believe that. I'm sure I had that same look when you came to my house." She smiled as she picked at her salad. "Now seriously. Tell me what kind of competition I've got out there."

Bren liked the sound of that. "If you're in the running, Natasha, there is no competition. I've never met a girl in my life who would stand a chance against you."

"Then consider me in the running," she said and filled her mouth with chicken salad.

Outside, the sun fell behind the hills and the moon took its place. Lights flickered on in the restaurant, and several waiters weaved throughout the tables, lighting candles that sat in red-bubbled glasses in the center of each table. Bren and Natasha's remained unlit.

"So why'd you break up with Harold?"

"He had a severe case of ego," she explained. "I honestly think he believes he's going to take over for God someday. 'Our Father who art in Heaven, Harold be Thy name.' He actually had that on a plaque on his desk. He always referred to it as a joke, but I think he secretly worshipped himself—sometimes not so secretly."

"His desk?" Bren inquired. "As in an office with a desk?"

"Oh, yes," she said as if absent-minded. "Harold was one of my professors." She opened her brown eyes wide and shrugged coyly at the information. "He was older, wiser, handsome. In truth, he was the father I never had," she said candidly. "I made the mistake of telling him my story about Windfield Manor. At the time I was still indoctrinated to its validity. I thought Harold would act professionally, but no, he found it hilarious. Every time we got together with some of his friends, I found myself the brunt of the joke, and it was always Harold telling the jokes.

"He's a very staunch member of the Church of England," she went on. "Not that there's anything wrong with the Church of England, other than the fact that they let Harold become a member. Anyway, you can't so much as mention religion without him preaching to you about God and the hierarchy and how bloody ignorant the world is when it comes to supreme truth." She stared down at her plate, still nearly full with lettuce, vegetables and slabs of chicken and pushed it over toward Bren. "You want some of this?" she offered, and Bren quickly accepted.

"My junior year, I had to write a paper for my final project in Harold's class. I decided, actually Harold decided for me, that I should write about the Windfield Manor Myth, analyzing the superstitions of Lurkdale. Not a bad idea, I thought, so I consented. I wrote a rough draft and ran it by him. He told me it was too simplistic and wanted me to compare it to other well-known superstitions, but you just can't compare the complexity of Windfield Manor with black cats, walking under ladders or breaking mirrors.

"One day, Harold and I were having lunch with two other professors and they were all talking theology. One of them was Catholic, the original sin according to Harold, who went on and on about how stupid this professor was for believing such nonsense. Well, later, he turned to his favorite subject: my gullibility. I don't know, I suppose it was the juxtaposition of the theology subject with my gullibility that clicked the light on for me, but there it was, my paper." She smiled, crossed her arms and leaned forward onto the table. "I paralleled the Windfield Manor Myth with religion. Brilliant, eh? I said that they're both based on hearsay from supposed eyewitnesses, and it's basically just one brainwashed generation brainwashing the next."

"You're an atheist?"

"No. I mean, I don't know. I'm agnostic, I suppose. I only wrote the paper to put Harold in his place, and he knew exactly what I was doing. I was saying he was just as gullible as I was, and it made him furious. He gave me an 'F' on the paper, which I suppose I expected. I went to Charles Stern, the Catholic I was telling you about, and he loved the paper, mainly because he could see the vein that had inspired it. He went to the school board and protested my 'F' and Harold denied any personal feelings for the paper. He claimed it was strictly academically weak. The school board ruled in favor of

Harold, and that night I hung a goat's head from the ceiling of his front porch."

Bren burst with laughter and the whole restaurant scowled at him as if his laughter were demonic.

"Remind me to stay on your good side," he said and ate in silence for a moment. "You ever introduce Harold to your mother?"

"Heavens no," Natasha said. "After he ridiculed me, he started interrogating me about my mother. I claimed that Mother had escaped the Lurkdale ludicrousness, but Harold was smart enough to know I was lying. His biggest flaw was that he was smart and knew it, that and his overbearing religious zeal. Apparently, he was torn between majoring in religion and psychology, but psychology won out. He figured he could cure all his patients by sending them to church. His favorite line was that when he died he would become one of the Herald Angels. A friend of mine is an artist, and after Harold and I broke up, I had my friend draw a cartoon for the school newspaper. It had a man, who looked remarkably like Harold, standing at the pearly gates, and God was turning him away saying, 'I don't care if your name is Harold, My angels have a reputation to uphold.' The faculty and the whole student body thought it was hilarious, but Harold was outraged. I had a copy of the cartoon blown up and hung it on the bulletin board in the foyer of the church he attended every Sunday. I still wish I'd have been there to see his reaction."

"You really take this breaking up stuff seriously, don't you?"

"Yeah. You watch yourself, Bren. I'll have cartoons of you all over Lurkdale."

"Heaven forbid," he said in mock horror. "You'll tarnish the God-like status these people hold for me."

The following day, Bren revealed the contents of the briefcase to Natasha as they sat in the gazebo beneath a cloudy sky. Vines twisted up through the wicker mesh and dangled overhead. The briefcase sat open between the two of them on the gazebo bench, and Natasha sat back with her feet on the bench and her knees pulled up into her chest as she thumbed through the photographs, stopping at the one of her mother and Stephen Bradson sitting on a garden bench. Natasha looked out through the arched doorway into the weedy garden, trying to locate the spot where the photo had been taken.

"She was beautiful, wasn't she?"

"Yeah." Bren nodded, but felt the mother's beauty paled next to the daughter who sat beside him.

Natasha flipped through a few more pictures, and then paused at the photo of Stephen Bradson staring from an open second-story window at the back of the mansion. It was a photograph that captured his darker side. There was horror in his eyes, as he stared below him at the photographer.

"That's the one that bothers me the most." Bren looked at the photo, then to the exact window in the house where the man had once stood. "It's that look on his face. He looks so—evil."

"He was evil. That man killed my grandfather and possibly my father. When I was young, I used to dream about finding him and cutting his throat, and Mother would be so proud of me."

"Wow." Bren gave her a long stare. "And I was always taught that girls were made of sugar and spice and everything nice."

"No. I was a homicidal little creature. You're lucky you never met me back then. I'd've gone right for the jugular."

"And to think that I was worried about you coming inside the house."

She smiled, but there was a seriousness in her eyes as she stared out the gazebo door, at the back of the house. "When I was sixteen, I started coming here to Lurkdale nearly every weekend. I'd pretend I was Nancy Drew out tracking down a killer. I must have read those newspaper articles twenty times. I even went around and interviewed people." She chuckled at the thought of it.

"And what'd you find out?"

"I found out I was one demented little girl." She tossed the photos back in the briefcase and pulled out a small black book, which Bren quickly snatched from her and tucked under his arm.

"Secrets, have we?"

"My diary. Nothing special." He tossed it back in the case, disturbed by the thought of her reading the lovesick passages he'd written about her over the last couple days. He retrieved the metal gadget and handed it to her, hoping to draw her mind off his diary.

"What is it?" she asked, examining the silver device.

"No idea. It came with everything else. No explanation."

# CHAPTER 17

※

*M*rs. Heather Chandler sat in her living room, waiting. This had become a ritual for her, spending her days worrying about her only child, and then staying awake into the night for that child to come home. She feared the night would come when Natasha wouldn't walk through that front door, but would lie slain in a dark room inside Windfield Manor. Heather trembled when winds beat at her doors and windows, for maybe it was Stephen Bradson come calling. She trembled when no sounds could be heard, for maybe her daughter wasn't coming home. She sat rigidly in the easy chair with the television turned on and turned low. The faint mumbles of the actors could barely be heard above the sound of the rain hitting the roof and the winds howling through the trees. When the doorknob turned, she quivered. When the door opened, she froze. When Natasha entered, she sighed. Natasha closed the door quietly, humming softly to herself.

"Happy, are we?" the mother said as though this were a sin.

"Would you rather I weren't?" Natasha locked the door.

"I'd rather you weren't off galloping through Lurkdale with that killer; that's what I'd rather."

Natasha walked over to the loveseat and sat down. Her face was moist with raindrops, but radiant. She and Bren had spent the better part of the afternoon wondering among the charred building that stood at the bottom of the hill, beyond the backyard garden and gazebo. The building had once been a stable where Heather kept her two horses. Now it was nothing more than burned wood covered in purple heather and yellow gorse. Two months after Thomas Windfield was stabbed to death in the study, the stable and corral mysteriously went up in flames. The general consensus was that Stephen Bradson had set the fire, his way of throwing salt on the family wound. It was one of the events that helped push the young Heather over the edge, since, at the time, the family was still dealing with the loss of Thomas and hadn't even begun to look for a stable in Scarborough where they could transport the horses. As it was, the horses had died in the fire.

"So how's Stephen Bradson?" Mrs. Chandler asked passively.

"His name's Bren Stevens."

"Not a very creative man, is he? You'd think out of all the possible names there are, he'd be able to come up with one that wasn't so blatantly obvious."

Natasha sighed deeply and fell back into the softness of the cushions. She felt the comment didn't deserve a response, so she gave none. Instead, she stared at the television, determined not to let her mother steal her joy.

"Do you love him, Natasha?"

She shrugged. "He's a very sweet man."

Mrs. Chandler studied her daughter's face. Seeing that joy ate at her. "So was Stephen Bradson. Clear up to the day he killed my father. And you're now seeing the same man, Natasha. I'm telling you it's the same man. You think I'm a crazy woman, but I know it's him. Have you ever in your life seen two people who look so much alike? Without being twins, it's impossible. And my father was wise, no question of it, but knowing a person's name and address five years before the person was born? Not even Dad was that smart."

"Bren Stevens is not Stephen Bradson, Mother."

"You think you know everything, but I saw him. Have you forgotten that? I saw him right before he slaughtered my father, and I saw him ten years later, and he still looked the same, not a day older."

"A lot of people hold their age well. But it's been thirty years now. This can't possibly be him."

"Well he sure is wearing his face!" Mrs. Chandler shouted.

Natasha watched the television again. She could feel the anger swelling in her, and she didn't want it to get the best of her as it had many times before. Her mother knew how to provoke her better than anyone else she'd ever met. She hated that about her.

"You said yourself that you saw the will after Grandfather died. And you saw the briefcase and the letter. So you know Grandfather willed the place to some unborn American." Natasha's words were spoken with complete control and gentleness, and this professional demeanor angered her mother. When upset, she despised the rational calmness of her daughter. She hated seeing Natasha remain cool while she lost control, and in her anger, she always knew which strings to pluck to bring her intellectual daughter to tears.

"He made Dad write that will and send him those things," said Mrs. Chandler. "Can't you see what a fool he's making of you? You walk around like you're so well educated and wise, but you're the biggest fool of us all. You always have been. I bet he goes to bed laughing about it every night."

"I'm going to bed." Natasha stood up, holding her tongue for now.

"You do that. You can run away from me. You can even run away from the truth. But you can't outrun a demon. Evil always knows where to find you."

She was walking toward the hallway door, tears rolling out across her checks. "You're a sick woman, Mother." Her chin was quivering. "These aren't the kind of things mothers are supposed to tell their daughters. Mothers are supposed to look out for their children and comfort them, and tell them that God is watching over them and that there's no such thing as monsters."

"I think the cruelest thing a mother could do is lie to her children. Why would you want me to do that? Your grandmother used to lie to me all the time. She used to tell me that God would watch over the righteous, that evil never wins. Yes, it's a beautiful theory. But you can only stay gullible so long, Natasha. After a while, experience straightens you out, shows you who's really got the power. Maybe God's out there watching, too; I don't know. But He doesn't interfere, does He? He just watches and lets evil track you down and have its way with you."

"That's a very cynical view of life."

"Is it? Perhaps you're right; it is cynical, but it's accurate, nevertheless."

# CHAPTER 18

Natasha didn't return to Windfield Manor for two days. She stayed home and let her mother spit her hate out all over her, chastising her for fraternizing with the enemy and for disobeying her sweet mother. Heather had grown comfortable in her insanity, and she'd raised a daughter who could share in her lunacy. Three years earlier, when Natasha had first announced her intentions of attending the university, Heather protested loudly. Outwardly, she claimed that education was for the poor who needed to go out and work for a living, something Natasha would never need to do. Inwardly, she feared the university would poison Natasha against her, by showing her how normal families interacted. It did just that.

During the two-day interim, Bren finished cutting the lawn and eradicating the weeds from the flower gardens in front and to both sides of the mansion. Though the large garden behind the house remained despicable, the front and side yards began to regain the old dignity they'd lost years ago.

He then went to work on the dead tree that stood in the front yard. His muscles flexed as he brought the ax forward with a thud, slicing into the dead trunk. Wood chips flung sporadically. As a lumberjack, he'd brought many trees to the ground. They were all insignificant and forgettable. Bringing this one down would be more noteworthy he thought as he buried the blade of the ax into the dead tree. He wanted the hideous thing out of his yard. With its gnarled limbs, it symbolized everything he hated about this house: death, loneliness and horror. A final blow with the ax and the cavity at the base of the tree split wide. It tottered, cracked and crashed to the earth, snapping its limbs beneath the weight.

"Well, well," a voice said at Bren's back once the clamor had died.

He turned around to find Mayor Tuttle, the wind toying with his gray hair and fluttering the sleeves of his sky-blue dress shirt.

"I didn't hear you come up." Bren looked beyond Tuttle to find no car sitting on the bricked parking area.

"I parked along the road. Thought I'd enjoy a breath of air and come up and see how our new resident is getting on. To be quite honest, I thought you'd've left by now." The mayor smirked. "This house isn't worth staying for."

"I kind of like it." Bren brushed his hand over the blade of the ax.

"To each his own." Tuttle loosened his tie and fixed his eyes on the gray granite house. "I must say, I've never cared for this place. Even when the Windfields lived here, I always considered it much too pretentious for my liking."

"Is that right," said Bren, looking over his shoulder at the house. "Thank you for sharing that with me, Mayor. I hold your opinion in the highest regard."

"And I hold your tongue in the highest contempt, young man," Tuttle snapped. "If it's an enemy you want, I can be a very formidable one. But I'd think someone like you would be seeking allies, not adversaries."

"I apologize. It's just that after our meeting in your office, I didn't realize becoming allies was an option."

"Making peace is always an option, Stevens. Great men always struggle with one another. The truly great ones then become friends." Tuttle smiled and Bren momentarily liked Mayor Tuttle, a true politician. "Before you invest any more time in this old antique, let me ask you this: how much you want for it?"

"I thought you detested this place."

"The house is worthless. Any fool can see that. But I've often thought that if a man were to destroy the house, it would still be a nice piece of property."

Bren set the head of the ax on the grass and leaned his weight on the wooden handle. "I'm not really informed on English real estate prices. How much do you think its worth?"

"It's not actually *English* real estate prices we're concerned with; it's Lurkdale real estate prices." Tuttle sat on the trunk of the tree that Bren had just fallen. The overweight man appraised the house, then the property around him and shook his head as if the sight had disappointed him. "I'll give you fifty thousand pounds."

"A hundred," asserted Bren. "And I collect my money from the bank immediately."

"Sixty," said Tuttle. "But there's nothing I can do about the money in the bank. That's out of my hands."

"Then the asking price for the house is four million pounds."

"That's absurd."

"Absurd?" said Bren. "I've got four million pounds sitting in the bank in Lurkdale, and all I have to do is sit in this house a year to collect it. I don't see how I could possibly accept anything less than that. I shouldn't even consider settling for that much, since I could wait out the year and still sell the house for a healthy sum."

"You think you'll actually last a year in that house?" Tuttle's congeniality transformed into contempt, and Bren's short-lived admiration for the mayor died with that transformation. "You'll be dead before the month's out."

"That sounds like a threat, Mayor."

"Just a prediction. This house has a reputation of creating corpses." Tuttle stood and dusted off the seat of his pants. "You consider my offer, Stevens. A house like this can be detrimental to your health."

"Well, if I decide to sell, I'll keep you in mind."

"Do that." Tuttle turned his back to Bren and started across the lawn toward the trees. Bren watched the mayor walking away from him and brought the ax slicing into the stump of the tree. The thump turned Mayor Tuttle on his heels, and he stared wide-eyed at Bren. He paused for a moment and said, "By the way, you never brought that key by my office like you promised."

"I've been a little preoccupied. But I've got it right here." Bren reached in his pocket and retrieved the key to the mansion.

Tuttle's face wrinkled with disapproval. "You're a real comedian, Stevens. A genuine Benny Hill. You and I both know that's not the key I'm referring to."

"No?" said Bren. "I must've misunderstood you. This is the only key I have."

Tuttle could see the lie in Bren's face, and he could see the faint smile at the edge of his lips. "I don't want you here."

"Well that's not your choice, is it?" Bren pulled the ax back out of the stump and set it on his shoulder.

"I can have you thrown out any time I want. You're not an English citizen. You have no right to this land. If you sell it to me now, I'll give you a fair price. Otherwise, you'll walk away with nothing." The mayor saw the worry sweep over Bren's countenance, and it pleased him.

"If you really want me gone," said Bren, "just allow me to get my money from the bank. I'll be out of here today."

"Can't do that. It'd be breaking the law to go against the specifications of the will." Tuttle stared at the house. His face darkened. The memory was an old one, thirty years old, but the juxtaposition of Bren's face and the house made it feel like it'd only happened yesterday, and the same emotions were fresh and intense. "I was here visiting at the time of the murder, you know."

"So I've heard." Bren had wanted to ask the mayor about that day, but had decided against it.

"In fact I'm the one who found him. I heard him scream, but by the time I arrived it was too late. He was already dead and that dreadful monster—" He looked discreetly at Bren. The resemblance brought a chill up his spine. "That dreadful monster was standing there with blood dripping from his hand. I chased him, but he got away."

"How?"

"He just—" The thirty-year-old secret sat on the tip of his tongue, but he couldn't speak it. He wanted to, but he just couldn't get himself to say the words. "He just got away, that's all." Not wanting his vulnerability to show, he turned away and started back across the cut lawn. This Bren Stevens was the same man and he knew it. He felt it. It went beyond resemblance. "Think about my offer," he yelled as he neared the spot where the lane cut beneath the trees. He turned toward Bren, who was still standing beside the fallen tree. "Think real hard. I want you out of this house."

# CHAPTER 19

*W*hen Natasha returned, she found Bren standing in the rain with a shovel, loosening the weeds in the backyard garden. His hair and shirt were soaked, but he looked up with a smile when Natasha rounded the corner of the house and wove through the garden.

"I thought you forgot where I lived," Bren said.

Beneath her red umbrella, Natasha looked sad and distracted. "I'd have called but you haven't got a phone. My mother's been overly crazed lately. I thought it'd be best if I stayed with her a while." She shivered beneath her yellow rain slicker. "How can you stand to be out here in this weather?"

"It's either that or be alone in my haunted house."

"Being alone in the house shouldn't worry you any. Unless of course you think you're not alone."

He looked at the dark windows at the back of the house. "I think I'm the only person who doesn't think I'm sharing this house with the bogeyman."

"No one thinks you're sharing this house with the bogeyman," she said soberly. "They think you *are* the bogeyman."

"Is something wrong, Natasha?"

"Of course something's wrong," she answered sharply. "Everything's wrong. I want to find him, Bren. I want to make him pay for what he did to my mother. And I want you to help me."

Bren started to grin, but thought better of it when he noticed her seriousness. He wiped the rain from his face. "I thought you said I'd be better off keeping my nose out of all this."

"Surely you feel you have some obligation to my grandfather." She was stern and unapologetic in her tone. "He gave you this house and his money; you owe him something. And he begged you to find his killer. That's why you're here, isn't it?"

"I'm here because your grandfather willed me his estate. That's the only reason I'm here. What do I know about conducting an investigation, especially when it involves something that happened thirty years ago? Professionals have tried and failed. What makes you think we're gonna have any better luck?"

"'Cause Grandfather thinks you can do it. Otherwise he wouldn't have asked you to avenge his death." The rain pelted her umbrella.

"The man never even met me. How would he know what I'm capable of?"

"He knew where to find you, didn't he? Knew your name and address before you were even born. If that doesn't give him some credibility, I don't know what does."

"Perhaps." He nodded, holding up a hand to shield the rain from his face. "Why don't we go inside?" He ushered her to the back door and into the kitchen, which was still in need of a good cleaning, but at least the pots and pans were put away and the lipstick message had been erased from the wall.

Natasha folded her umbrella and shook off the rain, watching as Bren hoisted his drenched body onto the kitchen counter while looking at her like he was waiting for the answer to a question he'd just asked. Her eyes were glassy, a little dreamy even, as she looked down at the Bren's shoes and watched the water dripping off him, onto the tile floor.

"So what's going on, Natasha? This doesn't seem like you."

She raised her eyes and shook her head slightly. "How would you know what's like me and what's not like me? The truth is, this is a lot more like me than anything else you've seen." She laid her umbrella on the counter and leaned up against the refrigerator in front of Bren.

"But surely you know this isn't rational."

"Don't talk to me about rational, Bren Stevens. You look like a man who's been killing the patriarchs of my family. There's nothing rational about any of this."

"Did your mother say something to upset you?"

"I don't have a mother. I have a psychopath who wants me to be just like her."

"I'd say you're giving her what she wants."

She gave him a cold stare. Her beauty abandoned her at that moment. Bren studied her. Surely this wasn't the same sensible young lady he'd been losing sleep over. She gritted her teeth and, without a word, grabbed her umbrella and stormed out the back door, slamming it behind her. He just sat for a moment, cringing, not sure if he should pursue her or not. Perhaps it'd be wise just to let her run off her steam and wait for her to snap back into the land of reality before trying to approach her. Certainly that would be best, yet still he went out the door after her.

When she heard Bren's footsteps in the wet grass behind her, she turned back and pointed her folded umbrella at him. She looked a lot like her mother had looked the day Bren had showed up at their home in Scarborough—unapproachable and obstinate.

"Stay here, Bren. I don't need another judgmental cynic slowing me down." She continued around the house toward her car, with Bren right behind her.

"What're you gonna do?" he asked.

She crossed the front lawn, with the rain pouring down across her face, and opened her car door. Bren thought perhaps she was crying; though he couldn't be certain in the rain.

"What're you gonna do?" he asked again.

"I've got plans," she replied and got in and slammed the door.

Bren hurried around to the passenger door, opened it and climbed in.

"Get out!"

"I'm going with you." He closed the door.

"No, you're not." She stared at him contemptuously with her keys dangling from her hand. "You're going to go back in your house and pack your ax around with you the rest of your life. And you're going to cower into a corner every time the wind blows. And if things get really tough, you're going to pack your bags and hightail it out of here. You men are all alike, a bunch of big macho wimps."

The rain was hammering at the roof and streaming down the windshield.

"I don't know which is worse, being a big macho wimp or a little deranged psycho."

"Get out of my car."

"I'm going with you."

She stared at him, fuming, her jaw tense, her eyes narrow, her body rigid, but she started the car. She refused even to look at him as she turned the car around and sped down the lane, through the grove of trees and out to Oswald Road, which led into town. He was certain now that there were tears on her cheeks, mingled with the rain.

In Lurkdale, she drove up one street and down another, going—as far as Bren could determine—nowhere. She crossed back and forth through the same streets, looking at buildings, looking at signs, but not looking at Bren. For nearly a half an hour, neither one spoke a word. They merely watched the windshield wipers flip back and forth as they listened to the rain strike the car.

"Where are you going?" Bren finally broke the silence.

"I don't know," she snapped.

"I thought you said you had a plan."

"I lied." She looked at him for the first time, and her eyes were dry, but red. She pulled the car up to a curb and stopped abruptly. "Okay, Bren. I let you come along for the ride; now make yourself useful. What shall we do?"

"I think we should take a few deep breaths and pretend we're rational human beings."

She took two quick deep breaths, and then said, "Now what?"

Shaking his head, he slid his fingers through his wet hair and stared ahead at the road. His only suggestion was that she pull herself together and gather her sanity, but he kept that suggestion to himself. "Have you ever talked to your grandfather's lawyer?"

"Yes." She brushed at her eyes. "And he's now dead. The lawyer who sent you the will is just someone who took over after the original lawyer died."

"Then I don't know who else to talk to."

"That's what I thought. You're useless to me." She drove again, took a left and passed over one of Lurkdale's three bridges, spanning the river, and wound down the streets toward the other side of town. The rain had slowed, but was still pooled in the cobblestone street.

"Where we going?"

"I'm taking you home."

When she pulled up in front of the house, Bren expected her to ask him to get out, and then drive away. Instead, she grabbed her purse, got out herself and started up the path toward the house. He followed her in through the front door and to the living room, where she plopped down on the sofa, which was now covered with a dark blue blanket to hide the ugliness. She again refused to look at Bren as he stood in the doorway watching her pout, so he went to the fireplace, put some fresh logs inside and set them ablaze. To the right of the hearth sat a stack of firewood that, only a few days ago, had been the dead tree that stood in the center of the front lawn.

"I'm sorry for my behavior, Bren."

He looked back at her and was happy that she'd been the one to break the silence.

"This is how I get when I hang around my mother too much. It's like the woman has the ability to suffocate every rational thought that enters her presence." She laid her head on the back of the sofa. "I don't think I even knew what a rational thought was until I moved away from her to go to university."

Bren put another log on the fire before coming over to the sofa where he sat down beside her and put his arm around her. He was afraid she might resent the gesture, but instead she laid her head against his chest and closed her eyes. Across the room, in the large mirror, he could see the reflection of the two of them. They looked like a pair of drowned rats with their wet hair and clothes, but he liked the sight. He kissed her on the forehead, then on the lips.

"I guess by now you know what you're getting yourself into," she said.

"You don't have a darker side, do you?"

"What you saw tonight is merely the surface." She stood and picked up her purse. Rummaging through it, she pulled out a brush and proceeded to run it through her hair as she looked in the long mirror. "I won't be here tomorrow. And possibly not the next day. I'm going to London to visit my uncle."

"I didn't realize you had an uncle."

"Yes. Uncle Justin. He's adopted actually."

"Would you like me to go with you?"

"That'd be great, but I'm going with my mother. I don't think she'd appreciate your company."

"I suppose not."

"I was wondering if you'd mind if I borrowed those pictures and the metal thing you showed me." She watched him in the mirror. "I want to ask Uncle Justin about them."

"Sure, no problem. Let me run upstairs and grab them." Before heading out the door, he went to the fireplace and grabbed his ax, which he'd placed by the woodpile.

"You take that security blanket with you everywhere you go?" she said as he walked to the corridor.

"When you live in hell, you've got to carry a little water with you to douse the flames." He disappeared through the doorway and up the stairs. Every time he wondered through the house, he had the habit of holding the ax over his right shoulder with both hands gripping the handle, just in case some evil force bearing his face happened to spring at him from an open doorway. He feared if Eric or Lug ever decided to play a prank on him by hiding inside the house, he'd have the ax buried deep inside their skulls before they had time to explain. It was an unpleasant thought, but that didn't stop him from sporting the ax around with him.

In his bedroom, he opened the briefcase and grabbed the photographs and key, at least the object that Tuttle had referred to as a key. When he came back down the stairs, he found Natasha standing in the entryway. In her hand, she held scrap of paper, and by the look on her face, it was something of significance.

"You've had company." She held the paper out to Bren as he reached the foot of the stairs. "It was in the study, on the desk."

Laying the photos, key and ax on a step, he took the note from her and read the short message, which had been printed in blue ink. "Dear Bren, I know the truth about you, who you are and why you're here. I know. Meet me tomorrow at Coalman's Pub, 7:00 P.M." He looked up from the paper and grinned suspiciously. "You wrote this."

"Oh, great, thanks a lot. I'm not just crazy, I'm also psychotic."

He looked at the note again. "It was on the desk, huh?" he asked earnestly.

"Yeah it was on the desk," she scoffed.

# CHAPTER 20

*A*t six-twenty the following evening, Bren set his flashlight just inside the front door of the mansion and hid his ax outside beneath a bush at the right of the steps. He then began his long trek into town, a journey he was well accustomed to by now, yet one he only made when absolutely necessary. At six-fifty, Bren sat in the pub, waiting. From the bar, he looked around the dimly lit room of Coalman's Pub and watched the eyes of strangers. The eyes of strangers watched back.

At five past seven, a thin man sat on a bar stool next to him, leaned his drunken face at him and said, "I seen your picture in the paper." He lifted a mug and sipped in a swallow.

"Yeah, me, too," said Bren and watched the bar again.

At fifteen past seven, a girl with green hair and a man shaved completely bald, with the exception of a long piece hanging down in front of his eyes, passed in front of Bren and left him with icy stares, but they didn't stop. At twenty past and still no sign of the stranger who had summoned him away from his home, Bren slipped back out the door into the night. He sauntered beneath the rising moon, and headed toward the edge of town. He'd gotten all the way to Oswald Road before he heard the engine behind him. Glancing back, he could see nothing but headlights. He felt he chest tighten and realized that he'd been set up. There were fields on both sides of the roads, and he wasn't sure how far he'd get across them in the dark.

He'd just started off the road when he recognized the knock of the engine. Squinting again at the blinding headlights, he could see that it was a pickup truck, and as it rolled up beside him he saw that the driver had a mop of red head.

"Need a lift, mate?" The driver's window was down and Eric looked like he'd either just pulled himself out of bed or was just on his way home from beer fest.

"Sure." He came around to the passenger side and hopped in. "You look like half a man sitting here all alone. Where's Lug?"

"In bed with flu, or so he's telling everyone. Truth is, the two of us went to Leeds a few nights ago and got so bleedin' drunk that we haven't been able to stand for two days. Me head's still spinning. A friend of ours brews his own whiskey, and I think we got a bad batch."

"I didn't think anything could sour Lug's rot-gut stomach," Bren said as the rusty truck bounded down the road outside of Lurkdale.

"What you doing out so late?" Eric asked. "Don't you know the bogeyman's out?"

"That's the best news I've heard all day, being how he lives in my home."

Eric laughed and said, "From what I hear, you're him."

The headlights lit the countryside out of town, turned through a grove of trees, and illuminated the face of the mansion, which filled Bren with dread. Walking through that door at night was something he always hated. Lately, as he noticed the sun fading from the sky, he'd go to his bedroom, barricade himself in and wait for morning. He didn't feel completely safe there either, but at least it was a smaller space and he could be sure that no one was in there with him.

He stepped from the truck, thanked Eric for the ride and waited on the front lawn as the truck turned around and passed beneath the trees. That sense of dread was back. The feeling that eyes were upon him, waiting for him. He reached beneath the bush and grabbed the ax. It felt good in his hands, secure. Staring out past the trees, he could see the truck turning onto Oswald Road. The wind was brisk and it made the branches sway and creak. He had a bad feeling, the sensation of worms crawling beneath his skin as the wind gusted around the house and fluttered in his shirt. He stared at the front door and hated the sight of it. The thought of walking through it make him feel weak inside. He raised his eyes toward the second-floor windows and felt his chest tighten for the second time that evening. Someone had been standing there, watching him. He'd seen the figure pull away. It was the bedroom where he spent his nights. He looked back at the road and could see the red taillights of Eric's truck headed toward town. Again, he looked up at the bedroom window and it was pitch black. He felt like running away. Forget about the money, forget about the house, just tuck tail and run. But that isn't what he did. Instead, he put the ax over his right shoulder and climbed the three steps up to the front door where he twisted the iron knob and gave it a shove. He hadn't locked the door. He rarely did, except at night when he was inside. He now thought he needed to reevaluate his procedure.

Inside the entryway, he snatched his flashlight and flipped it on. Footsteps creaked across the floor upstairs, then ceased. He looked up at the dark balustrade on the second floor and pointed his light into that darkness.

As he climbed the stairs, his palms were cold and his face pale. His nightly visitor had come early and had found the house empty. And now he was going to get the ax. When Bren hit the top step, he paused and listened. A door creaked down the hallway. He shined his flashlight and saw nothing, just the wooden floor and several open doors. He usually kept them open so that the light from the windows illuminated the hallway, but at night he always found himself wishing they were all closed.

Stepping lightly into the hallway, he flooded the walls with his flashlight. He could hear something move in one of the rooms. He steadied the ax over his shoulder. His muscles tensed. Shining the light into the bedroom where he'd been spending his nights, he could see his briefcase lying open on the bed.

"I know you're in here," he announced, trying to sound brave. "Come out and I won't hurt you."

In several of the rooms, a whistle of wind blew past the plastic that he'd tacked up over the broken windows. He could feel the eyes upon him again, just as he had outside. He darted the beam of light to several open doors along the hallway. If it could see him, he could see it, he reasoned as he scanned the walls, the cracks, the keyholes. Suddenly, his skin chilled as if someone had grated a fingernail file across his teeth and had hit a nerve. There it was: the eye, looking through the crack of an open door, between the hinges. Bren stared. It stared back. Every fiber of his being screamed for him to flee, but he couldn't move. There behind the door stood the person he'd been searching for. If he left now, the stranger would only disappear back into the hole he'd crawled out from, free to roam the house at will and return another day.

Letting out a scream, he attacked the door with the ax. The blade split into the wood, slamming the door all the way open, back against the wall with the person trapped behind it. Wood chips splintered. Still shouting maniacally, he jerked the ax free and let it fly again. The metal sliced through and inched out the other side, and a voice bellowed out a piercing scream from behind the door. Only the voice wasn't the quality he'd expected. It was frightened and higher in pitch. It was feminine.

He planted his foot against the door to steady it as he jerked the ax blade free. Stepping back, he quickly pulled the door back and raised the ax over head, ready to strike again.

"Please, don't kill me! Please!" the girl pled, crouching on the floor with her arms wrapped around her head.

He studied the cowering girl and dropped the ax to his side. For half a minute he stood speechless and numb. Had he found a man who looked identical to himself, he wouldn't have been more surprised than he was right now.

"Natasha?" He looked past the shielding arms at her frightened face. "What are you doing? You scared the wits out of me. You're lucky I didn't split your head open. I thought you were going to London."

She stared up at him with her eyes wet with tears and her body trembling. "I had to know."

"Know what?" He knelt beside her.

She reached behind her and held up Bren's black diary. "I had to know if you were him."

He fell back onto the seat of his blue jeans, the ax at his side, the flashlight on his lap, pointing at a bare spot on the wall. He wanted to laugh and cry and go back to New Hampshire. "Then it *was* you who wrote the note."

"Of course, you idiot." She wiped her eyes. "But now I know," she added, as if now all were fine. "I know it's not you."

"Of course it's not me." He stood and stepped away, shining the light around the nearly barren room. "You're right, I am an idiot, the biggest idiot to ever walk the streets of Lurkdale, and believe me, some pretty big idiots have walked those streets." He went over and leaned on a small white chest of drawers, the only piece of furniture in the room. "Here I am thinking we've got a great thing going, and all the while you're wondering if I killed your grandfather or not, thinking I'm some kind of freak who hasn't aged in thirty years. At least now I know where I stand."

"You have no idea where you stand."

"Oh, I don't, huh? So how am I supposed to interpret this? As a gesture of love?" He shined the light at her face as she sat crouched in the corner. She held up her hand to block the light.

"That's exactly how you're supposed to interpret it." She stood and held up his diary. "I read what you wrote about me."

"Oh!" he said strongly, but quickly the realization of what this meant fell over him and his expression changed, thinking of all the sappy lines he'd written over the past week.

"You know, you really should come right out and tell a girl all those things instead of just keeping them to yourself in your little black book." She walked over to him and grabbed his hand, which was sweating and trembling. "I've fallen in love with you too, Bren. That's why I had to know."

# CHAPTER 21

The moon glistened and painted shadows across the land as the wind blew through the trees and twirled smoke from the mansion chimney. Down at the bottom of that chimney, red and yellow flames crackled in the fireplace. It cast a scarlet glow throughout the darkened room, across the sofa, the curtains, and Bren's face, as he creaked back and forth in the rocking chair. He held a book on home improvement in one hand and his flashlight in the other, pointing its beam at the white pages. His eyes strained to read the small print as the wind beat at the plastic-covered windows at his back.

Beside him, the ax leaned against the wall. It'd become his third arm, always with him to ward away evil and ready to sink its heavy blade into unwanted guests. He'd already locked both the front and back door and had decided over an hour ago to go upstairs and barricade himself in his bedroom. However, with the cold seeping through the house, he hadn't been able to pull himself away from the fire. Setting his book on the sofa next to him, he rubbed his eyes and stared at the fire, which was beginning to burn itself to embers. He waited until only spots of light could be seen smoldering beneath the ash and smoke before standing and heading to the corridor.

In two days he could go to the bank and withdraw his first lump sum. The first thing he planned to do was install new locks on the outer doors and one on his bedroom. The second thing he planned to do was put glass in the windows. He had no idea how his guest had been getting into the house, but new locks and windows seemed like they'd do the trick. Unless, of course, the man lived inside his walls.

In the corridor, he flashed his beam of light down toward the kitchen, then up to the entryway. He hadn't heard anyone in the house for five days now, and if he could just hold on through two more, he figured he'd be home free. But apparently two days was just too much to ask.

Moving toward the twisting mahogany stairs, he heard the floor creak in the kitchen behind him. Not the sound of the house settling, he was certain of this. He darted the light back down the corridor to the kitchen and caught a glimpse of a large man scampering off to the left of the door. Adrenalin flushed through his body. In a split second his heart doubled its pace and sank into his stomach. There he stood, by the living room doorway, staring down the corridor at the kitchen. In his right hand he held his flashlight. In his left, he held—nothing. He turned the beam to the living room, over twenty feet of ugly tan carpeting to a spot beside the rocking chair where the ax still rested against the wall.

Down the corridor, the floor creaked again, and when he returned the light to the dark passage, he found a man standing within the kitchen doorway. One hand clinched in a fist, the other holding a frying pan. Bren raised the light upward to the dark face, which was covered in a black ski mask. The man raised his large hand and palmed the beam of light to keep it from shining in his eyes.

With a marksman's accuracy, he flung the pan down the corridor. It looked surreal hurling through the beam of light, a chunk of black metal whirling toward Bren's face. He lifted the flashlight to shield himself, and the pan slammed the light with a crash, shattering both glass and bulb. As the last rays of light fell from the air, the last thing Bren saw was this beast of a man hurrying through the dark toward him.

He felt the blood drain from his face, down through his torso. He bolted toward the dark living room, toward the ax, but he didn't make it far inside the doorway before a hand grabbed the back of his shirt and slammed him against the wall. The pain didn't register yet. He spun and pushed at the man's face as fists shot through the dark in quick succession, hitting him in the stomach and leaving him breathless. He buckled forward, and another fist ripped across his lips, straightening him up like a limp doll and slamming his head into the wall.

There was a dim glow in the room, cast by the smoldering embers in the fireplace. All he could make out was the arm of the rocking chair across the room and the shape of the intruder's head as he bore down on him and wrapped his hands snugly around Bren's throat and pressed his thumbs into the windpipe. Bren stumbled back against the wall. He could feel breath on his face and the coppery taste of blood in his mouth. His arms flailed wildly like a drowning man trying to fight his way to the surface of the water, but the grip remained firm at his throat. His eyes blinked. The dark room grew darker. His head became light from the lack of oxygen, and there came a moment of surrender—a moment that later he would recall as nearly peaceful. A pain twitched in his left temple. His arms relaxed. In his right hand, he still held the broken flashlight. His fingers refused to loosen their grip from the useless scrap of metal and let it drop to the floor.

The entire event, from struggle to surrender, had lasted no more than a minute or so, but it felt much longer. His right eyelid began to spasm and he was amazed at how quiet everything had become. The only sound to disturb the silence was a long groan that issued from the intruder's throat. It was the sound of satisfaction. The joy of killing.

He was actually enjoying himself.

Bren found it contemptible, the idea that his own life could be taken so lightly that this man was actually taking pleasure in snuffing it out.

He brought the flashlight up with a violent thrust and struck the man across the jaw, staggering him. He struck him again, and the hands released their hold from his neck. The flashlight fell to the carpet, and Bren dropped to his knees where he sucked strenuously for air, but he knew he couldn't afford the comfort of wallowing in his own pain. Briskly, he rose and stumbled out into the corridor and hurried to the front door. He fumbled to twist the lock, but his hands were shaky, his thinking frenzied. Behind him, the large silhouette stepped out from the living room into the corridor. Abandoning the locks, Bren leaped up the stairs, skipping every other one. His mouth was drenched with blood from his teeth-punctured lip, and his throat was strained and bruised. Gretchen Wicks had predicted he'd take the life of another, and he'd thought she was out of her mind, but if he had the chance, he'd take this man down, six feet under the ground.

He flung the bedroom door shut and shoved the dresser in front of it. It screeched across the wooden floor. He didn't honestly think he'd be able to get it all the way in front of the door before this devil barged his way in. But he did, and the bed, too.

He stood at the foot of the bed, panting. In spite of the cold night, he'd worked up a healthy sweat. Steam rose from his chest and back. His heart pounded and his head throbbed. Outside the door, he could hear the man climbing the stairs, hammering his fist against the wall and accenting every footstep to add menace to his approach.

"Come out, you coward! You worthless excuse of a human being!" His voice was full and strong. He came down the hallway and kicked one of the doors open, sending it crashing against the wall. He let out a deranged-lunatic scream before falling unearthly quiet.

From inside the room, all Bren could hear were the faint creaks of the floor. He sucked the blood from his numb lip and spit it out. The shouting had chilled him, but he preferred that to the brutal tranquility he was now forced to endure. Bracing himself against the foot of the bed, he prepared for the onslaught that was sure to come. The floorboards popped just outside his door. He knew the man was standing there; he could sense it. His eyes darted around the moonlit room, looking for something to protect himself with. Against one wall stood a stack of cans, cereal boxes, jars of peanut butter and jam and two loaves of bread. Hanging in the open closet were several shirts and a pair of nice dress slacks. Short of pelting the man with food or bending one of the hangers so he could poke it in the man's eye, he had nothing of any use. His one useful weapon, the ax, lay downstairs in the living room where it served no use to anyone except the man now standing outside his door.

Lightly and methodically, the intruder began tapping at the door, knowing precisely in which room Bren had hidden himself. Then, ever so softly, he began to whisper. "Little pig, little pig, let me come in." The doorknob turned. "I'm a huffing and a puffing, you little bleeding coward." He hit the door with full strength and the barricade moved forward.

Bren stiffened his body. The push was strong and constant. Bren curled his toes inside his shoes, trying to grip into the floor as his feet slid backwards and the gap in the door grew wider. Fingers reached inside the door and pried. The dresser and bed grated against the floor with a screech.

The man in the ski mask laughed villainously as his head popped through the large gap and stared in at Bren's figure silhouetted against the moonlit window behind him. Bren stretched his leg out, hoping to be able to reach the wall to give him more leverage. No such luck. Rather, he crouched and muscled the bed forward, which in turn pushed the dresser, which slammed the door up against the man's nose, pinning his head against the doorframe. The head wiggled out from the crack, and the door crushed in on the fingers. A scream echoed in the hallway, followed by a string of obscenities as the fingers pulled free from the doorjamb.

Bren abandoned his hold, threw up the window and crawled out onto the stone ledge that encircled the mansion's second story. The distant ground blended into the darkness. He shimmied along the wall toward the next room. Above him, clouds shielded the moon, leaving him with no more than a faint trace of light falling from the dark sky. Behind him, the bed and dresser clamored aside and the bedroom door crashed open.

The intruder lurched into the darkness. His eyes quickly scanned the room. Dropping to one knee, he peered under the bed. Nothing. He tipped it upon its side before rummaging the closet, where he pulled the clothes off their hangers and hauled out the two suitcases that Bren had sitting on the closet floor. Letting out a scream, he tossed both cases across the room.

Bren hurried.

The head emerged from the window and watched Bren shuffle away. "You're dead, mate." The intruder groaned and pulled himself back inside. He tore wildly at the room, hurling clothes, dresser drawers, and Bren's food supply. In the drawer of a small table, he found what he'd come looking for: the briefcase, which he opened and searched. He didn't like what he found, nothing but a black diary. That was all. It wasn't there. It should have been. He knew it should have been, but it wasn't.

Bren reached the next window. It had a stretch of plastic over it, which he punched at until he'd knocked one corner loose. Grabbing the edge, he yanked down, popping the tacks out of the wall. The plastic crumpled and fell to the floor. He reached in and grabbed the lip of the windowsill to hoist himself in, but he got no farther than that. Across the room, the door flung open, and standing inside the frame was his nemesis. A trail of moonlight fell across his black mask, causing the whites of his eyes to glisten. He came quickly, and Bren retreated from the window, scuffling along the ledge toward the corner of the house. An arm lunged out after him, the fingers brushing his shirt. He turned back and saw a leg step from the window onto the ledge behind him. The intruder didn't look any more at ease on the narrow lip than Bren did. He moved unsteadily, forcing Bren to the corner, which he feared would be tricky getting around. However, it turned out to be more manageable than he'd anticipated, mainly because it rounded over to the wall that was covered with dead ivy, which gave Bren something to hang onto as he maneuvered the turn.

Cautiously, as a light rain began to fall, the intruder held his body flush against the wall and slid his feet along the ledge. He peered around the corner and spotted Bren fighting his way up the tangled vines toward the third floor. He wasn't far above him. One good leap and he could grab his foot; he knew he could. Then all it would take was a hard pull and Bren would come crashing to the ground. Perhaps with a little luck he'd survive the fall, and with a little more, he wouldn't. Either way he'd be out of the house for good.

He slid one foot around the corner, up against the edge of the vines and found a thick stock that he hoped would support his weight before jostling upward and stretching his arm toward Bren. He got hold of one foot, and both men slipped down the wet vines a few inches. He held the American's life in his hands. It was exhilarating. One good tug and it'd all be over. The foot wiggled frantically in his hand, but he held on, all the while struggling to secure his own footing inside the vines, which he could feel pulling away from the stone wall under his and Bren's weight. He clung tightly to the ivy and yanked sharply at the foot he held in his hand. Once, twice, three times a charm. He felt it give. All over, he thought at first. Not only for the American, but for himself as well. He dropped about three feet before he managed to get a handhold on the vines and stop himself. He anticipated the blow that would surely come when Bren's body slammed against him from above, but it didn't come. Nothing but a shoe and one white sock glanced off his shoulder on their way to the ground. Looking up, he saw Bren climbing away from him. One foot now bare.

Bren scaled the ivy up to a third-floor window, fought his way through the tacked-up plastic and climbed in. The room was dark and nearly completely empty with the exception of three wooden stools that he'd saved, with the plan of sanding and varnishing later. He grabbed one of them and returned to the window, prepared to beat his pursuer with it once he came into range. He glanced down the outside wall. The vines below him were empty. The man had apparently gone back down through a second-story window.

The rain fell harder. He set the stool down and listened. The man scuffled through the darkness of the second story beneath him. The only way out of the room was down the flight of stairs, and that would surely lead him right to his assailant. On the other side of the room, he opened the unbroken window and looked out. There was no ledge wrapping the third floor, just flat rock and black space between him and the ground.

He gazed out toward Lurkdale, where a few streetlights glistened beneath the pouring rain. The village slept, unaware of the pursuit taking place at Windfield Manor. He wanted to cry for help, but he knew the only ears that would hear would be those of the stranger, come to rip out his life and feed his corpse to the mice. No one else would care even if they did hear. After all, they themselves had warned of such doom.

He grabbed the stool, went to the top of the stairs and waited, calculating the moment when the man's head would appear in the stairwell so he could smash it with the stool. He glanced over at the window he'd come in through and considered going back down the ivy, but he just couldn't make himself run again. He'd put an end to this right now—or die trying. In the hallway below him, he heard the approach of footsteps. There was a beat of silence, followed by the sound of feet hurrying up the stairs. He raised the stool. A dark face emerged and he made good on his word. He slammed the stool into the intruder's head with full power, sending the body tumbling backwards down the stairs. The clamor rumbled, and when it faded, he heard a faint moan.

"Who are you?" Bren yelled down the dark stairwell.

The only answer was a growl at the foot of the stairs.

The second time the footsteps came up the stairs, they were more apprehensive. The man in the mask was prepared this time when he saw the stool swing toward his face. He ducked, and as the stool struck the wall behind him, he knocked it out of Bren's hands. Bren backed away toward the open window, watching the dark figure emerge at the top of the stairs.

"What do you want?"

"I want blood," said the man. "Bright red American blood."

Bren considered his options and concluded that he had only two: lie down and surrender or fight. He chose the latter, which took his assailant entirely by surprise. Shouting like a crazed savage, he charged forward, tucked his head and planted it squarely into the man's stomach. The intruder flew back with the wind knocked out of him, giving Bren time to pelt him several times in the face and kick him a good one in the groin. When the man collapsed to the floor, Bren didn't let up. He seized upon him and lashed out at his face incessantly until a fist rose up from beneath him and caught him on the chin, knocking him toward the wall, toward the stool, which he grabbed and slammed against the intruder's head. One leg of the stool came loose, and when he struck the man a second time, the leg came off completely. He stepped back, tossed the stool to the floor, and held the leg above his shoulder like a baseball bat.

The intruder lay stiff on the floor in the shadows. His large arms twitched like a dying animal. Slowly, he rolled to his stomach, arched his back and pulled his knees beneath him, giving Bren a supreme opportunity to try out his batting ability. He brought the stool leg squarely down in the small of the man's back, which collapsed him. For good this time. The back of his head looked so vulnerable there in the trail of light. One good blow and Bren could end this forever. He actually considered it, but he couldn't go through with it. Self-defense was one thing, but killing an unconscious man was something different altogether.

Bren bent forward to catch his breath.

He'd seen a rope in the shed out back, and he figured the best thing he could do was bind the man's hands and feet, then walk into town and contact the local authorities. With any luck, this would not only put an end to the nightly visits but would also put and end to this whole Stephen Bradson affair, and Lurkdale would let Bren live in peace.

He was still staring down at the body when the head twitched. He strained at the dark, not sure if he'd actually seen movement or if it'd only been a glint of moonlight reflecting off the white tag on the back of the ski mask. Reaching the stool leg forward, he prodded the man in the back. Mistake. A hand snatched the leg so quickly that Bren didn't have time to pull it back. The body twisted, yanked the club from Bren's hands, then lunged forward and clasped him by the ankle. He should have split the back of the man's head open when he had the chance; he knew that now. In an attempt to flee, he turned toward the stairs, but the hand pulled his feet out from under him, and he slammed the floor face down. A second later, a sharp blow struck him in the back and he realized that the man had bludgeoned him with the stool leg.

The man stood.

Bren turned and slithered away on his back. With the club raised in his hand, the intruder approached, rearranging the ski mask so he could see out of the holes again. He staggered for a moment and looked as though he'd topple over, but he steadied himself and hovered over Bren, intent on inflicting the same fury that Bren had unleashed on him. The beating had dazed him, making it impossible to focus. Bren was nothing but a cowering blur, lying on his back and scooting toward the stairs. He hardly even saw the foot rise up, but he definitely felt it lodge into his groin. As he shrank to his knees, Bren rose and punched him in the temple, toppling him forward, but before he fell he swung rashly and was pleased to see the wooden leg catch Bren across the jaw.

The man's head struck the wooden floor, and the club dropped from his fingers. He listened to the long moan issue from his own lungs. It sounded distant, as though it were in no way connected to him. He couldn't believe how badly this had turned out. Here he was lying face down on the floor, and the American—where was he? He blinked at the darkness. A figure blurred and stammered before him, heading toward the stairs. Then he was gone.

Bren landed on every third step on his way down. In the dark maze of hallways on the second floor, he hurriedly felt his way. He could hear the man descend the stairs and stumble behind him, noisily pounding his fist along the walls as he came.

"You're dead, you bloody Yank! Dead!" The voice reverberated in the hall.

Somewhere in the distance was the stairwell, hidden around dark bends. Behind him came the silhouette of a madman, glowing within the frame of the window at his back. Bren had the advantage, and he knew it. The window at the back end of the hall made his pursuer easy to see, whereas Bren was hidden within the darkness, only betrayed by the sound of his own footsteps and his hands sliding along the wall to guide his way. He stopped and pressed his body flush against the wall. The figure staggered toward him.

Unsettled by the silence, the man paused and squinted at the blackness in front of him. He could see nothing. Bren was still there, though; he knew it. He'd heard him stop and he could feel his presence. This stupid man was lying in wait. What a fool! The man let out a shout and hammered his fist against the wall to see if he could frighten his quarry into betraying his position. Nothing moved.

Another shout and he forged ahead with his arms held stiffly in front of him to feel his way in the dark. To Bren, the man looked like a live version of Frankenstein's monster and the association sent a chill right through him. This devil had crawled up from hell and Bren had every intention of putting him right back down. When he drew near, Bren gathered his fear and put it all into his swing and landed a solid punch to the man's nose, dropping him to the floor.

He didn't stay down long. Rather, this insult had brought him faster now, following the footsteps that he could hear fleeing in front of him. The hallway twisted once, then again, and he grinned. The balustrade shimmered in a trail of moonlight, and he could see Bren rushing toward it. He had the edge now, with the light gleaming beyond the chandelier in front of Bren.

At the head of the stairs, Bren's focus shifted from the rain drizzling outside the window, past the chandelier, to the front door at the foot of the stairs. But a fist had him by the back of the hair. It nearly took him off his feet. The beast flung him against the wall, spun him around and belted him in the nose.

Bren dropped to one knee, holding his face in his hands as blood trickled over his lips. His eyes rose up and looked at the black mask. A foot shot up into his mid-section just before the large hands gripped his hair again, pulled him to his feet, and shoved him back against the balustrade.

His back arched. His hands, wet with blood and sweat, gripped the wooden rail as the large man inched him backwards, until he was hanging slightly beyond perpendicular with the floor. A slight tilt of his head gave him a clear view of the front door. His hands slipped an inch farther and he could see the dark floor, a neck-breaking distance below him. The only thing keeping him from falling was that his assailant was holding him by the collar, that and the fact that Bren had twisted his foot into the wooden braces of the balustrade.

The intruder flashed a smile and released his grip on Bren's collar. He'd anticipated a dramatic fall to the entryway floor, but instead, Bren latched onto his assailant's shirt, pulled himself forward and smashed his forehead into the man's nose. He stumbled back and clutched his face in pain as Bren shot three quick jabs at his face, knocking him backwards.

In the pale light, Bren could see the eyes glare at him. It was the look of utter madness. This beast of a man stared down at the blood on his hands and began to laugh. It started as a low growl, then began to swell as he bent forward and rubbed his hands on the front of his black jeans. If the laughter had been intended to intimidate, it was working brilliantly. Bren wiped his mouth with the back of his hand and blinked a line of sweat from his eyes. He circled around the man, toward the stairs. He still had a chance, he thought. A quick descent and perhaps he could make it into the living room to the ax.

The man stepped in front of him, blocking the top of the stairs. Blood smudged his mask and lips, and when he smiled, it even marred the white enamel.

"You want me?" Bren took a step toward his assailant. "Here I am." He twisted sideways, shot his foot in the air and landed it solidly in the man's chest, sending him toppling down the stairs.

His arms flailed, but didn't prevent him from crashing back first onto the steps and sliding down headfirst to the bottom. When he finally came to a halt, the only sound in the house, other than the rain pelting the roof and windows, was the low moan rising up from the entryway floor. He crawled to his feet. His ski mask, twisted and mangled, tilted up to the balcony and gazed at Bren. He mounted the first step, and then paused, debating his next move. For the first time all night, the man didn't seem so sure of himself. He pressed his hand in the small of his back and winced with pain before stepping off the stair and disappearing beneath the balcony into the corridor.

Bren gazed down at the empty entryway for a moment, unsure of what to do. His nose and lip were bleeding profusely, and he had a gash along his jaw where the stool leg had cut him. He considered going down after the ax, but thought better of it. Who knew where his visitor had gone off to?

He returned to his room, turned the bed back over onto its legs and placed the not-so adequate blockade back in front of the door. Moonlight came through the window, revealing the shambles of the room: clothes tossed, drawers dumped, and cans and packages of food scattered. He looked from the window to the ground, hoping to see the man abandoning the house, but all he saw was darkness.

# CHAPTER 22

*B*ren related the details to Natasha, Eric and Lug as they sat in a cafe eating lunch. The condition of Bren's face pretty much said it all. He had a black eye, a fat lip, and a gash along his jaw. On the table in front of him was the key, which Natasha had brought back from Scarborough, after showing it to her mother. Heather Chandler had taken one look at it and said that it proved without a doubt that Bren was Stephen Bradson.

"How's that?" asked Bren.

Natasha picked up the key and turned it around in her fingers. "She said Grandfather used to guard the thing like it was a family heirloom. He wouldn't let anyone else near it. She claims, though, that she once knew another man who had one just like it. He was a young man, about your age, went by the name of Stephen Bradson."

"You're kidding."

She shook her head.

Bren wasn't sure what to think of that. He looked across the table at Eric and Lug, who hadn't said much, but looked horrified by everything they'd heard. Outside, the sun broke through the clouds and swept in through the front windows of the cafe. Bren gazed across the nearly empty room and out the window. Across the street was the bank, and come tomorrow, he would be over there collecting his due.

"I did find out one thing," said Natasha. "You know that photo that bothers you so much, the one with Bradson staring from the upper window? It wasn't Grandfather who put it in the briefcase. It was my mother. And get this: she took that photo the same day Grandfather was killed—only moments before he was killed. The expression you see is of a man about to commit murder."

Bren had a headache, and it was getting worse. He took a piece of ice out of his glass of water and held it against his swollen lip. He heard the cafe door open and glanced over to see Mayor Tuttle walk in. This was the last person Bren wanted to see right now, but Tuttle headed straight toward the booth where the four of them were seated. Snatching the key up off the table, Bren shoved it into the pocket of his jacket, out of Tuttle's sight.

"How's life treating you there, Stevens?" Tuttle eyed all four faces. He knew all of them, including Natasha. He couldn't say he was fond of any of them.

"Grand."

"Good to hear. I see you haven't left the house yet like I'd asked." Tuttle put his hands on the table and leaned down at Bren's face, inspecting the damage. "What happened to you?"

"Fell down some stairs."

"Is that right?" The mayor gleamed. He stood tall and interlocked his fingers in front of his robust stomach. "Stay here much longer, I've got a feeling you're going to be falling down a lot more stairs."

"That a political promise, Mayor?" asked Eric. "Or one you intend to keep?"

Tuttle offered a sardonic grin and fixed his gaze on the redhead. "You were such a charming child, Eric Starkey. Whatever happened to you?"

That shut Eric up and put a smirk on Tuttle's lips. He glanced around the room at other patrons, who were happy to see the mayor in here handling the riffraff seated in the corner booth.

"You ready to close our business deal?" Tuttle asked Bren.

"Actually, I've got another buyer."

"You have, have you? Why don't you let me make a counter-offer?"

"I'm afraid you'd have a hard time beating this one, Mayor. Natasha here offered me one whole shilling. I didn't see how I could pass that up."

Natasha looked at Bren with confusion, but decided not to question him when she noticed how the remark had gotten under Tuttle's skin.

"You watch yourself, Stevens," said the mayor. "And be more careful on those stairs."

The modest home stood in a shadowy Lurkdale neighborhood. The slate-rock roof held in the heat and held out the cold, and the bushes along the front scratched at the windows in the windy night. A silver Oldsmobile came down the lane with its headlights shining through the neighborhood, then pulled up and parked in front of the house. A stout man with gray hair stepped from the car and listened to the bloodhounds barking in the backyard as they sniffed at the air. He strolled up the walkway and pounded at the door. When it opened, light spilled out into the darkness and a larger man stepped into the light. His eyes were black, and his nose and lips were swollen.

"Looks like our Yankee friend is staying," the stout man announced with displeasure. "You may have to pay him another visit."

"I ain't doing your dirty work for ya no more, Tuttle. I looked for your bloody key. I couldn't find it." Sean handed over the key that Tuttle had given him, a key that opened the back door of Windfield Manor.

"This isn't just my work you're doing. It's for the town. He's in the house, Sean. He tore down the fence. You of all people should know what consequences this could lead to." Tuttle put his hand on the wall and leaned into the doorway, toward Sean.

"Then *you* talk to him. I'm finished with it."

"Have you forgotten all about your kin? About your cousin?" Tuttle asked angrily. He swatted at a moth that fluttered into the light. "You watched him die, remember? Watched him fall from that second-story window with a knife in his neck."

Tuttle spoke the truth. Sean and his friends had spent that evening in a bar telling ghost stories to his cousin, and to make the night complete, they had taken a late night jaunt to the mansion. They drove their cars flush up against the outside of the fence, then stood on the hoods and looked over. They rattled on about the legends, how Windfield had died and his killer still remained. Yet Sean's cousin wouldn't believe. He'd been raised in London and knew better than to fall for small-town superstitions. So they dared him in, and he took the dare. Dropping over the fence, he marched right through the front door. "Come get me ghost," he yelled. "I'm here!" He went to the living room and looked out at his mates gazing over the fence at him. "Ooo, I'm scared!" he mocked, then grabbed his own throat as if being chocked. They all laughed as his face vanished from the window. Shortly, his head popped from another window, on the second floor this time. He laughed at the fools down below, standing on the hoods of three separate cars. Then his laughing stopped. "Hey, there's somebody in here!" he yelled and disappeared into the dark. There was a moment of anxiety, though a few of the boys commented that he was merely toying with them. Even when they heard his scream permeate the night, they had their doubts. Less than a minute later, all doubt was removed when he came sailing from an upper window and hit the ground with a thud. Horror stricken, they scaled the fence and checked the body, dead with a knife in the throat.

"If it's his fate to die, then let the killer take him." Sean lit a ciga-rette and blew the smoke at Tuttle's face. "I don't want anything more to do with this, Tuttle."

"Aren't there any real men left around here?" Tuttle scoffed. His cheeks brightened.

"Talk to Bren. He seemed to do pretty well for himself." Sean held his bruised nose. "What's that key go to anyway?"

Tuttle said nothing. His jaw tightened as he turned in frustration and walked away.

# CHAPTER 23

*B*ren withdrew his money for the month. He bought new locks and windows, and over the next few weeks, Lug and Eric helped him put them in place. The house was still without electricity, but it was at least secure. It was more than a week into August now, Bren's wounds had slowly healed. The anniversary of Thomas Windfield's death was approaching. The person who sensed it most was Gretchen Wicks. She'd fallen asleep on her sofa earlier that evening and had woken in a cold sweat. A window was open at the back of her rickety shack, allowing a slight breeze to cool the room. But even that couldn't stop the perspiration from trickling down her brow. She'd had one of her dreams. The kind that made her mouth dry and her heart pound. She rose and went to the kitchen's rusty sink where she splashed water across her face before filling a glass and rinsing the dryness from her mouth. There could be no mistaking what she'd seen. The man had to be stopped, and stopped soon. That awful man who now resided in the house where Thomas had died. It'd been more than a dream. It'd been sheer prophesy and she knew it. There had been blood on the living room mirror, and Bren Stevens had put it there with the unceasing swing of his ax. The time was drawing near, and when it hit, blood would run.

Stepping out the kitchen door of her one-bedroom shack, the seventy-two-year-old hag pulled a black cloak over her head and trudged into the dying light of the forest. Birds fluttered in the trees. She'd noted a decisive influx of crows in her area, beginning about the time that Bren had moved into the house. She took it as an omen of the darkest, most atrocious kind. This man had bad karma, and before all was said and done, the stench of death would stain his hands.

By the time she hit Oswald Road, the stars were out and a half moon was the only beacon that lit her way. The house stood off in the distance at the base of a hill that blocked one side of the manor from her view. But she could see the moonlight glinting off the new windows. She knew the man was home. She sensed it, as she sensed the company he kept. She dragged her feet along the gravel beside the paved road, and a thin sheet of dust hung in the air behind her. Past the house, she could see the lights of Lurkdale, a place she called home and despised at the same time. People here didn't appreciate her guidance. Her words were only spoken to enlighten, to keep the onset of evil from rearing its ugly head, but folks shied away from her knowledge. They treated it like a plague come to infect them with boils and rot their skin.

When she reached the back of the house, she kept to the trees. Bren and company were in the gazebo, but that was on the far side of the garden, away from the road, so she rounded the narrow end of the house where the dead ivy still hung. From there, she slunk around the front of the house and entered the other grove of trees and edged her way toward the backyard. She stood for a moment, staring out over the garden. The flowers, shrubs and hedges lost all definition beneath the light of the moon.

A murmur of voices drifted through the still air. Gretchen moved again. She watched her footing as she passed among the trees, careful not to snap twigs and draw attention to herself. As she neared the gazebo, she could see four figures sitting in the darkness. The sensation washed over her like a flood of warm blood. Her arms tightened with gooseflesh, and in her mind flashed an image of Bren Stevens standing at the living room mirror sporting his ax—the red paint that once covered the metal head now almost gone and now nothing but the shine of silver flickering.

She listened to the voices speaking in the darkness.

Gretchen emerged from the trees. She was standing at the backs of the four figures, which were staring out the front of the gazebo at the dark walls of the manor. Through the opening in the back of the gazebo, Gretchen could see that one of the individuals seated before her was a woman, and there was a familiar aura about her. This woman had roots here. She had a sense of belonging, much more than did the man who had been willed the home. Seeing the young lady cling to Bren Stevens gave Gretchen a chill. She took another step forward and felt a shiver run up her spine.

"Leave! All of you!" Gretchen shouted. "You're not welcome here!"

Four jack-in-the-boxes couldn't have sprung to life with more animation than did these four. They were on their feet and turned around before Gretchen had gotten three words out of her mouth. The chubby one with the shaggy hair and an unlit cigarette hanging out of his mouth fumbled to remove a crucifix from his earlobe, and when he got it free, he held it up like a madman with a dagger. Gretchen scowled at the gesture.

"What do you want?" Bren asked.

"Do you think this is a game?" Gretchen Wicks stepped through the opening at the back of the gazebo and all four individuals stepped out the front. "I bring you warning, but still you stay."

"What do you expect? You come around raving about how I'm gonna kill someone. You can't expect me to take you seriously?"

"Oh, but I am serious. I assure you. Of all the cursed words ever I spoke, these words are the most true: you *will* murder; you *will* take the life of another. These things *will* happen 'les you leave this house this night. Mark my words. This I know as surely as I see your face before me now. I'm giving you a chance to flee your fate—a chance most hell-bound souls never have. Take what's given you, dear lad. Take it and flee."

Gretchen opened her scabby lips and her teeth were as black as the cloak covering her head. She looked at Natasha and saw nothing but Windfield. There could be no question whose daughter this was. Even in the dark, the eyes gave her away. There was a time when Gretchen would have taken pleasure in feeling Heather Windfield's pain, when she would have gladly inflicted that pain herself, but thirty years of torment was all the penance anyone should have to bear.

"You of all people should know better than to be here," Gretchen addressed Natasha. "Run home to yer mother. Ask her to forgive you. Then beg God for mercy on yer soul. And while yer praying, pray fer this foolish lad. He needs more blessings than the lot of you together." She gestured to Bren, looked at the house and cringed with disgust, then turned her back and departed again into the trees.

They hadn't heard her come, and they didn't hear her go. But they felt her presence. It lingered long after she'd disappeared back the way she'd come.

"What the hell was that?" Natasha's jaw was slack.

"Hell is right," said Bren.

"Gretchen Wicks." Eric's eyes searched the darkness of the trees.

"Did you see her teeth?" Lug was still clutching his crucifix. A shiver twisted his face into a sour expression. "Caught the rot, they have, hang in her mouth like spoilage, buried behind those scabby lips of hers." He cringed and spit out his words and sadly watched his cigarette drop into the flowerbed.

# CHAPTER 24

By morning, Bren still hadn't killed a soul. He whistled though the corridor, carrying his ax with him into the kitchen where he grabbed a large knife and headed for the dead ivy on the side wall outside. It'd sprinkled during the night, leaving the grass and ivy dewy. The scent of rain and the light of day dulled the sharp dread he'd felt the night before when Gretchen Wicks had shown her ghastly face at the back of the gazebo.

He tossed his ax on the wet grass and pulled on his brown leather gloves before whacking the blade of the knife against the thick stocks of the ivy, near the ground. He'd made a three-foot-long incision before he stuck the knife in the soil and latched onto the cut ivy to see if he could work it away from the house. It took effort, but it peeled back, exposing the dirt-stained rock behind it. Getting it to lose it grip from the high wall would perhaps be more laborious. But that day wouldn't come for some time. The house had other things in mind.

He slashed his way toward the center of the house, folding back the dead plant as he went. He was a half hour into the project when he first saw it. At first, all he noticed was the edge of the wood framing and thought what he'd found was a piece of the support used to get the ivy started on its climb up the stone wall. Yet another four inches of cut ivy revealed it for what it truly was: the frame of a basement window. He carved a three-foot square in the ivy, exposing the entire window, which was caked with dirt. He grated it away with his glove and held his face down against the glass. He could see nothing. But there was a room in there, no doubt about it, a basement that he didn't know he had.

He left the knife sticking into the soil at the base of the window, but took his ax with him. From the front door, he marched up the stairs to his bedroom and retrieved his flashlight before heading back to the ivy, where he pointed the light down through the basement window. Cobwebs hung from the ceiling and stretched from wall to wall, a mansion for spiders. Hardly a place lived in by a hiding murderer or anyone else. From what he could see, the room wasn't very large.

He jabbed the blade of the ax into the glass, and it shattered down into the dank room. It smelled of mildew, like the wet carpets he'd pulled from several of the bedrooms. After raking the ax around the frame to clear away the jagged fragments of glass, he shined the light in again. Spiders ran through the webs and a large rat scurried beneath a bookshelf that stood against the right wall. The air was stifling. He poked his head in and looked down at the cement floor where the glass had landed. The light caught movement along the left wall. He jerked back and thumped his head against the top of the frame. He flashed the light up along the wall, only to find his own face staring back at him from a mirror.

He went in feet first and quickly pulled the ax and flashlight in behind him. Immediately he felt a spider crawling along his bare arm and he slapped it away, and then used the ax to clear a path through the maze of webs. In the dusty room there was a mirror, a staircase, bookshelves, a sofa and a desk. The walls were made of jagged reddish-brown bricks. The floor was gray cement and was mostly bare with the exception of a large rug that lay in front of the brown sofa. On the bookshelf, he found volumes of books about stocks, real estate, and investments, all of them between thirty to fifty years old.

He broke a path to the desk, where he opened a drawer and fingered through some papers: business forms and real estate contracts. From a second drawer, he withdrew a book that had a blank cover with plain blue binding. Peeling open the pages, Bren shined the light across the ink scribbles. Thomas James Windfield's life experiences were written upon the paper. Day by day, thought by thought, the secrets of the mysterious man stretched through the pages of the diary. Bren grinned and tucked the book under his arm before forging his way through the webs to the stairs. He felt all slithery with spiders, which were now swarming across the floor, and, he feared, inside the legs of his blue jeans.

At the top of the stairs, a wall obstructed the path. On the side wall, he discovered a latch, which he lifted and found that he could then slide the wall aside. It rumbled as it moved, revealing an oak desk and a large bookcase beyond it. Thomas Windfield's study. The very room where he'd been slain. Bren stepped out into the light and found the wall to be another bookcase. It was so obvious now. Where else would a man hide a secret door but in his own den? Stephen Bradson undoubtedly knew about this passageway and had used it to secure his escape, had perhaps used it to catch Thomas unaware.

After sliding the bookcase back into place, Bren went to the living room. He leaned the ax against the woodpile, removed his gloves, dusted off his clothes and beat four spiders to death before settling on the rocking chair with the diary open on his lap.

The first page started out detailing the history of the house, which had been built in 1830 by Sir Edward Oswald, a notorious squire of Lurkdale, who aptly named the manor Oswald Grange. Thomas took over the mansion in 1954. At which time, he gutted it, remodeled it, and renamed it in his own honor.

From there, Bren turned toward the end of the diary, where he found the last entry, dated August 15, 1964. It mentioned a trip into Lurkdale where Thomas met with his lawyer to discuss a modification to his will, one that now included a man by the name of Bren

Stevens. Seeing his name there in the diary made him feel a bit eerie. Where had Thomas gotten his name? And why had he included it in his will?

Bren flipped back one page and found an entry about Thomas teaching Stephen Bradson how to fence. "He's a quick study," the journal stated. "A natural athlete. Yet I've got a feeling Earl intends to do the poor lad in."

Teaching Stephen Bradson how to maneuver a sharp object was perhaps not the best move Mr. Windfield had ever made, Bren mused.

He turned back about thirty or forty pages. "I bought the Hayward house today as planned," he read from the page. Not interested, he flipped forward, scanned a few paragraphs and turned through several more pages. "Beth resents the boy, yet I can never explain. I'd like to blame it on being a naive youth, but I'm neither naive nor young." He turned ahead five or six pages, not really knowing what he was looking for, but hoping something would jump off the page at him. The next line he read did just that. "When I returned from speaking with myself, Heather nearly caught me." At first he thought he'd misread it, but he went over it again and found that it said exactly what he'd thought it'd said. Perhaps, then, it'd been miswritten. He read on: "It was the closest incident thus far. She was sitting near the window and questioned how I had got in the room."

Turning back a page, he found the beginning of the entry. "I went through the living room mirror today."

There it was, spelled out in black and white. Instinct told him this was what he was looking for. His eyes wandered up from the pages of the diary to the long mirror that stretched along the inner wall of the living room. The door behind the bookcase in the study wasn't the only secret passage in this house. The mirror held another. He went to it and knocked. It sounded solid. As he walked the length of the mirror, he rapped his knuckles on the glass, expecting to hear a change in the pitch when it hit the location where the wall behind the mirror opened up to an empty cavity, which led to who knows where. But it all sounded the same. Yet it was there. It had to be there. Finding it would make honest men of both Eric and Lug, who claimed Bradson had walked out of the wall at the back of the room.

Tossing the diary on the sofa, he pressed his palms against the glass to see if he could slide it up or down or to either side. It didn't even feign movement. He snatched up the diary again, which surely explained everything at some point within its pages. He skimmed a dozen entries while pacing the floor, until another passage came right off the page at him.

"Today was a near tragedy," he read. "I found Justin playing with the key near the living room mirror. I'd forgotten to lock my desk drawer and apparently he discovered it. Fortunately, I found him before he found his way through the mirror."

Bren's lips broke into a smile.

"Key." He laughed aloud, tossed the diary back on the sofa and sprinted up the stairs. Thomas wanted him to find the door. He wanted him to be sucked into whatever it was this house held secret. He grabbed the key out of the dresser and skipped steps on his way back down to the living room.

He examined the mirror again. There was no keyhole, just solid reflections stretching down the wall, with no visible lines framing a door. He reached toward the mirror, to try again to push it. But his hand didn't stop there. Rather, it sunk into the silvery reflection and disappeared inside the glass.

He pulled his hand back with fright. His heart raced and his stomach was all fluttery. He stared down at the key with fascination. Again, he stretched forth his hand. Again, it vanished into the mirror. He held it there this time. It felt lukewarm, a bit liquidy perhaps, but no more than a handful of air on an extremely humid day. For several seconds, he stood with his nose nearly touching the glass before he gathered the courage to go on. Closing his eyes and holding his breath, he pressed his face at his own reflection. The mirror pushed aside like tepid mercury, and his face vanished into the wall. He stepped one foot in but left one firmly planted on the carpet, afraid that once he entered completely he may never be able to return. What he found when he opened his eyes was nearly as startling as the idea of walking through a solid mirror: he was staring into his same living room, as though he'd just entered the reflection, entered some parallel universe. He half-expected to find everything in reverse, but this wasn't so.

But it *was* different. The thought simultaneously frightened and elated him. The tattered curtains were open, revealing the broken windows. The place was filthy again. And the sofa was sitting sideways in the living room, and two young boys were seated on it facing the doorway. He'd stepped back in time. It sounded unreal, but he could think of no other explanation.

At that moment, he had what he would later regard as one of the few premonitions he'd ever received. The feeling warned him not to come all the way through the mirror, that once entered, there was no turning back. But he stepped through.

The young boys, whom Bren had accurately appraised as twelve-year-olds, were puffing on cigarettes and blowing the smoke coolly at the ceiling. From the back, he could see nothing but the stringy brown hair of one and the red of the other. It had to be them, and here he was, the beast stepping through the wall.

Between puffs, the heavier of the two boys chewed at a Cadbury bar. He had a confidence that people twice his age didn't have, a confidence that was destined to endure for perhaps one more minute, two at the most. He feared nothing. At twelve, he owned the world. He took in a drag on the cigarette and blew out, trying for a smoke ring but ending up with a cloud. Relaxing back into the folds of the sofa, he glanced at himself in the mirror. His life of confidence vanished with that glance. His mouth gaped. The cigarette fell to his lap. In the mirror he'd caught the reflection of a stranger standing behind him in the room, and in that instant he knew that monsters really did exist.

He tried to speak and warn his friend of the evil at their backs, but no words would escape his lips.

"What's your problem?" the redhead mocked.

The chubby boy stood and backed away from the sofa, with his finger pointing at Bren. His friend had a smile on his face when he turned his chin back over his shoulder to see what had startled his mate, but the smile faded quickly. His eyes bulged.

The sight of the boys with the cigarettes awakened the memories of a conversation he'd had with Eric and Lug, where Lug told him that the devil who had chased them from the house that day had threatened to chew their eyes out if he ever caught them smoking again. As a result, neither of them had ever lit up another cigarette. Bren smiled, and that smile brought fear to the faces of the boys.

"If I ever catch you smoking again I'll chew your eyes out." He coughed out the most evil voice he could muster. "And I know where you live, Lug. You too, Eric."

Eric was a thin adult but an even thinner boy. His hair was short and parted on the side. At the mention of his name, his face grew long and narrow. He came out of his seated position with remark-able fluidity, ran to the window and dove head first through one of the frames that no longer held any glass.

Lug looked stunned, nearly petrified at the sight of his one good friend leaving him to die a lone death. He clearly had no idea what action to take.

Bren laughed sinisterly and stepped forward.

Lug moved to the window and gave a sick-toad leap at the glass-less frame, trying to imitate his friend's escape, but his overgrown body stuck inside the frame. He struggled like a fat slug wiggling through a pinhole, legs flopping, mouth bellowing.

Bren grabbed Lug's shoe, and the boy's lungs burst out a scream that put fire-engine sirens to shame. "He's got me, Eric! Don't leave me!" His foot jerked wildly.

Out in the yard, Eric was now squeezing his body through a hole in the fence. No camaraderie here. Lug was on his own.

Though he was certain Lug would disagree with him, Bren thought this was one of the funniest scenes he'd ever witnessed. It took all he had to suppress the laughter as he stood at the window holding the chubby boy's foot. The flopping of Lug's body and the sheer panic in his scream were comedy at its best. After about a minute, he felt the poor child had suffered enough and gave Lug a shove through the window and let him go. He dropped to the earth with a thud, but quickly recovered and sprinted to the fence, smashed his body through the hole and hollered all the way home.

Bren laughed so hard that tears filled his eyes. He'd scarred the two boys for life, but boy was it funny. Wiping tears from his eyes, he stared down at the cigarette that was still smoldering on the carpet. Another was sitting on the sofa next to a half-eaten Cadbury bar. He grabbed both cigarettes, tapped them out on the windowsill and dropped them outside.

"Oh good lord, I'm the ghost," he said as he glanced in the mirror. "I'm my own twin."

He was still smiling, not considering the dark undertones of his own words. He clutched the key with amazement, twirled it in his fingers and stepped back to the mirror. He could hardly wait to rush home to Natasha and tell her of his discovery. There was nothing to fear after all. The stranger in the house was none other than himself.

He walked to the mirror and closed his eyes before stepping through. The moist sensation washed over his face and arms, and then solidified back into a mirror behind him. When he opened his eyes again, his already pounding heart did double time. The same curtains still hung over the windows, but they were newer now, and untorn. The sofa was sitting with its back to the windows, which were unbroken.

This one felt more like a parallel universe than did his first trip through the mirror. He related better to the scene of the room in shambles since that was the way he'd first found it the day he'd arrived at the house. Now, however, the room looked respectable, yet disused.

From the corridor, he walked to the entryway, where a stack of boxes lay piled near the door. He could hear voices outside. Through the small entryway window, he could see that a large moving-truck had been pulled up close to the front steps. Three men were standing inside the back of the truck securing a dresser and a table so they wouldn't shift during transport.

Bren bit at his bottom lip. He'd gone back further, not forward. He could see the pages of the newspapers that he'd read in the Lurkdale Library. His first journey had obviously taken him ten years back in time, to the year 1984, when Eric and Lug were mere lads. Therefore, he now stood in the year 1974—another ten years back—when Heather Windfield Chandler had come to claim some of her possessions from the abandoned house.

He felt suddenly ill, realizing that he had no idea how to return to the present, and certain that the answers were right there in Thomas Windfield's diary if he had but taken the time to read it rather than hastily skim it and toss it aside. He'd trapped himself in the past. Or had he? A smile curved on his lips. The diary was still here, right now, twenty years in the past, locked inside the basement, right where Thomas Windfield had left it.

"All those boxes are ready to go," a gentle voice spoke at his back.

He turned. At the head of the corridor stood a beautiful twenty-nine-year-old Heather. Her brown hair was pulled back into a pony-tail, and she was wearing a blue and red flannel shirt, which was untucked and dangling over the waist of her jeans. She didn't yet believe in ghosts, but as the recognition set in, she was quickly converted. A sad horror darkened in her eyes as she stared at the face of the man who had slain her father—and had then disappeared without a trace. His blond hair was longer perhaps, but other than that, she could detect no change in his appearance. The man had not aged.

Her mouth dropped open as she took a step back. At first only a peep escaped her lips, then a cry of panic as she called for help.

"It's not what you think, Heather. I didn't kill your father." Bren tried to go to her, to console her, but she didn't want consoling, not from him.

"Please don't hurt me." She backed down the corridor, horrified.

"I'd never—"

The front door burst open. The three men had heard Heather's cries and had come to her rescue. Bren's face rotated from the surprised-angry men to Heather, then to the staircase. He sprinted, up, hurdling two, three steps at a time. The three men raced after him.

He should have gone to the living room, back to the mirror. He'd only chosen the stairs because at the back of his mind he remembered one of those stupid articles from the Lurkdale Gazette. He felt destined to climb the stairs, but only because he'd read the account in the newspaper, which had only reported what he'd done. It was maddening.

As he hit the top stair, one man dove forward with his arms stretched out and caught Bren's heel, sending him sprawling upon the hardwood floor. His body slapped the ground, and the key fell from his hand and slid down the hall in front of him. He scampered after it, but before he could reach it, a man kicked him in the ribs. He dropped to his side with a moan.

He didn't recall reading that in the newspaper.

Bren flipped over onto his back to fend off the man, who was crouching above him now, reaching for his throat. Bren kicked at the man's stomach, and a long breath wheezed from his mouth. But as one man buckled, another came forward. Bren's head was reeling.

The whole experience felt surreal to him. In a blink, he looked up to find a fist jetting toward his face. This was happening to *him*! Everything he'd read in the papers was happening to *him*! He pulled back and felt the fist brush past his nose. He got to his feet and hit the man on the chin, which stunned him long enough for Bren to locate the key and snatch it up. The third man didn't seem so eager to catch him. He came to the forefront, but did so slowly as Bren dashed into the bathroom at the end of the hall and swung the door closed. The force of the man hitting the door from the outside pushed it back open an inch, but Bren got it closed again and flipped the lock.

The door rattled and shimmied under the pressure of two, then three men charging at it. The flimsy lock wouldn't hold long. Bren frantically surveyed the room. No way out. But there had to be. The newspaper claimed that the men had found the bathroom empty once they'd finally broken their way in. But how? There were no windows, no other door—just a bathtub, sink, toilet and mirror. Mirror! His chest tightened with hope. He'd assumed that the key only worked on the living room mirror, but he had no basis for that. He reached for it with a silent prayer and felt a wave of relief when his hand passed through. He stepped upon the edge of the bathtub and crawled onto the sink, going into the mirror headfirst. His body disappeared into the silvery reflection like a man diving into a vertical pool of water, one that gently rippled when entered. As his feet vanished through the glass, the bathroom door burst open, and three bewildered men found nothing but a bathtub, sink, toilet and mirror. A moment that would forever change an entire village's perception of reality.

Bren materialized into the same bathroom he'd just left. He slid across the sink and dropped to the floor with a thud. The light blue shower curtain was drawn, and the shower was running beyond it.

"Is somebody there?" a female voice asked, and Bren stared up to see a hand part the shower curtain. Heather peered at the door. "Justin?"

Bren pressed his body flat to the floor. If seen, there would be no explaining this. The curtain closed again. He was going to be fine. Just fine. All he had to do was get out of the bathroom, creep down the hall, down the stairs, sneak out of the door and off Windfield property without being seen. No problem.

He quietly stood and twisted the lock on the door. It clicked open. He stepped back again, afraid Heather had heard the sound, but the shower had drowned it out. Turning the brass knob, he pulled the door open and stepped out quickly, easing the door closed behind him.

He stuffed the key into the pocket of his blue jeans and ambled timidly down the hall. With the exception of the water running behind him, the house was silent.

The place looked magnificent. Paintings lined the hallway. The wood floors were polished. The varnish on the doors and trimming had no scuffmarks or dings. It was August 11, 1964. Thomas Windfield was still alive. The Beatles ruled. And Bren Stevens hadn't yet been born. Nor would he be for another five years.

The sound of the shower turning off startled him. He hurried down the hallway to the balustrade. Peering over to the entryway, he witnessed a lovely woman of forty-three exiting the corridor beneath him. Her auburn hair was stylishly curled, and she wore a black and white dress. It was Mrs. Windfield, Thomas's wife.

Bren took a few steps back, still able to see below him through the wooden dowels that lined the balustrade. Heather would be exiting the bathroom soon, and he knew he couldn't still be standing at the front of the hall when she did.

Below him, Mrs. Windfield stopped just shy of the front door, turned and came back a couple steps. "Of course you're right, dear," she spoke to someone down the corridor from her. "Aren't you always?" She came to the foot of the stairs and paused to adjust her dress sleeve before continuing up.

Bren turned back to see the bathroom door opening. He hurried into the nearest room, the same room he'd claimed as his own, thirty years in the future: the master bedroom. He closed the door behind him and listened to the footsteps coming up the stairs. He scanned the room and didn't like what he saw. Beside the bed, on the dresser, stood a short stack of books, all about real estate. On the wall above it hung an oil painting of a small cottage next to a brook. All of these things were fine in and of themselves; however, they indicated that he was standing in Mr. and Mrs. Windfield's bedroom. The later of whom had now reached the top of the stairs and was coming down the hall.

He dove to the floor and slid under the bed as the doorknob turned.

From his snake-eye view, Bren watched two black high heels cross the room and stop at the dresser. He heard the scuffles of Mrs. Windfield picking up some earrings and putting them on, then the hiss of the bottle as she sprayed her neck with perfume. The feet stepped back to the bed, directly in front of Bren's face. A moment later, the springs above him pressed down against his ear as the lady sat down. His head was wedged between the bed and the floor. If she was waiting for her husband to come and apologize to her for whatever wrong he'd done, Bren prayed that Thomas Windfield wasn't a stubborn man.

Mrs. Windfield crossed her legs, removed one of her high heels, adjusted the lining that had been pinching her heel, and then replaced the shoe on her foot before rising and walking out the door. Bren rubbed his ear.

Once he heard the footsteps descending the stairs, he dragged himself from beneath the bed and beat the dust from his jeans and faded blue shirt. He opened the door a crack and peeked into the empty hall. It looked safe. Easing his way back to the balcony, he stared over the railing. He could hear voices, but they were far down the hall, too far to make out what they were saying. He took the steps gently, constantly keeping watch on the front door, the corridor below him, and the hallway above him. If he could just get outside. Even if they spotted him there, he could create some story about wandering up to the door of the wrong house.

At the foot of the stairs, he could hear the voices more clearly. They were faint but discernable as they drifted up from the dining room.

Bren put his hand on the knob, prepared to escape to the great outdoors, but at the last moment decided he'd best check that the way was clear first. Stepping to the small window, he parted the frilly white curtain that now hung over it and looked to the front lawn, where a thirteen-year-old was playing with a soccer ball. The boy's blond hair curled above his ears, and his face was tough and tanned. He manipulated the soccer ball between his feet and kicked it into the air.

"All I'm saying is that I'd like to be included in the decisions around here."

The voices sounded louder now, drawing Bren's attention away from the window.

"What have you against the boy?" a man's voice argued. "He deserves just as much chance in life as the rest of us."

"But why do *we* have to give it to him?"

Above him, Bren could hear the approach of footsteps in the hall. He quickly tiptoed down the corridor, to the door of the study.

Thomas Windfield exited the dining room. He was sharply dressed in a black suit and bow tie. His hair was dark brown with streaks of gray at his temples, and his face, which bore a disconcerted expression, was fortunately still facing into the dining room.

Bren eased open the study door and closed it behind him. He wasted no time locating the latch that released the bookcase from its position in front of the basement stairs. It made a gentle grinding sound as it slid away and then back in front of the opening. With the sound of the bookcase clamping back into place, he heard a second sound, that of Thomas Windfield opening the study door. Bren's heart was all a flutter. He didn't dare descend the stairs lest Thomas hear his feet on the wooden steps. Of course, if the gentleman decided to slide the bookcase aside, Bren imagined it would be quite the shock finding a stranger standing just inside the door.

He listened intently. There was the sound of a desk drawer being opened, the flutter of papers, the drawer closing, and best of all, Thomas exiting back to the corridor.

In the basement, Bren searched through the desk for the journal. There was a mirror hanging on the wall just behind him; all he had to do was figure out how to make the key advance him to the future, and he could walk right back to 1994 without anyone being the wiser. No one would ever even know he'd been here. But even before he opened the desk drawer and found the journal missing, he already knew that he was in for the long haul. The papers had said he'd been here; therefore, he was destined to stay. And do what? Kill Thomas Windfield? But why? Because Thomas had stumbled upon him hiding in his basement? Bren couldn't say.

He sat on the brown sofa, wringing his hands and staring at the mirror. He studied his own face. He was no longer the same man he'd been when he first came to England. But a killer? The papers claimed it was true, as did Gretchen Wicks. Even now, staring into the mirror, he could see her face, smell her breath, and, worst of all, hear her words of doom: *It will build your dreams, your passions, then it will warp your soul and twist you into taking out its vengeance for it.* The memory sickened him. This witch, with all her prophecies, could rot in hell for all he cared. In fact, he'd prefer it that way. If anyone deserved to die, it was Gretchen Wicks, just to put an end to all that condemning chatter of hers. And yesterday—had it only been yesterday? It felt an eternity away—she'd come blabbing again, speaking her words of ruin.

*Of all the cursed words ever I spoke, these words are the most true: you will murder; you will take the life of another.*

"I am the ghost," he mumbled, and the implications were now all too clear to him. Thomas Windfield had implored him to come to England, to avenge his death, to find a killer who was none other than Bren himself. And why would he commit such a heinous crime? Ask a question enough and you're bound to find an answer; and Bren thought he'd found his: if Thomas remained alive, then Bren would never receive the will and, thus, never inherit the manor or the money or meet Natasha. It appeared as though the only way he could ever meet the girl he loved was by killing her grandfather.

He remained in the basement the rest of the day, trapped in the past and listening to footsteps pass overhead. He studied the key. It was a simple piece of metal with a very complicated talent.

When the light filtering in through the live vines outside the basement window had faded, and the house fell silent, Bren climbed the stairs, slid open the bookcase, tiptoed through the entryway, unlocked the front door and sneaked out into the night. Out at last! He breathed in the fresh air. He'd made it out. But he felt anything but free.

# CHAPTER 25

*A* tomcat knocked the lid from a garbage can, and it fell with a bang. Bren opened his eyes. It took him a moment to get his bearings. He was in an alley, lying on a cardboard box behind a butcher's shop. The stench of spoiled meat scraps was wafting up from open bins. Rising, he wandered through the cluttered alley toward the street. The sunlight shining over Moorland Avenue was refreshing. Lurkdale was alive, more alive than he'd ever seen it. Lurkdalians bustled. Businesses thrived. Thomas Windfield's wealth sifted through the village like water through a sieve.

"Top of the morning to ya, gov." A man smiled on by.

"Good morning," Bren said, surprised. Someone in Lurkdale actually smiled and greeted him. It would be some time before he took something like that for granted.

At a corner newsstand, he lifted a paper and read the date: August 12, 1964. He thought of the newspapers he'd read in the library and wondered how many days of prosperity this happy town had left. How many days before Thomas Windfield would lie dead on the floor of his study? Two of the papers he'd read in the future bore the date August 12, telling of incidents that had occurred a day earlier. August 11, 1974, Heather Windfield saw the ghost. August 11, 1984, Lug and Eric saw him again. Yesterday! Every pass through the mirror had erased another ten years.

On August 17, 1964, the Lurkdale Gazette would release a paper announcing Thomas James Windfield's demise. In four days, the horror would begin, the murder having taken place on the 16th. Bren wanted to leave. The only glitch was that Thomas Windfield was the only man who could tell him how to return to the future.

He stopped at a cafe window and looked in at the people hunched over breakfast plates. His mouth watered. He hadn't had a thing to eat since yesterday morning, just before discovering the basement window. He pulled his wallet from his back pocket and counted the bills. He had sixty-two pounds, enough for breakfast, lunch and dinner for the next week, but since the oldest bill was dated 1981, the money was essentially no better than blank scraps of paper. So he walked away hungry.

He spent the early afternoon hours sitting on the hillside at the back of the mansion, staring down over the garden. The gray stones of the house shimmered in the sun, and the ivy along the side wall was alive and green, as were the trees in the yard. Everything felt wrong. He lay back on the grassy hill with his eyes closed, wondering how he could return to the future and bypass confronting Thomas Windfield. His only hope was in finding the diary, but that involved going back into the house and snooping around, something he wasn't eager to do.

He couldn't say how long he'd been lying there, perhaps as long as an hour, maybe more. He'd drifted in and out of sleep, dreaming about slipping through mirrors, only to awaken and remind himself that it *wasn't* a dream. Regardless of how unreal it felt, he had to accept the fact that it'd happened, that he'd traveled thirty years back in time and was lying in the grass of 1964. He lay there until a shadow fell across his face, and he heard the snort of a horse standing nearby. Looking up toward the sun, he found the silhouette of a girl on the back of a brown thoroughbred standing over him. He came to his feet quickly and put a hand above his eyes to block the sun. Her face was younger than when he'd met her in Scarborough, but there was no mistaking that face.

"Heather, you startled me," he said, then cringed at his own words. Seeing the way she squinted down at him, searching for recognition, he knew that it was already too late to undo the damage.

"How do you know my name?"

"Oh, I—" His mind raced for a logical answer and struck gold. "In town a man mentioned the Windfields had a beautiful daughter named Heather. I figured that must be you."

She smiled at the flattery and sat up straight with her chin raised high. Her dark brown hair was long, nearly to the small of her back. "You're an American, aren't you?" She seemed pleased with this, and grinned when Bren confirmed that he was indeed American. "Why are you staring at our house?"

"Just admiring it. I used to have one just like it."

"I'm sure you did." She walked her horse around him, examining his blue shirt, which was showing signs of having been slept in. "My father doesn't like strangers hanging around, especially Americans." She looked at him imperiously, then flipped her hair over her shoulder and turned the horse away.

"Wait!" he called after her. The horse stopped, but Heather never looked back. "Do you think perhaps I could have a look inside?" He couldn't be sure, but he thought he saw a slight grin upon her lips, a look of satisfaction, as though she enjoyed the sound of a pleading man. Yet when she turned toward him, there was no smile, merely a frown of disapproval. She gave no reply other than to start away again, slowly this time, perhaps giving him time to plead again.

When he didn't, she stopped and turned back to him, giving away no emotion. "On second thought, I see no harm in your taking a look." She said this casually, as though it really didn't matter to her one way or the other. Flipping the reins, she continued down the slope of the grassy hillside, making him hurry to catch up. "What else did the man in town tell you about me?"

"Well—" Bren trotted beside her horse as he searched for a lie. "He said you were very popular and charming."

"Did he now? And who was this man?"

"I didn't ask his name."

She offered a sly grin, and Bren wasn't sure if she knew he was lying or was merely pleased to learn that someone in town had been speaking highly of her. Either way, she was allowing him to tag along and was going to be his ticket into the house.

At the base of the hill, they turned toward the stables, which were painted white, with a corral of the same color beside them. Thirty years in the future, they would be no more than a mound of charred wood overrun with purple heather and yellow gorse. As they approached, Bren could see a man standing near the corral gate, throwing hay over the fence to another horse, which was yellow with brown patches on its face. The man was wearing a derby to keep the sun out of his eyes. As Heather approached with her horse, he came to her and grabbed the bridal, holding the horse steady while she dismounted.

"I expect you to do a thorough job brushing her this time, Berney."

"Yes ma'am." Bernard Phelps nodded politely at Bren before taking the horse away. He was taller than Bren had remembered him from their meeting in the used bookstore. Judging by the way he'd watched Heather get down from the horse, Bren was certain that he was stricken with her. This was something he hadn't considered before, yet it made perfect sense. She was a lovely young woman. A bit conceited perhaps but still striking. She flipped her long brown hair off her shoulders and led the way up the flagstone steps to the garden, which was full of colorful flowers and trimmed hedges.

"What's your name?"

"Br—Bradson. Stephen Bradson." Bren immediately wished he hadn't chosen the name that he'd read in the newspaper, one that sounded so much like his own, but it was already out of his mouth before he had time to consider it.

"How long you staying in England, Stephen?"

"I don't know. I haven't given it much thought."

"Don't you have a job you need to get back to?" There was a hint of loathing the lazy in her voice, as though she herself was used to grueling work and was tired of those who glided through life on the shirttails of their rich relatives.

"I'm in between jobs right now."

"I can't wait to introduce you to my father."

He wasn't sure what she meant by that, but it didn't sound entirely innocent.

Near the fountain, a lady crouched in a flowerbed, plucking weeds. At first Bren mistook her for Heather's mother, the auburn-haired lady who had smashed his head the night before. It dawned on him that he had no idea what her name was. When the woman stared up from the flowers, however, Bren could see that he'd done Mrs. Windfield a grave injustice. Just the sight of this kneeling woman made him quiver. Her eyes were dark and her teeth gray.

"Morning, Heather," she called.

"Morning, Gretchen," Heather said with that superior inflection of hers.

Gretchen Wicks lowered her witchy black head as if attending to her work, but her eyes followed Bren and Heather in through the back door. Something moved in her, something cold and foreign. She lifted a grimy finger and thoughtfully rubbed her teeth, certain that something was out of place, but not sure what it was or where it belonged.

In the kitchen, Mrs. Windfield was crouched before the open stove pulling hot mincemeat pies from the oven with steam rising from the crust. Her auburn hair was backcombed neatly, and she wore a white apron over her green blouse. When the door came open, she looked over at her daughter and then stood up when she saw Bren come through the door behind her.

"Mother, this is Stephen." She gestured to Bren, who was still in the process of closing the door. "He's from America." There was that tone in her voice again, like she had a little secret that she was keeping all to herself. Yet apparently it was a secret that her mother was in on, because there was a flash of disapproval in her eyes before she turned a smiling face toward Bren and lied about how nice it was to meet him. It was hot with the oven door hanging open, yet that didn't stop Bren from feeling the chill that these two women were giving off. It made him uneasy. The little smirk that Heather was now giving him didn't help any either. It said that he was standing at the center of a battlefield, and that she was using him as artillery, a position he didn't much care for.

"Perhaps he can stay for lunch. You hungry, Stephen?" Heather smiled at her mother.

"Well, I—" Bren began. The aroma rising from the mincemeat pies made his mouth water, but he knew he'd be better off declining this invitation.

"Good. Then it's settled," Heather spoke up before he could complete his refusal.

Heather helped cart the pies into the dining room where light falling through the large window sketched a checkerboard on the table, across plates, glasses, silverware, and the white cloth beneath them. When the three of them had settled around the table, Mrs. Windfield cut a slice from the mincemeat pie and placed it on a plate in front of Bren.

"We don't get many tourists in Lurkdale." The mother passed the pan to Heather for her to help herself. "Not exactly a popular attraction."

"I wanted to see the real England."

"Lurkdale is real all right—real boring," Heather spoke as if to herself.

"I actually find it rather interesting."

"Every place is interesting when you know you can leave." Heather was staring at her mother as she said this, and her mother showed no signs of offense to the comment. Mrs. Windfield was very much a lady. She had all the mannerisms that Bren associated with the filth rich. Even when she was rebuking her daughter, she kept her voice soft and retained a pleasant grin, as though she were talking about the lovely weather or a nice opera that she'd recently attended.

"Our home is such a prison." Mrs. Windfield took a roll and set it on her plate. "Wouldn't you agree, Stephen? Have you ever seen such a contemptible place?" She gestured to a painting by Rembrandt (a replica) and a small marble statue of a naked woman, looking like something from a Greek amphitheater.

"I think it's lovely."

"That it is. Our warden is a great decorator," said Heather, and then perked up when she heard the front door open and close. Her I-have-a-secret look was back on her face, and she gave Bren a thin smile.

Thomas appeared in the doorway, dressed in white shirtsleeves and dress slacks. He had one of those faces that looked liked it belonged on a soap opera. Prominent chin, strong jaw, and warm brown eyes that looked right through you. Justin lagged behind him with a scowl on his face. His blond hair didn't quite reach his ears, a length forced upon him by his adoptive parents.

"You two have fun?" Mrs. Windfield smiled uncomfortably at her husband.

"Splendid," Justin piped up sarcastically.

She ignored the boy. Bren could see that there was no love between Mrs. Windfield and Justin, both of them living under the same roof and despising each other. Bren was aware that the boy was adopted, but he had no idea how long he'd been here at Windfield Manner. Apparently not long enough to form a bond with his new mother, perhaps not even with his sister.

"Want some lunch?" she asked her husband.

"Go wash your hands, Justin." He patted the boy on the head.

"They're clean." Justin flashed his hands at Thomas to exhibit their cleanliness.

"Wash them anyway," said the mother.

"Yes, ma'am." Justin gave her a vindictive stare and left the room. Mrs. Windfield followed him out, going to the kitchen to fetch more plates.

"I believe this is an unfamiliar face." Thomas came to Bren and offered his hand. "Thomas Windfield," he introduced himself and glanced disapprovingly at Bren's blond hair, which came to the middle of his ears. It looked feminine to him, something those boys in Liverpool had started. The way Thomas saw it, only a hoodlum would wear his hair in such a fashion, and that wasn't the type of company he liked sitting at his dining room table with his impressionable daughter.

"Stephen Bradson," Bren said, then stood and shook on his lie.

"I'm sorry, Father." Heather tapped a napkin on her lips. "I should've introduced you. Stephen and I met at the top of the hill. I asked him in for lunch. Hope you don't mind."

"Of course not. Why would I mind?"

"If it's a problem—" Bren started.

"No. Stay. You haven't even finished your lunch," Heather insisted and the two men sat. She lifted a forkful of mincemeat pie and blew on it. "Stephen's from America," she said before taking her bite. She watched her father's face darken. The creases around his eyes deepened, just as they always did whenever she successfully planted a thorn beneath his skin.

"Over here dodging the draft, I suppose," he said to Bren, then stood as his wife reentered the room holding two plates, which he took and placed on the table.

"The draft?" His brain spun on the thought for a moment before thinking of the date and the war taking place in Asia at that very moment. "No. Just vacation."

Justin entered, displayed his clean hands to his mother and took a seat next to Bren. His first though was that Bren was a friend of the family that he hadn't met, but the tone Thomas was using made him think otherwise.

"Convenient, isn't it?" Thomas dished some pie for his son and himself. "That is, with America at war over in Vietnam and all. And here you just happen to be on vacation out of the country. Marvelous timing, wouldn't you say, Beth?" He looked to his wife for agreement, but got nothing but a disapproving shake of the head. "Yeah, I suppose you're right. He is Heather's guest after all, isn't he?" Thomas could see that his daughter was pleased with herself and that only added to his irritation.

"Are you staying in town at the tavern?" asked Elizabeth.

"Yeah, I suppose so."

"You haven't checked in yet?"

"You think there'll be a problem?"

"Then where's your luggage?"

Bren shrugged, glanced at Thomas and said, "It was stolen," thinking the comment would win him some sympathy from the middle-age gentleman, who clearly wasn't won over by his first impression.

"In Lurkdale?" Elizabeth asked, surprised.

"Yeah. This morning at the bus station. I set my bags down and went to help an elderly lady off the bus, and when I turned around, my bags were gone."

"An American getting robbed by an Englishman," said Thomas. "Now there's something new."

"They take your money?" asked Justin.

"Got it all, I'm afraid."

Thomas smirked. He could see it coming. The rich man's world was filled with beggars, all with a different sob story to tell and a different ploy intended to relieve the wealthy of their fortunes. "And this is where the gullible rich help out the poor lad in need, is that it?"

"I didn't come here for handouts."

"Then why did you come?"

Bren had no response for that, and a painful silence hung in the air, as thick as tar and every bit as unpleasant. He was looking at Thomas and it surprised him to find that he didn't like the man. Having Thomas will him a home and a large sum of money had biased him in Thomas's favor. Yet sitting at his dining table and listening to him speak had erased all the kind thoughts he'd ever had about the man. In fact he thought it entirely possible that he may end up killing the gentleman after all.

"You needn't be so blatantly rude, Father." Heather nearly sounded sincere in her admonishment. "I asked him here as a guest."

"Fair enough." Thomas dished some pie into his mouth, without taking his eyes off Bren.

"Have any American coins?" asked the boy.

"Justin, that isn't polite," said Elizabeth.

"Justin here collects coins," Thomas explained to Bren. "No sin in that, is there?" The comment was clearly spoken for his wife's benefit, and it silenced her just as he'd intended it to. It reminded Bren of the type of thing his father would do, which made him dislike Thomas Windfield all the more. The only difference he could see here was that Mrs. Windfield shrank beneath the criticism. Bren's mother would have erupted with some derision of her own, reminding Bren's father of what a useless husband he was and how she would have been better off marrying their drug-dealing neighbor. At least he had ambition.

"I may still have a coin or two." Bren stuffed his hand into the front pocket of his jeans. He fumbled his hand past the bulky mirror key and gripped onto a coin. Though he'd been in England for almost two months, he generally found a dime, nickel or penny mixed in with his change. He rubbed the coin between his fingers. *A dime*, he thought, bearing the face of Franklin D. Roosevelt and a date that would require more explanation that he cared to give. He let it fall from his finger.

"I guess I exchanged all my money after all. Sorry." He pulled his hand from his pocket, and the teeth of the key caught on the band of his watch and popped right out onto the floor. It clanked across the tiles, slid behind Justin's chair and came to rest at Thomas's back. Bren eased his chair away from the table, stood and casually bent down to retrieve the key from the floor, certain that a quick snatch would only add intensity to the already ridiculous situation.

"That's Thomas's." Justin looked up at his father. "That's yours."

Thomas turned in his chair to see what Bren had dropped. He didn't like what he saw. His upper lip snarled, looking like a cross between Elvis Presley and a mad dog. "So you didn't come looking for handouts, did you?" He glanced at Heather as if she were somehow involved.

She shrugged innocently.

"Well—it's, ah—" Bren could think of nothing to say. All eyes were upon him. "Could we talk? In private."

"Why of course." Thomas sounded all too willing to accommodate as he stood and placed at hand on Bren's back to escort him from the room. "I just love to hear you Yanks tell me lies. You're so much better at it than us English."

They came up the corridor, to the entryway, which was filled with the afternoon sunlight as it filtered down through the round window and past the chandelier. Thomas pushed the study door open and had Bren go in before him. He could see that the young American kept himself in shape, but Thomas was no slouch. And being older only meant he had a few more tricks up his sleeve. He locked the door, turned to Bren and slapped him hard across the face.

"Whoa, what the hell was that? Damn." Bren stepped away from the man. He had his hand clinched in a fist. "I thought we were gonna talk."

The forty-eight-year-old Englishman really wasn't in the mood to hear this longhaired man's fairytales. He proceeded to roll up his shirtsleeves as he eyed the blond man with contempt. He'd had a loathing for Americans ever since he was seven years old, ever since three New York brokers swindled his father out of his life's savings.

"I'll let you know that I have no tolerance for thievery." Thomas contemplated stepping casually over to the lad and snapping his nose with a quick jab. Instead, he went to his desk, picked up the phone and started dialing, ready to put the matter into the hands of the police.

"I didn't steal this thing."

"Did Heather give it to you?" Thomas kept dialing.

"No, actually," he replied and let the words hang in the air for a moment before adding, "you did."

Thomas looked up from the telephone and laid the receiver back into its cradle. There was a look in his eyes, one that said he knew the words that he was hearing made no sense, yet he believed them anyway. "Go ahead."

"Well, you haven't given it to me yet." Bren rubbed his cheek where the man had slapped him. It still stung. "I know it sounds ridiculous."

"Not so ridiculous." Thomas pulled a set of keys from his pocket, walked around his desk and unlocked the center drawer. As he pulled the drawer open, the expression on his face was priceless. It was very similar to the one Bren had had when he first watched his hand sink through the mirror. A whole new world had just opened up to him. Thomas lifted a key identical to the one in Bren's hands. His demeanor softened noticeably and he gave Bren a curious smile.

"You left it to me in your will."

Thomas set the key back in the drawer and closed it. For the first time all day, he looked like someone Bren could actually grow to like. "We really have to talk. But not here." He opened the study door, stopped and looked back at Bren. "Sorry for slapping you. Sometimes my emotions get the best of me." He waited for Bren to tell him it was all right, that it was understandable under the circumstance, but he got nothing but a slight nod.

Stepping out of the study, he ushered Bren toward the front door and called down the corridor, asking his wife to make up the guest room. "Stephen's staying the night," he said and opened the door for them to leave.

In the dining room, Elizabeth and Heather exchanged a glance that said more than either of them would ever be able to put into words. Thomas Windfield was an enigma, a man without convention, and neither his wife nor his daughter believed that they or anyone could truly comprehend him. He'd always been an unpredictable man, but he'd always stood firm on his anti-American issue and had always flown off into a rage whenever anyone touched that precious hunk of metal that he generally kept locked up in his desk. Yet here he was inviting this stranger to spend the night.

The August sun painted the hills green, yellow, and purple. They shared an odd kinship, one that they couldn't explain to anyone, nor fully comprehend themselves. Strolling through the countryside, Bren told of how he'd received the will, how he found the house in shambles, how he tore down the fence and elicited the hatred of the entire village. He told of his finding the diary hidden away in the secret basement, then journeying through the mirror three separate times.

"So there I sat in your basement, like a total idiot, with no idea how to return to the future."

Thomas laughed heartily. He was a handsome man when he laughed, with a broad smile and bright eyes. "I thought you said you read my diary."

"I did. I read exactly enough to get me in trouble."

Thomas had been spared the anxiety of such errors by having the key explained to him when he first received it. He took the passages in and out of time so much for granted now that it sounded inconceivable that one in possession of the key wouldn't understand how it worked.

"That's not a toy you have there, lad. You could get yourself killed popping around in time so haphazardly."

"How's that?"

Thomas grinned. He enjoyed the curiosity and his ability to prolong it. "In time," he replied. "In time, I'll tell you everything." Stopping, he took in a long breath of the warm country air. They'd walked from the stables to the slope of the hill, just below where Bren had first met Heather. They turned and faced the English moors, covered in lavender and yellow. Far to their left, a slight haze hung over the more boggy areas.

"Why'd I give so much to a total stranger?" A gentle breeze brushed Thomas's face and fluttered his hair.

"You don't wanna know."

"If I didn't, I wouldn't've asked." There was a firmness in his voice, and Bren could see that Mr. Windfield was accustomed to getting what he asked for. Bren could also see that he wasn't going to be the one to disappoint him.

"You asked me to avenge your death," he said and felt guilty for saying it, whether it was the truth or not.

"Why don't I like the sound of that?" He didn't expect an answer to that question, and Bren offered none. "How do I die?"

"It's not very pleasant."

"Death never is."

"I suppose not." Bren looked again at the moors and felt a knot in his stomach for what he was about to say. "You're murdered. Stabbed to death."

"By whom?"

"By—" A picture of himself in the town newspaper flashed in his mind, and the words beneath the picture read: *Windfield's Killer.* Yet he couldn't tell Thomas that he'd summoned his own killer, that he'd petitioned Bren to find himself, to seek revenge for an act that he himself had committed. "Some real ugly guy is all I know. They never do catch him."

"When does this murder take place?"

"I think I've said enough already." Bren spoke with firmness and by the look on Thomas's face, he could see that the man didn't appreciate the tone.

"No, I think you just got started." Thomas turned full face to Bren, and his voice was sharp again. "I don't believe in fate, Stephen. I don't believe history must be maintained and can't be changed. I've traveled back and forth through time enough to know what can and can't be done, and if I can twist time in my favor, you can bet I will. A man doesn't rise to my station in life by sitting back and letting events take their course. Now you answer my question."

"All right," Bren consented. "But after I do, you have to tell me how the key works. Tell me how to get back to my time."

"You have my word as a gentleman."

"You die in four days," said Bren. "In your study."

Thomas rubbed a hand roughly over his face. "You're positive?"

"One hundred percent."

"Would you know this man who killed me if you saw him?"

"Nope." Bren shook his head. "The description of his ugliness came from two guys who claim to have seen him. Now how does the key work?"

"I'll tell you after you save my life."

"But you gave me your word as a gentleman."

"And I'll keep my word as a gentleman," said Thomas. "I gave you my house and a million pounds. Now you're going to earn those gifts. For the next four days you're going to be my guest in my home, and you and I are going to become confidants. You understand me?"

"You're making me your prisoner?"

"No. I'm making you my friend. Consider it an honor." Thomas turned and headed back down the hillside, through the long grass.

Bren sighed, watching the man walk away from him and feeling a mixture of dislike and pity for him. *Let me go home and you'll probably live to see ninety*, Bren wanted to tell him, but of course he couldn't. The man was making a grave error; Bren knew this. The newspapers claimed it, Gretchen claimed it, and Bren felt it in the pit of his stomach. For the second time in two days, he'd had a premonition, and just like the first, this one would prove tragic.

# CHAPTER 26

$\mathcal{T}$he sound of metal clinking together rose up from the side lawn and woke Bren from his sleep. Looking from the window, he saw two men on the grass at the edge of the garden. They each held swords and wore masks as they sparred gracefully, exchanging jabs with their swords.

His sleep had been short and shallow. After Elizabeth had shown him to his room the night before, he'd pulled a wooden chair over to the window where he sat for nearly two hours staring down at the dark garden. When he felt sure that everyone else was asleep, he crept out of his bedroom, through the hall and down the stairs into the entryway. From there, he entered the study. Even with the door closed behind him, he didn't dare turn on the light. Working only by the light of the moon coming through the small window behind the desk, he scanned the books lining the many shelves in the room. He tried the desk drawers: all locked. Somewhere in this house sat the diary of Thomas Windfield, and somewhere within its pages was a passage telling him how to get home. But for now, he was stuck.

He came out the back door of the house and spotted Heather and Justin sitting on one of the stone benches at the edge of the garden watching the two men spar. Heather had been the one who had extended the initial invitation to him, but she didn't look overly pleased that he was still here.

"What've we got going here?" He stopped beside the bench.

"It's called fencing," said Justin.

"Is that what that is? I always thought this was boxing. I get those two confused."

Justin sneered at him.

"Who are they?"

"Thomas's the one with graying hair," said Justin.

"Quit calling him 'Thomas.'" Heather slapped at his arm. She was wearing a pair of black shorts and her tanned legs were crossed in front of her, and much to Bren's dismay, they were very attractive.

"And who's the other one?" Bren watched the slashing swords in the foreground.

"That's Heather's lover," said Justin.

"Mother told you not to talk like that!" She slapped his arm again.

"She's not *my* mother."

"She is now."

Justin spit on the grass and wiped his lips defiantly. He was a good-looking boy with an ugly chip on his shoulder, and from what Bren could see, the boy had accurately pegged this family as nothing but trouble. He walked off through the garden and kicked the heads off two flowers.

"He's adopted," Heather said.

"Ah," Bren replied, as if this had explained everything. He took Justin's seat next to Heather and she scooted away, making no attempt to cover the gesture and every attempt to emphasize it.

The metal clinked. The two men danced back and forth through the grass, grunting and breathing heavily, each trying to out-maneu-ver the other. The older man retreated, then pursued, then retreated again. Seeing his opportunity, the younger man stepped in and took a jab, but Thomas turned aside and slapped the sword from his opponent's hand. Before he could stoop to snatch the weapon from the grass, Thomas placed the point of his sword to the man's chest, declaring his victory.

As her boyfriend bowed with defeat, Heather offered a slow, obligatory applause.

After stripping off his mask, Thomas came over to the bench where Heather and Bren were seated. His face was glistening with sweat, and judging by his heavy breathing and glowing expression, you'd have thought he'd just taken on Goliath and had come out the winner.

"Ever tried any fencing, Stephen?"

"I once tore down a fence."

Thomas laughed, gentleman-like, while his daughter responded with a contemptuous roll of the eyes.

"No, never even held a sword before."

Thomas quickly turned the sword over in his hands and offered the hilt to Bren, who took it and admired it with novelty. He recalled the blurb he'd read in the journal about Thomas teaching him to fence. At the time he'd thought that Mr. Windfield had been unwise to teach Stephen Bradson how to maneuver a sharp object. It felt different now, knowing that *he* was that Stephen Bradson.

"Perhaps I'll have to teach you how to use that thing. See if we can make a fighting man out of the draft dodger." Heather's boyfriend was doing the talking. He came over and stood next to Thomas and removed his mask. The sight of those hazel eyes and that egotistical smile made Bren's skin crawl.

"Earl Tuttle," he said absently, pointing the tip of the sword into the grass.

"You know each other?" asked Heather.

"No. Just repeating the name you told me." Bren stood to shake Earl's hand.

"I don't think I mentioned Earl's name."

"Sure you did. Or perhaps it was Justin. Anyway, it's a pleasure to meet you, Earl."

"See you've met the love of my life." Tuttle grabbed Heather's hand, pulled her to her feet, and put his arm around her. The sight of them together looked as out of place as a priest in a strip club. "Ever seen anything more beautiful?"

Bren shook his head, more to flatter Thomas than either Earl or Heather. The truth was he found a very attractive, a bit conceited perhaps, but still very attractive. As for her being the most beautiful girl he'd ever seen, that's where he'd have to draw the line, since her daughter already held that title. The daughter outclassed her in the charm department as well.

"You're all sweaty." Heather removed Earl's arm from around her back and stepped away from him. "You need a shower."

"I smell like a man." Earl grabbed her hand.

"You smell like an animal. Both of you do." She pulled her hand free and wiped the sweat from it onto her black shorts.

Thomas stood back, taking it all in—not Heather and Earl's exchange, but the way Bren was watching Tuttle. He knew him all right, had most likely met him sometime in the future. Whatever their relationship had been it clearly hadn't been one of friendship.

"Stephen, would you care to run into town with us? Earl and I need to check on a few properties."

"Stephen and I are taking the horses out for a ride," said Heather. "Aren't we, Stephen?"

He looked at Heather, surprised. A moment ago, he'd have sworn the girl hated him. Now she was planning out their afternoon. But he went along with it, confirming her lie with her father by saying they were planning to take the horses up through the hills. Thomas didn't look delighted with this news, but he didn't protest either. He left that up to Earl. Not that he came right out and said that he didn't want her galloping through the hills with the new kid in town. Rather he told her to have fun with the draft dodger and left it at that.

# CHAPTER 27

"You're not only a liar, you're also very bad at it." She knew that neither she nor Justin had mentioned Earl's name, and hearing Bren repeat the lie the second time didn't convince her otherwise. She kicked her horse in the flanks and turned up the hill, through the cotton grass, heather, and gorse. There was something mysterious about this man. Something less ordinary than all the men she'd dated around Lurkdale, Earl Tuttle included. She kept one step ahead as she sat gracefully in the saddle, glancing back periodically to watch Bren bounce awkwardly behind her with his inner thighs rubbing raw against the saddle. He had a pained expression on his face, which pleased her greatly. She brought her horse to a run, wanting to see how Bren would handle a faster pace. Heading up the hill, she checked behind her again and found that Bren had stopped altogether and was merely allowing the horse to graze in a stretch of long grass. That didn't please her at all.

She huffed and galloped the horse down to him. Her hair bounced behind her. She had the expression of a mother who had told her son not to play in the street, but had found him there despite her warning.

"I see you're no horseman either." She walked her horse up beside his.

"My horse was tired."

"Is that right?"

"Yeah. He told me so himself."

"He's a she," said Heather. "And it looks to me as though she's in charge here rather than you." She watched Bren's horse pull up a clump of long grass. "If we wanted her to rest and eat, we could have left her in the stable. You've got to show these animals who's boss or they'll tread all over you." Her horse bent its face toward the grass and she pulled back sharply on the reins, and then gave Bren a nod, letting him know that she'd just demonstrated to him how it was done.

"I'll keep that in mind next time I seek dominion over the animal kingdom."

"You wear those clothes much longer, you're going to smell like a member of the animal kingdom. Oh, I forgot, someone stole your clothes, didn't they?" Her tone was condescending and sarcastic.

"That's right, they did," Bren said. "I considered putting on one of your blouses this morning, but I thought I should probably ask your permission first."

"Ha, ha," she droned and patted her horse on the neck. "So what happened between you and my father?"

"Nothing. Your father's a nice man."

"He can be. But I've never seen him take a liking to anyone like he did you."

"What about Earl? Surely your father took an instant liking to him. But then who wouldn't?"

"What was your last job, comedian? No wonder you're out of work." She yanked on the reins and brought her horse's head around until it faced downhill. "No one takes a liking to Earl right away."

"Not even you?" Bren walked his horse up beside hers as they descended the slope.

"Earl's okay. He irritates my father. I kind of enjoy that."

"Sounds like a solid relationship."

She grinned slightly. To their right, the roof of Windfield Manor peered out beyond the green hill.

"You have a girlfriend?"

"Yeah."

"Sure you do."

"I *do*," Bren insisted. "Very beautiful girl. You'd probably hate her."

"Then why isn't she here with you?"

"I left rather abruptly."

"Then it's true about you dodging the draft?"

"No. It's complicated."

Heather grinned. She pulled her horse up close to his and leaned toward him seductively. "You get her pregnant?"

"No! Nothing like that."

"Just checking. I hear American men have active hormones."

"All men have active hormones."

"And what do you do about them?"

"I control them," said Bren.

"Sure you do."

"I do. I'm practically a saint. You ever heard of Saint Stephen? Well that's me. Saint of the controlled hormones."

"Why control them?" she asked.

This was a definite come on, and it made Bren blush. She was lovely, no doubt about that, but she also happened to be the mother of his girlfriend, which was a recipe for trouble. This didn't seem like the same woman who had scolded him and thrown him out of her house in Scarborough.

"Could we change the subject?" Bren adjusted his weight in the saddle. His inner thighs were beginning to cramp.

"Why? Does this subject *bother* you?"

"Yes, it *bothers* me."

"Good." Heather brushed at nothing on her breasts and raised her eyes to make sure he was watching. He was. She grinned at him to let him know that she knew his thoughts. He was handsome and mysterious, but he desired her just like all the others.

"So tell me, what were you doing with my father's key?"

"It wasn't his. They just look alike."

"What's it go to?"

"You don't know?"

"Of course I know," she lied, and lied poorly. "I was just che—" She stopped herself, seeing that Bren wasn't buying her story. "Okay, so I don't know," she confessed. "It's Dad's big secret. One of them anyway."

"He has others?"

"Plenty. He's an enigma."

"Why do you say that?"

"I've lived with the man my whole life and he's still a total stranger to me. One-hundred percent unpredictable. For example, my brother, Justin." Her tone suggested that she'd just explained everything, that Bren should now understand completely the enigmatic quality of her father.

"And this makes your father an enigma?"

"It does when he leaves on a business trip and comes home with a son." She watched Bren nod with understanding. "He never explained himself either. Just returned home a few months ago and said, 'you now have a brother.' That, my friend, makes him an enigma." She looked out across the field. "So what's the key to?"

"It'd probably be better if your father told you about it. It's a man thing."

"Then what would you know about it?" she said.

"Oooh! One point for the spoiled little rich girl." Bren licked his finger and sketched a mark in the air.

"I'm not spoiled."

"Sure you are. I bet you've gotten everything you've asked for your entire life. If you were ever left to fend for yourself, I doubt you could even make a bowl of cold cereal."

"I bet there's a lot of things this little spoiled girl could do that you couldn't."

"Name one."

She gazed out across the lavender field, to the white stables resting at the short slope that descended from the garden behind the house. "I bet I could beat you back to the stables."

"I've never raced a horse before."

"I don't want to hear your excuses." She tucked her hair behind her ears before letting out a shout and kicking at the horse's flanks.

She'd already covered ten yards before Bren reacted by digging his own heels into the sides of his horse. As it bolted forward, he came up out of the saddle a good five inches and slammed back down with enough force to make him think he'd just crippled his entire posterity. Out in front of him, he could barely see Heather through the cloud of dust being stirred up by her horse's hooves. She'd pulled ahead another twenty yards. Steering his horse to the right to avoid breathing in any more of her dust, Bren couldn't help but admire how graceful Heather looked in the saddle. She moved in rhythm with the horse. Her bare legs were firm. He torso was pitched forward. And her long hair streamed out behind her. Compared to his own bounce-and-grimace approach to horseback riding, she looked like a pro jockey.

By the time Bren arrived at the stables, Heather had already dismounted and was tying the reins to a post.

"Oh I'm such a little pampered girl; I can't do anything by myself," she mocked as Bren walked his horse up beside hers and spit out a mouthful of dust. "I wish I were a strong man like you who's so good at everything. In fact I'll bet you can even make cold cereal by yourself, can't you, Stephen?"

"Yeah, yeah, yeah." He dismounted and tried to stretch the cramp out of his leg. "So you're good at one thing. Bet I could chop down a tree and saw it up into lumber faster than you."

"Now there's a skill I've always wished I had." She took his horse and tied it to the post for him. "What *are* you good at, Stephen? I already know you can't ride or fence or talk about sex."

"Talking was never my strong suit."

"Now that sounds like an invitation."

"It's not." He combed his wind-blown hair back with his fingers. "You've now met the one man on this planet who doesn't wanna sleep with you."

"Ooo that hurts." She held her hands against her breasts and laughed as she walked off up the steps to the garden.

He hated himself for it, but he couldn't help admiring her as she went. She had a gorgeous pair of legs, thin and firm. And by the looks of the back of her black shorts, he suspected her legs weren't her only good features. He climbed the stairs to the edge of the gazebo and watched Heather weave the path through the garden and go in the back door. She appeared at the kitchen window, where she filled a glass of water from the sink and drank it slowly. Dipping her fingers beneath the tap, she ran them over her hot neck and down the vee of her shirt as she smiled out at Bren.

"Stephen." Justin was cradling a soccer ball under one arm and gestured Bren over. Bren hadn't even noticed Gretchen Wicks kneeling among the flowers until he passed the hedge she was crouched behind. Her black hair was a sharp contrast to the colorful flowers that surrounded her. Even when she spoke, she kept her eyes to the ground, exposing nothing but the weedy hair that fell over her neck and shoulders.

"Away you scoundrel of hell; back from where the devil brung ya."

Bren paused and looked down at her. "Did you say something?"

"Just clearing me throat." She looked up and demonstrated before turning her face back to her weeding.

"That's what I thought." He went to Justin, who was leaning against one of the black lamps that lined the garden paths. He'd witnessed the interaction between Bren and Gretchen but had heard nothing of what they'd said. He was only thirteen years old, but that was old enough to know when things were out of kilter and that there was definitely something odd about Gretchen Wicks. The Windfields gave him grief. But Gretchen gave him the creeps.

"You have any cigarettes?" he asked.

"How old are you? Twelve?"

"Thirteen."

"You shouldn't be smoking."

"Who're you, me father?"

"Not that I know of."

"Oh, that's funny." Justin bounced his soccer ball once on the flag-stone walkway and stuffed it under his arm again. "I wouldn't have taken you for the type to come preaching at me."

"You don't like it here much, do you?" said Bren.

"You figure that out all by yourself?"

"Looks like you've got it pretty good to me."

"What would you know? This place reeks. And Elizabeth and Heather hate you as much as they hate me."

"I'm used to people hating me. Back where I came from the entire village hated me. They used to throw tomatoes at me and dump toilet water on me, and I'm not talking about the perfume either."

"Ah, you're just trying to make me feel good."

"Telling you that people dumped toilet water on me makes you feel good?" Bren said in mock contempt. "Wow, what a sadistic sod."

Justin smiled and he was a handsome boy. He'd been raised in Leeds by a single mother, whose factory job had never provided more than the bear necessities. He used to dream of the very things he now had; however, now he'd gladly trade it all if he could just have his mother back.

Heather still stood at the kitchen window, watching Bren and Justin converse. The fact that Bren hadn't followed her in irritated her slightly, but it also excited her. He was more of a challenge than most men. Average men were so predictable. She never let them have their way with her, not most of them anyway. She only led them to believe she would be an easy score. Once she was sure they'd fallen for her, she quickly lost interest and was on to her next mark.

Her mother entered the kitchen behind her and came up to the window.

"Why do you suppose Dad's letting him stay?" asked Heather.

Elizabeth frowned. Until Thomas acquired Justin on his business trip down South, she'd considered herself a complacent lady. Now she found herself frequently agitated, resenting the boy she was forced to raise and resenting her husband for bringing him. "Who can tell with your father?" she answered. "Maybe he plans on adopting him."

Heather frowned in response.

"You invited him in," Elizabeth reminded her.

"I only invited him because I figured Dad would disapprove."

"And you think your father didn't figure that out?" Elizabeth removed several plates from the dish drainer beside the sink and began putting them into a cupboard.

"What are you saying, that Father invited Stephen to stay just to prove I couldn't get the upper hand?"

"I wouldn't put it past him."

"And he thinks *I'm* devious." Heather bit lightly at her bottom lip. "Well this one's going to backfire on him, 'cause I think Stephen's kind of cute."

"What about Earl?"

"What about him?" Heather swallowed the last of her water, set her glass on the counter, and walked down the corridor, swaying her brown hair and narrow hips behind her.

# CHAPTER 28

Thomas and Bren stood before the living room mirror, looking in at their reflections as piano music flowed out from the conservatory, up through the corridor and into the living room. The song was "Moonlight Sonata."

"Heather's really quite good." Bren tilted an ear to the music.

"Indeed." The father nodded. "And she wants you to know it."

Bren smiled, realizing how well the father knew the daughter, and wondering if the daughter were so acute. He'd done his best to avoid her all afternoon while he waited for Thomas and Earl to return from town. As much as he disliked Earl Tuttle, he was happy to have him in the house, keeping tabs on his girlfriend. She'd made an overenthusiastic show of affection when Earl first returned, hugging her arms around him and giving him a long kiss on the lips, obviously intended to make Bren jealous. Bren had cringed at the sight. Seeing the two of them kiss was about as appealing as watching a choking fly feasting on a dead rodent's wound, as Lug would have put it. Yet what bothered Bren most was that he actually did feel jealous. That I'm-the-best-in-the-world-and-you-can't-have-me attitude of hers had a way of getting down under his skin and making him yearn.

"This key has made me a wealthy man." Thomas was holding the key that he'd willed to Bren.

"I don't see how," said Bren. "Now, if you could go ahead in the future, that might be useful. But what can the past teach you that everyone else doesn't already know?"

"It's not what the past can teach *me*; it's what *I* can teach the past." Thomas grinned. He could see that Bren hadn't yet considered the advantages of time travel, even if it did only allow him to review recent history. "Use your imagination a little," Thomas prodded. "I know plenty of things that ten years ago I didn't know."

"You're saying you go back and talk to yourself?" Bren smiled at the thought of it. "Can that be done?"

"Why not? I'm alive now. I was alive then. Why can't I go back and speak to myself? Feed myself knowledge? Tell me what to do, what not to do?" Thomas chuckled at the pure shock he saw on Bren's face. "Sounds absurd, doesn't it—me going through the mirror to talk to myself? But it *can* be done. Can and has been done—many, many times. A little investment tip here, real estate advice there. I'm my own fortuneteller, Stephen. And I'm right one-hundred percent of the time." Thomas tossed the key into the air over his shoulder, spun on his heel and caught it again with a childish laugh. "There's a fortune in there, my lad. And this key is the only way in."

As the words were falling from Thomas's lips, Earl Tuttle rounded the corner. His ears perked to the word "fortune," and he caught the glint of the key landing in Thomas's hand. He'd seen the key before and had had long speculative discussions with Heather as to what it went to. His suspicions had always bent toward it opening a secret door in the library where Thomas kept an inexhaustible cache of jewels, heirlooms, and money. His theory on what lay hidden didn't change; however, the location did.

"Thomas." Earl pretended he'd neither heard the comment about fortune nor seen the key. "I was wondering if you were up for a little fencing."

"Indeed." Thomas wrapped his finger around the key to conceal it, though he suspected Earl had already noticed it. "How about you, Stephen? You game?"

"Why not."

"Grab three swords and masks," he said to Earl. "We'll give Stephen here his first lesson at a true gentleman's sport."

Earl smiled and slapped his hand on Bren's shoulder. He cherished the chance to show his skills to anyone who hadn't already been bored with his talent. Showing up someone as unsophisticated as Stephen Bradson would be even more delightful. Bren followed Thomas to the door while Earl lingered at the mirror, combing his fingers through his hair. His eyes only left his own face long enough to spot Thomas casually passing the key to Bren. He didn't like the sight of that one bit. He stepped out into the entryway and retrieved the swords and masks from a closet beside the mahogany stairs. Following the two men down the corridor toward the kitchen, he stepped within the corridor that led down to the south wing where Heather still sat at the grand piano.

"We'll be in the yard fencing, luv, if you need me!" Earl's voice echoed through the corridor. When he stepped back around the corner, he found Thomas and Bren waiting for him just inside the kitchen doorway. He nudged Bren with his elbow and gave him a wink. "So, Stephen, did Heather talk you into a race while you were out riding?"

"As a matter of fact she did."

Thomas let out a hearty burst of laughter as they stepped out the kitchen door into the pale sunlight falling over the garden.

"Why's that funny?"

"Heather does that to everyone," said Thomas.

"Well she's good."

"The horse is good." Thomas followed the flagstones at the top of the garden that led around to the side lawn. "She, of course, had you riding Gypsy, and I wager I could run faster than *that* horse."

"Figures," said Bren.

"She's pulled that one over on the best of them, lad."

Earl paused beneath the shady branches of an elm and laid the swords and masks on the grass. "She's a con." He winked at Thomas. "But the kind of con you don't mind beating ya, eh matey?" He slapped his hand on Bren's shoulder and left it there as if they were old pals.

Thomas grabbed a sword and handed it to Bren, then took another for himself. "Let me show you how it's done." Lifting his left hand for balance, he demonstrated the proper stance. Bren imitated. Earl held the third sword and leaned against the trunk of the tree as he watched Thomas lead the American down the stretch of lawn toward the front of the house. Both men faced the same direction and looked more as though they were practicing dance than a routine utilized in war. They'd gone all the way to the edge of the house and had just started back when Heather yelled from the back door, informing Thomas that he had a telephone call.

"Go ahead and start without me." Thomas jabbed the point of his sword into the grass beside the wall that was covered with ivy. "I'll be back shortly."

Thomas jogged around the corner, and Earl Tuttle took his place on the grass. He had that sparkle in his eye, the same one Bren had seen thirty year in the future whenever the stout mayor knew he had the upper hand. Earl was studying him, watching the way he moved, the way he held the sword. He liked his odds. The newcomer looked strong and agile, but when it came to fencing, he was a mere child.

"Who exactly are you?" Tuttle could see the outline of the key in Bren's front pocket, and it made him angry.

"Stephen Bradson."

"That's not what I meant." Earl slid the flat side of the sword's blade along his fingers. "Why'd Thomas give you his key?"

Bren grinned. He could see that Earl was taking this personally, like Thomas had betrayed him somehow by sharing a secret with the newcomer that he'd kept secret from everyone else. "He likes me," said Bren.

Tuttle returned to the shade of the tree and picked up two of masks and tossed one at Bren, who snatched it before it slapped against his face.

"Put it on."

"Thanks but I think I'll wait for Mr. Windfield."

"Take it from me, mate, Thomas is a kind old gent, but you're not going to learn much fencing from him."

"As I recall, he beat you this morning."

"Just between you and me, Stephen, I let the old fellow win." Tuttle came insolently through the grass and paused a foot in front of Bren. "It keeps the relationship strong. Can't have the future father-in-law knowing you're better than him, now can ya?"

"Why, of course not." Bren rubbed a hand along the mesh face of the mask. "After all, if he doesn't like you, he may stop giving you investment tips, right?"

Tuttle's jaw tightened at the accusation. "If anyone's taking hand-outs around here, I'd say it's you." He slipped his mask over his face, took a few steps back and sliced the air with his sword. "I just humor Thomas with the investment deals. He used to be good. He could outguess the best of 'em. But that was years ago. Lately he loses more than he makes." He sliced the air again. "Now put on your mask. Let me show you a real man at work."

"Gee, I can't think of anything I rather see, Earl, but if it's all the same to you, I believe I'll still wait for Thomas."

"Don't worry, I'll take it easy on you. This is only practice after all, now isn't it?"

Bren stared hard at Earl Tuttle for a moment. He trusted him about as much as a man standing on the gallows trusts the hangman, but he pulled the mask down over his face anyway.

Tightening his grip around the sword's hilt, Earl stretched his back, and then danced back and forth, jabbing now and again. He glared at Bren through the mesh of his mask and had to smile at how inept the American was at handling his sword.

"Ready?" asked Tuttle.

"I guess."

Tuttle wasted no time. He moved in quickly and lashed out at Bren's chest. The sword came up instinctively and batted Tuttle's sword away. The metal clinked and Bren stumbled clumsily backward through the grass. The jabs came consecutively. First to the right, then the left, then up the middle, and Bren could do nothing but continue wielding and backing away.

"Hold on a minute!"

Tuttle paid no heed. In fact, he increased the onslaught. He had the stranger cowering away from him like a wimpy little mouse, and he wasn't about to let an opportunity like this slip away without milking every drop of pleasure out of it.

The blade raked Bren's mask, and he jerked back so hard that he nearly came off his feet. Tuttle couldn't keep from laughing. He'd never seen such a sissy reaction from a man.

"This ain't teaching me a thing, you stupid bastard!"

Tuttle's face went sober. He slapped his sword across Bren's arm for the obscenity. Today's lesson had become one on gentlemanship. Something this American obviously knew nothing about. He lowered his sword and shook a finger at Bren before bowing and removing his mask.

"What the hell was that all about?" Bren shouted, angrily ripping his mask away. He threw down his mask and sword and charged forward with his fists clenched, but a single slice in the air from Tuttle's sword stopped him cold.

"Uh, uh," said Earl Tuttle. "Always keep your temper. That's your first lesson in warfare." Tuttle remained calm and poised.

"You're an asshole! And if I ever want a lesson on how to be an asshole, I'll come to you! But you definitely don't know how to teach fencing!"

"Au contraire. I just taught you a very valuable lesson: if you're always retreating, you can never win."

"Don't flatter yourself." Bren's muscles were tight. Sweat beaded across his red face. He wanted nothing better than to rake his knuckles across Earl Tuttle's thick lips, but instead he padded off along the flagstones toward the back door.

"Stephen," Earl called out gently. "I don't want you hanging around Heather. She's much too well-bred for you." He stuck the blade of his sword into the ground and offered Bren a gentleman's nod.

Bren offered him his middle finger in return and went through the door into the kitchen. About halfway down the corridor, Heather emerged from the dining room. She smiled coyly, but Bren passed without comment. He continued on into the entryway and up the stairs while Heather watched.

The back door opened and closed, and she went in and found Earl standing at the sink helping himself to a glass of water.

"What's the matter with Stephen?"

Earl splashed a little water on his face and waved away the heat. "If he expects to play with the big boys, he's going to have to start acting like a man." He leaned back against the counter, satisfied with himself as a master teacher.

With the sun painting a red banner across the sky as it fell over the horizon, Bren stepped out the back door and stretched his arms above his head. Birds clamored in the darkening trees. Several butterflies still drifted above the flowers. Yet all Bren noticed was Gretchen Wicks sitting on one of the benches near the fountain beneath the dying light. She looked up at him as if she'd been waiting for him and was relieved that he'd finally come. She stood, and there was no mistaking that this was an invitation for Bren to come talk.

The last thing he wanted right now was to sit down with the village witch and have her confirm his murderous destiny, but he came down the path to her anyway. She was only forty-two, not yet so old and wrinkled, but God had not blessed this woman with beauty, nor hygiene.

"Evening." He wondered if she had sensed Thomas's upcoming death, just as in the future she'd predicted every ailment to befall Lurkdale.

"Why've you come?"

"Just came out to go for a walk. Get a breath of air."

She scowled. "There's something not right about you."

"I could say the same of you, you know?" Bren grinned, but Gretchen didn't share his humor. Instead, she glowered, with her twisted mind thinking twisted thoughts. Bren's whole being felt foreign to her. In her forty-two years of life, she'd encountered some odd folks whose very presence had given her the chills, but she'd never sensed anything so alien as Bren Stevens, a.k.a. Stephen Bradson.

"I see the way you look at me." She parted her lips and the yellow, twisted enamel shone dully in the light. "Like you know me. Do you?"

Bren shook his head. "Don't know you at all."

He wondered if she could tell he was lying.

She could.

Her fingers were black with soil, and in those fingers, she held a wilting weed. She twisted at it and tore off its fragile leaves. "What is it you think you've come to do?"

Bren shrugged as if he didn't understand.

She held up the weed and smelled it like a flower. "Life's so fragile, isn't it? It's everywhere, springing to life one minute, dying the next. We all try to do our part, but in the end, we change nothing. Life simply must be." She smiled her yellow smile as if she'd passed on great knowledge to the young American, who felt he understood but didn't like the words.

"I don't know what you're talking about."

"You know." She nodded. "You know more than is allowed to know. And your knowledge isn't welcome."

"And what about you? You also know more than's allowed. What gives *you* the right to interfere?"

"My knowledge is a curse—a curse I was born with. I can't escape it. You can. So take yourself away from here. Go back to wherever it is you came from."

"Am I the one?" he asked, wondering if it was indeed his destiny to kill Mr. Windfield.

She nodded ambivalently.

"Is that a yes?"

"Go home."

"Then I'm not the one?" Bren felt a shiver run the length of his spine, feeling that both his and Gretchen's words were merely for show and that the real conversation was going on clairvoyantly.

"There's nothing more you can do here."

"I say you're wrong. There's plenty I can do. Plenty I *will* do."

"And in doing, you will accomplish nothing."

"What's your part in this?" His question implied her guilt, implied that her ugly hands would hold the blade that would stop Thomas Windfield's life.

"I'm merely an observer of life. No more."

"Then what good are you?"

She gazed long at Bren, thinking, then turned and walked around the curve of the fountain where she bent and grabbed a spade and a handful of weeds that she'd left there before waiting on the bench for Bren's appearance. She swept the side of one hand over the black soil that she'd recently cleared of weeds so that flowers could grow. She smiled briefly at the work she'd done; then her dried lips fell closed. She glanced away from the soil, up at Bren, who was now reentering the back door of the manor. The most peculiar impression she'd ever experienced swept over her.

This man was going to kill another man.

Yet that thought wasn't the peculiar one. It was the time that puzzled her. It would happen in three days; she felt it strongly. Yet another part of her sensed that it was long, long away. A lifetime.

# CHAPTER 29

The following day was Sunday, and the Windfields were church-going people. At least Elizabeth was, which meant the whole family went. Bren wasn't any more keen on the idea than Justin, but he dressed in some of Thomas's clothes and went with them, as did Earl Tuttle. Dressed in a double-breasted suit, he showed up outside Windfield Manor in his Volkswagen Beetle and took Heather into town with him. He wasn't necessarily a religious man, but he enjoyed the social aspects of it, making small talk and discussing politics. By the time Bren and the Windfields arrived, Earl was already making his rounds through the chapel, looking like he was out campaigning for mayor. For someone with all the charm of a goat, he appeared to be fairly popular.

When it was time for the service to begin, Bren took a seat with Justin and the boy's new parents, while Heather and Earl sat a row up from them and over to the right. Throughout most of the sermon, Earl gnawed at his fingernails, thinking about how Thomas had handed the key over to Stephen Bradson, a man he hardly even knew. He worked himself into a good anger over that. The American hadn't even been there three full days, yet somehow he'd already weaseled himself into the family fortune.

Halfway through the service, Bren looked over and caught Heather staring at him. Even when his eyes met hers, she didn't look away—or even so much as blink. She just kept looking, not caring who else saw her gaze. Bren felt a fluttering in his stomach, the kind most men get when a beautiful woman seduces them with her eyes and refuses to look away. He grinned. She didn't. She just batted those long lashes of hers over her brown eyes. The thoughts that crept into his mind weren't fit for church. In fact, they weren't fit for him at all, being how he was in love with Heather's daughter. Yet he didn't look away, not until he saw Earl glance at Heather, and then at him.

Earl gave a little nod and a smile, but it was clear that he was far from happy. He put his arm around her and gave her a kiss on the forehead, then looked once more at Bren. He felt sick inside. Poisoned. It was bad enough that Thomas had given the man his key, but to have Heather acting like a schoolgirl with a crush on the new boy in town was more than he could stomach. But he kept his cool. No use making a scene. Not here in front of everybody.

After church, Earl walked outside with the family and watched as Thomas introduced Stephen Bradson around like he was some sort of long lost relative who would someday inherit the throne. The long-haired coward. Came to England to dodge the draft and now he was being treated like royalty. Earl could feel the hatred festering inside of him. One more round with the swords and he'd show him who was truly king.

He couldn't stand the sight of it anymore. "Come. Let me drive you home." He grabbed Heather by the hand.

"That's okay. Why don't you go home and change. I'll ride with my father."

"No. You ride with me." There was a note of hostility in Earl's voice. No one around appeared to notice, other than Bren. He'd been chatting with the minister and had now turned toward Heather, not sure whether or not it was appropriate to butt into their quarrel. Earl gave him a sharp stare and motioned toward Thomas, who was walking toward the car. What he wanted was for Bren to go with

Thomas and butt out of his affair, but clearly Bren was too thick headed to understand the gesture, for he remained watching them, until Heather nodded that it was okay for him to leave. She didn't want to make a scene in front of all her friends, so she allowed Earl to take her by the hand and escort her to his car. She felt like a child being led by a parent, but she didn't protest, not even after they got in the car and followed her father's Rolls Royce out of town. She sat quietly next to Earl, knowing that her silence would make him reevaluate his behavior. But Earl wasn't always the fastest learner.

He drove down the lane to Windfield Manor and watched the family enter the house while Bren stayed out on the front lawn, waiting for Earl and Heather to pull up and get out of the car. The man needed to be taught a lesson; Earl could see that now. He'd plainly told the man to say away from Heather, but instead he makes eyes at her in church and waits for her on the lawn. Earl came around the car to open Heather's door for her, but she got out on her own. She wouldn't even let him take her hand and lead her to the door.

"Heather," he said, following her up the walk.

She stopped on the steps and pointed her finger at him. "Don't you ever treat me like a child."

"I don't like the way you've been acting."

"Why don't you go home, Earl?" She went through the door, and Earl followed.

Bren stood there on the lawn and watched the front door close. He wasn't sure if he should go in now or wait outside a while.

Inside, Earl started up the stairs after Heather, and then stopped. His nostrils were flaring and his teeth were gnawing at his bottom lip. One way or another, Stephen Bradson had to go. If he needed a little prodding, then so be it, but Earl had no intention of standing idly by and watching some foreigner steal everything he'd worked for. He opened the closet at the side of the stairs and removed two swords, which he promptly took outside with him. Upon exiting, he found Bren climbing the front steps, unrolling the sleeves of the white shirt.

"Stay out here." Earl snapped the door shut behind him. "Perhaps I can teach you a few lessons." He leered. "In fencing, that is." He held out a sword to Bren.

"I don't feel up to it right now." Bren refused to take the sword.

"How're you ever going to improve if you only practice when you feel up to it? Consistency, my friend, is the key to perfection." He held out the sword again.

Bren gave him a stare and hissed his breath between his teeth in a mocking gesture before walking around him.

"Take it!" Earl demanded and shoved the handle into Bren's stomach. He was going to get a fight out of this man yet.

Bren snatched hold of the sword with a moan. Raising his eyes up coldly to Earl's face, he wrapped his fingers around the hilt. He wanted to take that blade and ram it through Earl Tuttle's fat heart.

But before he could do anything, Earl swung and slapped his sword across Bren's bare forearm and chuckled at the pain that was bright on the flesh. He swung again. Bren shielded it this time.

"See. You're learning," said Earl.

Bren reached for the doorknob and Earl whacked the outstretched hand with his sword, producing a welt just below the knuckles.

Slicing the air several times, Earl forced Bren from the steps and down into the grass. Earl came at him, first with a few casual jabs, then intensifying the blows until he had Bren cowering like a mouse being pursued by a cat.

Intimidation, that was the only thing people like Stephen Bradson responded to.

Metal smashed against metal as Earl carefully manipulated Bren to the side of the mansion, away from peering windows. The family would be upstairs changing their clothes, but it wouldn't be long before someone came back down.

Bren stumbled backwards under the assault, staving off the blade that snapped at him. The metal clanged. All he needed was one good thrust into Earl's thigh and he'd put an end to this assault right now. He backed away, flinching at the sight of the blade whirling at him, yet managed to bat it away. Then he saw his moment. Earl paused just long enough for a breath, but that lull was all Bren needed to make his move. It felt wrong, perhaps even evil, but he felt he had no choice. He stepped in and jabbed his blade with full force, focusing his attention on a spot just below Earl's hipbone.

He hadn't even halfway extended his elbow when he felt the blade slice through the flesh of his forearm. His sword dropped into the grass, and the tip of Earl's sword immediately caught him under the chin and backed him up against the granite wall.

"Can you take a little friendly advice?" Earl panted out the words. "Go home. You're not welcome here anymore."

"I don't think that's yours to say," Bren said boldly, considering his position.

Earl forced a pinhole into Bren's neck and said, "I think it is."

Apparently he'd gotten his point across, because he received no more argument from the American, who stood motionlessly with his eyes wide and his heart pounding.

"You think you're such a big man, making goggly eyes at my girl-friend, playing me for a fool. Well I'm no fool. And I could pop out those eyes of yours with one little flick of the wrist." If he'd thought he could have gotten away with it, he would have done it right there on the spot. Instead, at the sound of the front door slamming, Earl lowered the blade and took a casual stance in front of Bren.

Heather rounded the corner of the house, already changed and adorned in tight jeans and a tan blouse. Seeing that Earl was still hanging around displeased her, but she made no show of it.

"You two at it again?" she said. "Like a couple of young lads with new toys."

"Yeah." Earl cut the air with a quick slice. "Stephen here wanted me to teach him a few lessons. Didn't you, Stephen?"

Bren said nothing, just pinched at the pinhole in his neck as a trail of blood ran from the cut on his arm.

"You're bleeding." Heather took his arm to examine the wound, which only broke through the first few layers of skin. "What happened?" She directed her question at Earl, in an accusatory tone.

"I guess I'm just used to someone with a little quicker reflexes."

She scowled and Earl pretended sorrow by dropping his shoulders and offering a slight shake of the head. Yet, as soon as Heather turned her attention back toward the cut, Earl made puppy eyes at Bren and stuck out his lower lip as if he were going to cry. Had he still been holding his sword, Bren would have taken this opportunity to change history by relieving Lurkdale of one of its future mayors.

"Want me to bandage that for you?" asked Heather.

"No, it's just a scratch. I'll take care of it." Bren applied pressure to the wound and walked off toward the front yard.

"Sorry about that, Stephen," Earl called after him. "I feel terrible about it. I truly do."

The third-story loft was immaculate. A snooker table sat at the center of the room, its colored balls scattered upon green velvet. Thomas, cue stick in hand, calculated his next shot. Bren leaned on a wall, chalking his own cue stick, a bandage on his arm. He was wearing one of Thomas's pullovers, a royal blue one with white collars, and the same dress pants that he'd worn to church. Bren studied the forty-eight-year-old gentleman. He appeared exceptionally calm for a man who knew he was destined to die in two days. Perhaps he wouldn't have been if he'd known his killer was standing in the room with him.

"You still do a lot of investing?" Bren thought of what Earl Tuttle had said about Thomas having lost his knack for fortunes.

"No. Nothing big anyway." He jetted his stick forward, and a red ball rolled off into a pocket. "I tell everyone that I already have more money than a man can spend in a lifetime—which is true. But—" He set the end of his stick on the floor and gave Bren a serious stare. "I haven't come back to visit myself in some time. I still go back, mind you, but my future-self no longer visits me. I think it's been about ten years since he's come. And I guess we both know why, don't we?"

"Ten year increments," said Bren, referring to how the key propelled its possessor through time ten years with each pass through the mirror.

"That's right. Ten year increments." Thomas nodded. His failure to continue communicating with himself during the past ten years could only mean one thing: some major event was approaching, one that would prevent him from ever visiting his former-self again. A major event called death.

Thomas rounded the table to prepare for another shot while Bren went to the window and gazed down to the garden. It was glowing beneath the light of a full moon and an occasional electric lantern rising along the garden pathways. His eyes followed the path that ended at the gazebo. Heather had forgiven Earl his insensitivity and was now seated with him in a passionate embrace. Bren cringed at the sight.

"What do you think of Earl?" His eyes were still staring out the window.

"Arrogant, superficial—but very motivated. Most of all, I know he makes Heather happy, and that's all that counts."

"But do you like him?"

"I tolerate him. Heather finds pleasure in making me miserable."

Bren had to smile at the father's insight.

"I think the only reason she started dating him is because she knew I didn't like him. So I started being nice to him to see if that would change her opinion of him. Unfortunately, it never did." Thomas cracked the balls again, and again found a pocket for one.

"She's very strong-willed," Bren said.

"Is that the American term for it? Around here we call it spoiled. What she needs is someone to take her over their knee." The father went to the window and looked out, not overly pleased with the view. "But she's always been my little girl. Never could say no to her. By the time I realized how badly she needed a spanking, she was too big to spank."

"Apparently Earl's father never spanked *him* either."

Thomas smiled and went back to his snooker game. "No. I guess not."

"Unfortunately, he's too big to spank, too," said Bren. "Otherwise I'd love to do the honors."

"Wouldn't we all." Thomas chalked his cue stick and shot in another ball. "I noticed you knew his name upon your first introduction. You met him in the future, didn't you?"

"Yes. We didn't get along then either. He's the mayor."

"Well now, isn't that a revelation?" Thomas stood up straight and looked at Bren. "And Heather? Is she a mayor's wife?"

"No."

"Thank God. Miracles do exist after all." The father raised a cue stick to the heavens for a silent hallelujah. "Who does she marry?"

Bren bit at his lip and looked back out into the night, not knowing how to answer, wondering if he should tell this man of the painful life destined for his daughter and of the recurring theme in her life. "Somebody from Scarborough," he answered.

"I take it you've met him? Is he a good man?"

"Yeah. Yes, he is," said Bren. "And they have a beautiful daughter named Natasha."

Bren didn't face Thomas when he spoke his lie. Instead he kept his face toward the window where his words could conceal themselves from this clever man who cared so deeply for his daughter's happiness, a daughter who sat below in the dark, cuddling a man whom she held like a toy to make the other children jealous. Her brown eyes gazed up at the stars, and, in their gazing, noticed Bren watching from a third-floor window. This pleased her. The American desired her. She grinned to herself as she laid her head on Earl's shoulder, knowing it would make watching eyes yearn.

# CHAPTER 30

*T*he grass on the green hillside was wet the next morning when Heather and Bren climbed it together. At first he'd refused her invitation, but Heather was a convincing young lady. All it took was her tying the bottom of her pink shirt into a knot so that her thin waist was exposed and Bren quickly decided that a morning walk in the fresh English air would do him good. Especially after the night he'd had. He'd woken up twice in a cold sweat. The first was accompanied by a dream of him sinking a long knife into Thomas's abdomen. The second was of him doing the same to Earl Tuttle. He much preferred the second.

"I saw you watching me last night," Heather said with pleasure as she strolled a step behind Bren.

He glanced back in confusion.

"In the gazebo. I saw you staring from the game room window."

"So I was looking."

"I thought you had a girlfriend." She moistened her lips as they topped the hill and walked in a sea of flowers all lit with sunlight.

"I do."

"Then why were you spying?"

"I wasn't spying." He turned back and looked down over the house below them. "I just happened to be looking out the window and there you were. That's all. It's not like I was hiding."

She squinted over the roof of the house where the sun was glisten-ing above Lurkdale off in the distance. The blue sky was broken up by occasional puffy clouds.

"You really don't like Earl, do you?"

"What's not to like?" Bren shrugged. "He's warm, gentle, thinks he God. Hell, I love the man."

"You're jealous." She bent and picked a yellow flower, which she put in her hair above her ear.

"Yeah, that must be it," Bren intoned. "I've always had this desire to be the world's biggest ass, and I'll be damned if Earl doesn't have me beat."

"No, I mean you're jealous because you wished it was you down in the gazebo kissing me."

"That's not true."

She stepped seductively close to him. Staring into his eyes, she slid her arms over his shoulders and stroked the back of his neck. She let her mouth fall open slightly in a gesture that indicated that she was preparing for a kiss.

Bren's stomach fluttered.

"Now tell me you don't want me." Her voice was smooth and seductive.

"I don't want you." He tried to sound convincing, but his voice betrayed him.

She leaned closer with her lips nearly touching his. "You sure you don't want me?"

"Yeah." The word was barely audible.

She pressed her lips against his. He pulled back slightly, giving a feeble fight before surrendering. Caressing her hand around his neck, she could feel the beat of his heart. His face flushed red, and all the world went dark for a full half minute. Heather pulled away with a smile.

"Now say it," she said.

"I—" His tongue could find no words.

"That's what I thought." She turned away with her hands clasped together behind her back as she looked to the sky and walked away as if nothing had happened. She was cool, no doubt about it. This girl knew how to work a man and leave him feeling needy and despondent.

He followed after her through the flowers and grass. Neither of them took note of the car emerging from beneath the trees down the lane and disappearing around the front of the house. It was a white 1955 Volkswagen Beetle. Earl's car.

He pulled up next to Thomas's black Rolls Royce and shut off the engine. A sense of confidence swelled up in him in a way that he hadn't felt for the past few days, ever since the arrival of Stephen Bradson. But last night's talk with Heather in the gazebo had changed all that. She'd been warm and affectionate, and when he'd made derogatory remarks about Stephen's swordsmanship, she'd laughed just like the Heather he'd always loved. Things were looking up again. In fact, he knew that this was one of those special days in a young man's life that drew a line between past and future. Today would mark a giant step in his life. Today he would ask Heather to be his wife.

He strutted up the walk, prepared to knock, when Elizabeth called to him from the far corner of the house where she knelt, tending to a small group of flowers. This was Gretchen's job, but on sunny days, Elizabeth often enjoyed wiling away the hours working with nature. She found it meditative.

"Is Heather around?"

"She went for a walk with Stephen." She pointed to the hill, and Earl's eyes followed. His sense of well-being plummeted. He squeezed his hands into fists and bit down on his bottom lip. Heather was near the top of the hill, running childishly through the tall grass, and Bren was chasing behind her. Their laughter and joy was visible even from a distance, and it ate holes in Earl's stomach.

Elizabeth had watched the two ascend the hill but hadn't paid much attention to them since. Now, looking up and witnessing the scene, she actually felt sorry for Earl; something she'd never felt before. Her feelings toward Earl had never been as harsh as those of her husband's, but he still had never been the type of man she foresaw her daughter marrying. Of course neither was Stephen Bradson. Not that Stephen was a bad man. He just had that certain edge to him that bothered her. He reminded her too much of her husband.

"I'll just wait for her if you don't mind." Earl still had his eyes fixed on the hillside. He walked to the back of the house, to the garden, where he sat on a bench making himself more miserable as he watched his future bride play kissing tag with the stranger.

For forty minutes, he waited, sat on the bench thumping his hand against his leg and working himself into a good rage. He pulled a small white box from his front pocket and opened it. The diamonds set in the face of the gold wedding band sparkled in the sunlight. He'd purchased it just this morning. At nine o'clock, when Dean Myrick unlocked the front door of his jewelry shop, he'd found Earl Tuttle leaning against the bonnet of his Volkswagen beetle. This was a man with a mission and it had taken him just under fifteen minutes to decide upon a ring. This day was going to be so perfect.

He snapped the lid shut and returned his gaze to the hill. Twice he'd warned the man to stay away from his girl and leave Lurkdale, but here he was, frolicking across the hillside like a little girl. Apparently cutting his arm and holding a sword to his throat wasn't enough to convince him that this was a serious matter. Very well then. Next time he'd surely get the point—every inch of it.

Earl watched as the two descended the hill and strolled along the garden pathways. Composed, he sat back listening to their laughter, which grated his spine and made him want to punch somebody. But he didn't let it show, except for the subtle gritting of his teeth.

"Where have you two been?" Stuffing the white box back into his pocket, he stood and forced a smile.

"We went for a walk." Heather got a sadistic pleasure from Earl's pain.

"Maybe next time you can let me know so I don't have to sit here waiting." His congenial tone was forced and unconvincing.

"You don't own me, Earl."

"No, of course not." His chin trembled lightly as he strained to keep his composure. "I was just concerned is all."

He offered Bren a glance, the kind that communicated that he had some personal issues that he wished to discuss with his girl in private and, therefore, wanted Bren to excuse himself. It wasn't that Bren didn't catch the meaning of that glance. It was just that after being prodded around by the point of the sword, he didn't have any respect for Earl's wishes. For this reason, he didn't budge. He stood, straight-faced, watching Earl's face redden as he stared him down.

Heather was enjoying herself, watching the two men fight a silent battle and knowing that she was the cause. She let it go on for a few minutes, and then said, "I'd like to speak with Earl alone, if you don't mind, Stephen."

So he went in the house.

"I was wanting to talk to you." Earl was thumping his hand nervously against his pants pocket, the one containing the white box. "You mind if we sit in the gazebo?"

She didn't look overly enthused, but she went with him. At the back of the garden—beyond the archways, hedges and statues—they sat in relative seclusion. The woven wood of the gazebo painted cross-stitches of light on their faces and accented Earl's solemn countenance. The setting was perfect, just as he'd pictured it last night when he came up with the idea of asking her to marry him today. The mood wasn't quite as romantic, however.

"You seem so serious." Heather was sitting crossways on the bench with her legs creating a barrier between her and Earl so he couldn't scoot any closer.

"It is rather serious." His heart was pounding, and in the back of his mind he heard that still small voice tell him not to go through with it. But to Earl, voices in one's head were only meant for prophets and schizophrenics, so he reached in his pocket and pulled out the tiny box. His hands trembled as he held it before her and slowly opened the lid.

Heather stopped breathing for a moment. The ring was indeed beautiful, despite Earl's haste in buying it. She put a hand to her chest and offered the most ambiguous smile Earl had ever seen. There was no way of knowing if she was pleased or horrified.

"Earl, you shouldn't have," she said, and she meant every word.

"I love you, Heather. I want you to be my wife." Earl's hands were quivering now. Taking the ring from the box, he held it out to her. "Heather—will you marry me?"

Hesitantly, not knowing what else to do, she took the ring and admired it. This was an absolute nightmare. It felt unreal to her, like some dream sequence in a movie where everything becomes hazy and slightly askew.

"This is so sudden," she said.

"We've been together since you were seventeen, nearly two years. I would hardly call that sudden."

"I mean, you just caught me by surprise."

"It's not like we've never talked about it." Earl put a reassuring hand on her knee. He knew she only had a case of cold feet. They'd spoken of marriage many times, and Heather had always led him to believe that when the question was asked, she would happily accept.

"But not recently." Her throat was dry and tight.

"Why? Have your feelings changed recently?"

"It's just a surprise."

"Then?" Earl waited for an answer, but she just sat there in silence. "I'm asking you to marry me, Heather. I want us to be together—always." Her hesitation should have been answer enough, but he pressed on. "This is not a difficult question. It's a simple yes or no."

Again she didn't respond. She couldn't look him in the face. Instead, she kept her eyes on the ring, hoping he would just walk away and save her the grief of giving him an answer.

"Heather?" he pursued.

"No," she replied and forced herself to look at him. Her face was pale. She could hardly believe she'd said it.

Earl believed it even less. "What do you mean no? A few weeks ago you were practically begging me to ask you."

"Things have changed," Heather said sadly.

"It's him, isn't it? It's that bloody American!"

"No, Earl, it's you." For the first time in her life, she tried to sympathize, but there was nothing she could say to ease the sting of her rejection. "I don't love you, Earl. I thought I did once, but I don't. I'm sorry."

He snatched the ring away angrily, and she jumped at the sudden aggression.

"You can keep your damn apologies," he chided. "You're a whore."

"What?" she said, hurt.

"You think I don't know what you two've been up to?" He rose to his feet and the gazebo shadows fell sinisterly across his face. "Staring at each other in church, acting like school children up there on the hill. Heaven knows what you do when you two are alone at night in your bedroom."

She stood and slapped his cheek. "Stephen's right! You *are* an asshole!"

"He said that?" He looked at the house as if searching for the stranger. "He's turned you against me. I should've stuck a sword through him when I had the chance."

She reeled with shock, finding it hard to believe that these words had come from Earl Tuttle's mouth. "You're evil. I never want to see you again!" She ran from the gazebo and up through the garden path, with tears welling up in her eyes.

Earl didn't bother to pursue. He just stood at the gazebo door and let his hate swell. His left cheek was bright pink from where she had slapped him. With a shaking hand, he put the ring back in the box, closed the lid and returned it to his front pocket.

Heather burst through the kitchen with tears now streaming down her cheeks. She ran the length of the corridor, past the study and up the stairs. She had entertained thoughts of ending her relationship with Earl, but had never dreamed that it could end so badly. She loathed him more than she ever thought possible.

Bren stepped from the study door and looked to the stairs, but all he heard were Heather's footsteps running down the hall above him. He'd been sitting in front of the desk, waiting for Thomas, when Heather had hurried passed. Though she'd gone by too quickly for him to see her tears, he could tell that something was sorely wrong. After climbing the stairs, he traversed the hall and stood for a moment in front of Heather's closed door. He could hear the strained sound of her sobbing. Without knocking he turned the knob and pushed the door open, where he found Heather lying face down on her pillow, weeping. Gently, he closed the door and sat on the bed beside her.

"What is it?" He stroked her back.

"It's terrible!" Her voice was muffled by the pillow.

"Did Earl hurt you?"

She looked up and her eyes were red and puffy. "He asked me to marry him."

"No wonder you're crying."

She smiled. "I told him no."

"Well that's good."

"You think so?" She sat up and looked earnestly into Bren's eyes. What she wanted was some indication that he felt for her the same way she felt for him, and to her, his not wanting her to accept a marriage proposal from Earl was a sign of his affection.

"Yes, don't you?" he answered, oblivious to the message she was reading into this.

"Yes, I just wasn't sure how you felt." She hugged her arms around him.

He returned the embrace. The girl obviously needed reassurance after such a harrowing ordeal as being proposed to by Earl Tuttle. Her tears were wet against his cheek. She sniffed back her sorrow and pulled back far enough to gaze upon his face. He was so handsome and kind, so unlike Earl Tuttle. She tugged at his shoulders for him to lie on the bed with her, and Bren knew that he was now in over his head. He knew it was wrong, but that didn't stop him from lying with her, embracing her and kissing her passionately. She felt good in his arms, so soft and titillating. This was a big mistake. The fact was he liked it. She had those beautiful brown eyes, that smooth skin and toned body. Just like her daughter's. The thought got his thinking straight again. He pulled away, but Heather merely moved with him and rolled her body on top of his, rubbing her hand up under his shirt against his firm chest.

"The door's not locked," Bren said with worry.

"Our doors don't have locks," she whispered. "Father forbids them. He doesn't want any hanky-panky going on in his house." Lying beside him now, she smiled as her hand slipped to his belt buckle and pulled it loose. She undid his pants, slipped her hand in and—

He stopped her and sat up quickly. "Listen, your dad—"

"Don't worry. He never comes in without knocking." She pulled at his arm, urging him back down, but he pulled away and got to his feet.

"I'm supposed to be waiting for him in the study right now. He's probably looking for me. I'd better go." He didn't wait for a response. She was much too convincing for him to risk hearing her side of the argument on why he should stay. He went to the door and exited abruptly, leaving Heather sitting on the bed completely confused.

Bren was breathing heavily and shaking his head in disbelief at what a fool he'd become. He leaned against the doorframe and wiped his mouth. His belt was hanging loose and the button and zipper of his pants were wide open. As he did up his fly, the bathroom door opened and Justin stepped out. His blond hair was mussed and his face wry, looking repulsed at the sight of Bren leaning against Heather's door, fastening his pants.

"I was just—Heather was crying and—" Bren stammered, trying desperately to justify his standing outside Heather's door with his pants undone.

"What do I care?" The boy scowled, rounded the corner and headed up the stairs to the game room.

Bren hurried to the end of the hall and down the stairs. He knew Thomas would be in the study waiting for him. Just after Bren had entered the house, leaving Heather and Earl to talk marriage, Thomas had stopped him and informed him that they had business of their own to discuss. The gentleman had left him sitting in the study while he went to the library to retrieve some documents he'd left on one of the tables there.

When Bren entered the study, he indeed found Thomas sitting behind his desk. He was checking some papers he'd written, making sure the wording was just right.

"Where were you?"

Bren wiped his face again to destroy any remaining evidence of what he'd done with the man's daughter.

"Heather was crying and—" Bren paused, haunted by Thomas's wise stare that looked as though he knew what had happened in his daughter's bedroom. "Earl asked her to marry him."

"And?" The father became concerned.

"She said no."

"Smart girl. Takes after her father."

"Yeah." Bren wiped his mouth again and sat down.

Thomas handed a piece of paper over the desk to him, which Bren took and examined. It was blank.

"What's this for?"

"I have a little business to discuss with my lawyer this afternoon. Something about a will, I believe. I'm going to need your home address."

Bren nodded, knowing this day had to come. He took a pen and wrote the name "Stephen," paused, scribbled it out and wrote "Bren Stevens," then continued on with his New Hampshire address. He passed the paper back over the desk to Thomas, who glanced casually at it, then did a double take.

"Bren Stevens?"

"That's my real name."

Thomas narrowed his eyes as an inquiry into Bren's previous deception.

"I made the other name up." Bren leaned back in the wooden chair as he looked across the desk at Thomas's bewildered expression.

"Why? Why would you use another name when you're here thirty years before your time?"

"I—" The truth was he didn't want his real name to appear in the newspaper stating he was Thomas Windfield's killer. But, of course, he couldn't tell him this. "Like I said, I know Earl and Berney in the future. I thought it might be odd, me showing up thirty years later with the same name. As it is, everyone wonders why we look alike. They'd really be confused if we had the same name."

"Smart thinking." Thomas folded the paper and stuffed it into the pocket of his shirt. He opened his desk drawer and removed his mirror key, which looked identical to Bren's, since they were one and the same. Thomas wasn't comfortable with the idea of giving up the key, but he knew he would have to give it to his lawyer, so that it could be sent on to Bren Stevens in thirty years. Otherwise none of this could ever take place. He stood and put the key in his pocket. "That should do it. I need to open a new bank account, too, as I recall. A million pounds, you say. Quite a bundle for someone your age."

Bren followed Thomas out into the entryway. He looked up at the balcony, certain that once Thomas had vanished into Lurkdale, Heather would lure him back to her lair and he would find himself in the same predicament he'd escaped earlier.

"You mind if I come with you?" Bren asked.

"Not at all. There are a couple of shops I've been wanting to take you to."

# CHAPTER 31

$T$he Nook was on Archer Street, tucked away among the many shops lining the cobbled lane. It was one of the few shops in town that specialized in men's clothing, since most stores catered to the female population, who tended to spend more time shopping and more money on clothes. As one of the Nook's regular customers, Thomas took pride in appearances—both his own and those he associated with. It only took him fifteen minutes to pick out two outfits to replace the wardrobe that Bren had brought with him through the mirror.

The new attire made him look dignified, as Thomas put it when they left the store. "Much more suitable for a man about to be willed a fortune."

Bren nodded, feeling neither dignified nor comfortable. He was wearing a white shirt, blue vest and tan trousers. None of these were what brought on the discomfort. What he didn't like was the fact that in the gazebo photograph, which had been taken the day of Thomas's death, he (Bren) had been wearing clothes similar to those he was now wearing and those in the bag he was carrying. He didn't have a clear recollection of the exact shirt and pants, but they were close enough to make him nervous. According to the date printed on the back of the picture, it had been taken tomorrow. August 16, 1964.

"You don't seem too happy with your new clothes," said Thomas.

"They're fine." Bren followed Thomas down the narrow sidewalk, which was bright in the midday sun. "I was just thinking about tomorrow—wondering what will happen if things don't—work out?"

Thomas paused at the corner and waited for the traffic to pass. "Are you worried that I might die or that I might live?" When he turn, he was sporting an impish smirk, one that said he knew too well the predicament he'd put Bren in by not letting him return to the future. "For if I live then what comes of the poor sod who spent all his effort coming back in time to save me? Namely you. This is the question, right?"

Bren didn't answer, but yeah, Thomas had pretty much hit the nail on the head. If Thomas lived, what would become of the will? And, thus, what would become of Bren?

"It would hardly be fair to give you nothing, now would it?" Thomas continued as they crossed through the street. "So I must give you something. But what? Money perhaps? My mansion? No, I'll be needing that, won't I? And I must say, if I'm still alive, I would hate to part with the one thing that has given me all that I have—the key." He patted his pocket. "Yet without the key, you could hardly come back in time and save me. Such a dilemma. What do you suggest?"

Bren shrugged. "You still haven't told me how it works."

"And you still haven't saved my life." Stopping by his car, Thomas opened the door for Bren to put the bags of clothes inside, and shut it again before leading the way through a street that opened onto Moorland Avenue.

"What if I fail? I hate to be a pessimist. But if you die, I'm gonna be stuck here in nineteen-sixty-four."

"Then I guess you'd better make sure I don't die, hadn't you?" Thomas stopped and patted Bren on the shoulder before motioning to the door they'd stopped in front of. A barber shop.

"You getting a haircut?"

"Not me. I've got an appointment with my lawyer, remember?"

Bren had to admit that his hair had gotten shaggy over the past few months and was in need of a trim, but Thomas indicated that he wouldn't be satisfied with a mere trim. He wanted respectability, and in his world that meant a complete view of a man's ears and the back of his neck. Long hair was for women and hoodlums, and by no means should it grace the head of a gentleman. Bren didn't like the idea of it, but he obliged. He sat in the barber chair with his blond hair falling abundantly to the floor while Thomas took care of business down the street. A long mirror hung on the wall in front of Bren so he could watch himself being shorn. The more hair that fell to the floor, the more he resembled the photograph of himself that he'd seen in the Lurkdale Gazette. It was eerie actually, seeing that likeness emerge before him. This was the second time he'd experience that sickening tug at his gut today.

He walked back to Thomas's car and waited. He felt an incredible guilt that he really couldn't associate with anything other than Thomas Windfield's upcoming death, and the fact that all signs pointed at him as the killer. He no longer trusted himself. He wanted the house; he wanted the money; he wanted the relationship that he'd begun with Natasha Chandler. Yet if Thomas lived, all of that would be lost. Thomas was currently off signing all the proper documents at his lawyer's. Now all that was left was for him to die.

Bren sat in the front seat of the Rolls Royce on the passenger side, inspecting his new haircut in the rearview mirror. It was a sight that Thomas would love, but one that Bren found unnerving. The driver's door opened and he glanced over, expecting to see Thomas, but finding Earl Tuttle instead, sliding in behind the wheel. He had a large scowl on his face and a large chip on his shoulder.

"You think you're a big man, don't you, Stephen." His fists were clinched and the veins in his neck were pulsing.

Bren popped open his door, but Earl grabbed his arm and pulled him back down.

"Not so fast, lover boy. I've got a score to settle with you."

"This has nothing to do with me." Bren pulled away.

"It has everything to do with you. I told you to stay away from Heather. But instead you're off turning her against me, calling me names, making her think I'm some sort of fool. You're out of line and you know it." He pointed his finger at Bren's face and was happy to see him flinch. "I try to be your friend and this is how you repay me?"

"The only person out there turning people against you is you, Earl. You open your mouth and people can't help but hate you."

Earl's hand come up quickly, intent on popping lover boy in the mouth, but Bren saw it coming, snatched Earl by the wrist and gave it a hard twist.

"You're not so tough without your sword. You try something like that again and I'll break your fat nose."

"Don't you dare threaten me." Earl pulled his wrist away. "I've worked hard to get in tight with this family. They're my friends. And you, you filthy sod, you've been here a couple days and already you've got it all going to hell. I want you out, and I want the key that Thomas gave you."

"I don't really care what you want."

"Get the hell out of here. You get in my way, I'll go right through you. I mean that literally." Earl glared out the windshield, where he spotted Thomas approaching down the street. He gave Bren one last stare before hopping out and scurrying away.

Thomas had been walking at a leisurely pace, but the sight of Earl brought him hurrying. He stopped beside the car and watched Earl disappear into an alley before leaning his head in through the open door.

"What'd he want?"

"Just wishing me happiness and a long life."

"I'll bet he was." Thomas climbed in and shut the door. He stared a while at the stranger seated beside him, a stranger he'd just willed a fortune and opened a bank account for. Two things that didn't exactly fill him with comfort.

"I'd be careful of him." Bren was still looking at the alley where Earl had gone. "He's top on my list of suspects." In truth, Bren himself was at the top of his list of suspects, but Earl was running a close second.

"Earl's harmless," Thomas reassured.

"I wouldn't bet my life on it."

Thomas cocked his head in thought, started the car, and drove off down the lane.

"He knows about your key. Maybe not how to use it, but he asked me to give it to him." Bren slid a hand in his new trousers and pulled out the key. It was one of those items that he carried with him everywhere he went. It was his ticket home. Losing it would be assuring his permanent stay in 1964.

"I feared he'd overheard us in the living room the other day. I suppose he and Heather have speculated about the thing many times. I see them watching me sometimes, seeing if they can find my hidden treasure—as if there were one."

"Where did you get this thing in the first place?" Bren turned the key over in his fingers.

"Now that there's an interesting story." Thomas looked over with a smirk. "Almost as interesting as the way you came into possession of it." He drove down one street and up another, past cottages and shops, all the while grinning to himself, amused by the story he was about to tell, a story he'd kept bottled inside him for twenty-four years. He stopped the car on Pepperfield Land, across from Coalman's Pub, which didn't look much different than it did last time Bren saw it, thirty years in the future. It was open but empty.

"That there's where it all began." Thomas pointed over to the Tudor style building. "When I was about your age, I was in there with some friends, drinking a bit, telling lies, eyeing the girls, the usual thing." He drove the car slowly along the street and pointed at the sidewalk. "On my way home, I walked down this street here. I became aware that someone was following me. It was dark, a bit foggy, and I was in no condition to fight. Anyway, this dark figure was following me in the fog, so I ran ahead a ways, sure that someone had chosen me as an easy target for a mugging."

He parked by an alley and turned off the car. "I ducked into that alley and hid behind a barrel, certain the man hadn't seen me. How could he have? But before long, here came the footsteps, right down the alley. I was a shivering mess, crouched there in the dark, waiting to die. The figure stopped directly in front of me. He knew right where I was as if he could see in the dark. Or as if someone had tipped him off as to where I was hiding, which turned out to be the case. With nowhere to run, all I could do was plead for him to spare my life.

"And while I was pleading, the man started to laugh, as if he were enjoying himself—which he obviously was. He said, 'You don't think I'd commit suicide, do you?' and stepped forward into the light, where I could see his face. And so help me if it wasn't *me* standing there in the dark, a bit older and looking sharper than I'd ever looked, but the man was me." Thomas's eyes were glistening.

"Are you saying you gave the key to yourself?"

"Indeed I am. As bizarre as it sounds, I was that man. Believe me, I had a hell of a lot more fun years later when I was the older man standing in the alley, scaring the life out of my younger self."

"But—" Bren stared over at the alley, confused by the details. "If you, that is your older self, gave the key to your younger self, how'd your older self return to the future? After all, you no longer had the key."

Thomas grinned. This was the most intelligent question he'd heard out of Bren's mouth yet, and he had no intention of answering it. "When I explain to you how the key works, you'll understand."

"But the key had to come from someplace."

"It would seem so, wouldn't it? It's like the thing just appeared into existence—which of course isn't possible." He shrugged. "I've stayed awake many nights trying to make sense of it. So far I haven't. If you come up with something, please let me know."

Thomas started the car again and drove down the cobblestone roads and out toward the mansion. He watched as Bren sat back and rubbed the key between his fingers, studying it. He knew how he felt—mystified, yet empowered. It was the same way he'd felt when he first received the key. It opened up so many possibilities. Good *and* bad. He'd made a fortune with it, but had alienated himself from his family in the process.

Bren reached his fingers toward the rearview mirror, certain he could reach right through the glass and touch the past. But Thomas snatched his hand away.

"That's no toy!" Thomas shook his head at him. "Never enter a mirror unless you can be absolutely certain it was there ten years ago."

"Why?"

"That mirror isn't only your entrance; it's also your exit. If that mirror wasn't there ten years ago, where would your hand go?"

Bren shrugged. "Where?"

"I don't know. That's the problem. No one knows. No one *can* know. Don't go experimenting when your life's at stake, Bren. It'd be better to limit yourself and be safe than to find yourself trapped inside a mirror with no means of escape."

"Is that possible?"

"Maybe." Thomas was looking through the windshield, out across the green fields at Windfield Manor, sitting at the base of the hill. "Is someone watching the house while you're here?"

"I didn't even know I was leaving."

"It's one of the fears I always have when I travel in time—that something will happen to the mirror while I'm gone, or that the house will burn down. I suppose that it's just one of the risks one must take."

"And if something does happen to the mirror?"

"I can only speculate," said Thomas, glancing periodically at Bren as he drove. "I have no way of being certain. But it seems to me that it would be like stepping into an open door and finding no exit on the other side. Perhaps you'd be suspended in time—or trapped inside the wall. I honestly don't know. But I'd be careful."

# CHAPTER 32

$\mathcal{H}$e lay back on the bed in the guest room wearing new clothes and fiddling with the key. By this time tomorrow, Thomas would either be dead or Bren would be on his way back through the mirror. At least that's the way he saw it. He figured there was also a possibility that both events would happen, since according to the accounts in the newspapers, he'd simply disappeared after the murder. The most logical explanation was that he'd escaped into the basement, found Thomas's diary and read the passage that explained how to get the key to take him back into the future.

He still had a hard time accepting the fact that he was going to kill a man tomorrow, but he didn't want to risk it either. What he needed was Thomas's diary right now, not tomorrow after it was too late. Stuffing the key in his pocket, he left the room and walked to the end of the hall where he stood at the balustrade and peered down into the entryway. The coast was clear, or so he thought until he started down the stairs. Justin was standing in the corridor near the living room entrance, listening in on an argument not meant for his ears. He looked over at Bren guiltily, then went out the front door.

When in the corridor, Bren could hear Thomas and Elizabeth arguing inside the living room. He knew immediately why Justin had taken an interest in the conversation, since his fate was the topic of debate.

"He's had a rough life," Thomas was saying, "but he's a good boy. Give him a chance."

"He's not my son, and he'll never be my son," said Elizabeth. "I've already raised my family."

Bren leaned against the corridor wall, out of sight of Thomas and Elizabeth, and looked at the front door and felt sad for Justin. If things went according to fate, he'd be orphaned once again and left in the care of a woman who despised him.

In the living room, Thomas leaned on the mantle of the fireplace with his arms folded in front of him. He knew what he needed to say that would make her understand, but he also knew that these were words that he'd never speak.

"Why must you let all these strangers into the house?" Elizabeth paced. Her face was tired and her eyes were red from recently wiped tears. "First the boy, then the American. You have a family—me and Heather. Isn't that enough? Do you think we don't notice you, that we don't love you? Do we bore you? What? Why is it that you feel you must bring strangers in off the street?"

"Why does everything I do have to reflect on you?" said Thomas. "Why can't it be just another aspect of my life, a kindness I'm showing to a stranger?"

"Because everything you do does reflect on me; it affects me." Her voice softened and she sat on the sofa. Her auburn hair was ruffled from rubbing her hands in it with frustration. "Sure you're being kind bringing them in, but I'm the one who has to feed them, who has to clean up after them, who has to rearrange my schedule to entertain them."

"What schedule? Before Justin arrived, you went out and helped Gretchen in the garden, not because you needed to, but because you had nothing better to do. You sat on the sofa, knitting. And knitting what? A blanket for the extra room where nobody stayed. You climbed all those stairs up to the game room to shoot a game of snooker with me, not that you like the game, but to keep me from playing alone. So I don't see how my inviting a couple of boys in has messed with some great schedule you had."

A single tear trailed down over her cheek and she brushed it away. "Have you ever stopped to think that I enjoy doing those things? That I like helping in the garden, that I like knitting, that I like spending time with you in the game room? Because I do. It's simple, sure. But I enjoy it. I was content with things the way they were, you and me and Heather all alone. We're a family. Why can't you be content with that?"

Bren tiptoed into the study and closed the door behind him. He tried the desk drawers again, but they were still locked and he couldn't force them open. He went through the sliding bookcase and rummaged through the basement desk, but the diary wasn't there. Not yet. He sat on the brown sofa and examined the key, questioning how the same thing that took him back in time could also take him forward. There were no movable parts, so it wasn't a matter of flipping a switch.

As he sat there pensively looking at the vines outside the basement window, he heard the bookcase slide open, then close. Footsteps descended the stairs. He quickly scanned the room for a place to hide. There was none. He considered crouching behind the sofa, but figured he would still be found and would only look more suspicious for doing so. So he remained on the sofa and smiled at Thomas when he rounded the corner on the stairs and glanced at him with surprise.

"What are you doing down here?" Thomas was already in a bad mood from his discussion with his wife, and finding Bren in the basement didn't set well with him.

"I just needed a little privacy."

"This isn't your house yet, and I'd rather you not come down here without my permission."

"Sorry."

"Were you looking for my diary?" Thomas came around to the back of the sofa, watching Bren through the large mirror. "Or just trying to figure the key out on your own?"

"No. Just thinking," Bren said.

"Please don't patronize me with your lies. I find it very demeaning to have someone think I'm foolish enough to buy into their deceit. Now what are you doing down here?"

"Looking for your diary," Bren confessed.

Thomas nodded. "While you're a guest in my home, Bren Stevens, I'd like you to act like one. And I don't want you up on the hill chasing my daughter around, or doing anything else to her for that matter."

"I did nothing. I assure you."

"Make sure you continue doing nothing." Thomas paced the cement floor. He looked older now, his shoulders hunched, his eyes heavy. "Since you're already down here, let me show you something." He stepped along one wall, counting the bricks, then removed one brick, which exposed a small cavity in the wall. "Even if they found the basement, they wouldn't find this place. A hiding place in a hidden room. Toss me your key."

Bren didn't like the idea of giving up the key, and he didn't like the way Thomas was motioning for it, like Bren had no say in the matter. He hesitated a moment before concluding that he really *didn't* have a say in the matter, not if he expected Thomas to tell him how the stupid thing worked. So he tossed it over and watched as Thomas placed it inside the hole, then replaced the brick, which blended brilliantly with the others.

"There, now it'll be safely waiting for you."

"Waiting for when?"

"You'll see."

Bren walked across the floor over to the window where dying light still bled through the vines. "Anybody else know about this?"

"The key or the basement?"

"Either."

"No. They all think I'm a genius. Why spoil it for them?" Thomas sat on the sofa, where his face glowed under the basement's naked bulb. "So what exactly *is* going on between you and my daughter?"

"Nothing." In Bren's quick reply, he revealed his guilt, and Thomas's face was grim with understanding.

"That's twice in the same evening," Thomas chastised. "You're losing my trust, Bren. Beth saw you on the hill with Heather. And Heather seems to think things are getting rather serious between you two. I don't want to see her hurt."

"Don't worry."

"I'm her father. It's my job to worry. I have experience in this. Something about going back in time makes you feel invincible—like you can do anything you want and not have to worry about the consequences. After all, you can walk away anytime you want. But these are real people's lives you're dealing with. *They* can't just walk away."

"Well I have no intention of hurting anyone."

"Perhaps. But sometimes we do things we don't intend on doing. Justin is a prime example." Thomas could see that Bren didn't understand what he meant, so he added, "He's my child."

"Adopted child."

"Real child," said Thomas and saw the lights go on in Bren's eyes. "About three years ago, while I was back in time, I took a jaunt down to Leeds. I met this girl in a bar and thought 'what the hell, I'll have myself a bit of fun, then vanish.' I saw her a couple times actually, over several months. I was a fool. We men truly are pigs. Sex destroys all logic and makes a man irrational."

Bren nodded with understanding, went to the wooden steps and sat down.

"After I'd been seeing her for a couple months," Thomas continued, "she informed me she was pregnant and that it was my child. What could I do? I couldn't stay. I had a family back here to care for. So I left." He cupped his hands behind his head and leaned back into the cushions, looking ashamed of the story he was telling. "Over the past three years, I lived with the guilt of what I'd done. So a few months back, while I was in Leeds on business—present day this time—I decided to check up on her, hoping she'd made up the story about being pregnant. Not only did I find she was telling the truth about the child, but I also found that she'd recently died of cancer."

"And so you adopted Justin."

"It was the responsible thing to do."

"Does Elizabeth know about this?"

"Heavens no. Though I think sometimes she suspects. Of course she would think the affair took place thirteen years ago, but—" Thomas cocked his head, then leaned forward with his elbow on his knee and his chin in his hand. "So what I'm saying is that you don't need to go back through that mirror if you don't want. But if you do intend on going back, don't lead Heather on."

"Okay." Bren nodded. "I like Heather. It's just that I—"

"You don't need to explain it to me," Thomas interrupted. "Explain it to her."

"I can't. You see I'm in love with her daughter."

Thomas started to laugh, then covered his mouth and looked at the ceiling, afraid someone might hear him and investigate where the sound came from. "What a fine fix you're in."

"Tell me about it. Your daughter's great, but I love your granddaughter. And she's from my generation."

"She must be something."

"She is." Bren rubbed his fingers through his freshly cut hair. "She's beautiful. More beautiful than anyone should be allowed to be. And she's got your stinging personality. She makes me feel like hell sometimes, just like you do, but I love the girl."

Thomas grinned. He liked the sound of that, and liked Bren for saying it. "We'll have to see to it that I meet this granddaughter of mine."

"Yes, we will," Bren agreed. "I've been giving this a lot of thought. I think you'd better leave town tomorrow. If you're not here, it can't happen, right?"

"My thoughts exactly." Thomas was on the edge of the sofa. "You been to London yet? We could make a day of it."

"Actually, I kind of had my heart set on Blackpool."

"What's in Blackpool?

"The Beatles."

"Good lord, not that long-haired rock band?"

"Their hair's still short," said Bren, and Thomas moaned at the thought. "If you want some investment advice from the future, buy stock in the Beatles if it's possible. It's a sure thing. Trust me on this." He could see that Thomas wasn't convinced. "Here I am in nineteen-sixty-four England," Bren continued. "If I didn't go see The Beatles, my friends'd think I was the biggest idiot to ever walk the earth—and they'd be right."

"What makes you think The Beatles are in Blackpool?"

"Front page of the Lurkdale Gazette. Justin was looking it over earlier. It gives a full outline of The Beatles' current tour. August 16, 1964, Blackpool Opera House."

Thomas leaned his head back and stared up at the ceiling. He had an amused grin on his face. "Me at a Beatles' concert. I think I'd rather stay here and die."

# CHAPTER 33

*A*t five A.M. on the morning of August 16, Thomas James Windfield was already up and dressed and sitting behind the desk in
his study. He'd had one of the worst night's sleep of his entire life. A
dream had disturbed him around three in the morning, and his
thoughts had disturbed him from then on out. The dream hadn't
been overly sinister really, but its eerie mood had left him feeling
depressed. In it, he'd floated weightlessly through the house as if he
were having an out-of-body experience. Drifting into the living
room, he found that someone had painted a large red cross on the
mirror. Across from it, Elizabeth and Heather were sitting on the
sofa crying. He floated down the corridor, through the kitchen, and
out into the garden, where he spotted Justin chasing a soccer ball
down a pathway. A light mist moved hauntingly through the flowers
and hedges. Near the fountain, Bren sat on a bench laughing hysteri-
cally as he counted mounds of money, which was falling around him
from everywhere.

Thomas had bolted the study door before unlocking the desk
drawer and removing his diary, which now sat opened on the desk.
Hunching over it, he scribbled out several paragraphs. He'd never
been faithful at keeping his diary up to date, but this seemed like a
worthy occasion—the day he was destined to die. He wrote a bit
about his willing the house to Bren Stevens, but said nothing about

his imminent death. He then slid the bookcase aside and went into the basement, where he put the diary in the second drawer of the desk that stood against the front wall, next to the stairs. He took the brick from the wall and withdrew the key. He looked at the mirror. He had a strong impression that he should step right through that mirror, back to 1954, where he'd be safe. He'd just recently started using the basement mirror for his travels back through time. When he bought the house ten years ago, the living room mirror was already there. He hung the rest of them later so he could have easy access in and out of time regardless of which room he was in. Yet he had to wait ten years before he could use any of them, so the mirror would be there in the past for him to exit from. Right now, this mirror would make a perfect escape route. With the key in his possession, no one would be able to follow him through, not even Bren Stevens. Thomas's dream had spooked him. He considered it a prophecy rather than a dream, and he was certain he knew its interpretation.

By ten o'clock, all four Windfields and Bren Stevens were on the road to Blackpool. Thomas had made several phone calls trying to secure five tickets to the sold-out performance. A business acquaintance from Liverpool had put him in touch with a scalper from Blackpool who agreed to part with five tickets for thirty pounds each (around six times the going rate). He reluctantly accepted the offer.

Blackpool lay on the coast of the Irish Sea, almost straight across the narrow width of the country from Lurkdale. Many considered it the entertainment capital of Europe. Its seven-mile beach had three piers that hosted carnival-type rides and arcades. It had a zoo, a trolley, a plethora of nightclubs, and dozens of theaters. Yet despite its popularity with the tourists, it was a city that Thomas ranked right up there with the Beatles. He insisted that the name Blackpool was Old English for cesspool.

When they came up over the rise, the first thing that caught Bren's eye was Blackpool Tower, which bore a striking resemblance to the Eiffel Tower, though it was about half the size.

"Kitsch on the beach," said Thomas as he parked the black Rolls Royce just south of a large amusement park called Pleasure Beach. The entire city was swarming with people and the air smelled of the sea and cotton candy.

Stepping out of the car, Bren squinted at the strong wind blowing in off the Irish Sea. He was jittery with nerves. Partially because he was going to witness a part of history today, and partially because this was the day he was destined to kill someone. He had a terrible feeling that Thomas still wasn't safe. Being at home or off in Black-pool didn't seem to make much difference when Thomas had brought the killer along in the back seat. Still, there was always the off-chance that someone else had actually committed the murder and Bren had merely taken the blame. Earl Tuttle was still in the run-ning for potential suspects. Though, for all Bren knew, it could be anyone, and he wasn't taking any chances. Before leaving Windfield Manor that morning, he'd sneaked into the kitchen and retrieved a steak knife from the silverware drawer. Wrapping the blade in a dish-cloth, he stuffed it into the front waistband of his blue jeans and pulled his white pullover down over the protruding black handle. It had made it difficult to sit while he rode from Lurkdale to Blackpool, and now, as he wandered the promenade overlooking the Irish Sea, he feared that it was rather apparent that he was storing something beneath his shirt.

Thomas was walking ahead of him, holding his wife's hand. He wasn't hiding his anxiety well. Rather, he looked like a man strolling down a long prison hall, heading off to the electric chair. His move-ments were tense and unnatural. He kept looking back over his shoulder at Bren as if he were expecting a knife in the back. Yet Bren suspected he was the only one who noticed. Justin was too busy gab-bing about the Beatles, and Heather was watching Bren and making sure he noticed how all the other men around were watching her. She grabbed his hand and gave him a smile. Her long brown hair was tied back with a white bow, and she was sporting a black button-up shirt, which accented her dark features.

Thomas glanced back again and stopped. He stared out to sea while a breeze blew through his hair and fluttered beneath his black and white jacket. He cuddled his small wife in his arms, and she looked happier than Bren had seen her since his arrival. She was a lovely woman when she smiled, though most of the time she appeared to live under a black cloud that followed her wherever she went. Right now, however, it looked as though that cloud had shifted over to her husband.

"Anybody ever die at a Beatles' concert?" asked Thomas, glancing down at Bren and Heather's interlocked hands.

"Not that I know of."

"I think Justin will be the first," said Heather. "Look at him. I think he's about to explode."

Justin hadn't stopped with the rest. He'd continued on up the promenade and was now staring impatiently back at them. His foot was tapping incessantly at the walkway, and he didn't seem to know what to do with his hands. He spoke the words "Come on," but they were drowned out by the sounds of the crowd, wind and waves. The noise of screams and a coaster sailing down a decline brought Justin's attention back around to the amusement park behind him.

"You go see to it that Justin doesn't explode," Thomas said to the two ladies. "Bren and I need a moment alone." He removed his wallet from his back pocket and handed several bills to Elizabeth so she could keep the boy entertained for the time being.

As the ladies walked on ahead, Thomas put his arm around Bren's shoulder and slowly led him up the promenade behind his family. The bulge that he'd noticed beneath the front of Bren's shirt distressed him as much as his dream had. He had no way of knowing for sure that it was a knife, but he suspected that it was. He suspected a lot of things, and the more he mulled it over, the more his paranoia grew.

Right now he had his arm around the shoulder of his own killer, and he knew it.

"I think it's time for you and Heather to have yourselves a little talk."

Bren breathed a little easier now that he knew the topic at hand. He'd imagined much worse when Thomas had sent the ladies away. He'd feared he'd noticed the knife.

"Does that mean you're ready to tell me how to get back home?"

"I suspect you already know how."

Bren stopped walking. Thomas was obviously accusing him of something, but for the life of him, he couldn't figure out what. "Had I known that," said Bren, "I'd have left before you ever saw me."

"And your name would have never appeared in my will." Thomas gave him a knowing pat on the shoulder and walked on ahead a few steps before turning back and adding, "I'll tell you how the key works tonight. But right now, I want you to end this with Heather. A true gentleman won't leave without letting a lady know where things stand."

"Are you angry with me for some reason, Mr. Windfield?"

"Of course not." Thomas narrowed his eyes at the wind. "Why would I be?"

Thomas had scheduled to meet the scalper outside the front door of Blackpool Tower. He was a burly fellow with a ragged beard and a more ragged derby. Thomas half-expected him to jack up the price or run off with the money without handing over the tickets, but it went off without a hitch. Thomas was pleased, for Justin's sake. The boy had had little his entire life, and now all he had was an illegitimate father and a stepmother who was struggling to find a place for him in her heart. With any luck this would turn out to be one of the best days of the young boy's life, rather than just another bad one where he was left with one less parent.

He put the tickets in the inside pocket of his jacket and hurried away from the beach, toward the shops that stretched out past the tower and carnival atmosphere. He'd promised Elizabeth that he'd meet up with her and Justin in a half hour at the base of the roller coaster at Pleasure Beach, so he still had time to do what he felt he needed to do. The city evolved around glitter and manmade amusements, but it was also a seaside resort, which meant it catered to fishing enthusiasts as well. He figured he wouldn't find much more than cheap souvenirs along the promenade, but he was bound to find a place in town where he could buy a fishing knife.

Down the beach from Thomas, along the promenade where scores of shops and arcades indulged whatever tourists they could lure inside their doors, Bren and Heather purchased a basket of fish and chips and strolled the walkway.

"So, what'd you want to talk to me about?" asked Heather.

Bren tossed the remaining portion of his fish in a garbage can and wiped the grease from his lips and hands with a napkin. "Do you believe in fate, Heather?"

She smiled. "Certainly."

Bren winced, realizing that she'd misinterpreted his question as a sign of his affection. "Well I don't," he said. "I don't believe in anything. Not anymore." He took her hand and led her over to a bench that faced the beach and the ocean beyond it. "You're one of the prettiest girls I've ever met in my life." He took a seat beside her, facing her and still holding her hand. "And I hope you know that I would never do anything to hurt you. Nor would I ever hurt anyone in your family." He wanted her to believe what he was saying, but more important, he wanted to believe it himself. "No matter what happens in the future, no matter what lies you may hear about me, remember that I would never hurt any of you."

"What are you talking about?"

"I just wanted you to know what kind of person you're dealing with here."

"And this is what you couldn't say to me in front of my family?"

"That's one half of it." He squeezed her hand and smiled stiffly. "The rest is that I'm leaving tomorrow."

She laughed, or rather let out a breathy sigh, and pulled her hand away from him. "And that's that?"

"I'm afraid so."

"Well that's just great." Her voice had taken on a edge, and her eyes had darkened considerably. "You realize I broke up with Earl for you, don't you? You nearly raped me in my bedroom, and now you're just going to walk away like nothing ever happened?"

This drew the attention of a man and woman who were lying on beach towels in front of them.

"It wasn't me doing the raping," Bren protested.

"Oh, please. Don't flatter yourself."

"And don't blame your breakup with Earl on me. You were using the man to irritate your father. You said so yourself."

"Which was precisely how I intended to use you. You're nothing, Stephen. Nothing. You're a second-rate bum who will never amount to anything. I pity you. I really do." She stood and dusted the seat of her pants with her hand. "You know what bothers me most about stupid people? They're too stupid to realize they're stupid."

Bren shrugged gently, wanting to console her. "I'm sorry, Heather."

"What are you apologizing for? You think this hurts me? You give yourself far too much credit. I can have any man I want, and I sure as hell don't want you." She turned and started away up the promenade, then added, "I don't know who's worse, you or Earl."

"Oh, now that hurt." Bren held his hand over his heart. "Compare me to Hitler, to Attila the Hun, anybody, but please don't compare me to Earl."

She made an obscene gesture and walked away.

# CHAPTER 34

*A* buzz of energy electrified the air. It was unlike anything Bren had ever witnessed or, he figured, would ever witness again, no matter how long he lived. Their seats weren't the best, but they were in, which was more than hundreds of fans crowded outside the front door could say. The only enjoyment Thomas Windfield would receive this night was walking through the throng on Church Street up to the Opera House and being able to present his ticket to the usher, to the envy of the ecstatic teens who hadn't managed to obtain entrance to the performance. Once the music started, however, he entertained the thought that he should have given his ticket to one of those teary-eyed fans, who would have undoubtedly taken more pleasure in this hysteria than he did. It distressed him to think he'd shelled out thirty pounds per ticket just to come listen to a bunch of kids scream, because that was all he heard. He could see John, Paul, George and Ringo bobbing their heads on stage, and he even caught a word or two, but for the most part he heard nothing more than a multitude of fanatics shouting their throats raw. He doubted that, come morning, anyone in attendance would be able to hear or speak.

Girls had already started screaming before the Beatles took the stage, but it wasn't until they actually showed their faces that the wailing began. A flood of teenagers swarmed the stage, and it took a few dozen policemen to hold them back. Tears streamed down the faces of young girls, who were biting at their fists and handkerchiefs. Bren recalled reading that after many of the Beatles' concerts, those cleaning up had found hundreds of the seats wringing wet, and that many of them actually had puddles of urine beneath them. People simply lost control within the delirium.

Justin hadn't lost control of his bladder, but that was the only thing he had under control. He couldn't stay in his seat. Several times he'd attempted to get past Thomas and Elizabeth, trying to get into the aisle so he could storm the stage right along with the rest of his peers, but Thomas kept him contained. He was torn, not sure if he should repress the young lad or let him run free. Both options had their downsides. The previous month when the Beatles' first movie, *A Hard Day's Night,* had been released, Justin had convinced Thomas to let him go to it alone—three times. Thomas had had trouble getting the boy to sit down for a hair cut ever since.

"Me mates will never believe I saw the Beatles," Justin shouted.

"Neither will mine," said Bren.

Through the mayhem, Thomas kept an eye on his guest. Before last night's dream, he'd actually considered him someone he could trust. But he knew better now. Even if the dream hadn't tipped him off, he would have still had the whole situation figured out by mid-concert. In all of the standing and sitting, and raising his hands above his head as he added his voice to the screams, Bren had forgotten about the knife stuffed in the front of his jeans. Its handle worked its way to the outside of the white pullover, and Thomas recognized it as one of his own steak knives. He shuddered to think that one of the very knives he'd used at his own dining table would be used to cut open his belly. This was an insult. He blinked at the bright lights above the stage as sweat trickled across his temple and down his jaw. The crowd was intense. The shear volume was enough to shatter glass. Yet, beyond the shouting and the pulse of the music, he could hear his own heartbeat pounding in his head.

He saw the whole picture now, and it made him feel stupid. He'd always considered himself an intelligent man, and it angered him that someone would attempt to play him for the fool. Worse yet, Bren had all but pulled it off. A few knife jabs in the abdomen and the ploy would be complete. He'd be dead and Bren Stevens would be walking back through the mirror a rich man.

Stupid, stupid man, he said to himself at least twenty times as he rotated his attention between the band on stage and his would-be killer.

He'd been conned, just like his father before him. But he wasn't beaten yet. He still had a trick or two up his sleeve—and a fishing knife in his pocket. The way Thomas saw it, what those New York businessmen had done to his father was unforgivable, but what Bren Stevens was doing to him was down-right evil. He wasn't sure how he would deal with Bren, but what he did know was that as soon as he got back home to Lurkdale, he would pay another visit to his lawyer so he could strike his killer from his will.

That night at 11:30, after they'd checked into their hotel, Thomas came to Bren's room and asked him to join him for a walk. Heather had already shut herself up in her room for the night, probably moping. Justin was in Thomas's room with Elizabeth, talking her ear off about the Beatles. It was by far the most he'd said to her in the two months he'd been in Lurkdale, and probably the least she'd spoken back. But then again, his topic wasn't something Elizabeth knew much about, nor cared to. When Thomas mentioned that he was going out for a walk, his wife gave him one of those looks that screamed *betrayal*.

The night air was pleasant. Pockets of teenagers stood on street corners and sat along stone walls, still discussing their glimpses of the Fab Four. Their battery-operated radios sounded tinny as they cranked out the newest hits: "A Hard Day's Night" and "You've Got

To Hide Your Love Away," songs that were considered golden oldies to Bren's generation.

Thomas walked with his hands stuffed inside the pockets of his black and white jacket. The left was clinched nervously into a fist. The right gripped the handle of the opened fishing knife. He hoped he wouldn't be forced to use it. But just in case, he took streets that veered away from the ocean and Wintergarden (the city center where the concert had taken place), figuring that most of the night owls would be carousing the beach or the clubs. If Bren made his move and Thomas was forced to retaliate, he wanted Bren's blood to flow in solitude, rather than in the midst of star-struck teens.

They passed up a quiet narrow street, lined with brick complexes that stood flush with the walkway. Though it was approaching midnight, the neighborhood wasn't entirely dark. The soft glow of the nearly full moon, which hung in the sky before them, painted the buildings in romantic highlights. Streetlights glared at both ends of the lane, and at the top of one of the stoops that led up from the street, a bulb shone above a closed door.

"I take it you had a pleasant little chat with Heather." Thomas had noted that his daughter had said little all evening.

"Yeah. She loves me," Bren intoned. "She compared me to Earl. It really wounded me."

Thomas grinned congenially. Away from the noise of the crowd, he could think more clearly, and that clear thinking told him to quit second-guessing himself. This was no nice young man standing before him. Sure he had his polished charm and rehearsed wit, but the man was pure evil. Besides the knife beneath his shirt, the man also had something else no one else had: a motive. He was the only one who stood to benefit from the murder.

In one of the darker stretches of the lane, Thomas stopped and checked his watch: 11:50. "I've got ten minutes and I'm home free." He grinned darkly over at Bren, knowing full well that Bren could have lied about the date. As far as that went, he could have lied about everything: the death, the will, his granddaughter—you name it. He was just toying with him now. Looking at Bren standing in the shadows beside the wall, Thomas could see the cogs turning behind his eyes. He was plotting all right. Give the man a clear shot and he'd have the knife out and be doing an excellent Norman Bates impression right here on the sidewalk.

Thomas stepped off the curb and moseyed to the center of the empty street. "You think we can change fate, Bren?" His hands were inside his pockets.

"It would appear we already have. Your fate was to die today in your study. Yet here you are alive in Blackpool."

"Yes." Thomas stared solemnly up at the moon. It looked so beautiful and peaceful up there among the stars. "When I was a child, some men convinced my father to give them his life's savings. Did I tell you that?"

"Yeah, I believe you did."

"They promised to make him a rich man," Thomas went on as if he hadn't heard Bren's comment. "But the only people they made rich were themselves. My father was devastated. The poor gullible fool. They not only broke him financially, they broke his spirit as well." He gazed off down the street. "When I got the key, one of the first things I ever did was go back in time and talk to my father. I pretended to be a private detective. I told him that I was running surveillance on the men who had asked him to make the investment, and I told him—practically begged him—not to give the men his money. I thought I'd convinced him, but when I returned to the future, I found that I hadn't changed a thing. The old fool went ahead with the deal despite everything I said. Fate has scared me ever since. Perhaps it was my father's fate to die a poor, broken man."

"You have no control over your father's actions," said Bren.

"And I have no control over my killer's actions either," Thomas said sharply. "If some cruel sod has it in his head to do me in, there's not a bloody thing I can do about it. There's nothing more aggravating than being totally helpless. And the worst of it is that I'm sure my killer is just some sniffling little brat who plans to kill me for my money because he's too lazy to work for a living." He gave Bren a hard stare. He looked so damned innocent, and that just aggravated the hell out of Thomas, who knew without a shadow of a doubt that right now, standing there on that darkened sidewalk, Bren was plotting how he could get the knife out from under his shirt and into Thomas stomach.

"You following what I'm saying, Stephen—or Bren—or whatever your name is?"

Bren grinned nervously. Thomas was looking a bit shaky there, and his tone of voice wasn't the least bit reassuring. He'd assumed this meeting in the street was intended to enlighten him on how to return to the future where he belonged, now that the crisis had passed. But now, he wasn't sure what to think. He leaned back against the brick wall of one of the buildings, folding his arm over his stomach to keep the handle of the knife from showing. He'd considered leaving it back at the hotel, but nighttime in a strange city seemed the most likely of places where such a weapon would be needed.

"I don't see how killing you is going to make anybody rich."

"Don't you?" asked Thomas. "Surely you can think of at least one person who would profit from my death." He stepped toward Bren and stopped just short of the curb. His accusatory stare was unmistakable.

"Surely you don't suspect me," said Bren.

"Why not? You're the only person with a motive. You just had me will you my home and a million pounds, and, best yet—you convinced me that it was my idea. It's brilliant. It really is. I applaud you."

"It's ridiculous, that's what it is."

"Why?"

"It just is."

"Indulge me, please." Thomas stepped upon the curb, closing the distance between him and Bren. He felt inclined to draw his own knife and kill Bren before he had a chance to commit his heinous act. "I want to believe it's ridiculous. Honest. But I've been racking my brain all day, and so far I've come up with nothing. So please—enlighten me."

"Well, first of all, I warned you about your death." Bren slid his hand over the front of his shirt, feeling the handle of the knife beneath it. He was no killer; he knew that now. The papers were wrong, and so was Gretchen. *Please, God, let them be wrong.* "Why would I warn you if I was planning on killing you? Why not just stab you and be done with it?" Bren glanced to the end of the narrow lane where two people were passing beneath the streetlight. He hoped they'd turn down the lane and interrupt this insanity. Judging by the glint in Thomas's eyes, this little meeting wasn't going to have a happy ending. He feared the old man would force his hand, and he'd end up proving the whole insane population of Lurkdale correct.

Down the lane, the two people continued on beneath the street-light and disappeared down the crossroad.

"Had you killed me right away, you'd have never been in my will." Thomas was watching Bren's hands. "You had to warn me first, so I'd feel your presence here was warranted, so I'd give you the key—the very thing that allowed you to come here in the first place. But warning me wasn't what you had in mind, was it?"

Thomas moved menacingly close. His eyes were darkened by shadows, but Bren could see that they held no warmth. Bren's right hand slipped up under his shirt and groped for the knife. He didn't want to do it, didn't want to put an end to the gentleman's life here on the streets of Blackpool, and hoped it wouldn't come to that. His fingers shot up past his belt buckle, but got no farther before a knife jetted up under his chin, pricking the skin. His head flinched back and thumped against the bricking that he was leaning against. The quiet of the street filled him with terror.

"You little peasant," Thomas chided. "I brought you into my home, and this is how you repay me?" He lifted Bren's white shirt and retrieved the knife hidden there.

"I wasn't gonna kill you."

"No?" Thomas held the steak knife in front of Bren's eyes. His hands trembled, causing the fishing knife to dig into Bren's neck.

"I brought it for protection." Bren's voice was thin.

"Against whom?" Thomas's breathing was quick and shallow. He knew he could kill this young man right now and get away with it. No one would miss him. It was 1964; the man hadn't even been born yet. Every search the police could run—fingerprints, dental records, missing persons—would all turn up nothing. He may have to explain Bren's sudden disappearance to Elizabeth, Heather and Justin, but that wouldn't take much. The only flaw he could foresee was the media, who would no doubt broadcast Bren's death on the television and in the newspapers. If no one in the family came forward, perhaps someone else from Lurkdale would. That may present a sticky situation.

He pulled the knife away.

"Tomorrow you're walking through that mirror and don't you dare come back." He closed the blade of the fishing knife and stuffed it back inside his pocket.

"Just tell me how to go and I'm gone."

Thomas stepped back—giving Bren some breathing room—and tapped the blade of the steak knife in his palm. He glowered. He despised being lied to, and Bren's pretending not to know how to return to the future was nothing but a grotesque lie. He wouldn't have come back in time to commit murder without knowing how to escape.

"You'd better not be toying with me." Thomas regarded him thoughtfully. "I'm generally a very reasonable man, but if you so much as startle me between now and tomorrow, I'll have no choice but to cut you wide open."

Bren shook his head and walked down the lane, back the way they'd come. He wasn't a drinking man, but what he needed right now was a shot of the strongest whiskey he could find. "I'm trying very hard to like you, sir, but you sure aren't making it easy." Bren paused in the center of the street and looked back at Thomas.

"I'm not looking to make friends. All I want to make is my next birthday."

"Well, you've nothing to worry about from me."

"Haven't I?"

"No." Bren turned and ambled down the lane. What he needed most of all, more than the taste of hard liquor, was to put some distance between himself and Thomas. If he had to live out his life thirty years back in time, then so be it. Just get him as far away as possible from this madman. The whole experience had left him feeling filthy, violated, the kind of emotion he imagined a woman would experience after being raped. He wanted to hit somebody—or do something far worse. The way he felt right now, he just may have one good murder in him after all. Stupid, bullheaded old man. Bren rubbed at his throat and found a trickle of blood. That was twice someone had jabbed him in the throat with a sharp object.

"You don't need the key to get back home, Mr. Stevens." Thomas Windfield's voice resounded in the narrow lane. Before continuing, he waited until Bren stopped and faced him. The streetlight was at his back and shadows fell across his face. "In fact you can't get home with it, only without it." Thomas traversed the length of the lane, pausing three feet in front of Bren. "The key only takes you back, not forward. Time has a way of knowing where you belong. With the key, you go back in time. Without it, you return to the present—your present."

"Are you saying I could have just walked though any mirror any time I pleased?"

"I wouldn't necessarily say any mirror." Thomas motioned for Bren to continue walking and they started down the road again, keeping a cautious distance between them. "Perhaps I shouldn't reemphasize this, but on the off-chance that you are just an innocent pawn in this whole bizarre mess, I wouldn't want to see you do anything that might get yourself killed. Mind you, I still consider you my best suspect." He could see no amusement in his companion's face. "You want to make sure the mirror you walk though is still there thirty years from now. Because without an exit, you're stuck; and without the key, you can't turn around and come back out into the past."

The air was stagnant, sheltered by buildings. But as they approached the ocean, it began to cool again. A salty breeze was coming in off the breakers, and down beyond the promenade, there were voices wafting up from the dark beach. The sound of a foghorn moaned, and out in the darkness, the faint lights of a ship could be seen moving south toward Liverpool.

"So now what happens?" asked Bren as they approached the hotel.

Thomas offered a knowing smile. "What you're wondering is how much I'm going to alter that will after you're gone."

"It has crossed my mind."

"Of course if I say I'm going to leave you nothing, that gives you all the more reason to kill me before I can make any changes, right?"

"If you left me nothing, I wouldn't so much as mess up your hair, Mr. Windfield." Bren paused at the bottom of the stairs that led up to their hotel doorway. "Not that I want you to leave me nothing of course."

"I'll make you a deal, just to keep you honest. When you walk through that mirror tomorrow, I'll be waiting there in the future to greet you when you come out the other side. I'll write you out a check on the spot. I figure the least I can do is give you the million pounds I originally willed to you."

"You do realize that after thirty-years interest, that original million turned into four, don't you?"

"Don't press your luck," said Thomas grimly, and climbed the steps to the door.

# CHAPTER 35

$T$he drive back to Lurkdale was long and disquieting. Justin appeared to be the only one with nothing to brood about. Thomas's eyes constantly wandered to the rearview mirror, checking to see that Bren was securely seated behind him and not leaning forward ready to draw a knife and slit the throat of the driver. He'd lived to see another day, but he wouldn't rest easily until Bren had stepped through the mirror and he'd had a chance to drive into town and alter the will.

When he pulled up onto the redbrick area in front of Windfield Manor and shut off the engine, Thomas gave a long sullen look at his home, the place where he was to have died the day before. It showed no sign of evil lurking about or of knife-wielding maniacs itching to cut away his life. Instead, summer drifted through the yard and brought with it the fresh smell of grass that had been dampened by rains the night before. The oaks and elms, fanning out on both sides of the mansion, spilled shadows out across the lawn beneath the afternoon sun. But amidst all that light and beauty, Thomas felt a dark tumor on his soul and an incredible weight upon his heart.

Along the drive from Blackpool, he'd pondered on how to have Bren depart through the mirror and, at the same time, fool his family into thinking that he'd taken a bus out of town. He could suggest that some photos be taken in the garden, with the hope that while the family tarried out back, he could escort Bren into the house, say goodbye at the mirror, then drive into town to talk to his lawyer. When he returned, he could always tell the family that Bren hadn't wanted a teary goodbye and had thought it would be best if he left quietly.

The backyard garden was filled with color and the scent of summer. All the flowers had blossomed to their fullest, had swollen with life, and the birds were singing in the trees. Bren felt it was the picture of death. Regardless of the date, Thomas Windfield was going to die today, and there wasn't a thing Bren could do to stop it.

Weaving the garden paths, he shot a glance at Thomas. He should say something. Remind the man about the photographs that had been sent in the briefcase. But he said and did nothing, merely stood at the gazebo's opening, along with Thomas, Elizabeth and Heather, while Justin snapped the photo. He then traded places with Justin and took another photograph himself.

He felt the anxiety ebb. This wasn't the scene from the photographs he'd received from Dan Adams. Things had changed. Two men, Bernard Phelps and Earl Tuttle, were missing from the picture. Thomas may not have altered his father's fate, but he'd altered his own. Bren looked at the gentleman and knew that things were different, that this wasn't going to be the sorrowful day that he'd predicted. About this time Berney Phelps rounded the corner of the house. He was dressed in a pale green shirt and filthy jeans.

"I thought you'd all moved away," he said as he passed along the hedges toward the family. "The place was like a graveyard yesterday."

Thomas looked at him harshly for his choice of words but responded kindly. "Heather's been complaining about us keeping her imprisoned here in all this squalor. We thought we'd take the inmate out for a day of freedom."

"But as you can see, they brought me back." Heather was sitting on the edge of the fountain. "I've been waiting for a knight in shining armor to rescue me, but all I keep getting are moronic peasants who can't even make it over the moat." She glanced at Bren.

"The problem is that when they see the damsel in distress, they realize she isn't worth saving," Justin chimed in and Bren smiled.

"You find that amusing, do you?" Heather chided. "Berney, go saddle the horses. Me and my moronic knight are going to have a race."

"No problem," said Bren. "As long as you ride Gypsy."

"Father." She wrinkled her nose at him, knowing he'd betrayed her secret.

"I think we should limit humiliating our guests to only one time per visit." Thomas sat beside his daughter on the fountain's edge and patted his hand on her knee. "I think Stephen's starting to feel that no one in this family likes him."

"Why should he get special treatment? You used to love it when I humiliated Earl."

"Earl's ego isn't as fragile as mine." Bren was standing next to Justin and Berney on the flagstone walkway while Elizabeth picked a few dying leaves from some flowers. Bren looked past Heather and Thomas, at the statue that stood in the center of the fountain. A large crow had lit upon the statue's head. It let out a guttural squall. Heather dipped her fingers in the blue water behind her and splashed some up at the crow, which sent it fluttering away.

"While you were gone yesterday," said Berney, "the horses were out down by the road. Had to chase 'em for nearly an hour. Gate was wide open."

Thomas glanced accusingly at Heather.

"It was closed when we left yesterday. I'm sure of it," said Heather.

"Thanks for taking care of things, Berney. You're a good man." Thomas didn't look well. His skin had become all pasty and he had a vacant gaze in his eyes as he stared up at the sky that was nearly all blue.

"I'd say there's the man who let your horses out." Bren was facing the side of the house, looking at a young man dressed in a white shirt and black trousers, looking like he owned the world.

Heather looked back over her shoulder at Earl Tuttle and groaned. "Has the man no pride?"

The poised young man weaved the garden walkways. He looked sharp, even Bren had to admit it. The collar of his shirt was open a couple buttons and he had a white T-shirt on underneath it. If it weren't for the smug expression on his face, he would have even been handsome. Stopping in front of the fountain, he put his hand on Berney's shoulder and grinned.

"Good day, everyone. Stopped by earlier but you were away."

"Come by yesterday, did you?" Bren asked.

"Yes...terday. Why no. This morning, it was."

"What do you want, Earl?" asked Heather.

"Must I want something? You're all like a second family to me. No reason to become strangers just because you and I aren't getting along, now is there?" He gave her a cheesy grin and a wink, then glanced at the girl's father and said, "Eh, Thomas?"

The gentleman sighed. He put his arm around his daughter's shoulders and gave her a squeeze. He loved her. She was an absolute jewel. But the girl had a knack at bringing home garbage. Like a cat that you adore that's constantly dragging dead birds or rodents into the house. She'd outdone herself this time, though. Standing before them were two of the most despicable men on God's green earth, and his lovely daughter, bless her heart, had invited both of them.

"Earl, perhaps we should have a talk." Thomas had already made an appointment to rid the household of one of the unwanted guests; he may as well do a thorough job while he was at it. He led the young mayor-to-be to the other side of the garden, away from the gazebo, where they sat on a bench facing the others.

"You know I've got nothing against you, Earl," Thomas said. "But in light of recent events, perhaps it'd be more comfortable for Heather if you didn't come by for a while."

"Actually I was hoping you and I could discuss a few business dealings? Surely my standing with Heather wouldn't affect that in anyway."

"No, of course not." Thomas was looking toward the gazebo, where Bren now sat on a similar bench, watching them.

Bren didn't like having all the members of the gazebo photo gathered together in the garden, nor did he like the way Thomas appeared to put more trust in Earl than he did in him. The two of them over there chatting like old buddies just didn't set well with him.

Heather—who had remained seated on the fountain's edge twirling her fingers in the water—got up and casually worked her way over to the bench where Bren was sitting and took a seat beside him. She said nothing for a moment, just stared out across the garden beyond the statues, fountain and flowers to her father and Earl. When she'd turned on Bren in Blackpool, he'd responded with sarcasm, but nothing nearly so heartless as calling her a whore—as Earl had done. If the truth be known, she still had feelings for Bren, but what little spark had remained between her and Earl had been snuffed out with that one proclamation.

"I'm sorry about comparing you to Earl," she said. "That was overly cruel."

"It was outright brutal," Bren agreed and nudged her with his elbow. "But I suppose I deserved it. I should've told you earlier that I couldn't stay long. Your family's been very kind to me, but a man can only take charity so long before he starts losing respect for himself."

Bren and Heather looked up to find Elizabeth standing before them with her camera at the ready. She snapped the button, and the knot in Bren's stomach grew heavier and acidic.

Across the garden, Thomas laid his jacket over his lap and scratched at his chin in thought. "Maybe it's time you tried a few things on your own, took a few of those brilliant ideas of yours and put them to the test," he advised the young Tuttle. "An eagle can learn to soar much better in the air than it can under its mother's wing."

"Yes, I suppose so." Earl disliked the reference of him hiding under his mother's wing. Thomas was no mentor. He liked the man, but he'd lost whatever talent he once had at making money. He was a has-been with a pot of gold stuffed away somewhere inside his mansion. On top of that, he had a very lovely daughter, who Earl adored. "You mind if I hang around a spell?" Earl forced a smile and straightened his brown hair. "I'll excuse myself shortly, but I'd like to leave with dignity. You understand."

Thomas nodded, though he didn't like the way Earl had made his request. It was much too Earl-Tuttleish for him. Cocky and assuming. In fact, it didn't sound like a request at all, more like a statement of the way things were going to be, like it or not. But Thomas thought it'd be best to let things slide for now. When Earl and Bren left, he'd be rid of them both.

Rising to his feet, he put his hand on Earl's shoulder and escorted him around the fountain and through an ivy-covered arch, back toward the gazebo. "You ever need a reference, I'd be glad to vouch for your character. You're a real ambitious young man, Earl. And ambition is all that really counts out there in the business world."

Earl gave no response. He was too busy eyeing the way Heather was cuddling close to Bren. He saw it for what it was: a ploy to make him jealous. You don't date a girl for two years and not get to know her cunning ways. And Heather had many. Even the way she laughed at nothing as Earl and Thomas approached was nothing but a dig at him. But knowing didn't make it any less painful. In fact it made it worse. He wanted to walk over and slap her pretty face.

"Heather," said Thomas. The word came out sounding much harsher than he'd planned. "Go get your mother's camera." He scorned his daughter with his eyes, also knowing perfectly well why she and Bren were suddenly good friends again. "No, better yet, let's all go," he added, looking to the gazebo, where his wife, son and Berney were seated in the shade of the white structure. "Earl can't stay long, and I want a photo of the lot of us before he takes off."

Bren grimaced. Whatever good they'd done yesterday by leaving town was apparently being nullified today.

*And in doing, you will accomplish nothing.* These nauseating words kept ringing in his ears. Where was that witch now, that doomsayer? "Gretchen Wicks, you ugly hag," Bren muttered under his breath as he followed the flagstones to the gazebo. He felt physically ill.

Thomas rallied the seven of them at the mouth of the gazebo, took the camera from his wife and handed it to Justin, before centering himself and his wife in front of the white gazebo, which made for a great backdrop with the green vines weaving up its side and over its top. Mopping his brow with a white hanky, Thomas glowered at Bren. He was a grown man of twenty-five, yet he was acting petty about the positioning of the group, as if it really matter who stood next to whom.

Thomas hugged his arm around his wife. Tomorrow morning, after a good night's rest, he planned to set her down and tell her all about the key, his journeys through time, Bren's true identity, everything. He'd even tell her about Justin. He frowned at Bren and Heather, who were insistent on not having Earl stand between them. Yet he wormed his way in before the shutter snapped.

They traded around several times, taking turns being the photographer. But it didn't matter now, not to Bren. That first picture had sealed it. Everyone was disbanding, and he thought it'd be best to go to the house, head right into the living room and step through the mirror.

Earl grabbed him by the arm and yanked him back toward the gazebo.

"I ought to rip your bleeding heart out," he whispered and kept a smile on his face for show, just in case anyone else was watching. He patted Bren affably on the shoulder before walking off through the garden, toward Heather, who was walking with her mother.

Bren stared up the path to Thomas, who had paused beneath one of the archways in a pool of shade. He pointed at Earl and nodded, trying to convey the message that if Thomas was intent on worrying about someone, he should be worrying about Earl. He'd now passed up Bren on his own list of suspects. But Thomas merely squinted his eyes, not comprehending the reason for the gesture.

"You know, Heather," said Earl, "last time I was here, I believe I left my jacket in your room. You think maybe we could go up and get it?"

Heather stopped by one of the lanterns and looked back at Earl. "I don't think you were wearing a jacket last time you were here."

"I'm quite sure I was. You mind if we at least check?"

"Yes, I do mind."

"Heather." Elizabeth folded her brow disapprovingly.

"He wasn't wearing a jacket, Mother."

"But what could it hurt to go look?" She put her hand on her daughter's arm.

Heather glowered. The only thing worse than being manipulated by Earl Tuttle was having others ally with him. The man was a leech. The last thing he needed was someone else helping him latch on and drain the blood out of her.

"Why don't *I* go check?" Bren came up behind them. "I need to go in and get some aspirin anyway. I've got a bit of a headache."

"Would you, Stephen?" Heather asked.

"No problem." Bren saw that look in Earl's eyes, the one telling him to keep his nose to himself and not to interfere. He happily disobeyed that look and trailed off up the path.

Earl had to struggle to keep his composure, but he did. He retained his calm smile and kept his hands steady. But he felt bad. He hadn't realized how much he loved Heather until now. She was so beautiful, so elegant, so spoiled rotten. She had that way of making men feel like they couldn't live without her, and right now, Earl Tuttle thought that if he lost her, he would break down and cry. He loved her so much that he wanted to beat her black and blue until she came to her senses and loved him back. He grabbed her by the arm, and his hand was shaking. She allowed him to escort her a short distance away from the others before resisting.

"What do you want, Earl?"

He picked a rose from the garden and handed it to her. "For the lady." He gave her a wink that looked as though he'd practiced it in the mirror.

"Spare no expense, eh?" she scoffed.

"It's the gesture that counts."

"Precisely, and giving a girl what is already hers isn't exactly a *good* gesture." Heather tossed the rose to the ground.

"The truth is, Heather, I just wanted to talk to you. Alone." He sounded needy. "You think perhaps we could just talk, so I can apologize for my behavior when I was here last?"

"I don't want to hear your apologies, Earl. I don't want to hear anything you have to say, and I certainly don't have anything to say to you."

"Why must you be such a bitch?" Earl's voice reverberated, and that last word hung in the air, snuffing out every other conversation that had been going on at that moment. All eyes turned to Earl, and none of them looked kind.

Thomas came calmly along the path. His ears and checks had reddened slightly, but other than that he looked completely self-composed. "Earl." He had his hands clasped together in front of him in a priestly manner. "I'm afraid I'm going to have to ask you to leave."

"Fine!" Earl's composure had vanished. He pointed an accusing finger as he spoke. "You've changed! All of you. Ever since that damn American showed up!" The veins of his throat pulsated and his face turned blood red. His thick face contorted with anger, and he marched through the garden, not bothering to keep on the path, but going right through the flowers, stomping extra hard and twisting his feet a little. He'd reverted all the way back to a three-year-old throwing a tantrum. Things were now beyond repair, and he knew it. If he came back tomorrow and apologized again, all he could possibly do was dig himself deeper into the ground and look that much more needy and pitiful.

By the time he rounded the corner of the house and headed for the parking area, he was fuming. Everything became hazy and dark. He wasn't sure where he was going or what he'd do now. He opened the door of his ragged VW, a car he despised. His life as he knew it was now over. And he had no one to blame but—

The American.

Staring back at the house, he shut the car door, without getting in.

He should have run his sword though the man's throat when he had the chance. He could have passed it off as an accident. These things happen. Some people break their legs learning to ski. Others come out paralyzed during rugby practice. A hole in the neck while attempting to master the art of fencing wouldn't be totally inconceivable.

He skulked to the front door and went in, closing the door gently behind him. From the entryway, he shot a gaze up the stairs to the balcony. Somewhere up there Stephen Bradson was vainly searching for a jacket that wasn't there. Earl crept down the corridor and into the kitchen, where he gazed out the window. The family disgusted him. Heather with her camera, taking pictures of her stupid brother, whose hair looked like it belonged on the end of a mop. Thomas and Elizabeth chatting with the moron Berney Phelps, who most likely only hung around so he could sneak peeks at Heather. Earl shivered at the sight. He opened the silverware drawer and grabbed a butcher knife. Its handle fit comfortably in his palm. Its sharp blade glistened in the light, short enough to control and conceal, yet long enough to slay its victim. He walked back down the corridor, calm and intent and ready to rid his life of the man who had destroyed it.

Out in the garden, Thomas excused himself from his conversation with his wife and Berney. He stared up at the back windows of the house. He'd sent away one of the unwanted guests. It was time to bid bon voyage to the other. He'd see Bren Stevens safely through the mirror, then take that drive into town and have a talk with Glenn Ward, his lawyer. Or, perhaps he should call Glenn first and tell him to begin alteration now, just in case Bren didn't go quietly.

Earl had nearly reached the entryway when the sound of the back door opening sent him scampering for a hiding place. He vanished into the study and crouched behind the desk. His heart raced. Footsteps traversed the length of the corridor and paused just outside the study. He held his breath. Someone was standing in front of the open door. He knew because the light coming in through the entryway had dimmed when the footsteps stopped. It was still dim. He lowered his head so that he could peer beneath the desk. Thomas was just standing there, looking puzzled. He was pinching at the skin of his neck as he stared at the stairs, and then glanced in the study at the phone.

Earl pulled back, afraid Thomas had glimpsed him staring out from under the desk.

# CHAPTER 36

*U*pstairs, Bren sat on Heather's bed. There was no jacket up there. There *was* a mirror, however, that he could walk through. Only, he couldn't recall if that mirror was still in this room thirty years in the future. What he should do was go back to the living room and leave right now. He stared at the open window. Someone had called his name, or at least the name they thought was his: Stephen. At the window, he gazed down into the garden, half-blinded by the bright sunlight. Slowly, as his eyes adjusted, he felt a horror sweep over him like nothing he'd ever felt before. There was that moment, which he'd remember all his life, when everything suddenly clicked into place. He knew, without a doubt, that the murder was taking place downstairs in the study at that very second.

Out in the garden, Heather was sitting on one of the benches and pointing the camera in Bren's direction. Earl and Thomas were both gone. Bren's face contorted with dread. It was happening. This was the picture he liked least, the one that had been taken moments before Thomas's body was found dead on the study floor.

He bolted from the room and raced through the hallway. When he hit the stairs, he didn't slow down. He was flying, only landing on every third step. Gripping the banister, in an attempt to keep from stumbling, he rounded the twisting staircase and hit the bottom at full speed. It felt like a bad dream.

He could see the back of Earl's white shirt even before he got to the study door.

"No!" The word came out involuntarily, and the timbre of its anguish echoed through the corridor.

Earl's back hunched in the air, crouching over Thomas's dying body.

In all their scheming, their running away, they had only managed to add one day to Thomas's life. Still the final outcome remained, spilled in red rivers of blood on the study's carpet. Only the date had changed.

Thomas gazed up past Earl. Bren could see his face so vividly. His eyes were dull and distant. He tried to say something, but all that came out was a gurgling sound. His hands and chin began to quiver, and he let his head fall back against the carpet where he stared blankly up at the ceiling. A gagging sensation caught at the back of Bren's throat.

Earl raised his head up from the horror he'd done. His eyes looked both frightened and malicious as he twisted around and faced Bren, the person the knife had been intended for, the person he wanted lying there in Thomas's place.

"Why—?" Bren began, but the sight of the crimson knife pointing his way stopped his question. He backed away from the door, slowly at first, then quickly as Tuttle advanced toward him, looking as though he intended to give him the same treatment that he'd given Thomas. Bren scurried across the entryway, where he tore open the closet door at the back of the stairs and grabbed hastily for a sword, spilling most of them across the floor. Spinning back around, he swung his sword in a haphazard fashion.

Earl stepped cautiously back into the mouth of the corridor and grinned. Bren was now holding the sword up with both hands, trying to steady it. For a moment, they did nothing more than stand facing each other in silence. The house was deathly quiet. Other than an intermittent bird chirping outside in the trees, the only sound

Bren could hear was the beating of his own heart, which was doing double time at the moment.

Earl inched forward with his knife, and Bren swung again, forcing him back to the shelter of the corridor, where a tormented smile quivered over his lips. Blood was dripping from the blade onto the hardwood floor, and Earl had a smudge on the midsection of his white shirt. At the sound of a heavy sigh, he looked back over his shoulder, in through the study door, where he saw that Thomas had turned himself over onto his stomach and was struggling to get to his knees. But his effort only resulted in a strained moan as he dropped back down onto his face.

"*C'est la vie*," said Earl, looking back at Bren. "Or should I say, '*C'est la morte*'?" He tried to find humor in his own joke, but found it difficult to produce a genuine smile. He rubbed the back of his hand across his eyes, and Bren was certain the man was going to cry. But he didn't. Instead, he worked his head one way and then the other and started bouncing on the balls of his feet, doing a little fighting dance to taunt his opponent. Earl lunged forward slightly and shifted from side to side. "You're going to have to be a lot better with that thing than you are to beat me."

Bren feared he was right. Even with the long sword in hand, he feared that the well-practiced Englishman could out-maneuver him, could somehow step within reach and stick his shorter blade inside, leaving him dead and cold before he was even born.

Bren advanced, taking a few liberal swings. Only the aggressor ever wins. Earl himself had taught him that.

Tuttle retreated farther back into the corridor.

"Why Thomas?"

"It wasn't him I was coming for." Earl painted a devilish smile across his face, and his confident gaze worried Bren, but that didn't stop him from inching forward and jabbing at Earl's stomach.

Immediately he knew it was a mistake. Earl slapped the side of the sword with his hand, shoving the blade against the wall and giving himself room to close the gap between him and Bren, who saw the knife jetting toward his stomach. The cloth tore. Earl thought he had him. It should have been a clean kill, and would have been if Bren hadn't pulled back so sharply. Instead, the blade merely cut a slit on the side of the shirt and left a line of Thomas's blood along the frayed edges.

Bren stumbled backward, trying to get his sword between him and Earl, as he pulled back into the entryway. Earl moved with him and lunged again. This time, however, rather than making a full-hearted attempt to wound his victim, he dropped his shoulder to the ground, rolled across the floor, and sprang back to his feet with sword in hand. It was something right out of an Errol Flynn movie. And if Bren hadn't been so horrified by the swift and flawless maneuver, even he would have been impressed.

"A whole new game now, isn't it?" A crazed grin worked its way into Earl's eyes, eyes that foretold Bren's future, and this future had blood spilled all over it. He swung confidently and approached.

Bren backed into the living room, careful not to catch his feet on the carpet. Every move was vital now. Though his chances of triumphing over Earl were bleak at best, he wasn't ready to go down without a fight. He glanced back over his shoulder. The windows were closed, and if he attempted to dive through them, he imagined he'd only make it halfway through before his body got stuck in the window frame, just like the twelve-year-old Lug's had. Yet somehow he doubted Earl Tuttle would be as gracious to him as he'd been to Lug.

Bren cowered backwards through the room, past the armchair, sofa and wooden rocker. The ticking of the grandfather clock that sat near the fireplace sounded loud and somehow appropriate, as it ticked off the seconds that Bren had left to live.

Earl knew he could take the man at any moment, but where was the sport in that? Here was the man who had destroyed his life; the least he could do was prolong the agony and enjoy the kill before the paddy wagon came and hauled him off to the big house, where he'd get a cozy little room with bars on the door. He planned to make a run for it, of course, but he knew he couldn't get far. He lived on an island after all. At best he'd make it all the way to Scotland before the police caught up with him. And with his beat-up Volkswagen Bug, he wouldn't be outrunning anyone.

Earl shrugged nonchalantly when Bren stopped just short of the fireplace. He had no place left to go except six feet under.

"Poor little Stephen. Looks like you've backed yourself into a corner." Earl let out a playfully sinister laugh and raised one hand out to the side for balance and showmanship. "I told you you'd regret coming between me and this family, didn't I? You just didn't know how much you'd regret it."

Earl swung, putting no real effort into it. He was just toying with his prey for now. Bren batted it away and the metal clashed. The second swing was just as casual, as was the third and fourth. His attitude was pure mockery.

It was Bren who increased the tempo, choosing to be the aggressor again. He thought if he could just get their positions turned around so that Earl's back was to the fireplace and his was to the living room door, he could make a dash out into the corridor, through the kitchen and somehow elicit the help of the family and Berney out in the garden. But that wasn't to be. Earl had already considered it, and he just wasn't going to let it happen.

The swords interlocked, and each man tried to out-muscle the other. Their eyes were intense as they held each other's gaze. When they separated, Earl had decided the time for fun and games had come to an end. His thrusts became violent now. His teeth ground and his nostrils flared. Bren was at his mercy. He could do no more than cower away and fend off the attack the best he could. The sound of the swords slapping against each other rang in his ears. He couldn't hold on much longer. He was already panting like the winner of a fat-man's race and his hands were becoming slick with sweat.

His face glistened and the dampness around his armpits was growing.

One final swing and it was all over. Bren's sword flew from his hand, and he had time to mentally reminisce about what a fine life he'd had before he heard the dull thud of his sword landing on the carpet.

Earl smiled and offered a courtesy nod.

Blood throbbed in Bren's temples. He couldn't believe what was happening. A nightmare had broken loose, turned to flesh, and stood before him with a sword in his hand, ready to make his final lunge.

"Well, well," Earl said and had to take a few long breaths before continuing. "I'd say it was a pleasure knowing you, but it wasn't."

Bren had resigned himself to death. He would have graciously taken the blade in the heart if Earl had been just a trifle less narcissistic. He glanced over Bren's shoulder at the mirror, perhaps checking his hair, or making sure his expression had the proper amount of menace in it, one of those important little details often overlooked by the average killer. But that casual glance was all it took for Bren to see his way out. And he took it. He turned sharply and dove into the mirror.

Since that day, Bren had often thought that he must have looked like a complete lunatic, throwing himself at the mirror like that. That was, until he vanished through it.

Earl didn't even have time to lunge. His face went slack. It was as if the cosmos had just dealt him a severe slap in the face.

"Can't be," he muttered. But it was. He'd just witnessed a man disappear into solid glass. Tuttle would have been no more amazed had the man walked on water and then turned it into wine. He tapped the mirror with the point of his sword and had to consciously keep his mouth from gaping open. What had started out as a very bad day had just become very bizarre.

Setting the tip of his sword on the carpet, he reached out and felt the cold mirror with his finger. Solid. He scanned the room with bewilderment before bending down and grabbing Bren's fallen sword, not sure what to do next. He could still make a run for it in his VW.

In the entryway, he gathered all the swords and put them back in the closet. He picked up the bloody knife from the floor and stared down the corridor into the sunlit kitchen. He must have stood there for at least ten minutes. Not thinking really, just standing there half numb. He looked down at the knife in his hand and felt a repulsive tug at his stomach. He'd killed somebody. Not just anybody, but Thomas Windfield. But he hadn't done it. Stephen Bradson had forced him. Stephen had come in and ruined everything. It was all Stephen, he thought. All Stephen. And he grinned weakly.

He took the knife to the study and wiped the fingerprints away with Thomas's shirt. He laid it beside the body.

Back in the living room, he looked again at the mirror and rubbed his mouth with trembling fingers. He felt physically sick. He was obviously dealing with some form of black magic here and somehow it was going to come back out and bite him. But he'd deal with that when it came.

After looking in at Thomas's dead body again, he calmly walked the length of the corridor and stopped at the kitchen window, where he looked out at the family. The news he bore was devastating, but at least he had somewhere else to place the blame.

He stepped out the door.

Heather looked up at him.

"He's dead," he said as he stepped forward, into the garden. "The American killed Thomas."

# CHAPTER 37

$\mathcal{B}$ ren came jetting out from the mirror, back into 1994 and landed face down on the carpet, thirty years away from the sword-wielding Earl Tuttle. His hands still shook and his breathing was still heavy, but he was away from the nightmare. And he was happy to know that the mirror was still intact in the future to provide a hole for him to exit through. He sat up on the carpet and rubbed his face, massaging color back into his dead-white skin. He closed his eyes and regained composure. Then, filling his lungs with air to calm his nerves, he looked up, and the fear returned to his face. He'd escaped nothing. In front of him in the rocking chair, calmly rocking back and forth, sat Mayor Tuttle, and cradled in his palm was a pistol with its barrel pointed at Bren's head.

"Hello, Bren." Earl Tuttle offered a half-hearted smile. "It's been years since we last met in this room. I wish I could say it's nice to see you again, but under the circumstances, you and I both know it would be a lie."

Bren nodded and rubbed at a carpet burn on his elbow where he'd landed. His hands were all tacky with sweat.

"I'd hoped this whole thing was behind me, that I'd never see you again, but unfortunately for you, you couldn't leave it alone."

"Leave it alone?" Bren barked and started to his feet. "You speak as if I've been off dredging up the past."

"Uh, uh!" said Tuttle. "I'm quite comfortable with you where you are, thank you." And watched Bren sit back down on the carpet. "It *is* the past," Tuttle continued with the light coming in through the window behind him, "for me anyway, and for the rest of the world. There's no use digging up buried memories and stirring up hurt feelings again. It was so long ago. Perhaps we could just let the whole thing die."

"It was only today, only moments ago."

Tuttle stopped his rocking and bent forward. The thickness of his face went dark with shadows as he leaned out of the rays of light. "For you maybe, but not for me, not for the rest of the world. Your recent past is ancient history for everyone else. It's been thirty long years, Bren—thirty years! The whole ordeal has passed from everyone's minds long ago, everyone's but mine. I've lived with this terror all these years, every moment, every day for thirty years. Believe me, I've suffered plenty. My memory has made sure of that. I was a foolish child then, full of greed and anger. I acted hastily. I didn't know what I was doing, but my debt has been paid now. If I could take it back, I would. But I can't."

Bren pulled his legs up into his chest and hugged his arms around them. The mayor sounded sincere, and what he said made sense. It *was* ancient history for everyone else in the world. And Tuttle had to have felt some remorse for what he'd done. Even callous men like him have a heart in there somewhere. Don't they?

"So you're asking me to forget everything I just saw?"

"Not forget, just dismiss. Let it pass. I'm a changed man now. I don't want to repeat my terrible mistake once again, but I'll do what I must. I've created a good life for myself now. I can't just let you take that away, Bren. I have a wife and children to think about. Try to understand my point of view here."

Bren smirked. It sounded ridiculous. A moment ago, this same man was ready to impale him with a sword and now he was pleading for understanding.

"Besides," said Tuttle, "you never should've been there in the first place. You were out of your place, out of your time. It was as much your fault as it was mine."

"No way." Bren shook his head adamantly.

"Oh yes," Tuttle said sharply, looking at his reflection in the mirror behind Bren, the same kind of glance that had betrayed him a brief thirty years ago. "If you hadn't come, things would've never happened the way they did. Everybody's life was fine before you showed up. So don't go pointing that all-righteous finger just at me." He resumed his rocking.

Bren stared at the gun. "You've been waiting thirty years for this day? So you could come and meet me here on the other side of the mirror?"

"No, actually, I haven't." Tuttle scratched at the cleft in his chin. "As a matter of fact, I didn't begin figuring the whole thing out until you showed up at my office over a month ago. Even then, I must say, you had me quite baffled. But the more I thought about the whole thing, the more the pieces began to fall into place. So I came out to have a chat, and—since you didn't answer the door, I invited myself in. Strangely enough, you never came home. And I must say, it was just too much of a coincidence—your disappearing exactly thirty years from the time you mysteriously showed up at the mansion. What I hadn't figured out on my own, good ole Thomas filled me in on while you were gone." He held up Thomas Windfield's diary, which Bren had left lying on the sofa before taking his journey through the mirror. Then, laying the diary on his fat lap, Tuttle rocked some more.

"It made good reading while I sat here waiting. It would appear that our good friend Mr. Windfield wasn't a genius after all." He chuckled with pleasure, happy to know that given the same circumstances, he too could have prospered as well as the late Thomas Windfield. "It all sounded quite preposterous, I do say—your traveling back in time through the mirror. But I figured it was no more ridiculous than the day I saw you disappear into the mirror—thirty years ago."

"Yeah, I suppose that would be quite baffling, wouldn't it?" Bren grinned at the thought.

"Oh yes. I was certain there was some sort of witchery involved, and I questioned how I could reveal your unnatural powers when you returned to point the finger at me for the murder. But you never returned. I always thought that was curious."

"So you placed the murder on me instead?"

"It was the reasonable thing to do. Thomas Windfield is stabbed while only two other people are in the house, me and some stranger that appears to have come from nowhere. Then, after the murder, the stranger mysteriously disappears. That was convenient for me."

"And how did you explain my disappearance?"

"I didn't have to. I claimed I heard Thomas scream, and when I came running, I found him dead. The blame naturally went to you. They searched the house and the woods for days. It was uncanny how you came and left without anyone noticing. It was a splendid escape. Almost."

"Yes, that it was." Bren looked out the open curtains behind the mayor, thinking again about having to dive through the glass if worse came to worse. He wouldn't be escaping through the mirror this time, not without the key. "But you proved to be the wiser."

"I did, didn't I?" said Tuttle. "Course all I had to do was look to see which day Thomas died, and that automatically told me the day you'd be coming back through the mirror."

"But I changed that date." Bren wrinkled his brow in thought.

"Pardon?"

Of course Tuttle didn't understand. How could he? He only knew one past—the past that sent Thomas Windfield to his grave on August 17, 1964. The other past had been annihilated, erased and replaced.

"As I was saying," the mayor continued. "The newspaper gave me the date. The only thing it didn't tell me was what to do with you once you returned."

Bren stared up at the black hole in the gun barrel, wondering how long it would be before sparks flew from that barrel, before a bullet came out with those sparks and lodged itself into his skull. He'd saved his own life just as he had Mr. Windfield's, and just like with Mr. Windfield, he'd added but a few simple moments to that life.

"I see you've given up the sword," Bren commented.

"Yes. Too old for that now." The sunlight was glowing on the back of Tuttle's gray hair. "This is much simpler. Still leaves a mess, I suppose, but you don't have to get any on you."

"Wouldn't want that, would we?" Bren glanced at the ax sitting by the woodpile and wondered how far he'd make it across the room before Tuttle shot a few slugs into him. "Did you kill Heather's husband, too?"

Tuttle frowned and lifted the pistol as if ready to shoot the idiot for his offensive mouth. "What difference does that make to you? You never even knew the man." Lowering the gun, he crossed his legs and checked his hair in the mirror again. "I was looking for the key. Figured Heather had taken it with her to Scarborough. Unfortunately her husband walked in on me. And he was such a handsome fellow, too."

"And the boy, here in this house? He walk in on you, too?"

"Don't use that tone on me, like I'm some kind of barbarian." Tuttle stood and paced a few steps. "It was the key I was after—all this time, just that stupid key! With it, I can be just as brilliant as Thomas Windfield. The only person who knows any better is you. And soon there won't even be you." He pulled back the hammer on the gun. "I am sorry. Honestly. It's not the way I would choose for things to end. But I've given it a lot of thought, and there are no other options. It's time to bid adieu." He leveled the gun at Bren.

"I won't talk," Bren spoke as quickly as a politician moments before election day, and just as believable. "Like you said, you've changed. It's been thirty years for you and everyone else. That's plenty of time. I mean, look at you—you're the mayor for crying out loud. What more proof could I want?"

"You almost sound convincing," Tuttle said. "Course this gun wouldn't be influencing you in any way, now would it? Yet when I'm not standing here with a gun, can I trust you then? I wish I could be certain, but you know as well as I do that I can't. And I can't have you going around spoiling my good name, now can I?"

"Who would believe me?" Bren leaned back with his arms behind him to brace himself. His heart was pounding. "Think about it. Who would believe that I walked through a mirror and saw you kill Mr. Windfield? I hardly believe it myself and I'm the one who did it."

"You have a point, I suppose. But what's to stop you from walking back through the mirror in front of witnesses?" Tuttle knew the answer to his own question, but he asked it anyway, wanting to justify the deed. He had disliked Bren from the moment he first laid eyes on him thirty years ago. He liked him even less now.

"I no longer have the key." Bren could feel a plan starting to bud. The mayor could never pull the trigger when doing so would cause his lifelong quest to continue.

"This key?" Tuttle lowered the gun and pulled the metal contraption from his pocket and held it in front of him.

"You found it."

"Thomas's diary lead me right to it."

*That stupid diary,* Bren thought. The very one he should have read days ago before blindly stepping into the mirror. So far the thing had given him nothing but grief.

"Have you tried it?"

"No. There's still plenty of time for experimentation." Tuttle kissed the dull metal key and pocketed it.

"Which key do you have?" asked Bren. "Not the one from the basement, I hope."

"Of course the one from the basement." He eyed the young man curiously, looking for flaws in the poker face. "You take me for a fool?"

"I'm—" Bren stopped himself as if holding back a secret. A lump had formed at the base of his throat. "You're right; I'm just being stupid."

Tuttle pointed the gun.

"Go ahead and shoot me, but you'll never find the other key—the real one. I guarantee it."

"You're lying." Tuttle didn't believe him. This man was pure garbage and every word out of his mouth reeked of deception. But he had to be sure. "You're saying this one doesn't work?"

"A replica. A decoy. Try it. You won't get far."

Tuttle suspiciously went to the mirror, keeping his eyes and gun upon Bren, who was sitting on the floor with his knees pulled up into his chest. He watched those blue eyes, expecting them to betray him. But Bren gave nothing away. Tuttle reached his hand out toward the mirror, half fearing it wouldn't pass through, and half fearing it would. He watched Bren through the reflection in the mirror now. His patience worried the mayor and made him think that Bren had spoken the truth about the false key. But the worry was short lived. His fingers dipped into the mirror, and the mayor grinned nervously with amazement, marveling over this impossibility. The cretin had lied to him about the key after all. Okay, so the lie had bought him a few minutes, but it only made his death that much more justifiable.

He raised his eyes with a sneer, to scorn Bren for his deception, but what he saw filled him with terror. Bren Stevens was rising rapidly toward him. He moved like a tiger, going in for the kill.

Earl Tuttle didn't have time to react, other than readying himself for the impact.

Bren hit him with both hands, and the force sent the mayor sailing toward the mirror. But he didn't stop at the glass, despite the fact that he put his hands out to brace himself. The wall simply swallowed him up, from his head down to the soles of his penny loafers. Ten years erased in a single second.

It would only take a matter of moments for Tuttle to hide the key somewhere in the past and then step back into the mirror and return to the present. Bren had no intention of standing by waiting for that to happen. He quickly grabbed the ax from beside the woodpile that sat next to the fireplace and began smashing the glass, hoping Thomas had been right with his theory about the mirror being both an entrance and an exit. With the exit gone, who could say where Tuttle would end up? Suspended in time perhaps, or trapped inside the wall forever. Not that the thought of Earl Tuttle living inside his wall brought him any comfort.

As the blunt end of the ax hammered at the mirror, lines split across the glass and a shower of broken mirror cascaded across the carpet. It only took a few short minutes, but to Bren it took far too much time. Every second the mirror remained intact was another second that the mayor could step back through with his pistol cocked and aimed. He beat the ax over and over again against the wall, looking slightly like an out of control Lizzy Bordon, and feeling a bit like her, too. He had a madman's grimace on his face. Destruction had never been so pleasurable. When there was no more mirror to hammer at, Bren surrendered the head of the ax onto the ground and gazed at the few silver fragments of the mirror that remained glued upon the wall. Tuttle wouldn't be exiting through those.

He should have been comforted, but instead a shiver rushed over him. This was a house of mirrors. One large enough to walk through hung in nearly every room, and all Tuttle had to do was pass through one of those. The man was a monster, but he was no fool. If he'd read anything about Thomas's theory in the diary, he would no doubt guess how Bren would react and, thus, choose the mirror of a different room. But which one?

Bren hurried toward the door, and that was when he heard it: a muffled cry straining from the wall behind him. He turned back. It was grotesque and yet, at the same time, reassuring. The wall was bowing forward as if an animal were trapped inside a rubber cage, trying to break free. The shape of the plaster and wood distorted for a moment, then retracted. Another faint cry bled from the woodwork, the agonizing moan of a man sealed up inside his own doom, a man who had stepped into a door and found no exit waiting on the other side, and, without the key, couldn't go back. Hanging from the wall, one remaining sliver of glass dripped a drop of blood, which dribbled slowly along the wall. Then all was silent.

❀

"It's a maggot-infested carcass of a putrefied pig, that's what I say." Lug stared out from the gazebo at the back of the house, with its gray walls dulled by the overcast sky. He had that same disgusted look on his face that he'd had the first day he'd entered the house. His eyes had grown bulbous and enraptured while listening to Bren retell his tales of horror.

Though the general consensus was that Bren was telling the truth, there had been misgivings about the details of the story. Natasha—who sat on the wooden bench with Lug and Eric on the opposite side of the gazebo, facing Bren—had difficulty swallowing the idea that her grandfather had originally been killed on the sixteenth, rather than the seventeenth, as she remembered it. She couldn't count the number of times she'd read the newspaper account of her grandfather's murder, and to her recollection, it'd always given the date August 17, 1964. Was she to believe that this important detail had suddenly been substituted in her mind within the last couple days? She had her doubts.

"Now the walls truly are haunted," said Eric, his red hair stringing across his face.

"Yeah, I suppose they are," Bren conceded.

"I'm never going in there again." Lug stood now, facing out the gazebo's opening. "What if he starts to decay?" He turned toward

Bren. "What if his stench starts seeping out through the cracks? Some putrid corpse oozing its bile out inside the wall where you can't stop its decay, can't stop its foul breath from breathing in on you at night while you're trying to sleep." He shivered.

"Don't start with that, Lug."

"He's got a point, Bren." Natasha stood. She stared past the flowers, hedges and statues to the curved windows of the conservatory, then to the back door. "Tuttle never smelled that good when he was alive."

"I don't think he's actually in the wall," said Bren.

"But you can't be sure. He could be in there still breathing at this very minute, just waiting to die and rot."

They were just toying with him; he saw that now. But his sense of humor still hadn't recovered from the trauma of having witnessed Thomas Windfield's death and having sealed Earl Tuttle up in the wall forever. Most likely his sense of humor wouldn't recover for quite some time.

Eric was still sitting on the bench looking at Bren, thinking. "The man we saw in the house that day—it was you."

Bren nodded.

"You knew who we were. You called us by name. Yet you went right ahead and scared the life out of us." He looked up at Lug and frowned. "What a bloody cowardly thing to do."

"Not nearly as cowardly as running home while your best friend dangles from the living room window."

"I did no such thing."

"You sure as hell did."

"I knew it," said Lug. "And all these years I've been calling you me mate. Off and leave me for the buzzards to pick me eyes out."

"I was twelve years old. What did you expect me to do—fight the ugly beast?"

"Hey, watch who you're calling ugly," said Bren.

Eric shook his head at him. "Bet you had a good laugh about that, didn't ya? Bet while you were watching us crawling out through the hole in the fence, you were standing there at the window grinning."

Bren shrugged. "I was half tempted to chase you home, but I didn't know if your little hearts could take it."

"You're a real chum, you know that?"

Natasha stood beneath the overhanging ivy that drooped from the roof of the gazebo. She stared a long time at the mansion, not paying any attention to the men arguing behind her. It'd begun to rain, but she didn't notice that either. She gazed out over the garden to the large mansion sitting before her, its gray roof flickering with little splashes of rain as the drops popped against the shingles. She thought of Mayor Earl Tuttle, shoved through the mirror with the key in hand.

"Where do you suppose Tuttle hid the key?" she asked.

That quieted them for a moment. They could see exactly what she had in mind.

Before walking to town and speaking with the police about Mayor Tuttle's car, which was parked in front of the manor, Bren had searched the living room, but had turned up nothing. That was two days ago. Last night he'd looked again, searched every inch of the living room and study. It was doubtful that Tuttle had gone farther than that to hide the key. But the search was far from over. The damn thing had to be somewhere, and by the look on Natasha's face, there wasn't going to be rest until they found it.

0-595-24949-3

Printed in the United States
26956LVS00003B/127-135